Once Upon a
CHRISTMAS

55 Heartwarming Short Stories Bring
Meaning to the Season

Once Upon a
CHRISTMAS

Sharon Bernash Smith
Rosanne Croft, Linda Reinhardt

SHILOH RUN PRESS
An Imprint of Barbour Publishing, Inc.

© 2015 by Barbour Publishing, Inc.

© 2010 *Once Upon a Christmas* by Sharon Bernash Smith, Rosanne Croft, Linda J. Reinhardt.
© 2011 *Always Home for Christmas* by Sharon Bernash Smith, Rosanne Croft, Linda J.
Reinhardt, with guest stories "Along for the Ride," © 2011 by Darlene P. and "Santa Saves
Christmas," © 2011 by Yasuko Hirata.
© 2012 *Starry, Starry, Christmas Night* by Sharon Bernash Smith and Linda J. Reinhardt, with
guest stories "When Christmas Came to the Dog-Trot," © 2012 by Sylvia Stewart and "Special
Delivery for Christmas," © 2012 by Betty Ritchie.
All titles are Reality Fiction™ *Faith Meets Imagination,* a registered trademark of Sharon Bernash
Smith.

Print ISBN 978-1-63409-067-4

eBook Editions:
Adobe Digital Edition (.epub) 978-1-63409-627-0
Kindle and MobiPocket Edition (.prc) 978-1-63409-628-7

Author photographs: Sharon Bernash Smith, © 2011 Will Smith; Rosanne Croft, © 2008 Bill
Burns; Linda J. Reinhardt, © 2011 Paul, Stephen Paul Photography; three coauthors group
photo, © 2010 Caeli Croft

Published by Shiloh Run Press, an imprint of Barbour Publishing, Inc., P.O. Box 719,
Uhrichsville, Ohio 44683, www.barbourbooks.com, in association with OakTara Publishers,
www.oaktara.com.

*Our mission is to publish and distribute inspirational products offering exceptional value and biblical
encouragement to the masses.*

 Member of the
Evangelical Christian
Publishers Association

Printed in Canada.

Contents

Once Upon a Christmas

20 short stories to bring delight,
reverence, and meaning to the season

Reality Fiction™ *Faith Meets Imagination*

Sharon Bernash Smith, Rosanne Croft, Linda J. Reinhardt

Dedication

"Joy to the World, the Lord has come."
I dedicate this book to all who long for joy.
May you find it this Christmas as you reach out
and embrace the Breath of Heaven, born in a lowly manger,
for He *is* the Lord Jesus, Savior of the World.
—Sharon Bernash Smith

The Memory of Professor Karlis Kaufmanis (1910–2003),
who inspired many young students to look up
and really *see* the stars.
—Rosanne Croft

In the celebration of the greatest gift ever,
I dedicate this book to anyone
who wonders about God's love and pray that someday you will find:
There is no way to measure the love God has for us,
or the gift God gave to us—His only Son.
There is no way to measure the difference between
the throne room of heaven, to the manger in Bethlehem, to the cross.
There is no way to measure how much love God has for *you*!
Merry Christmas!
—Linda J. Reinhardt

Once Upon a Christmas
CONTENTS

What Christmas Is All About

Sharon Bernash Smith

Some say Christmas is just for children. Some celebrate in excess, even going into debt. Others are overwhelmed with preparation and exhausted even before it's all over.

But Christmas celebrations don't have to be that way. It's certainly not what God intended when He sent His only Son as the Breath from Heaven to "save us all from Satan's power." The Bible says that Jesus came for *all* mankind, so that *all* might know this God-made-man. We're to celebrate His birth, life, and death, to joy in His resurrection, and to wait in hopeful expectation for the day of His triumphant return.

Bypassing the commercialization of Christmas and the frenetic activities that cling to us isn't easy; it takes a conscious decision to do so. Focusing on Jesus' birth is the beginning of creating a God-centered celebration full of the peace we crave and the joy God meant for us to possess during the season.

Throughout *Once Upon a Christmas,* you'll find all kinds of stories about the impact of Christmas in the lives of remarkable characters, most of them fictional. However, the truths revealed are universal. Each story invites the reader to a place of delight and reverence for our most cherished Christian holiday.

So merry Christmas, dear reader. May the joy of Jesus live in your heart this Christmas and all year long.

The Train Baby

Sharon Bernash Smith

Two German cousins playing in the snow discover a mysterious brown bundle lying next to the railroad tracks on Christmas Eve, 1943. It's a baby! Where did she come from, and who could have left her there in the middle of nowhere?

Their bravery is soon tested when they realize just who the baby is and why she must be hidden from a Nazi neighbor in order to spare her life and possibly even their own. . . .

This story led the author to write The Train Baby's Mother, *a novel about a Holocaust survivor.*

Somewhere in Germany

L isten!"

"I hear nothing, Ellie. Your imagination's once again getting the best of you."

"I tell you, I heard something, Fritz. What if it's a wounded animal caught in a hunter's trap?"

"They hunt only for food. How many times must I tell you this?"

"Tell me a thousand times, and I will still think it cruel."

Another sound rose from the direction of the rail tracks that ran through the back part of their grandparents' farm.

"Fritz!" Ellie's head jerked in the direction of the wail.

"I heard it. Maybe the train hit an animal."

They moved as fast as the knee-deep snow would allow, straining against the heavy restriction. Cousins brought together by misfortune, living in the country for safekeeping while their fathers fought for the homeland, they found comfort in the camaraderie that kept fears about war at a distance.

Fritz, whose long legs gave him an advantage over the younger Ellie, arrived first. "I see nothing here, Ellie. Winter plays a trick on us. See for yourself."

Ellie, her braids now loosed from a red wool stocking hat, grabbed her heaving sides. Misting breath almost crystallized in the fierce December cold. "Oh, Fritz, you are always so wise, far and above any boy in all the land." She waved her arm and bowed in mockery.

Suddenly the stillness collapsed with a cry, plaintive and intense.

They turned in unison toward the sound. It came from the embankment directly on the other side from where they stood. Climbing up the bank for a better look brought them to a standstill. There, in the sooty snow, lay a half-buried bundle of reddish fur. It was moving.

"Ellie, quick. Take my hand, I'll help you down." A slippery slope made their progress slow. In places the drifts came to Ellie's waist. At the bottom, they nearly fell onto the pile that was still moving.

"Fritz," Ellie whispered, "it sounds like a. . ."

"A baby? Yes." He bent over, curiosity pushing aside fear. He picked up a corner, lifting it with utmost care.

"Ahhh," the cousins exhaled together. There, before them, lay an infant. . .tiny and pale, but alive, like a rose plucked from Grossmutter's summer garden.

"Pick it up, Fritz, before it freezes, for goodness' sake. Oh my, where could such a baby have come from?"

"The train."

"What?"

"From the train, Ellie. Someone threw this baby off when the engine slowed down to make the curve ahead."

With the child in his arms, Fritz looked closer. *Not very old,* he thought. But what did he know of babies? Calves, goats, and goslings, those he could tell you about, but a baby? This one was swaddled tightly with blankets, snuggled inside a shabby remnant of ratty fur.

Some fierce emotion within the twelve-year-old boy emerged. Never had he understood the meaning of innocence until that very moment, staring into the face of something so fresh to the world. "Ellie, you are maybe too young to understand about this train. . .this baby." His words were a whisper.

"I'm about to be eight, may I remind you. Just because you're older doesn't mean I am stupid."

"Silly girl, listen. This baby is a Jew." A chill went through him. . .and not from the cold.

"And just how could you know that, Herr Fritz?"

"Because I know what this train carries inside the boarded cars that have been rolling through our backcountry."

Ellie stared at him, eyes wide. "Fritz, I've heard our mothers' whispered prayers in Grossmutter's kitchen. Those trains are filled with people, aren't they? They're being sent to work camps, are they not?"

Fritz glanced at the infant's thin but cherubic face, then quickly wrapped the baby's head beneath the coat again and turned toward home. He motioned for Ellie to follow. "Only the place to which they go is not a place of work at all, Ellie. What they say in the village is. . .is unspeakable."

"Fritz, please tell me. I'm not so little that you have to protect me all the time."

He peeked again at the perfect face now sleeping in his arms and shuddered. He'd long ago lost his innocence when the war began. And now, if he told Ellie the truth, she would lose more of hers. But it was time.

"Ellie, the Jews are being taken away to die. Someone threw this little one from the train to save its life." There, he'd told her, but he couldn't look at her face.

She was silent for a moment, taking in the meaning of what she'd heard. "Poor baby. Poor, poor little baby," she cried in sympathy. "Fritz, maybe the baby is Jesus." She stumbled, falling to her knees.

He stopped and turned toward her. "Ellie, you just told me that you were a big girl."

"*Ja!*" She picked herself up while he waited.

"Then think like a big girl. This is not baby Jesus. Besides, it's a girl. I saw a pink sweater."

Ellie began to sob. "Oh, Fritz, what if she got hurt in the fall? What if she dies after all?"

He, too, was worried. "She landed in a soft snow bank, and the train passed only minutes ago. See, she sleeps like a lamb, but soon she'll be hungry. Hurry, before it snows again."

He knew that his grandmother, mother, and Aunt Margot would help without question, but their neighbor, Herr Hoffman, hated the Jews with a passion. This might not go well. Fritz had no idea what somebody who hated Jews would do to a tiny baby, but he knew full well what had happened to Jesus.

He fought back tears. He was much too old to cry, but this small bundle of blamelessness tied him to something bigger than himself. He didn't have a name for it, but the fierceness of the emotion made him feel old.

Welcoming lights from the farmhouse beckoned ahead, releasing a strong resolve within his very soul. Whatever it took to protect this little Jew baby, he would do.

"Mein Gott, mein Gott!" His grandmother could hardly contain herself for the horror of what might have happened to this baby from the train. "Oh, how must the mother feel, tossing her own child to the wind? To the wind."

"Mama," Fritz's mother chided, "she had faith to believe that God would protect her baby. Perhaps she saw the children in the snow. Maybe that's when she made her decision."

Still, they all struggled with tears at the thought of such a desperate act. This child and that mother would never meet again this side of eternity. It was a horrible thought, but they could not take time to dwell on sentiment.

The women had the baby unwrapped and were looking her over for any injuries. Relieved she had none, they did discover she had a wet diaper.

"How old, do you suppose?" the grandmother wondered aloud.

"A few weeks, no more," offered Fritz's mother.

"Fritz, Ellie, bring me that pile of flour sacks behind the stove. We'll tear them up for *windels*; she's soaking wet."

The children gladly obeyed.

"Now what do we feed you, *mein schatz*? Cow's milk will not be good for you, but thank Gott we have a good goat."

His mother turned to Fritz, but he was already out the door, headed toward the barn to milk their sweet, productive nanny. He was grateful for the new snow, knowing it would keep Herr Hoffman from making any friendly visits.

Too friendly, thought Fritz.

Herr Hoffman had been stopping by on a regular basis, and not out of unselfish motives, as far as Fritz could tell. Their neighbor flirted openly with his mother and Aunt Margot, despite their lack of reciprocation. Larger than life in his own mind because of all the land in his possession, he was arrogant and rude. The older man didn't care that Fritz's father and uncle were at war; he cared nothing for their honor. Fritz knew Herr Hoffman was powerful and, therefore, dangerous.

The man was open about his hatred of the Jews, being a staunch supporter of Hitler, and made mention of the fact whenever he came. He brought game he'd killed and anything else he could think of in order to gain access to the Schmidts' kitchen. Fritz was sure that, despite the extreme weather, Herr Hoffman would find a way to make a stop. How would they explain the baby to him?

Fritz focused on the task ahead when he reached the barn, preparing the stanchion, and placing the goat on top. Rich milk sang into the bucket, raising comforting steam against the boy's face. Still, his mind was on edge. Fritz leaned closer into Nanny's warm side; they had to have a plan, or Herr Hoffman would surely discover the train-baby secret.

After finishing, he turned the goat loose into a stall rich with hay. Grabbing the milk bucket again, he spotted a couple of brown nipples left over from when they had to bottle-feed an orphan lamb last spring. Relieved they at least had a way to feed the baby, he only hoped they'd be able to protect her from the living, breathing hatred residing a few kilometers away.

His grandmother was pacing when he arrived back at the house. "Thank Gott, Fritz, she is starving. Your *mutter* has cleaned a bottle we found. And ja, I see you thought to bring the nipples. So big are they, but we will make them do."

After a few adjustments, the baby nursed with vigor, stopping only to burp.

"Oh, mein schatz," his grandmother repeated over and over, "mein schatz."

Ellie stood as guardian. Fixed on the entire process, her eyes welled with fear. "Grossmutter, will she live?"

"Oh, I'm sure, Ellie," Fritz's mother, Gretchen, spoke up. "See how she eats? As long as she can tolerate Nanny's milk, she'll do just fine. Wait until your mother arrives from town. Won't she be in for a shock?"

Fritz came to attention at his place by the huge stone fireplace. "How's Aunt getting home, Mutter?"

"Well, she didn't want to, but she accepted a sleigh ride from Herr Hoffman. Otherwise, with the storm getting worse, she'd be forced to stay in town. Who knows how long this could last?"

He thanked God for the information and for the old oak telephone that brought the news of his aunt's impending arrival. "But Herr Hoffman will surely come inside. He'll want to know about the child."

The room went silent except for the baby's hearty eating noises and Ellie's crying. "Herr Hoffman hates Jews, Auntie, even tiny ones. Fritz told me." Now her cries turned to sobs, and she buried her face in her aunt's shoulder.

Fritz's mother stood with the baby and began to pace in front of the living room window, looking out at the foreboding sky. "They'll be here soon," she whispered. "We must be ready."

"I'll take her to the barn," offered Fritz. "She'll be safe and warm in the loft."

"Nein," said the grandmother. "What if he stays. . .invites himself to dinner besides? You and the baby could not be out in the barn too long. The cold would be dangerous. There has to be another way."

Fritz darted to the back door, grabbed his drying coat, and announced over his shoulder, "I'll be back in a moment. Pray while I'm gone."

Before his mother could question him, he was out the door and making his way back to the barn. Even since the last trip, snow had drifted higher, and he struggled to open the reluctant barn door.

He first took time to night feed the animals held up inside. There was Nanny, a last year's baby, and the surprise kid, born only weeks ago, now dubbed Gus.

Fritz threw grain down for the few chickens a marauding fox had missed, then milked the cow bawling for relief for her extended udder. He hated to take the time, but it needed to be done. Still, he shook with nervousness over the creeping darkness outside. His aunt would be home soon.

He prayed again out loud: "Dear Lord, help us protect the baby, and keep us safe from Herr Hoffman."

The cow must have thought he was talking to her, because she lowed in response. His mouth watered and his stomach growled at the sight of the foaming bucket, half full of sweet Guernsey milk. He hoped dinner would be ready when he returned, then chastised himself for the petty thought because he knew matters of life and death loomed before him.

With a pitchfork, he pulled hay down from overhead, filling all the racks double full, in case the storm got so bad he couldn't make it back in the morning.

Chores done, he looked around, grabbed another bottle, and picked up what he'd come for in the first place.

Head down against the wind, Fritz wrapped the protesting animal he carried inside his jacket. He could barely make out the lights from the house for the snow and ice pelting his head and face. Despite the noise of the wind and shutters banging against the house, he heard the familiar jingle of sleigh bells in the distance. He pushed harder against the elements and the pounding fear in his chest.

His feet slipped on the house stairs, tumbling him against the back door. The struggling animal protested the jostle with all four feet.

His mother opened the door to help him inside. "Fritz, have you gone mad? What were you thinking. . . ?" She stopped midsentence when she noticed what was under his coat. "Now I know. For sure you are mad!"

"It's Gus."

"I recognized him immediately, Son. What's this all about?"

"I have a plan, Mutter. Here, take him." He handed the thrashing kid over to his bewildered mother, flung his coat over the back hook, and yanked off the barn boots filled with snow. The fire beckoned, but he checked first to make sure the baby was all right.

Ellie squealed when she saw the kid and ran with delight to take it from her aunt. Frau Schmidt came from the back room carrying a quilt for the baby.

"What is that in my house? Another guest now, I suppose?"

"Nein, Grossmutter, he is part of my plan. Let me explain." He retrieved the goat from Ellie. "Here's the idea. Please, there's not much time, so listen carefully."

Seconds after the explanation, cries from Herr Hoffman reached inside. "Whoa!"

The children grabbed the goat, lifted the baby from the couch, and headed for their sleeping loft directly above the living room. Ellie needed to use the bathroom, but Fritz shot her a look that said there wasn't time.

Fritz made a makeshift pen for the goat from an old blanket surrounded by leather suitcases pulled out of the wardrobe. He shoved a nursing bottle into its mouth, praying for cooperation.

Ellie looked as if she'd fall apart any second, but she'd have to be as strong as he needed her to be. He realized how much he loved her despite the difference in their ages. She was more like a sister than a cousin.

Down below, his mother was greeting her sister and Herr Hoffman. Just the sound of his voice frightened the children, but a scripture from Sunday school ran through Fritz's mind. *"Ist er grosser, der in mir als er ist, her in der Welt ist. Greater is he that is in you, than he that is in the world"* (KJV).

Immediately his aunt asked for Ellie. Up above, Ellie's face went pale, melting into what Fritz feared would become a big cry.

"Ellie," he whispered, "you are the bravest girl I know. God will give you strength to do this." He took her by the shoulders and knelt before her, looking into eyes the color of spring skies. "I know I've not always treated you with kindness, but I tell you now, I believe in you." He gave her a sound hug, which she returned with a deep sigh.

She sniffed, smoothed the front of her sweater, and swallowed. "I'm here, Mutter," she called downstairs. "Up here with Fritz." She touched the side of Fritz's face and mouthed, "Thank you." He watched her turn and go below, carefully placing stocking feet onto slippery rungs. As she descended, her face changed before him. What was that look? Courage!

Fritz listened to the downstairs conversation, alert to any movement from the baby or the goat. So far they both slept, but he noticed the baby stirred in her sleep. Was she hungry again. . .so soon? Dreaming, perhaps. She stretched, rolled her perfect fuzzy head from side to side, and settled. He hadn't realized he was holding his breath. The reality of what could have happened to this child struck deep into his being. He reached over and stroked one tiny hand, resting out of the covers, before turning his attention back downstairs.

According to the plan, his mother and grandmother kept Aunt Margot and Herr Hoffman in the kitchen by the cookstove. Even a few feet away from the hiding place could mean the difference between life and death.

"Herr Hoffman, thank you so much for aiding my sister as you have." Fritz heard the strain in his mother's voice. Grossmutter was strangely silent. Praying, no doubt.

"It's no bother, Frau Miller. Anything to help out a lady." The loud voice startled the baby and the goat at the same time, but neither woke. Herr Hoffman boomed on: "Such a storm, eh? I must press on to my own farm, or my animals will starve. All the servants but one are off for the holiday. Sorry to burden you with my problems, but with the war and the elements, I struggle. So much land brings great responsibilities."

"Yes, I imagine it is a weighty challenge." Fritz could hear the mock seriousness of his mother's comment. "You'll be on your way, then?"

"Now, Frau Miller, surely you would not send a good Samaritan on his way without some heated refreshment?"

Grossmutter ended her silence. "Herr Hoffman, I've some hot cider simmering here. I'll get you a cup. . .for the road." Fritz heard the tension in her high-pitched timbre.

"How very kind, Frau Schmidt." He paused, then turned his attention to Ellie. "My, little girl, how lovely you are. Just like your mother, eh?"

Ellie did not respond.

"Well now, cat got your tongue. . .Ellie, is it?"

"No, Herr Hoffman. I, I mean yes." Ellie was flustered, and Fritz prayed for her resolve to return.

"Well now, which is it? Yes or no?" Herr Hoffman's laugh was short and edged with cruelty over Ellie's awkwardness.

"The cat does not have my tongue, and yes, my name is Ellie, Herr Hoffman."

"And where is your cousin, that boy?"

"Fritz is napping; he's not. . .uh. . ."

"Not well," interrupted his mother.

"Oh, my, sorry to hear that. . .so close to Christmas and all."

"Really?" said Aunt Margot. "He was fine this morning, was he not?"

Grossmutter interrupted now. "Herr Hoffman, sit, enjoy the cider."

"May I remove my fur before I partake?"

"Of course. Here, let me help y—"

Behind Fritz, the baby cried one long wail. He rushed over to pat her little back. She would not be comforted. He rolled her over and coaxed a warm bottle into her mouth. *Lord, please make her content.* He propped the bottle with a folded blanket and relaxed for a second when it seemed to work.

Below, silence screamed for an answer to the upstairs cry.

Herr Hoffman spoke first. "What was that?"

"It sounded like a baby." That was Aunt Margot.

"Oh, Mama," Ellie said, "Fritz and I have a secret."

"Ja?" It was Herr Hoffman. Fritz heard a chair scraping away from the table and heavy steps coming closer below. He jumped into action.

Glancing at the baby to make sure the bottle was stable, he reached down into the makeshift animal pen, grabbed the kid, and brought it up to his chest. He moved quickly to the stairs and was halfway down when the others met him at the bottom.

"This is your secret?" Aunt Margot laughed.

"I told you, Mama." Ellie jumped up and down, looking into Herr Hoffman's questioning face.

"Explain this animal in my house," Grossmutter scolded.

Quite the actress, Fritz thought admiringly.

"Oh, Grossmutter, look at him. It was so cold in the barn when I did evening chores, I could not leave him. His cry means he's hungry, but I have a bottle upstairs. Please, may I keep him in for the night?"

Grossmutter nodded toward the loft. "Go."

"Hmmph, your boy is too soft," growled Herr Hoffman. "He needs a man's hand to his backside. When he's old enough to join the army, working in a Jew camp will toughen him up. A goat in the house, indeed." He turned in obvious disgust.

The family took a deep breath, but no one exhaled. Fritz looked at Ellie. Her lower lip quivered like a leaf in the wind.

"Surely the war will be finished before Fritz must serve, Herr Hoffman." Fritz's mother walked over to her son. She stroked the goat, winking at Fritz.

Worried the baby would finish her bottle any second, Fritz put a foot on the bottom rung of the ladder.

"Wait!" Herr Hoffman stomped toward him, and Fritz tightened his grip on the kid.

"Ja?"

"It's amazing how this kid sounded exactly like a human baby, eh?"

"Ja, amazing."

The goat bleated right on cue.

They all laughed, Herr Hoffman the loudest. "This creature reminds me of my animals at home. I must attend them immediately." He turned from Fritz and saluted to the others before making his way to the door.

Fritz tore up the ladder, arriving at the exact moment the baby finished nursing. Deftly, he lifted her to a shoulder. *Be calm,* mein liebchen, *be calm.* He patted the tiny back and stifled a laugh when she burped in his ear. Her breath, like fluttering bird wings next to his cheek, caused a single tear to fall in compassion. *How cruel the world has already been to you. I'm so sorry.* In that moment, he knew something beyond explanation. . .a soul-knowledge.

Somehow he would be bonded to this child for the rest of his days. He knew it with the same certainty of faith that reminded him daily that God was real. He stayed put until he heard the sleigh bells fading into the distant night.

"Fritzie, come down." Grossmutter's voice was excited, but he heard relief as well.

He backed down the ladder, carrying the baby with great care.

Aunt Margot stood behind her mother, mouth agape with shock. "Is that a baby?" She walked over to her nephew with a look of wonder. "It is a baby! But. . . ?"

"Mama, we found her in the snow. She's a miracle—just like Jesus, Mama, because. . ." Ellie took a deep breath. "Because she's a Jew." The last part was a sigh. "Fritz and I want to keep her. Can we, please?"

"Children," Fritz's mother explained, "we will keep her until it is safe to let her go."

"What do you mean, Mutter?"

"Fritz, there are people in the village who will take this liebchen and get her safely out of the country."

"Sister, you know people in the Jewish underground? This is extremely dangerous. You'll have to be careful, especially with Herr Hoffman sniffing around like some evil animal on the prowl."

"Ja, I know. But we cannot let him get his hands on this tiny one. Her life is worth any risk. How proud I am of our children." She walked over and hugged them both.

Frau Schmidt had the baby now, rocking before the blazing fire, singing close to one ear.

"What's that you're singing, Grossmutter?" Fritz asked.

"The same song I've sung to my grandchildren since they were born. . .see how it calms her?"

The clock struck the hour.

"Soon it will be Christmas Day, and we have a baby in the house. I cannot believe it," said Ellie's mother. She walked over to the fireplace, gazing down at the baby, swaddled in one of her childhood quilts. "Remarkable, isn't it, how one so small can sleep through such trauma?"

"See," cried Ellie, "it's like when Jesus was born. He left his home and was born in the cold on Christmas. Oh, Mutter, a baby for Christmas. If *Vater* were here, he would help us save her, isn't that so?"

"You're right, of course, Ellie. Come over here, and let's take a closer look at our little Christmas surprise."

She unwrapped the sleeping infant, and in the glow of the fire, they took turns admiring each and every delicate curve. The few strands of hair she possessed were dark and bound to be curly. Behind one ear they discovered a tiny birthmark in the shape of a star. Although she was a little on the thin side, they all agreed she was quite the beauty.

"I think we should call her Star. What do you think, everyone?" Ellie looked around for approval. The agreement was unanimous.

"Ja." Frau Schmidt laughed. "She is our Christmas Star."

They carefully rewrapped her and prayed that God would pour out His blessing upon Star and the family who'd shown such faithful courage in letting go of their child.

Even though they had no idea what the future would hold for this tiny survivor, they took comfort in knowing there was One who kept them all in the palm of His hand, through this silent night...and beyond.

Mama's Christmas Harp

SHARON BERNASH SMITH

Living with a houseful of seven siblings is a costly proposition, and when your father is a pastor in small-town Texas in 1951, it's a given that Christmas presents are not a guaranteed commodity.

When Mama announces with great enthusiasm that another child will be added to the roster, Christmas looks even slimmer in the gifting department.

Despite their bleak material circumstances, though, the Osterminders are in for an unexplainable surprise when an awkwardly shaped gift arrives on their front porch exactly on Christmas Day. . . .

It's remarkable how holidays stir up a memory. . .like a gentle wind moves a pile of fallen leaves. It happens every year without fail and, frankly, it's part of what makes Christmas special for me. I've been considered an adult for longer than I care to admit, but once a year my heart takes a journey that yet retains the bountiful remembrances of my youth. I can't for certain separate facts from sentiment from all my memories, but the recollections of the Christmas I was nine remain clear and uncluttered. . . .

When my papa took the new pastor's job, he said things were looking up. And they were. But not for long. Now, I don't mean to sound disrespectful, but there was a reason things started looking downwards, right after things were looking up: my parents were having another baby. A baby! It was probably more of a surprise for my youngest brother, who thought he'd be the baby of the family forever.

We should have known something was up when our mother started spending a whole lot of time with her head over the porch rail. And then there were all those sudden trips to the outhouse.

We found out real soon that any extra money Papa was bringing home went right into the "baby fund." See, Mama had figured she was done having babies and, therefore, had given away every single baby thing to the neighbor lady, who had even more kids than we did. Which, I think I should mention, was a passel. Eight.

Eight! I already had seven brothers and sisters, and before Christmas there'd be one more. Really!

First there was Nyla Ray. Then Mary Ray, followed by Michael Ray, then me, Buddy Ray. The next two came as a pair, Lonnie and Bonnie. . .Ray. Most people would have stopped right there, especially since we're not Catholic or Mormon (two questions my parents were often asked). But wouldn't you know we were surprised. . .again. . .by Susan Ray and, one year after her, Audie Ray. You couldn't really say Audie Ray was a surprise. After all, how surprised can you be after being with child seven times previous?

Probably, by now, you've guessed my Papa's name is Ray. Raymond Lee Osterminder. We're German. Well, half. Mama's kin came from jolly old England. That's what my grandma, her mama, used to say: "jolly old England," real cheerful-like.

Although times were hard, and money scarce, all happenings in our home centered on one thing: love. First, God's love practically burst right out of my mama. Papa was more reserved in the display of his emotions, but never did we doubt the love and affection he had for God or his family.

Papa said the church was supposed to be the outpouring of Christ's love in human flesh, and we found that to be true wherever we went. Each church we were called to folded us into their lives like blood kin.

With so many mouths to feed, you'd think my parents would have been all stressed over the drain on funds in Papa's new appointment. Papa said, though, "God always has a plan." We don't always see it like God sees it—a point he never failed to tag onto the "the plan" lecture. That was obviously true where the size of one's family was concerned.

I have to admit, I spent a lot of my childhood in quiet expectation of how God's "plan" would unfold in my family. Over the years I was never disappointed.

But that Christmas in the middle of my ninth year, my young faith was tested.

Whispered rumor went through the house like a Texas tornado the first Monday in December 1951. "Mama's with child again."

"What?"

"How do you know?"

"Saw her pukin'."

"Soooo?"

"Twice, on the way to the outhouse."

"Yep, Mama's havin' another one."

"Well, I want a puppy."

"You're getting a baby."

"Bet Papa doesn't know."

"Audie Ray will not be happy about this."

It went on like that right up to when we were called to breakfast. You could have heard a pin drop while our mama doled out our morning ritual of steaming oatmeal. This gave her a big hint that something was up. Every one of us, except Audie Ray, stared at our mother like she was a foreigner among us.

"Well, ya'll are sorely quiet this fine morning. Makes me thinks aliens from outer space stole my children and replaced them with somebody else's." She briefly looked us over. "Yes sir, a big ugly alien."

Silence. The only sound in the room besides Audie Ray's little voice was the oatmeal hitting one bowl at a time.

"No sirree, I don't recall any of my children being this quiet since...? Well, I cannot recall such a time ever. Can you, Mr. Osterminder?"

Papa looked around the table at each of his offspring and smiled a lopsided grin, before beginning the blessing: "Dear Lord, I thank You for the food You have brought to our table in faithful abundance. Thank You for the hands that prepared it. I thank You for each child You have blessed me with. And thank You, too, for"—the pause filled the entire room—"the new life that You have seen fit to bring to this family...again. In Jesus' name I pray. Amen."

Usually the amens went all around the table, but that morning only Mama and Audie Ray responded. The rest of us remained silent, too stunned to say anything after the factual revelation had been declared: that indeed one more Osterminder would soon be with us.

"Well, darlin's, eat up," Mama said, trying to be chipper, before excusing herself to stretch over the back porch railing.

"But, Papa," Nyla Ray said, ignoring Mama's retching noises behind her, "where's one more baby going to fit?"

It wasn't a selfish question but a practical one. Truth was, we couldn't imagine squeezing in another human being anywhere. . .even if it did have a bitty body.

"Nyla Ray, God will provide."

We waited for further explanation. None came.

Mama came back in, pale as fresh milk. She glanced at my father with love and devotion before sitting down. "Children, I know this news must come as a surprise to y'all." She looked at Papa again. "Truth be known, it's a bit of a shock to me as well." She kind of giggled, little-girl-like. "But I am so excited."

Then she threw her head back and laughed out loud. She meant it. She was downright happy!

"Well," Mary Ray said, quiet and resolute, "maybe Nyla Ray and I could fit a pallet in between our beds. After the baby leaves your room, I mean."

"You girls always come through in a pinch," Papa said.

Mama's big tears spilled down onto the cheeks that were now pinking up again. "Thank you, Mary Ray," she whispered. "Thank you for being the sweet gift you've always been."

The table erupted.

"I want another girl."

"Me, too."

"It better be a boy," one of the others shouted.

"We'll talk more at dinner," Mama said. "Ya'll better hurry or you'll miss the bus. Daniel Ray, help your brother out of his high chair, please."

Audie Ray was oblivious to how his life was about to change, but the rest of us knew exactly, since we'd had more practice. In a family our size, "sharing" had its own special meaning. We shared everything from underwear to shoes. Some of us even shared beds. My first pair of new, never-been-worn oxfords didn't come until I graduated from high school. They hurt, too, because up until then, my shoes had always been well broken in by Michael Ray.

But now, because Mama had given away all her baby hand-me-downs, there wasn't one thing in our house small enough for the "poor little thing." That's what I heard Mama call our newest addition one day when she was talking to one of the church "sisters" on the phone.

"The poor little thing will have to stay naked as the day it comes into the world, I guess. No, I'm not worried, sister. God always provides. I'm surely amazed at how He's provided even my wants over the years. Why, who knows? He might even bring me an ol' harp someday. I've been thinking about it for years. I mean, I haven't played one since our hill country assignment, but my, a girl can still dream, can't she? Sister Neoma, I wish you could hear 'Silent Night' played on such a fine instrument like that one. Truly, it was heavenly."

I had to turn away from the conversation, because sudden sadness cut through me all the way to my backbone. My mama was the best, least selfish person I knew. To hear such longing in her voice depressed me all to pieces. I had no idea she even thought of the beat-up harp, left behind in the hill country church. She'd never, ever said a word about it in front of us kids. Poor Mama. I had to tell Papa about this.

He already knew when I brought the subject to his attention. "Mama didn't even know she could play that thing," he explained to me. "Seemed like some kind of divine gift in her eyes. She said it always made her feel closer to the Lord when she sat down to plunk at it. I can testify that the entire congregation felt the same when those wonderful melodies poured forth Sunday after Sunday. Truth is, I wanted to buy it from the church, but it was a landmark of sorts, so we had to move on without it."

My papa was the same kind of optimist as Mama, and he said he'd take her request to the Lord for sure. I did not hold to the same amount of faith as my parents, so I was entirely skeptical of the "harp" prayer from the beginning. I didn't know then that "the Lord works in mysterious ways" is not some old saying but a heavenly truth.

After a few weeks, Mama stopped throwing up and remained just as lark-happy over the newest Osterminder child that would make its grand arrival sometime in late summer. She said if it was a girl, my sisters could name it. If it was a boy, then me and the others could choose. Of course the middle name would be "Ray." My sisters settled right away on "Cassie, after our grandmother on Mama's side." I was leanin' toward the name Skeeter, but Daddy said no child of his would be named after an insect designed to suck the life out of you whenever it could. Audie Ray got into the process by suggesting "Spot." Which, of course, was ludicrous, since that was the name of every dog we'd ever owned, even an all-black one.

Michael Ray's best friend Harold had died when they were in the third grade, so he suggested for the baby to be Harold Ray, if it was male in gender. That was okay with me, and the other boys agreed.

Any house with eight children is noisy, night or day, but Christmas Eve in our home sounded like the Fourth of July. Seemed everyone talked at once, though no one listened, until Mama put two fingers in her mouth and whistled one of her infamous, ear-splitting, calls-to-attention. Silence! (Mama grew up with seven brothers, so she knew how to handle us.)

"Children, I'd like ya'll to sit around the Christmas tree, if ya'll would not mind."

We tripped over each other in obedience.

"Each of you has been sweet and loving about the news of another baby, even after you knew we'd have to set aside money for the arrival. I thank you for that. It's meant a lot." She cleared her throat and dabbed at her eyes with the edge of her apron. "As your mama, it pains me to see you go with less than you might have because of the need for sacrifice, but—"

She cleared her throat again. By now, we were all squirming.

"I have a surprise," Mama said.

We started talking at once. "What is it, Mama?"

"Don't tell us you're having twins again." This came from Audie Ray, causing an uproar of laughter.

"Far as I know, Audie Ray, there is only one, but we'll see, won't we?"

That brought a groan from the rest of us.

"Shush now, let me share my surprise. Your granddaddy always said we should save a little money for a 'rainy day,' and well, I thought long and hard about what that means to this family." Audie Ray left our group and climbed in Mama's lap. "For sure we are not in dire straits, 'cause our family has plenty to eat and clothes on our backs, but Christmas is special. Therefore, I determined our absence of money for presents to be that 'rainy day'. . .so to speak."

By the look on Papa's face, I think Mama's surprise came as a revelation to him, too. But he said nothing—just grinned from ear to ear.

Mama asked Papa to drag a huge box from back of the pantry. It had Sears and Roebuck written on every side. Mary Ray started to squeal, and the twins jumped up and down like a couple of little puppies. The rest of us waited in quiet expectation. We knew that our mama had a whole list of things she could have bought from the Sears catalog, but she'd laid aside her own desires for her children, as usual.

I had a huge lump in my throat as her face lit up with joy, brighter than the Christmas tree, for the chance to make her children happy. Oh, how I wished at that moment to be rich, with money enough to buy Mama the harp she still dreamed of, the one she knew she'd never have.

My papa stood beside her and gave each of us a "God bless" when we came up for our gifts. The things Mama bought were mostly practical in nature, but she knew her children well. Therefore, we each had something unique, reflecting who we were deep inside. For me, it was a thick tablet and a box of number-two pencils, with a sharpener shaped like a cowboy boot.

My brothers and sisters were blessed as much as I was, but Mama's rainy-day fund had something for her husband as well. His Bible had nearly fallen apart at the seams, but Mama knew he'd never part with it for a new one, so she'd done the next best thing. She'd bought him a beautiful cover for it. . .one with a zipper and a handle.

Papa' eyes went all misty, soon as he saw what his special gift was all about. He tried to speak, but nothing came out. He reached out his hand and pulled our mama into a real tight hug. Her hands touched his face, and she whispered something in his ear.

My papa, never at a loss for words, could not get a sentence out of his mouth without a struggle. "Darlin'," he managed, "I have nothing for you. Nothing at all."

"Raymond Lee Osterminder, don't be stealing my joy by worrying about your lack of funds. It's only 'cause I'm sneaky that I've been able to keep my little secret. Please, I mean it. I'm fine."

Mama meant what she said, but Papa still looked somewhat like a bitty ant crushed on the sidewalk.

A pounding knock at the door interrupted our festivities. Mary Ray was sent to open it.

"Hey, Papa. Come here, quick! There's something queer-looking on the porch."

Papa walked to the door, peered outside, and scratched his head. "My goodness" was all he managed to say. "My, my, goodness. Lydia, I think you should take a look at this," he yelled.

She craned her neck from the living room to see what all the fuss was about. "Just tell me, Raymond."

"No, you need to come out here and look."

We walked her to the door in one tight group.

"What is it?"

"Dunno, looks weird to me."

"Why's it shaped so funny?"

"Dunno."

"Mama, there's a tag with your name on it."

"It's for you, Mama. You got a present after all."

Mama had not said a word, for unlike the rest of us, she had recognized the odd-shaped gift right away. Both hands covered her mouth, unbelieving eyes gone big as moons.

"Mr. Osterminder, is this your business?" Now her hands went to her hips.

Papa shook his head. "I'm bewildered, Lydia. I'm telling you the truth. I've no idea how this got here."

Finally, she pulled the velvet cover off. "But it's the same one, Raymond. I'm positive. It's the very same one."

"One what?" Audie Ray was walking all around Mama's Christmas present, not recognizing it to be a harp.

And not just any harp, mind you, but the hill country harp she'd never forgotten.

"Oh, oh," she repeated over and over, walking in circles, stroking its shininess with a soft touch, like it might disappear if she took her hand off it. Her fingers went across the strings. "It's all tuned up!" she squealed with delight. "But, Raymond, how in heaven did you get this here?"

"I tell you true, Lydia, I've no idea how this harp got here, or who could have brought it. It's a mystery to me."

"God's mysterious ways," we began to shout. "It's God's mysterious ways!" Then we begged for a song. "Mama, please, just one."

Papa brought a chair from inside, and Mama put the strange, heavenly instrument into position. Resting her face against one side, it looked like she was hugging the thing. Nice and slow, with eyes closed, my mama began to play. Even though her fingers were red and worked raw, she plucked the many strings with delicate strokes.

Right away, we recognized our family's favorite Christmas carol, "Silent Night." Despite the bitter west Texas wind blowing dust round our front porch, no one moved. We could have listened to our mama play that harp until the following Christmas.

From that day to this, no one has ever figured out how that hill country harp landed on our front porch on Christmas Day, 1951.

It's rare that all of us get together in one place anymore, but with modern communications, we remain close. And that includes Harold Ray. Amid our continued wonder of Jesus' birth, the timely mystery of Mama's Christmas harp has become an integral part of each and every family discussion. If Mama and Papa ever did find out how that old instrument got way across the great state of Texas, they never shared it with their children.

The lesson I learned that Christmas has stayed with me. I'm able to testify, without question, that God continues to work in mysterious ways, His wonders to perform.

Only One Wish for Me

Linda J. Reinhardt

It's the first Christmas without Grandpa Schooster for Andrew and Marie. Along with Marie's daughter, Caroline, they search the house for his special Christmas decorations and stumble upon his old journal.

Much to their amazement, they read all about their first Christmas with Grandpa Schooster after their own parents died and he took on the responsibility of raising his grandchildren, whom he adores.

He had taken them up to his cabin in the mountains. Upon arriving, he discovers the children have asked for a gift that only God can give to them. What could this gift be?

Together Andrew, Marie, and Caroline enjoy once again the story of how Grandpa spends the night discovering a gift that cannot be put under a tree. . . .

"Only One Wish for Me" was first performed as a play.

I know he had to have stored them up here. I've looked all over the house, and I can't find them anywhere," Marie stated. Her voice sounded weary. She pointed the flashlight down the narrow stairwell to help Caroline climb up through the attic door.

"I hope so, Mom. I'm getting tired. It seems we've looked everywhere." Caroline laid back across an old trunk parked in the middle of the attic and, with a flare of drama, threw her arm over her face.

"Oh, I know, honey. This can't be much fun for you. You've been a lot of help, though." Marie leaned over and tickled Caroline's stomach, causing a giggle.

"Mom"—she held on to Marie's hands—"it has been fun. I'm just tired and sad about Grandpa. But I like being able to help you and Uncle Andrew."

"Yeah, I'm feeling tired, too." Marie straightened and stretched with a quick look around the attic. "I think I'm going to start over in that corner and see if I can find the missing ornaments."

"Hey, Mom, can I take a look in this trunk?"

"Sure! You should find a lot of interesting things in it."

"Great!" Caroline rolled off the top of the trunk onto the dusty attic floor and grabbed the old rusty latch to open the lid. Marie continued on the hunt for Grandpa's Christmas decorations, but Caroline forgot all about those things once she became completely absorbed in emptying the items out of what her imagination called "the treasure box."

An aah escaped her lips when she pulled out an old, worn notebook. "A diary?" Caroline whispered. She leaned back against the trunk, soon lost in whatever secrets the diary held.

"Marie!" Andrew called before poking his head in the attic entrance. "I finished looking in the garage, and I didn't find them. Did you find any up here?"

Caroline looked up at her uncle Andrew. "I don't think she's found them yet."

"Oh! Andrew! Caroline! I think I finally found them! I can't believe it." Marie reached toward a box that was sitting on a high shelf.

"Yay!" Caroline exclaimed. "Now we can finish decorating the tree."

"Finally. I think we should have just gone and bought new ornaments," Andrew grumbled. "Hey, Marie, those are pretty high. Don't you think you should use a. . ."

Crash! The box and everything else on the shelf fell to the floor.

"No!" Marie fell down beside the box, scrambling to open it. It was nothing but broken pieces. "No!"

Andrew and Caroline hurried over to Marie.

"Mommy!" Caroline called.

"Marie! Are you all right?" Andrew bent down near her. "Did you get hurt?"

"No," Marie sniffled.

"Phew! I was afraid you'd hurt yourself." Andrew rubbed her back in an awkward gesture.

"These are irreplaceable, and now I've broken them." Marie sat back.

Andrew picked up one of the pieces and took a look at it. "These are just ordinary ornaments. There's nothing special about them. We can buy them at any store."

"No we can't, Andrew. These were Grandpa's. The ones he used to decorate the tree. But now he's gone, and we can't replace them."

"Oh, well, I wasn't thinking about it that way." Andrew's voice was sad.

"No. . .really?" Marie's voice dripped with sarcasm.

Both sat for a moment lost in their thoughts.

Marie exhaled slowly. "I'm sorry, Andrew. I just miss him so much. He's been there for us no matter what, ever since our parents died. I don't know how to deal with him being gone."

"Yeah, me neither."

"I'll never forget how scary it was the night our parents died," Marie whispered.

"You remember that night?" Andrew asked.

Marie nodded. "I'll never forget it." She gave a little shiver.

"I'm sorry, Marie. I only vaguely remember it."

"Well, you were pretty young. I'm surprised you remember it at all. We had a babysitter, and after Grandpa left the accident, he came home to stay with us. He tried not to wake us, but I heard him talking to the babysitter before she left. I thought it was strange Grandpa was there instead of Mom and Dad."

"You do remember that night!"

"I stayed in bed until after the babysitter left, but then I heard crying. It was Grandpa."

Caroline interrupted. "Mom, Grandpa wrote it all down. It's all in the old notebook I was reading by the trunk." She went back to get it. "Look!"

Caroline handed the book to Marie. She glanced over the pages. Tears rolled down her face unchecked onto the book. "Grandpa's journal," she whispered.

All three sat on the floor together. Andrew held on to Marie and read over her shoulder until she released it for him to hold. "Go ahead, Andrew. You read it for us. I can't." She wiped at her face.

Journal of Matthius Schooster

Tonight is the hardest night of my life. I thought I would go before my child. Part of my heart feels like it has been taken from me. If it wasn't for my precious grandchildren, I don't know what I'd do. They own the other part of my heart.

I had no idea how to tell the children their parents were gone forever. As usual, they surprised me. They seemed to understand all of this horror better than me. Even though they're sad, they have an unexplainable sense of peace about them. I don't understand it.

When I got to their house, I tried to be as quiet as possible. I went and checked on them and decided to let them sleep. I was in the living room when grief overwhelmed me.

"Grandpa?" I heard. "Grandpa, what's the matter?"

I couldn't talk. I was so overcome with emotions. My daughter was gone, and her babies were left without her.

Marie kept asking me over and over what was wrong. "Grandpa, why are you crying? Where are my mom and dad? Please, Grandpa, tell me what's wrong."

I pulled her close and started to say the awful words, but somehow, some way she knew. The poor little one fell into my arms sobbing. My heart ripped into even smaller pieces. Why is life so cruel?

We cried together until early morning. Then Andrew woke up, and it was time to tell him. Marie amazed me by asking if she could tell him. I wasn't sure about it. That's a lot of responsibility for a little girl. But I could see in her eyes it was very important to her.

When he entered the room, he was so excited to see me. "Grandpa!" He ran and dove onto my lap, giving me one of his wonderful hugs. I clung tight, knowing in just a few short seconds, his life would be forever altered.

Finally, he loosened his grip and held my face to rub noses together as is his little custom with me. Then his eyebrow raised, and he looked me in the eye. "Your eyes are all red. What's the matter, Grandpa?"

"Andrew." I could see Marie take a big gulp as she fought for composure. "Do you remember what we learned in Sunday school this week?"

I wondered what on earth they were teaching in Sunday school that would help this little girl tell her brother their parents were dead.

"Yes. Since Jesus lives in our hearts, someday we get to go and live with Him forever in heaven," Andrew answered proudly.

"That's right. It's a beautiful place and, best of all, Jesus is there." Marie gently touched Andrew's leg.

"I love Jesus!"

"So do Mom and Dad," Marie choked out.

"Hey, where are Mommy and Daddy?"

Marie positioned herself real close to Andrew and held his arms. "Andrew, they went to heaven. To live with Jesus just like we learned at Sunday school." Tears poured out of the sweet girl's eyes when she broke this news to her baby brother.

"What? When are they coming home?"

Marie shook her head and held Andrew tight. Andrew called out for his mommy and daddy repeatedly for what seemed like hours until he slipped into a merciful sleep. . . .

Andrew stopped reading the book and, just like the kid he'd been back then, wiped his nose with his shirt sleeve. "Wow, that was hard to read, especially today, without Grandpa here."

"Mom, how come you wanted to tell Uncle Andrew about your mom and dad dying?"

"Well, because Grandpa didn't know Jesus then. I wanted Andrew to know our mom and dad were with Jesus."

"Grandpa knew Jesus."

"Not then," Marie answered as she reached for the journal from Andrew. "Don't you remember Grandpa's story about how he met Jesus at Christmastime?"

"Sort of." Caroline snuggled closer to her mom.

"It's a very interesting story. Let's see if Grandpa wrote about it in his journal." Marie sifted through the notebook, stopping now and then to read a few pages. "Oh my goodness, here it is! Andrew, isn't this exciting? We get to hear the story again from Grandpa!"

Andrew scooted over to peer over her shoulder as she read.

Journal of Matthius Schooster

It was snowing like crazy this Christmas Eve night. I brought the kids up to my cabin in the mountains. The two of them are now in my care since earlier this year, when their parents died in that awful accident. I knew this Christmas would be hard for them, being the first one since their parents died, so I brought them up to the cabin to get away from it all. I love them so much I want to make the holiday as special as it can be.

Andrew and Marie were all cozy, huddled together on the floor in front of the fireplace. They were busy doing what they call "night devotions." Every night they ask me to read with them, but I'm not into that kind of stuff. They do it because their parents wanted them to read that book every night, so I won't take that away from them. But me, naw. I don't understand what all the fuss is about.

I could hear Marie, forever the teacher of her brother, say, "Okay, Andrew, last night we read in the book of Matthew, part of chapter 21. Tonight we'll read some more of it. We've almost finished the whole book."

"Wow! How much more is there?" Andrew responded.

Marie flipped through that Bible and counted. She announced they only had seven and a half more chapters to go. Then they would be done with the whole book of Matthew.

I don't know why it takes so long to get through that thing. I found my daughter's old Bible all worn and torn. She'd written all over it. Don't understand it.

Well, I like to listen to Marie as she reads since she's such a good reader. Don't pay attention to everything she says, but. . .she read something like, whatever things you ask in prayer, believing, you will receive. The two of them whispered and giggled together, then finished with the words "in Jesus' name, amen."

Hmm, I wondered what that was all about. Oh well, it was time for them to get to bed. I told them to start wrapping things up. They needed to get to bed so Santa could come with their gifts and still have time to stop at all the other kid's houses too.

Marie answered me with, "Santa can't bring what we want, Grandpa."

Oh, for crying out loud, it broke my heart. Of course Santa can't bring them what they want. They want their parents here for Christmas. I scooped those cute things up and swung them into the room, dropping them on their beds, giving them both tickles on their tummies.

Once Marie was able to talk again, she informed me that only Jesus could bring what they wanted for Christmas. And she informed me that she and Andrew had prayed about it. Since they knew it was God's will, they knew what they were getting for Christmas.

Andrew nodded. I didn't know how to answer. I mean, I thought they believed their parents were in heaven. Why would they think God would let their parents come back?

I had the two of them hop into their beds, but they insisted on praying before being tucked in. *How many times do they have to pray?* I wondered. I rubbed the top of my head, feeling a bit impatient. *Enough is enough.* But I played along and told them to get on their knees by their beds like they were taught. Andrew asked me if I was going to pray. And I said, "No, I'm not into that stuff, Andrew."

I can see I'm disappointing the boy, and it breaks my heart, but maybe someday they will forget all this nonsense. For now, I'll just play along with it.

I stood and listened for when they would finish. They really are quite cute prayers. Marie asks God to forgive her for not being nice to Andrew. And Andrew always does a funny little rib about Marie, like, "Thank You that Marie wasn't cranky." And then Marie will nudge Andrew. It's cute. I'm sure their prayers are smiled upon.

But then tonight I stood up straight when I heard my precious Marie say, "Please watch over us as we sleep. And, God? What we prayed about earlier, You remember, what Santa can't bring us for Christmas. . .well, we look forward to it as You promised. Thank You. In Jesus' name, amen."

Whoa, whoa, whoa, that disturbed me. *Surely these kids don't believe God promised to bring their parents back home for Christmas!* My eyes brimmed with tears, and I was filled

41

with a strong protectiveness.

I tried to tell them God may need more time than just one night to answer their prayer. God may need more notice than that. They didn't want to hear it. The two little kids informed me that, in the morning, they knew their special present would be here and Santa *could not* bring it. God promised in the Bible that *all* they had to do was ask, and they would receive.

How do I argue with that without hurting their memory of their parents? I thought. I felt sick. I didn't want those baby darlings' hearts broken any more than they already had been.

I tucked them in with a kiss and one more attempt to convince them not to expect anything to happen right away. "Give God some time," I said.

But Marie came back at me with, "God can do anything. He can answer our prayer right away."

I said good night and turned out the light. With heavy steps, I found my way over to my rocker. I rocked back and forth, troubled and wishing God would answer their prayer. I wanted life back to normal. Christmas without my daughter is heart-wrenching. I'm so glad I have these two. Marie looks so much like my Natalie.

I picked up that old Bible they had lying on the floor by the rocker. "Darn book, causing a whole bunch of trouble." I looked up toward heaven. "And so are You. Not that I think You have anything to do with it, but they do. This here book says whatever they ask God for, He will give to them. Well, what about tomorrow morning?"

I was so disgusted.

So, what, they ask, and then what? Tomorrow He'll produce their parents. Oh, these poor little ones. Tomorrow is going to be a tougher day than I thought.

I flipped my way through the pages. The book looked overwhelming to me. I stopped where the kids had a book marker and started to read that particular section. It was actually quite interesting. Different, but interesting. Funny thing, I actually got caught up in what I was reading and lost track of time. I got startled by a knock. I felt like I had been awakened from a deep sleep. I couldn't figure out where the knocking came from. It continued. It took me a minute to figure out someone was at the door.

How strange! Up here in the mountains on a snowy night, someone is knocking at my door?

When I opened the door, a man stood in what looked like a big white blanket wrapped around his head and it went all the way down to his feet. He had sandals on. Tonight of all nights! We stood and stared at each other. Neither of us said anything until I asked him to come in. I don't know why I asked a complete silent stranger in a blanket to come into my home, but I did.

For a minute I thought I might still be sleeping and was in the middle of a dream, but when I gave myself a pinch, it hurt. So this was real.

The man had a nice smile. I offered him my rocker by the fire. I figured he must be cold, considering what he was wearing.

But the man said, "No, that's all right. You can sit in your rocker. I'll just sit over on this stool."

We sat facing each other. I have no idea why, but for the first time since Natalie died, I felt happy inside. The place felt all warm and homey.

I stated this to the man, and he just continued to smile at me.

I felt confused because, as I said to the man, "I feel like I know you, but I know I don't."

The man had a sad tone to his voice when he answered. "Yes, a lot of people think they know me, but they don't. I do know you, though. I've been trying to get your attention for fifty-two years now."

What? I thought. *Fifty-two years? That's how old I am.* "Why didn't you just do what you did tonight and knock on my door?" I asked aloud.

The man said he had but I'd never heard him before.

I thought that was ridiculous, and I told him so. "Never heard you!? I heard you fine tonight! You must not have been knocking very hard!" I rocked back and forth in my rocker, very agitated.

The man answered in a calm manner. "Oh yes, I have. It took those two little children in there to soften you up to listen. They love you a lot, you know."

I smiled and nodded. "Yes, I know those two love me." Then I sat up with alarm. *Hey, how did he know my grandchildren?*

The man chuckled. "They were introduced to me when they were real young. After your daughter and her husband met me, they made sure those two knew who I was. Ever since, day and night, that family has been asking me to introduce myself to you."

"Isn't that a bit of an exaggeration? Those kids have been with me every day since earlier this year. There's no way they could have called you without me hearing them."

The man acted like he had a fun secret when he let me know they had. Like he had a private joke or something. I bristled.

Then the man leaned over to me and let me know that they called him whenever I left the room and at night right in front of me. He said I didn't pay attention, though, until tonight. Tonight the kids really disturbed me.

How on earth did this guy know all of this? I sat, deep in thought, in my rocker.

The man asked if I would like to talk about what's bothering me.

For some reason I can't explain, I poured my heart out to him. I told him about losing my daughter and her husband, Andrew and Marie's parents, earlier this year. I explained how this is the first Christmas without them. How hard I knew it would be not only for them, but for me. And how they read this book here, called the Bible. I lifted it up for him to see. He didn't take it from me, though.

I also told him, "You might not believe this, but they think God talks to them through this, and I am almost positive they got it in their heads, from what they read tonight, that if they ask God, He would let their parents be here tomorrow."

The man said firmly, but with gentleness and kindness, "They know their parents live in heaven now."

I nodded and agreed that is what they say. I mean, who doesn't say things to make themselves feel better? I didn't believe the kids believed it, though. I stood and poked at the fire. My insides were in turmoil.

Once again the man said with gentleness, "They believe it; I know they believe it. It's not their parents they're praying for."

"What?" I sat down, shocked. "Then who or what else are they praying for?" I put my hands over my face and moved them down slow, with a look at the man.

He simply said, "You."

My mouth flew open in shock. "Me? What on earth could trouble those kids about me?" Then I slapped my forehead with my hand when an awful thought hit. *Those poor kids must be afraid I'm not going to be there for them. That I'm going away, too.*

I had a strong feeling I could trust this man to help me work this out, but then he gave me a strange answer.

"No, they're afraid no one is there for you."

"For me? For me?" Oh! Then I got it. How funny. I chuckled and was filled with delight. I gave the man a wink. "They've been praying for me to have a match made in heaven, huh?"

The man chuckled along with me. Then he changed the subject, which I didn't mind because now I knew Marie and Andrew were okay. They wanted Grandpa Schooster to have a Grandma Schooster. I thought that was simply adorable.

"So, Mr. Schooster, how do you feel about Christmas?"

"Christmas? I love Christmas! It's one of my favorite holidays." *Isn't it everyone's?*

He asked me why. . .and why do I celebrate this holiday?

What? Did the guy go nuts? Hello? It's Christmas. "I've always celebrated Christmas. It's a tradition. What's December 25th without presents, food, decorations, and Christmas carols. It just couldn't be!"

"That's how some people have gotten to feel through the years. Christmas is only a tradition." The man nodded.

I explained it's also more than a tradition. It's a feeling a person gets inside this time of year. A feeling of hope and a feeling of giving!

Then the man said something that gripped my heart and made me see so clearly. "It's more than a tradition, and it's more than a day on a calendar. That hope and feeling of giving comes from the reason Christmas is celebrated. That reason is me. Without me, there is no Christmas."

I sat back in my chair, staring at the Bible. "Without you? You. . .oh my. . ."

Yes, I could almost feel Jesus smile as He answered me. I knew He stood with me as I opened the Bible and read the story of the baby in the manger, the baby named Jesus.

I now understood what Christmas was all about. Jesus came to earth, to live among us. God gave His Son for me, and if I believed, I would be saved.

I read until the night turned into morning.

It was quite hysterical when Andrew and Marie woke up in the morning. They poked their sweet little faces out their door, their hair all mussed up. I watched them come over to me with shocked expressions as they looked at the tree. That's when I realized I'd forgotten to put their gifts under the tree. But then I saw their shocked looks turn into smiles when they saw me reading the Bible. The book they believe God talks to them through. And now I know He talks to me through it, too.

Those children were right: Santa couldn't bring this gift or fit it under a tree. I gave them big hugs and said, "Merry Christmas, children, from Jesus and me!"

Normally, a parent leaves behind a legacy for their children, but instead my children left behind an eternal legacy for me.

Marie closed the journal. The three of them smiled at each other through their tears. "And look what a legacy Grandpa Schooster left for us."

"We know, as much as we miss him, Grandpa is with Jesus. He's having the best Christmas he could ever have."

"Isn't that the truth! He gets to spend Christmas in the presence of God. It makes missing Grandpa just a little easier, knowing he's celebrating Christmas in heaven."

"He's probably singing with the angels."

"Or making a joyful noise?"

They all laughed, knowing Grandpa could *not* sing.

Caroline started softly, and then, as Andrew and Marie joined in, she elevated her voice louder and louder. In the dusty old attic, they sang their own Christmas songs with the angels.

No Room for Jesus

Sharon Bernash Smith

It's hard enough growing up poor, but growing up without a mother who left only a note before leaving can make a child's heart grow hard, even a young child.

Bella won't admit her heart condition to anyone, but a neighbor knows, and soon her father will as well.

"Just because I hate my mother doesn't mean I don't love Jesus," Bella declares when confronted.

But God uses the celebration of Christmas and a younger sister's deep love for Jesus to break through the pain and sorrow of abandonment. That's when things begin to look up for Arabella, better known as Bella Jean.

December 27

Nobody I know would want to be me. I'm too tall, too skinny, and I'm pretty sure I'm coming down with acne. And, a few days ago, I was positive I'd be gettin' nothing for Christmas. See, my dad broke his leg when he fell from a scaffold at work. He's laid up for a goodly amount of time, and there's no mother here to make any money.

Don't think I'm feelin' sorry for myself, even though most people would have to agree I have good enough reason to be blubbering a fair share of the time. Oh, my mother's not dead or stashed in some hospital, ailing away. Nothing like that. Truth is, one day my sister and I came home from school, and Donna Jean—that's my mother—was gone.

Her note said: *Can't stay.* Not, *I hate you all. . .you're driving me crazy. . .*or, *I have me a boyfriend.* Two words is all she wrote.

My sister and Daddy cried for days, but not me. Donna Jean couldn't make me cry when she was here, and for sure I wasn't gonna cry after she'd gone.

I did feel sorry for Cassie, my sister, because she was so little and really needed a mama. Not that I even think of Donna Jean as anyone motherly. Now, Mrs. Pyland, the neighbor lady, she's the motherly type and has been real nice to Cassie and me ever since Donna Jean snuck away. Since the note, she's been extra nice to all of us.

Donna Jean left two Christmases ago, and you'd think by now, my dad would have gotten over her and all that. But just the other night I heard him praying with Cassie, and he actually said a prayer for Donna Jean: "Lord, bless Donna Jean wherever she is. Amen." I say, "Amen" all right, amen to anything having to do with her. Funny, the more I try not to think of her, the more her face kind of floats into my mind. I wonder why that is?

Well, back to Christmas. Whenever I try to talk with my daddy about the "problem" of Christmas—specifically, no money—this is what he says: "When times get tough, the tough get going."

I don't even have a clue what that means. I'm pretty sure Cassie doesn't, either, but she always says "yeah" when he says it. He told her the Lord would provide. That's another thing he's always sayin'. He's real determined for Cassie to believe it, especially this time of year. And I'll tell you why.

See, Cassie loves Christmas more than any human being I know. Which is why she was so intent to bake her special cake.

"We should have a birthday cake for Jesus," she announced, all happy-like.

"Why are you telling me?" I asked.

"Because I can't make one by myself, and you know it."

"Soooo?"

"I hate it when you say that."

"Soooo?"

That's when she dissolved into a bucket of tears.

"Shut up, Cassie. I'll help you make the stupid cake."

"Shame on you, Sissy. You shouldn't say anything about Jesus is stupid."

"Cassie, get real. Do you think Mary and Joseph had a birthday cake for Jesus?"

She got real quiet. "Do you?"

"No way. Don't you know anything?"

"Hey, I got a whole lot of thinkin' going on in my head."

"Yeah, right!" She started to cry another bucket, so I said "sorry."

We had to borrow some stuff from Mrs. Pyland but ended up with everything we needed. Cassie proudly announced to Dad that we didn't want any help when he offered.

Cassie got more flour on her dress than in the bowl, but she was having a great time, judging by her constant toothless smile. I don't get it. I don't get her.

Once I asked Mrs. Pyland why my sister was so dang happy all the time. She said, "Girlie (that's what she calls me), it's because she knows Jesus."

I shook my head in hearty disagreement. "No, that can't be it. 'Cause I know Jesus, too."

"But"—she let out a long sigh—"not in the same way."

"What's that supposed to mean?" I said, both hands on my hips. (I'm really frustrated with someone when I do that.)

She took my hand and sat me next to her on the creaky porch swing. "Girlie, there are lots of people who say they know Jesus. But some of them know Him with their head, and others know Him in their heart." She patted herself on her big, apron-covered bosom right about where her heart would be. She had this faraway look in her black eyes when she said all that. "There's a big difference."

"Don't tell me you're thinkin' I don't have Jesus in my heart!" I screamed. I jumped off the swing and stood right in front of her, madder than a hornet. " 'Cause I do, you know. I prayed that prayer with my daddy. . .years ago."

"Oh now, girlie, I ain't sayin' you don't, but—"

"That's an awful big 'but.' But what?" Now I was jumping up and down on her old porch.

"Well, I think that you got some strong emotions in your heart. . .stuff that don't leave much room for Jesus." She looked at me with big ol' cow eyes.

"Like what emotions?" I was shoutin' now.

"Like a whole lotta fury." When she said that, she was shakin' her head back and forth, slowly like.

I could tell she had something left to say, and for sure, I knew it had to do with Donna Jean.

I ran off the porch then but got the last word anyway. "Just because I hate Donna Jean does not mean I don't love Jesus." I was halfway home when I said it, but trust me, it was loud enough for even an old, hard-of-hearing black woman to make out.

That was weeks ago, but watching my sister while we were baking her Christmas cake made me remember the whole conversation.

The minute that cake came out of the oven, Cassie started singin' happy birthday to Jesus. By the look on her face you'd think He was right in our dilapidated, pea-green-painted kitchen. At first, I thought her face was lit up from the heat of the oven and all. Then I realized the glow was coming from her insides. For some unknown reason, big hot tears poked at my eyes. I blinked about half a dozen times and put the heels of both hands hard against them.

"Oh, Sissy, thank you." Cassie's voice was soft as cotton candy.

When I tried to talk, my voice sounded real peculiar, like when I'm close to gettin' a cold. "What in blue blazes for?" I croaked.

"For helping me make the most bee-u-tee-ful cake in the whole wide world."

"Cassie, we've not put one bit of decoration on this cake."

"I know that, silly," she said. "But in my mind, I can see it all finished. Jesus will be so happy."

I couldn't hold back those stupid tears right then, though I tried with all my might. Instead, I ran out the back door and hid behind a musty-smellin' camellia bush. I didn't know what was happening. I guessed I must have let my guard down for a second or two. But I could not get that look on Cassie's face out of my mind.

Pure love. That's what got my eyes to waterin' like they did. My little sister's face was full of pure, sweet love. Despite having no mama and dim prospects for Christmas, Cassie could still love. I'm amazed I recognized it, seeing as how my heart really was like Mrs. Pyland said. Full of fury, I mean.

In the dark behind that dirty bush, I realized the truth about me, Arabella Mead. My eleven-year-old heart was holding enough fury to fill ten of the ugly boxcars that rolled through town every couple of hours. I crouched down with my back resting against our house and covered my mouth with both hands, so nobody inside would hear me. Then I wailed like a baby for the hurt I could not keep in.

I was ignorant to the fact that a human being's tear ducts could pour out so much salt water. Finally exhausted, I must have fallen asleep despite the cold.

🎄

Next thing I know, my daddy was pulling me out as gentle as he could manage, hefting me up into his arms to carry me inside, which wasn't easy, him bein' in a cast and all. I thought he'd be mad, but he kept whispering, "Poor little Bella, my poor little Bella," over and over. The smell of him was Lava soap and mothballs. They comforted me just like the smell of Donna Jean used to. Once he laid me down next to my sleeping sister, I started to bawl all over again.

"Bella Jean, tell me why you're crying, my special girl?"

Every time I opened my mouth to speak, a big old sorrowful sound came busting out. Was it really me, crying like some big, fat baby?

"Are you hurt, Bella, sick or something? Tell me."

Daddy's voice was sweet as spring well water. I was beginning to think I might not ever be able to speak. I pointed to my chest and whispered, "My heart hurts."

Daddy took me up out of bed and limped over to the rocking chair. He sat down, me hanging over his lap a good ways. He never said a single word, just rocked and rocked until I finally stopped crying and could breathe mostly normal.

"I'll tell you what's wrong, but you've got to promise not to tell a soul, Daddy." I hardly recognized my raspy voice.

"You know I'm a man of my word, Bella Jean. You can trust me. I promise not to tell anyone."

"I. . ." How could I tell my daddy what I had only just admitted to myself? Must have been something about the comfort of the rocking that coaxed it right out of my mouth. "I. . .miss. . .Don. . .my. . .mama." There—I'd said it.

Daddy rocked awhile longer in silence, me resting against his front, every beat of his heart keeping time to the rockin'. Then he whispered to the top of my head: "Bella Jean, it's okay. A girl your age needs a mama. God made children to love their mamas and daddies."

"I did love her, even when she did unmotherly things," I cried. "Even when she embarrassed me in front of the whole third-grade class and Mrs. Sweeney, I loved her. It's when she left that horrible note that I had to stop. If I did still love her, it would plainly hurt more than I could possibly stand."

"That's when you decided to hate her."

"Yes sir, exactly. How long have you known?"

"Well, I have to admit," he said, pushing me back to look full in my face, "it's taken awhile to figure it all out, but I've been prayin' for you and Cassie. I been prayin' for me, too. . .that God would help me be a wiser daddy." He gave me one of his bear hugs.

I know my daddy will keep his word, because he's that kind of man.

Funny, right after my breakdown things started turning around. Like I said, a few days ago I thought for sure Christmas would be a pitiful celebration. Boy, was I surprised.

Christmas Eve, Daddy, Cassie, and me were enjoying Jesus' birthday cake, exactly like Cassie wanted, when a booming knock at the front door brought us all out of the kitchen. Cassie got there first and started jumpin' up and down like a scared-up jack rabbit the minute she saw who it was, and what they were carrying. It was the Reverend Carmichael and a couple of fellas from church, loaded down like the wise men's camels. Me and Cassie had never seen so many presents in all our years combined.

I noticed Daddy had tears in both eyes when Reverend gave him a big, Merry Christmas kind of hug before leavin'.

Most daddies would have made their little girls wait until the "official" Christmas to open gifts, but my daddy's not like other fathers. We opened them all just as soon as the Reverend left.

Cassie got tons of stuff, including a doll that wets her very own diapers, which has kept my sister busy, since she feeds the doll at least once an hour.

I got some smell-good cologne, a stuffed black poodle with a silver collar, and about twenty-seven different colors of hair ribbon. I also got the most perfect gift for me. . .a pink diary. It has a lock with a key. It's how I'm able to write down all this stuff.

Even though I'm only eleven, I think all this writing has helped me sort out some things in life. The number-one thing I know for sure is this: God is real. I only have to look into the face of my sister to know that. He made me her sister for a reason.

Then I know that *I am loved*. For sure, my daddy loves me. Cassie tells me she loves me every single night before we go to sleep, even before I sing her "Silent Night." Mrs. Pyland loves me enough to tell me the truth when I don't want to hear it. And, oh yes, I know Donna Jean loves me.

My mother sent me and Cassie a postcard from Florida that came the day after Christmas. On the front it had a smiling dolphin, jumping out of really blue water. On the back it said:

Hope you have a nice Christmas. It's hot down here.
Love, Mama, XOXO

Well, Diary, that's all for now.
Sincerely, Arabella J. Mead*

*P.S. Better known as "Bella Jean"

The Night Visitors

SHARON BERNASH SMITH

With a husband at war on Christmas Eve, putting together toys for two children becomes a monumental chore for one young mother in the 1940s. William's letters have stopped, and she's in tears over missing him but becomes distracted by carolers singing in the rain outside her door.

How precious were the words they sang about the baby Jesus. Invited in from the cold, they make light work of the toy assembly and leave, having lightened a woman's heart as well as her task.

After they've gone, she discovers they've left something behind. . .a miracle. . .heaven-sent and heavenly delivered.

Christmas Eve, 1944

Every time she made a little headway on Hayley's tricycle, tears blurred her vision, and she'd have to stop. Yet there was still Noelle's dollhouse to finish. Getting up from the floor, Catherine walked to the window, pushed back the drapes, and stared at the rain. It hadn't stopped for days, making getting the tree a muddy mayhem, instead of the cheerful trek she'd wanted it to be.

Pressed against the pane, her thoughts turned to William. *Her* William, faithful husband, father, and soldier.

It'd been over a month since she'd heard anything from him. This was the longest it had taken for a letter to reach home, and her mind cluttered with the worst thoughts possible. Still, she had hope. Hope in the God of the Universe, who watched over them always. She believed that if it was William's time, and the Lord allowed it, His strength would get her through. How, she couldn't imagine, yet there was peace in the knowledge of God's sovereignty just the same.

Now if she could only get through Christmas. Hopefully a little red trike and a two-story dollhouse wouldn't send one lonely woman over the moon. William's parents had provided both toys for their only grandchildren, and she was grateful but regretful for turning down William's father's help.

"Lord, please forgive my whining. And please, wherever William is right this moment, touch his heart with courage and protect his life. Amen."

She looked up just as a group of people made their way along the driveway to the house. Who in their right mind would come out on a night like this? That's when she heard the singing, clear and rich through the glass. Carolers.

They waved as they got closer. Catherine waved back before heading to the door. They were singing "Joy to the World." Standing in the miserable downpour, every face reflected the sentiment of the words being sung. The entire picture was joyful to behold, enveloping her with a wash of Christmas spirit.

When they'd finished, she begged them to come in out of the weather. She had hot cocoa on the stove and even some homemade cookies Hayley, Noelle, and baby Silas had helped her make earlier.

The carolers apologized for dripping on the entry floor, but she assured them it didn't matter in the least. After the soggy coats were laid by the fire, one of the group noticed the unfinished toys spread out near the Christmas tree.

"Looks like you could use some help with these."

"Yes, I'm not very handy, as you can see. That's my husband's forte, I'm afraid."

"Is your husband at war, then?"

"Yes, yes he is." Despite her brave efforts not to, Catherine broke down into tears. "I'm sorry. It's just that I've not heard from William for over a month, and well, with tomorrow being Christmas, I guess..." She couldn't finish before more crying took her breath.

"Would you mind if we prayed for you now?"

Before she could answer, she was surrounded by bodies, with words of comfort falling upon her spirit. Peace, like a gossamer veil, swirled round and round her head. She couldn't recall ever having the same degree of serenity in her entire life.

When the visitors finished praying, they offered to help with assembling the toys.

Singing in perfect harmony as they worked, the task was completed in less than fifteen minutes. Catherine's elation had no words, but her smile said it all, and they told her so when she tried to thank them. Each gathered their rain gear, and she walked them to the door. Gigantic snowflakes surprised them all. Already they were covering the neighborhood.

"Oh, how perfect!" she exclaimed.

The carolers agreed and waved good-bye before heading down the street and out of sight.

"Merry Christmas, merry Christmas, and thank you," she called after them.

Suddenly the hot chocolate came to mind.

"Oh my." She ran down the driveway, slipping and sliding to the end. Looking up and down the street both ways revealed nothing. The entire neighborhood was still. . .and empty. Perhaps the snow had covered any footprints. But that quickly? She wondered.

Standing beneath the falling loveliness, she turned round and round in admiration before returning to the house. On the porch she paused for one more look. "God, mighty is Your handiwork." A shiver ran down her spine. She turned, stomped her feet, and stepped back inside, closing the door tightly.

"Brrr, I need to stoke the fire." Passing the hall table, an object caught her eye. Strange. Perhaps one of the visitors had forgotten something.

Stepping closer, she recognized a letter. . .an airmail letter. Grabbing it, she stared at what her mind could not comprehend. Blood pounded in her head. It was from William! The entire envelope, tattered and torn, was covered with water spots front and back. In shock, she realized something was missing as well. . .the address. It was obliterated, except for a few faded numbers.

"But how. . . ?" Her mind raced with possibilities.

The night visitors! Completely mystified, Catherine held up the letter to lamp light, slowly opened one end, and reached inside to take out the precious message.

My darling Catherine,

I am safe and, as always, wishing I was with you and the children. Is it so terribly hard for you, my sweet? I promise to make up for every day we have to be apart, even if it takes the rest of my life. . . .

"Oh William, William. . .I miss you so," she whispered.

These days seem darker than a man's soul can bear, but with God's mercy, I continue. My only hope is in Him, and my endless, intimate thoughts of you and the children.

Chances are, you might not even get this letter before Christmas. I know the day will be difficult, especially since I have no way to send you anything. But remember me, knowing I am with you in spirit. Place your hand over your heart. . .that's where I'll be. . .forever.

There isn't much time to write. If I want this letter to go out today, I must close. Merry Christmas, sweet Catherine.
Your loving husband,
William

P.S. I pray every day that God will give His angels charge over you. . .Christmas angels, of course.

Of course! The night visitors were angels, the very ones who'd brought William's undeliverable letter. . .her own Christmas miracle.

"I should have known," she whispered. "I should have known."

The clock struck midnight.

Catherine placed a hand exactly over her heart. "Merry Christmas, my darling William. Merry Christmas, and hurry home."

Starlight and Snow

Rosanne Croft

Keeping their tradition, a young girl and her family suffering from the pain of divorce go to see the Nativity scene on Christmas Eve. In spite of her pain, the girl reaches out to her little brother and tries to keep her faith in the midst of her own hurt. God allows her to see, for a moment in time, the reality of Jesus' birth.

What she learns in that dreamlike moment will never leave her. . . .

T he five of us whined and complained, but Mom wouldn't listen. She'd always had a stubborn streak. I must have been louder than everyone else, because she spoke to me first.

"Ruth Anne, we're going as a family to see the Nativity scene at church, like we do every year." Her voice cracked a little. "I'll be right back. I'm going to warm up the car."

I paced in front of the living room window, watching as Mom started the station wagon in the driveway. The snow came down in penny-sized flakes, sticking to the sidewalk.

It was the first Christmas Eve since Dad had left our house to marry someone else. Christmas loomed ahead with a big dark hole in it.

Mom rushed back inside with snowflakes on her brown hair.

I met her at the door. "It's snowing like crazy, Mom. We could just wait until tomorrow, when we have to go to church anyway," I ventured.

She was ready for my opposition. "No. Call the other girls and Tommy, and get your coats on."

I helped four-year-old Tommy put on his coat and hat. His face had worn the look of an old man ever since Dad had left. He reached up to tap me on the shoulder.

"Ruth Anne, is Daddy going to be there?" he asked.

I shook my head. "Just us," I told him.

His face crumpled. He didn't say anything but furiously pulled on his mittens.

Six-year-old Kathleen whipped her scarf around her neck. "Sorry, Tommy. You're the only boy in the family now." Her two front teeth were loose and landed in weird angles on her lips as she talked, faintly whistling.

Chrissy never said much. She stood motionless, leaning on the doorjamb, her wool coat buttoned to the top. She was the only one of us with brown eyes, and they said it all. Tonight her eyes threw darts of lightning. "I hate Christmas this year," she mumbled into the collar of her coat. "It's never going to be the same."

Terri, our only teenager, thought she was too cool to go anywhere with us younger kids. She pouted but slipped on her coat. She never wore a hat, because it messed up her carefully ratted and sprayed hairdo. Her lips were tight with annoyance.

I put on a long stocking cap, inappropriate for my age, but Dad had bought it for me a few Christmases ago. It was warmer than my other one, and I refused to give it up.

"Maybe when we come home, we can make hot cocoa," I said, yearning for an inkling of a cozy Christmas feeling.

Kathleen looked ecstatic. "With marshmallows?"

"Maybe," Mom said.

Snow lay in three-foot piles around our driveway where Chrissy and I had shoveled it the day before. That was one of the many jobs we'd taken on since Dad had left. Now the wind swirled snow around our faces as we climbed into the car and sat on the brittle seats. It was my turn to be in the front, and in spite of the heater blowing full blast, I could still see my breath.

I peered at Mom. Her face was determined and almost happy.

The enormous Gothic doors were always open at the cathedral, even in the dark of night. We hustled ourselves out of the cold car into the sparkling night and piled inside the glowing church, snow melting instantly off of our coats and landing in puddles on the yellowed linoleum floor. Surrounding the marble holy water fount, each of us removed a mitten and dipped a hand into the chilly water, touching the sponge on the bottom of the bowl. We crossed ourselves with proper solemnity and looked around. There were a few winter-wrapped people in the front pews.

The warmly lit interior smelled of candle wax and pine needles. Our eyes adjusted to the candlelight, and there it was: an outsize Nativity scene on the right of the center of the church. The regular old statue of Saint Joseph had disappeared from his niche. In his place was a forest of dark evergreen trees, smelling of juniper and pine. We followed Mom and tiptoed all the way up the nave, feeling like pesky little birds under the Gothic canopy. It was a relief when we got to the cushy kneeler directly in front of the crèche.

The Sisters decorated with tiny glittering lights on the lush evergreens behind the wooden stable. Fuzzy gray moss from Woolworth's lay on the shingles of the stable roof. A pearly angel in swirling clothes and feather wings hovered over the scene where the timeless faces of Mary and Joseph beheld the infant. Mary, her blue veil framing her face; Joseph, one hand on his heart and one holding a lamp; the shepherds, looking shy and hesitant. Animal eyes peered through the darkness of the stable, lying in the same straw shared by the ceramic child in the manger. In the forest of trees, the wise men strode toward the peaceful place to lay their wealth at the feet of the baby.

Silently we knelt there, and a hush emerged in the starlit trees. In the quiet arose a sound: the wispy rustle of angel wings against the rough wooden roof of the stable.

"Over here, Tommy," I whispered, seeing his eye level hit the marble railing square, so he couldn't see too well.

He slipped his wet boots off and stood on the kneeler beside me. "Shhhhhh," he said, one finger to his mouth, "it's holy in here."

I nodded. I felt it, too. Mom's eyes were shut, her lips moving. The annoyance on Terri's face had disappeared, and she stared just as intently as the rest of us at the apparition before us. Chrissy's liquid eyes reflected the soft candlelight. Her head tilted a little, and her hat was askew, showing dark wet hair clinging to her forehead. Kathleen wiggled her loose teeth and sniffed as she gazed at the baby Jesus.

"See," I whispered to Tommy, "there's the baby Jesus."

"Where's His daddy?" he asked.

"That guy there, standing by Him. That's Joseph, His father on earth. But really, His dad is God."

"Where's God?"

"You can't see Him," I said slowly, "but even if you can't see Him, He watches over us all the time."

"Even when our daddy's gone?"

"Yep." I bit back the lump in my throat. "That's why the baby Jesus came—because we belong to Him."

A candle sputtered and went out, releasing a pleasant smokiness in the air. Something in the air changed, and I stared as the scene before me rippled and moved. The panorama lived and breathed! I could smell the smoke and straw; the cold nipped my nose, and the wind rippled the angel's lush garments and my bangs. Mary smiled tenderly, gazing at the Baby with star-filled eyes, and Joseph held the lantern up a little higher so I could see. The donkey snorted, and the sheep pawed at the hay with their hooves before they abruptly lay down, scattering wisps of it around the stable. I saw Jesus, sleeping in the manger, His little chest rising and falling, snug and magnificent at the same time. And the break in my heart filled with joy.

Out of the murky night, the tiny sparkly lights and the wavering candles swelled up like a song, swirling into a divine impressionistic painting. I had a radiant feeling that all would be well—that it was safe to rejoice because Jesus was here. His little flesh-colored ceramic hands seemed to direct the whole world from that bed of straw.

Christmas really had happened. Jesus knew about us and our daddy. He wasn't just a baby. He was God's Son, and He loved us, and I knew it. And in that moment, I realized that everything was right in the world, even as earthly circumstances would argue with me that it wasn't.

I blinked hard, and the air changed again. The lights on the trees still sparkled, but I could see they were electric, not stars. The ceramic figures stiffened into the two-foot statues they were. A lone feather floated down from the luminous angel, landing like a snowflake near baby Jesus' glass head. The enchantment was gone but my joy wasn't. That moment in time was carried in my heart for the rest of my life.

Mom steered the station wagon back home as the snow stopped, and we looked from the car windows at the stars in contented silence. There were no tears that night, no more angry scowls or whining.

The stars twinkled back at us. "All is well," they said. "Jesus is with you."

Christmas in Pippa Pass

Sharon Bernash Smith

There's poor, and then there's poor. Things can't get much bleaker financially when you're poor in Pippa Pass, Kentucky, at Christmas.

With the wind pushing cold and despair at a young mother's door, she prays for God's intercession in order to bless her family in the dead of winter.

What she receives proves that God's faithfulness can be found anywhere, even in the midst of poverty, and especially during the early hours of a Kentucky Christmas morning.

December 24

She laid another piece of seasoned hickory into the stove. Pungent smells of snow-damp wood heating in the fire rose to meet her. She hoped the flame would be enough to dry it out.

"Not many pieces left," she said. Words spoken to no one.

Her back ached. Overworked fingers were chapped from the cold, making them old too soon. Even with the stove going full blast, Kentucky wind blew through the cracks around the door, keeping the air stinging. She draped another quilt over the baby's cradle, careful to leave his face uncovered. Wilson T, already dubbed "Button" by his sisters, was baby number five. He slept on, oblivious only to night's long slumber.

How'll we make it, Lord? I don't mean to be lackin' in faith, but this Christmas is a test fer sure without no money. Even if I had hundreds, I couldn't git to the store in this bad a weather anyways. She shook her head.

The baby woke, and she grabbed him before his cries stirred any of the others. Despite deep poverty, despite the snow blown in piles to the roof, her heart refused to give up. Rocking and nursing her first boy gave Hattie Jo Ross purpose. Because purpose existed, her life had meaning and something more. There, in the deep recesses of her worn being, an ember of hope smoldered steadfast against despair.

She settled into the feeding, felt her milk let down, and relaxed. Her eyes swept the room that had been her home since she and Wilson Lee Ross married when she was only fifteen. Nothing had changed much in ten years.

Lavender, pennyroyal, meadowsweet, and at least a half-dozen other herbs were drying next to a hand-painted sign: *Love grows here.*

She brushed baby Wilson's perfect little ear with a kiss. "Sure does, right, Button?" Her head went back against the chair.

She'd been so eager to grow up. Wilson Lee had waited for her to do just that, confessing many times that he'd fallen in love when she was in the sixth grade and he in the ninth. She smiled, thinking of him. He loved her and the children but, like every other man on the mountain, suffered from depression brought on by the cruel poverty that stalked most of them like Satan himself. Some had left Pippa Pass to other parts of the state, but some had escaped Kentucky's borders altogether.

They'd stayed. "Too much Ross history in the hills," he'd said. "Too many buried kinfolk to pack off and leave, Hattie Jo."

She'd reminded him, "'Twas the living bein's that mattered most," just in case he'd missed that fact.

That was then. But after the bitter winter, still unfinished, Wilson Lee just might be about changing his stubborn mind. She switched the squirming infant to the other side.

Lord, I need a plan for my children's Christmas, she prayed. At least they had more food than a week ago. The Pippa Pass Primitive Baptist Church had hauled groceries by mule-drawn sled all the way up the mountain to their front door. Brother White and Brother MacPherson had made the journey nearly seven miles one way and wouldn't even except a thank-you for the effort.

"No thanks needed, Hattie Jo," they'd said. "Merry Christmas."

Tired of the same old venison and possum, she'd needed Wilson Lee's help to keep the children from eating everything at once. Fresh oranges from who-knows-where were the favorite, and she'd peeled one, cold and tangy, right off.

They had their own larder, of course, full of "staples" that wintered them over most times—dried apples, early vegetables canned from the garden—but the fall had come too soon, catching the mountain dwellers by surprise. At least half of the harvest lay frozen solid, a cold reminder that poverty, overtaken by harsh weather, means disaster. Hattie Jo suspected some might even die, especially the elderly lacking enough fuel for warmin' old bones.

Button was full and satisfied. *Praise God for my good, healthy milk.* She kissed the baby before tucking him back in the wooden cradle. When she straightened, Christmas ideas started to pop in her mind. "Thank Ya, Lord."

She pulled her gray wool coat off its peg and grabbed the sewing shears from the treadle machine whose label now read INGER, instead of SINGER. After securing the gate legs under the kitchen table, the coat was laid out, backside up. She began to hum "O Little Town of Bethlehem."

Using a pattern made from newspaper, four long pieces of wool, intended for neck scarves, were deftly cut. After hemming them, the names of the girls came to life with a running hand stitch: Amy, Sue Ann, LaRue, and Frankie Mae. How surprised they'd be! That smoldering hope stirred.

The clock chimed 2:00 a.m. The scarves looked wonderful, but they could use another touch.

Instantly, the trunk under the stairs came to mind. Her life tokens were stored there. That trunk was her memory keeper. Tonight she hadn't the time for long sentiments, so she shuffled right to the bottom. Wrapped in yellowing tissue, the remembrance lay waiting. . .a bright red velvet muff, soft as goose down. Her daddy had brought it home from the war, a wildly extravagant gift for the hills of Kentucky. Tears stung her eyes. This was the only tangible thing she had left of him after he died in the mines at age forty-two. Swallowing against the lump in her throat, Hattie Jo removed the muff.

Excitement erased most of the fatigue from the long day. Four perfect hearts cut from the soft velvet went directly under the name of each girl. "Oh my. . .they're beautiful, exactly like my little darlins'." One more thing to do, and they'd be declared "finished." She placed a few stalks of lavender into a paper bag, and put the new gifts inside. After a good shake, they smelled of springtime and romps in high mountain meadows. The heady aroma, full of more inspiration, led to another idea.

Linen hankies, found tucked inside the muff, took only minutes to fashion into dainty mountain dolls. . .a trick her Memaw taught her years before. French knots formed tiny black eyes and upturned smiles.

There was enough tissue left to wrap each gift. Tied with red and green hair ribbon she'd bought weeks ago with egg money, she'd use the leftovers to fix the girls' hair into festive braids for the holiday.

They'd gotten a Christmas card from Wilson's sister in California, and even though it had palm trees on it, she used the backside for individual nametags, signed: *Love, Mommy and Daddy*. Wilson Lee's pride often got in the way of accepting help from the outside, but these gifts came from the inside, with the Lord's driving force.

The gifts fit just perfectly under the tree they'd cut yesterday morning before the storm had moved in. Strings of popcorn and individual pinecones hung from branches, sharp with fragrance. Homemade stars and "pretties" created by four-year-old Frankie Mae, which weren't readily recognizable as ornaments, looked beautiful just the same. Even the oranges from church added to the bright and cheery atmosphere pushing against the poverty howling at the door. Wild beeswax candles glowed better than any storebought kind. They were not, and never would be, poor in spirit, and that's what mattered most to Hattie Jo.

Button woke again. Gathering him to her breast, she deftly nursed him from a sling while finishing the Christmas treats. Breakfast would begin the celebration, so she added cinnamon Red Hots, kept secret from the children, to homemade applesauce. The pot of bubbling comfort turned a soft pink as the candy treats did their trick. Mouth watering, she couldn't help laughing out loud for the delight of her efforts. One of her biddies had given up a rare winter's egg that would be used to make flapjacks. Smothered with the applesauce, it'd be a feast. Already, the children's squeals of delight rang in her head.

Sitting down to finish the baby's feeding, that smoldering ember of hope burst into full flame. Her mind had gone from despair, only hours ago, to full-on Christmas joy. "Thank You, Lord." Her eyes roamed around the transformed room. "Thank You for loving this family to such a degree that You'd give me all this to share."

The baby stretched and opened his eyes, looking directly into his mother's face, a warm little hand resting right where her heart beat against his cheek.

"Good mornin', Button."

The girls' squeals weren't just imagined anymore. She turned to see the entire family tumbling down the stairs to embrace her night's efforts.

"Oh, Mama, how'd ya do it all?"

"I had a heap of help, to tell the truth. Merry Christmas, everyone."

Wilson Lee was staring at her across the room. The love she saw in his eyes was her Christmas gift. It would last a lifetime.

A Dr. Dobson Christmas

Sharon Bernash Smith

Have you ever tried to micromanage something? How about Christmas? Did it work out like you planned?

Claudia loves the Lord with all her heart, and she loves celebrating His birthday. Nobody tries harder or works longer at preparing for the Christmas celebration than she does.

Only every year, all her hard work and good intentions end up in frustration, late greeting cards, and sometimes even a disaster or two. Not very glorifying to the Lord of lords and King of kings, that's for sure. When one of her sons declares that his most profound memory of Christmas is her "freaking out" every year, she's devastated.

How will this year be different? Well, for one thing, she's going to take Dr. Dobson's advice and do something she's not done before: prioritize the real meaning of Christmas.

The powerful lesson she learns will help her celebrate the holiday with renewed passion.

Dr. Dobson would be so proud.

❦

She was stuck in holiday traffic ten blocks from the entry to the mall. "It gets worse every year," she muttered to herself. The familiar melody of the Focus on the Family radio broadcast came on. "Let's Make a Memory" was today's theme. Claudia reached to turn up the volume. Dr. Dobson's sage advice was the highlight of her day. Today's program was dedicated to the "real" meaning of Christmas, while creating lasting memories, built on shared family preparations.

She wished she could write down all the ideas covering the entire season. But by the time she reached the parking lot and found a spot on the back forty, the show had ended.

Yet now she was pumped! Inspired! This would be the year of the "Dr. Dobson, Perfect Christmas." She had a head start. She'd already made a list. It was complete, too. . .before today's ideas, that is. Never mind, she'd make a new list when she got home. No one put more thought into Christmas than Claudia Smith. But somehow, no matter how much thought or effort went into the preparations, she felt frazzled every single year.

Perhaps *frazzled* didn't quite describe the true state of her being at the end of the Christmas season. Charbroiled-burnt-out rang truer. But wasn't it the thought that counted? After all, she agonized over every single gift, every single decoration, and since nothing said lovin' like something from the oven, she agonized over dozens and dozens of homemade cookies. One year she'd fallen asleep at the kitchen table, her face nearly in the frosting bowl. . .spatula in hand.

Once inside the mall, she realized she'd left her checkbook and credit cards in the glove compartment of the car. This was the story of her life. *I don't get it, Lord. Why am I so disorganized? You know I have the best intentions, right?* Something about the road to hell being paved with good intentions ran through her mind, but she guiltily dismissed it.

The shopping trip interrupted, she sighed and elbowed her way out of the mall, trying to remember where she'd parked. In the dark, everything looked different. It took her five minutes to find the SUV, and another five to dig through her oversized purse for the keys, only to realize she'd locked them inside. To make matters worse, her cell phone was dead. She'd have to walk back inside and find a pay phone to call her husband. Hopefully, he was still at work, because he'd be very upset if he had to drive fifteen miles from home to bring a spare key.

He wasn't. "Claudia, I just changed my clothes and wanted a nap before dinner. Are you sure you don't have the keys?" Don's patient voice made her feel even worse.

"I can see them in the ignition. I may be absentminded, but I'm not blind." Her voice was shrill and loud.

"I'm not deaf. I'll be there as soon as I can. Cheer up. At least you'll have more time to shop."

"Right." She didn't have the guts to tell him about her inability to buy anything. *Well, it won't hurt to window-shop.*

She hung up the phone, turned, and bravely faced the crowd. The whole sight was disconcerting. Something was wrong with these people. Did they not know that Christmas was about Jesus? Looking at most faces, you'd think they'd just seen *Nightmare on Elm Street*.

Another thing bugged her. Not a single decoration in the entire mall gave even faint homage to the real meaning of Christmas, with the exception of the Christian bookstore.

Exhausted, she dug change from the bottom of her purse, made her way to Starbucks, and waited in a long, surly line for the pick-me-up she felt she deserved. Suddenly a chill of realization ran up her spine. Don had no idea where she was in the vast expanse of the Vancouver Mall.

"Now what do I do?" She was near tears when she spotted her husband's head above the crowd, making his way toward her with staunch determination. She'd never loved him more. "How in the world did you find me?" She hugged his neck in gratitude.

"When I realized you didn't say where you would be waiting, and you didn't answer your cell phone, I figured you'd need reinforcement. I knew you'd head for Starbucks."

"I'm so predictable." She sighed.

"Good thing, too." He kissed her on the cheek. "I fed the kids pizza before I left. Let's you and me go on a date, mall girl." He took her hand and squeezed it.

The "good intention" saying kept going around in her head all the way home. The entire afternoon and evening had been a complete bust. *I don't get it, Lord. I can only be missing an organizational gene or two. And if that's the case, I'll blame it on heredity.* Only she knew that wasn't true, because both her sisters were models of the "a place for everything and everything in its place" mentality. She hated them.

Don was asleep when she finally got the kids settled. She could use some feedback to sort things out.

There was no way her frantic preparations every year at Christmas could bring any glory to the Lord. "Peace on Earth" never quite rang true in her household, but it wasn't because she didn't try. *What goes wrong every year, Lord? Show me.*

Last year she thought for sure she'd made enough memories to last a lifetime. Everything in the house was "homemade": all the gifts and, of course, every Christmas card. She didn't realize until New Year's Eve that not one card ever got mailed. They'd lain hidden under leftover wrapping paper she'd hand-stamped and piled in the corner of her bedroom. Not only did she find the cards under there, but also a missing earring, Zak's shot record, and the hamster's exercise ball.

That was the same year she'd invited Zachary's Boy Scout troop over to surprise their mothers with gingerbread houses made from scratch. From the beginning it had gone badly. . . .

They rolled out and cut over one hundred pieces of homemade ginger dough and placed them in the oven. No one noticed when one of the boys accidentally knocked the oven regulator to broil. The fire was easy enough to extinguish, but what happened next was worse.

Never lacking in creativity, Claudia cut up cardboard boxes to make the individual house components. She also substituted superglue for the traditional icing used to keep the parts together. It all went quite well until Andrew Wolgemuth glued his right hand smack in the middle of his forehead when he pushed his glasses from the end of his nose back onto his face.

It took only a minute for the ER people to get him unstuck, but who knew a nine-year-old could be so allergic to superglue? In every Wolgemuth family picture that year, Andrew's swollen face made him look like a holiday alien. His mother didn't speak to Claudia for at least six months or more.

Despite the many failures on her "Christmas" record, Claudia was sure of one thing: she'd succeeded in showing her family all the love and devotion she could muster. Hands down, she got an A for effort. Her motivations were straight from the heart.

A good night's sleep perked up her Christmas spirit, and by 7:30 she couldn't wait to get started on another year's holiday memory.

When Zak came to the breakfast table, she asked him what his most prominent Christmas memory would be. "Take your time, honey. I want to know what you remember most." She stirred her coffee with anticipation.

"Uh, I don't know." He seemed reluctant to share.

"Come on, Zak, what is it?" She leaned across the table to push a lock of thick hair back off his forehead.

"Well. . ." He hesitated before getting up and running to the back door. He grabbed his backpack, opened the door, and shouted: "What I remember most. . .is. . .every. . .single. . .year.. . .YOU FREAK OUT!"

The door slammed behind him, but his words echoed in the kitchen, bouncing off the walls like rubber balls of condemnation.

Claudia was speechless. What she'd heard could not be true. Her youngest son, the one on which she'd spent twenty-two hours of labor and then delivered backward, had just broken her heart. She shook her head in disbelief. *Lord, only You could know how hard I've tried.*

She got up, put a Kenny G Christmas CD into the player, and took a cup of coffee to the living room. Tears of disappointment threatened, and she grabbed an old Kleenex from the pocket of her chenille robe before sitting down.

Her daily devotional Bible lay on a table next to the chair. She opened it. There, for the day's scripture, she read: "Lay up for yourselves treasures in heaven (NKJV)."

But isn't that what she'd been doing? Years of frenzied efforts flashed back. Somewhere in the midst of harried Christmas after Christmas preparations, she'd not given the Lord God of the Universe His due. Oh, He'd had a place, but not *the* place. She had meant well, but the need for perfection overwhelmed her, and time and again she gave in to the complexities of trying to compete.

But what was she competing against? Some pie-in-the-sky image of perfection, set by whom? An old family script rose to the surface: "For heaven's sake, Claudia, why can't you be more like your sisters?"

There it was! Truth! All those years growing up there had been one comparison after another. Her sisters were wonderful, beautiful women of God. And she loved them. But the three of them were all different, each with special gifts. Their mother hadn't meant to be cruel in the comparisons, but the comments created a deep-seeded drive in Claudia.

Somewhere in her mind existed a scale. On one side was her life, her efforts; on the other side were the lives of her sisters. No matter how much of her she placed on the effort side, the scales never evened out, and thus went the years.

"Lord, I know You love me regardless of my failures or efforts."

"Enough to die for you, child," He said.

She began to weep. Big waves of grief washed over her for childhood memories that condemned her to failure. Today, this moment, she realized she'd always felt inferior. Somehow that feeling intensified during the holidays. Of course she was flawed. No one is perfect. . .not even her sisters. She needed to change, but how?

A strong voice pressed in: *"Come to Me, all you who labor and are heavy laden, and I will give you rest"* (NKJV).

"Oh, Lord, I need to rest in the knowledge of You. I know I'm loved just for me, and not any of my works. Help me let go of all my expectations. May they be only on You."

Claudia spent an hour in prayer and worship. Afterward, her heart felt lighter than she could remember.

The weeks that followed were filled with peace because she went to the Lord first thing before launching into a new day. By slowing down and changing her focus from performance to worship, time flew by with gratitude, instead of grinding on with lists and shopping.

To begin, she created a Christ-centered Christmas card, then sent it online. Ah, Christmas in the new millennium. . .wonderful. An act of love instead of drudgery.

Next, she looked at the family gift list and decided that everyone on it had more "stuff" than any one human needed. *A chance for a new tradition, if ever there was one,* she thought. Instead of material gifts, she took the money that would have been spent and gave it to the local Pregnancy Resource Center in the name of each person on the list.

The burden of performance never once landed on Claudia's shoulders, having been replaced by a blanket of comfort created by God Himself. Even the "perfect" tree was turned entirely over to Don and the children because she wasn't anywhere near home while they decorated.

When she did return, and peeked in the window, everyone was sound asleep on the floor, faces glowing in the twinkling reflections of the most beautiful tree she'd ever seen. Oh to be sure, there were some things that could have been done. . .but not by her, not this year. . . not ever.

My, my, she thought, opening the front door, *Dr. Dobson would be so proud.*

Merry Christmas, Lord.

Remember Me

Linda J. Reinhardt

On top of the pressures from work, directing a play, and trying to get her Christmas list checked off, it is Janet's turn to help her grandma put together the traditional family dinner. Janet thinks someone else should take care of it—not Grandma, and certainly not Janet. She has things to do.

But during her Christmas play, thanks to one little girl, Janet is reminded of what she's missing during Christmas.

Then, suddenly, her list isn't so big and time with her grandma doesn't seem such a burden. In fact, it might even become a joy.

Janet blew at the piece of hair that fell into her eyes as she stood in line with all the other last-minute shoppers. Arms overflowing with merchandise, she sighed loudly when the same old Christmas song blared over the store speaker. *Does every store have the same CD to play over and over again?* If she could scream, she would. *If I ever hear another Christmas song played again after today, it will be too soon.*

Her hands grasped her items tightly as she was shoved rudely from behind when somebody squeezed through the line to get to an item on the other side of her. Ugh! She turned to glare at whoever shoved her, but it was wasted on the back of the person's head. *So what else is new? Just one more thing I did today that's a waste.*

It had been difficult to get this day off from work. For the last two months she'd had to work extra due to other employees' illnesses. She'd gotten up early to get her shopping done but instead had spent the entire day looking in vain for items either out of stock or not the color or size she needed. Then, when she did find something, the lines were astronomically long. To top it off, at every store she remembered yet another person to buy a present for and found items for them, but not for those originally on her list. So she had dozens of packages, and no one checked off.

"I wonder what's taking this line so long? I feel like I've been here forever," she muttered.

Shifting the items, she tried to get a glance at her watch. Her goal was to get her shopping done and pick up her grandma's tree before having to be at the church tonight for the children's Christmas play she was directing. *If this line doesn't move, I won't have time to get the tree. Grandma will be so upset. . . .*

Just then another clerk came to help. *What a relief.* Sweat trickled down her neck. Her hands were too full to take off her coat. All the things that had to be accomplished before Christmas filtered through her mind. Tonight she could check off the play. *That'll free up some time for the next couple of days. How did I ever get nominated for that play, anyway?*

A frown creased her brow when she thought of Christmas Day. Every year someone stayed with Grandma to help her prepare her fabulous Christmas. This was Janet's year. There was a traditional dinner, with certain desserts, plates, decorations. Big to-do. This year had been hard on her grandma, and Janet couldn't figure out why someone else didn't volunteer to do all the work for Christmas. Why leave it on Grandma's shoulders? Grandma didn't need any more stress.

Neither do I. Janet's agitation grew. *Why does Grandma have to do all the things she does, anyway? It's ridiculous.*

Ah! Okay, my turn. Janet tried to smile at the slowest-moving clerk in history. With another glance at her watch, she realized it would be a quick stop at the tree farm. She'd have to wait until tomorrow to put up the tree because, after the play, she'd need to run back to the stores to finish shopping.

Grandma would be disappointed. She'd planned a special evening for the two of them decorating the tree. But Janet had things to do.

After she paid, Janet grabbed her bags and marched out of the store to the parking lot. What greeted her put a lump of frustration in her throat. Tears stung her eyes. *I can't take anymore.* Cars were at a standstill in the parking lot! Exasperated, she threw her bags down. *This is more of a hassle than I can deal with.* Defeated, she picked up her bags and slowly walked to her car. She didn't need to hurry now.

Another line! Another Christmas song! *How wonderful is this?* She dug through the pile of bags to see if she could find her CDs. No such luck. *Ah, a break in traffic.* Janet pulled out of the line and pulled onto the freeway. The clock on the dashboard let her know she had just enough time to still get a tree and throw it in Grandma's front yard and make it to the church. Good thing for her she had a change of clothes in the back of her car. Things were starting to look good.

The tree farm had only a few trees left, so the tree was an easy pick. Not the best, but it would work. The guy tied it to her roof and off she stormed to drop it off. At home it wasn't all that hard to untie it from the roof and drag it to the side of the house. She ran in to say a few nice words to her grandma and be on her way.

It took effort to ignore the hurt on Grandma's face when Janet explained decorating the tree would have to wait because of the way her day had gone. With a shrug and a kiss on her grandma's cheek, Janet walked out to her car.

As she drove to the church, her conscience bothered her. *Oh well, she'll just have to understand I have a lot to do before Christmas. Someone else should take over the preparations.*

At the church, everyone was doing their part. *Oh, good.* Janet went and changed her clothes.

Allie, one of the cast member's daughters, had somehow turned into Janet's helper. At times the girl was cute, but tonight Allie got on her nerves.

Allie had question after question: "Miss Janet, where is the baby Jesus?" "Does baby Jesus sleep in the manger, like the song?" "Miss Janet, is baby Jesus a real baby like my brother?"

Janet had trouble concentrating on the final touches and instructions to the actors. She tried to shut out Allie's chatter while helping everyone get ready.

Still Allie would tug and tug at her shirt. "Miss Janet, can my brother play baby Jesus?" Janet pried Allie's fingers loose from her shirt and gritted her teeth in an effort to smile. "Miss Janet, can I put baby Jesus in the manger?"

"Allie, please stop asking me so many questions about Jesus. I'm trying to get everyone ready," Janet blurted out.

Allie's lip stuck out. "But what about baby Jesus?" The girl looked like she would cry.

Janet closed her eyes to compose herself. "Allie, why don't you go and take care of that issue, okay? I'm going to trust you."

Allie nodded and skipped away, happy to oblige.

Janet breathed a sigh of relief.

Janet peeked out the makeshift curtain to see the audience. Grandma was sitting in the front row with her brother. A pang of guilt went through her when she realized she hadn't offered her grandma a ride to the play. *Oh well, she might have been bored getting here so early. Not to worry, time for the play.*

One by one the cast members went out, saying their lines and singing their songs. Janet relaxed against a wall with a view of the stage, still very well hidden from the audience. Her job was done. Wow, and Allie hadn't been glued to her side for quite a long time. Janet decided to take this time to close her eyes for a much-needed break just as Mary and Joseph took their place in the makeshift barn.

Janet's eyes sprung open. Horror filled her whole being. Baby Jesus! That's what Allie was hounding her about. There was no Jesus in her play.

Her shoulders slumped. *I can't believe it. I blew it. I'm in charge of a traditional play about Jesus and forgot Jesus!* The main character of the whole event, and the person the entire play was all about. Janet put her hand to her mouth. *Oh my! I not only forgot Him in the play, I forgot Him in the entire holiday. I've been so busy with my list I forgot the real meaning of Christmas.*

Janet peeked at her grandma, who wore a big grin while she watched the play. *I don't even have time for Grandma. I wanted someone else to do Christmas when it was my turn.* Janet realized what she almost had missed. Every year when someone took their place helping to organize the family dinner, they spent time, valuable time, out at the farm with Grandma.

Is Grandma building memories for us? Are her traditions a way for her to have time with each of us?

Janet prayed silently for forgiveness. *Is my list more important than spending time with Grandma? Maybe Grandma would like to come with me and share in the whole shopping experience. Maybe we can decorate the tree after we got home.*

Everything started to look different when Janet remembered not to forget Jesus. Much to Janet's delight, Allie had borrowed her little brother and put him in the manger. So Jesus ended up in the play after all.

Afterward, when everyone gathered for punch and cookies, Janet, with her arm around her grandma, deemed Allie the best little helper ever. For Allie had helped remind Janet to put Jesus into Christmas.

Merry Christmas, Ada Rose

SHARON BERNASH SMITH

Jennifer has moved to the Washington coast to "start over" after a divorce she never wanted. In the midst of winter rain and a grand pity party, she discovers something long forgotten in the house she's rented. A quilt and a good-bye note, written by a previous occupant, leads her to introduce herself to a complete stranger with a daughter named Ada Rose.

Ada Rose has special needs, and though different, so does Jennifer. In a small beach town, right before Christmas, God meets her needs in a way she never expected. . .and will never forget.

December 22

The drive from Longview seemed lonelier this time. *Better gas up here,* Jennifer thought. With a pounding headache and a left leg numb from the knee down, a break would be good.

She pulled her van into the first station after the ENTERING NASELLE sign.

Everything outside was dripping, and neither the overhang covering the pumps nor her jacket hood gave enough protection. She shivered. Was she crazy to move all the way down here? Who in their right mind wants to spend winter on the Washington coast? It had seemed like a good idea when she signed the lease agreement in October. But then the sun was shining and the breezes off the Long Beach Peninsula were a balmy 73 degrees. Rain? What rain?

"Me, the long-term thinker," she muttered to the indifferent pump, now clicking off. She shook her head in disgust at the total price. "Hope my money holds out."

She put the gas cap back and looked around for a bathroom before heading out across Willapa Bay. Despite the rain, she looked forward to every mile of that ride. It never disappointed.

Once back on the road, with an espresso from a drive-thru in hand, her spirits lifted. At the spot where the Naselle River flowed into the luxurious expanse of the Bay, a great blue heron pushed upward with a fresh catch of fish, headed toward shore for some secret feasting place.

"Lord, thank You for this creation that proclaims Your glory, even in the rain. Forgive my whining." She flipped the CD player on, increasing the volume of a familiar praise album until the windows of the van rattled.

She didn't see the family of deer until they jumped in front of her, not ten yards away. Slamming on the brakes threw the van into a sideways skid, and for a second she imagined launching into the icy salt water. At high tide, she'd probably drown.

Just as fast as the drama began, it ended, the vehicle now sitting nonchalantly on the side of Highway 4 like she'd planned the abrupt exit all along. The three deer followed the water's edge, oblivious to what they'd caused.

She rested her head on the steering wheel, taking deep breaths. "Oh Lord," she whispered, "thank You for Your protection." She reached to turn the CD volume down.

A sharp rap on the window made her jump, and she bumped her head against the visor. It was the Washington State Patrol.

"Brother, now what?" Rolling down the window let in slanting rain. "Yes?"

"Morning, ma'am. I was behind you just now. Are you all right?"

"Yes, Officer, I'm fine. A little shaken, but okay." She took a tissue and made an effort to sop up some of the water.

"Maybe you should take it a little slower, with the rain and all. May I see your driver's license, please?"

"Surely." Rummaging through an enormous purse exposed her wallet at the bottom. Digging out the license, she handed it over. The trooper scanned it, then walked back to his patrol car.

Jennifer's head went back on the wheel while the open window dumped more rain into the interior.

He was back in a minute. "Ms. Carter, your license has expired."

"What?"

"I'm afraid you've let your license expire." Persistent rain dripped from the plastic covering his gray Stetson.

"Why am I not surprised?" Her hands went into the air in exasperation. "I know this is not an excuse, but I'm recently divorced, and in the process of moving down here, I forgot. I just forgot." She looked up at him, ready to cry.

"Well," he began, looking over the contents of the van. She braced herself for the super-high ticket she deserved. "Well, Ms. Carter, how 'bout I give you a warning this time?"

"Really? Oh, thank you so much." Things were looking up.

"Just make sure you get this taken care of at the DMV tomorrow." He handed a soggy ticket through the window. "Drive carefully now," he said and tipped his hat.

She put the van in gear, signaled, and pulled out onto the highway. The ambiance of the Bay now escaped her attention while she concentrated on the wet road. Long Beach was just ahead, and then she'd head north up the peninsula to Ocean Park and her new home. Her new home. "Mine," instead of "ours." It still sounded strange after nearly a year.

Her husband's departure had been a surprise only because denial had kept her from reading the writing on the wall. After the fact, Jennifer had spent months beating herself up for not questioning the frequent out-of-town stays and unexplained phone calls taken in other rooms, away from the family. Business, he'd said. Yeah. . .unfaithful business. She wanted to work at their marriage. He wanted out.

The timing was brutal. Ed left the same month BJ, their son, was deployed to Iraq. Her girls were gone at college, so for the first time in her life she was truly alone. Alone and menopausal. How fair was that? She laughed out loud at her own drama.

They'd "settled" things financially, and in the end she couldn't complain. She did, of course, to all her friends at church, until even she was sick of the story. Sick of introducing herself to new people, as "Hi, I'm Jennifer, the loser. . .my husband left me. . .blah, blah, blah."

It went on for months until she'd finally sought some Christian input. Her counselor had directed her right into the Word. She studied, prayed, and sought the Lord's face as never before in her life.

One day she'd come away from studying, walked into her kitchen, and realized something. She was back! Well, not all the way, but she could feel the fragmented pieces of her life coming together again. It was refreshing and hopeful. God was more real than ever before, and for that she'd be forever grateful.

Years ago, she'd dreamed of moving to the coast and writing a series of adventure books for children. Then her time and energy had gone into her own three kids 24-7. But now...? Well, now she had time; the energy she'd leave to the Lord.

She'd searched online for several months before choosing this part of the coast. Real estate was affordable and selection plentiful. Instead of committing to a mortgage, she would lease—with option to buy—a perfect cabin in Ocean Park, Washington, sitting on Loomis Lake, partially furnished even. This gave some leeway in case her plans didn't work out. In a year, she'd know if the fit was good...or not.

That was in the fall, but now as Christmas approached, her courage waned. She convinced herself a little sunshine might bring back her resolve. As if in response, the clouds parted and a bright shaft struck the side of her face.

Long Beach was all decked out with Christmas decorations, but Jennifer ignored them. Now headed toward Ocean Park, she looked for the lake turn ahead. A sigh escaped. This was it...the beginning of a whole new chapter in the life and times of Jennifer Carter. She fought back tears for the sadness that welled up within. Signaling, she made the turn. Rain fell from the tree-lined road, dropping a familiar litany. Alone...alone...alone. Sometimes the sadness that still remained was tremendous.

Pulling into the driveway brought some cheer when she saw the landlord, Mr. Rude, waiting on the porch. A welcoming plume of smoke rose from the red chimney into the evening sky.

"Hope you don't mind me going inside, Mrs. Carter." He removed a Mariner's baseball cap and stuck out his hand to help her down from the van. Though near eighty, his grip was strong and comforting.

"Oh, Mr. Rude, I don't mind at all. I love the smell of wood smoke. It's perfect. Thank you for thinking of it."

"Well, I have an extra set of keys and a few instructions for you." He handed her an envelope. "My son's phone number is in there—not that I think you'll need it, but you know...better safe than sorry." The cap went back on with an agile adjustment on his snow-white head.

"When are you and your wife leaving for Florida?"

"A week from tomorrow. Not sure if I'm ready for that much sunshine. But my brother and his wife like it all right, so I guess we'll be on a new adventure." He extended his hand again. "Thank you very much for making our departure worry free. I hope you enjoy the lake as much as we have."

"Well, I'm on a new adventure as well. Thanks for choosing me; I know I'll love it."

"Not at all, Mrs. Carter. I've left the things you said you could use, including a big bag of cat food for the cat. Me and the Mrs. appreciate you taking him. It'd be too hot in Florida for that guy. If there's anything you find you don't want, just carry it out back to storage, and it'll be good. I'll say bye now. God bless you."

"Oh, and God bless you, Mr. Rude. Take care." She waved as he backed out and watched his tail lights for a second or two. She jumped when something brushed against her legs. "Oh, I almost forgot about you, Mr. Man." A huge orange cat, with a stub of a tail, meowed his welcome. "You'll be good company." She bent to pick him up. "Hey, you and I could use a diet."

Jennifer stood for a minute, sizing up her new home. Weathered, yet charming for its age, the house was what she called "beach quaint." Mellowed gray shakes adorned the front, and ocean-blue shutters with starfish cutouts flanked all the multipaned windows. A wind chime jingled a friendly welcome. Yes, this would suit her just fine.

Inside, a large picture window summoned her to the water view. Fading light created a mystery of the trees and snags on the opposite shore. Jennifer cracked the window, inviting the settling sounds of evening into the living room for company. A huge osprey circled overhead, calling out a feral cry to a mate before making its way to a tryst.

"Awesome. Lord, please bless this home and bless me with. . .peace." Mr. Man meowed. "I'm taking that for an 'amen,' but maybe you're just hungry."

A low-key excitement lightened her initial loneliness while she emptied the van. After some of "her" things were placed around the cabin, it began to feel like home. She checked to make sure the phone was working and put more wood on the fire before mixing up tuna for a sandwich.

Chamomile tea after dinner made her too sleepy to make up the bed, so she threw a sleeping bag on the couch and snuggled down. A shimmering silver moon hung over the lake, suspended from the heavens like a gigantic, opaque globe. Clouds drifting across the expanse cast mysterious, dancing shadows on the wall.

"Oh, the long beauty of the winter moon. . .oh, the everlasting beauty of You, Lord. May Your light shine on my son, so very far away. Keep him and the girls safe."

She woke with the feeling someone was watching. Turned out it was "something." A cat-sized raccoon peered into the French doors leading to the deck. It didn't even flinch when she got out of bed and padded to the window. A few loud raps on the glass ended the surprise morning visit, and Jennifer watched it waddle away.

"Well, nice meeting you, too. Brazen little varmint." She shivered. "Good thing I slept in my sweats, 'cause it's freezing in here."

A little prodding rekindled the fire, and things warmed up, giving Jennifer renewed enthusiasm for the day ahead. Sunshine soon exploded all over the lake vista. How lovely. The osprey was back maneuvering above the mist with graceful sweeps, while a solitary duck swam near shore, calling out a greeting to no one in particular.

She could not resist walking outside. Now the duck's calls sounded a scolding. "Okay, okay, I get the hint." She went back inside to fix some breakfast and plan her day.

After finishing scrambled eggs and a comforting cup of fresh-ground Starbucks, she pulled a "to do" list out of her purse. At the top, she checked off *put away clothes and supplies from van.*

Her brother and his two girls were driving a U-Haul truck down on the weekend with the rest. They'd be fun company, and she'd surprise him with some homemade clam chowder or a batch of fresh oysters, fried just the way he liked. Maybe she'd even bake them all a chocolate cake.

After a while, though, sadness tugged at her initial enthusiasm. It was the nostalgia surrounding her belongings. She could have sold everything she'd shared with Ed from their old life, but she was too frugal.

Jennifer prided herself on being a "make the most of things" kind of person. But today not even the crystal sparkle of sunlight bouncing across Loomis Lake dissuaded the downslide.

Taking another cup of coffee by the fire, she reached for her Bible and opened it to the book of Psalms: "The Lord is my shepherd; I shall not want." What comfort those words brought. Then she remembered the scripture the Lord had given her the day Ed moved out. "I know the thought that I think toward you, says the Lord, thoughts of peace and not of evil, to give you a future and a hope" (NKJV).

"Lord, You are so good to me. Thank You for speaking to the depth of my pain. Thank You for never leaving or forsaking me." She turned on the CD player. "The Battle Belongs to the Lord" poured forth. It was too easy to forget that the battle in every day belonged to the Lord. Every day, regardless of how many days the battle raged, He promised to be her Shepherd, Lord, and King. What more could a person need?

Encouraged, she was now ready for a "plan." She'd start in the back with the guest room, working forward to the rest of the cabin.

The bedroom, small but cozy, had a "shabby chic" feel. Jennifer thought it could use some tweaking, but for now a good cleaning and airing out would suffice, starting with the closet.

The doors stuck a little but opened after a tug, releasing the tangy smell of long-forgotten seashells. On the top shelf she found a handful of sand dollars next to a paper grocery bag filled to the brim with skeins of hot pink yarn and a stack of Christmas cards.

It felt odd to rummage through the Rudes' belongings, even if they'd left them behind. She guessed they'd run out of energy after so much packing. All the remnants went into a bag for the Goodwill. An old towel made an ambitious dust rag and worked wonders on spider webs as she went.

In the farthest corner of the closet, a remnant of wallpaper covered with tiny rosebuds still clung to the wall. Jennifer thought it gave testament to her idea that perhaps this room had once been a nursery. She wondered who had lived here before the Rudes, sure they weren't the original owners.

When all the critter remnants were removed, she reached for the vacuum. That's when she noticed the small door.

"A door?" She pulled on the knob, but it came off in her hand. "Bummer. Now I'll never get it opened. Hmm. . .I think I saw a tool box in the kitchen."

Returning with a large screwdriver, Jennifer pried at the door until it popped open. The darkness was dense. Bravely she felt around until her hand rested on something. A cardboard box? Moving it into the light revealed nothing.

"What was I expecting anyway?" Though the plainness of the box didn't give a hint, its weight bore witness to something inside, so she removed the top.

Layers of white tissue held a beautiful hand-stitched quilt, folded with attention. Maybe it was just her writer's imagination, but Jennifer had the strangest feeling it had been waiting for discovery. Her fingers stroked the top in admiration.

"How perfect," she whispered. It was a crib-sized blanket flowing with shapes of blues and sea-foam aquas, imitating the surface of Loomis Lake, or maybe the ocean. But who would leave something so precious in an obscure closet? Intrigued, she carried the bundle into the living room, hoping better light might shed some clues in her direction.

Dexterous hands had created these thousands of even stitches, a labor of patient love. Just then something from within the folds dropped to the floor. She stooped to retrieve an unsealed vanilla envelope. A piece of lined paper with writing on it was inside.

"More mystery." To read or not to read? Temptation had its way, and Jennifer removed the paper. When she opened it, there was a tiny lock of reddish-blond hair still taped to the bottom. She began.

My sweet baby girl,

They say you're going to die. Every fiber of my being cries out in pain with the knowledge of how frail you really are. I'm drowning, caught in a riptide that holds me captive. I can't breathe. Maybe I don't want to. I've prayed, but you're still sick, sick beyond what medicine can heal. If you go, I want to go with you. What life would I have if I stayed? I love you, sweet precious baby. In my heart, I will always be your mother, Ada.

Tears covered Jennifer's cheeks. Poor, poor Mama. Had her baby died? Whatever happened to the grieving mother? Compelled to find out more, she went to the phone and punched in the Rudes' number. She hoped they wouldn't think she was a busybody, because for some reason, she just had to know what had happened.

Mrs. Rude answered the phone, and after listening to Jennifer's story of discovery, she expressed her amazement at what was found. Jennifer didn't mention the letter.

"My, my, Mrs. Carter, in all those years, I never thought to open that door. Dunno what I thought was behind it, but seems to me, you were the one meant to find out."

"Funny you should say that, because that's exactly what I felt."

"Well, you'll be glad to know that the first owner, Ada Rose Rafferty, still lives on the peninsula."

"Really? That's fantastic. Do you think Mrs. Rafferty would mind a visit from me?"

"I'm sure she'd love to know you found the quilt, dear. It'd give you a chance to meet someone new down here. Let me know how it works out."

"Oh, I will. Thanks for the information."

After hanging up, Jennifer looked in the small peninsula phone book. There was only one Rafferty, but instead of calling, she wanted to go in person. She wrote down the address, picked up the quilt and letter, and headed out.

The place was easy to find, but second thoughts kept her in the car for a few minutes. "I must have been crazy to think that a complete stranger would talk to me." Exiting the van, she clutched the quilt to her chest, tentatively walked to the front door, and rang the doorbell. Not sure if the doorbell actually worked, she gave the door a good rap. This got a response from someone in the house.

When the door opened, an attractive woman in her midthirties, with hair the color of goldenrod, stood smiling. Her eyes matched the earlier crystal blue of the lake.

"What you want?" she asked.

"I'm very sorry to bother you, but I'm looking for Ada Rafferty."

"That's me, I'm Ada. That's me!" She clapped her hands together, and that's when Jennifer realized that although a woman stood before her, she was actually talking to a child. Ada Rafferty was mentally disabled.

A few seconds later, an older woman appeared from another room and came to stand behind Ada.

"Hello, I'm Ada's mother. . .Ada Rose, but I'm called Rose." She extended her hand toward Jennifer, and her daughter did the same, pulling her into the house.

"I'm Jennifer Carter, and well, this is very awkward, but I believe I have something of yours." She offered the quilt in the women's direction.

"My stars, I haven't seen that in years. But I must be getting old, because I don't remember why I left it behind. Goodness," she said as she took it from Jennifer, "however did you come by it?"

"I found it in a closet at the Rudes' place. I've got a year's lease there." Jennifer's heart skipped a beat. "And, uh, there's something more."

"Really? Another quilt?"

Jennifer drew the letter from her purse. "No. There's this."

"Oh my." Rose's hand went to her throat when she saw the envelope. "I'd totally forgotten." Ada was jumping up and down. "I wanna see, Mama. Can I see?"

Rose's eyes met Jennifer's. "Will you excuse me for a minute, please? Have a seat while I find something to keep my daughter busy."

"Certainly."

Jennifer looked around the comfortable room. Feeling less awkward, she relaxed. Ada's happy chatter came from somewhere in the back of the house after her mother started a movie. This was a home filled with love. There were photographs everywhere that testified to the fact.

"Sorry about that." Rose returned with a tea tray in hand. "Hope you like Earl Grey. I was just about to have some." She paused. "Oh my, how rude, I didn't even ask you if you drank tea. Most younger people like Starbucks coffee."

"I'd love a cup of tea, Rose. You're very kind. You don't even know me."

"Ada says she likes you. Truth is, whoever she likes seems I do, too. She's never met a stranger."

"I think she's charming."

"Oh, she's that and more. She's a blessing. Not that I thought that when she was born."

"Really?"

"No ma'am. Do you use sugar?"

"Thank you, yes."

"Would you like the rest of the story, as they say?" Rose paused in the tea ritual and nodded toward the letter now resting between them. "The rest of the story about that, I mean. Have you read it?"

"Well, yes, I did." Jennifer's face blushed with the confession. "And, Rose, I don't quite know why, but I think I need to hear the whole story."

The older woman leaned back into a chintz rocker, teacup balanced on the arm. She took a loose strand of hair captive behind one ear and began....

I'd about given up on ever getting married. Not that I didn't have a couple of chances, but my dad said my standards were too high. I guess maybe he was right. But I was happy, just so you know. Perhaps *contented* would best describe me then. I loved the Lord, and I loved my nursing work at the Ilwaco Hospital. My life was rich on a daily basis, while time kind of just...slipped away...you know, like the tide.

Then, one day, I woke up and I was in my late thirties. By then I really thought that I'd continue in the status quo, gliding into my later years, with the Lord by my side. Little did I know how quickly things would change.

I first saw him on the Fourth of July. I'd gone down to the docks to get some fresh fish, and there he was, bigger than life: Daniel Rafferty. He stood on deck of the *Lady Lorraine*, tossing a rope to a mate on shore, laughing at one of his own jokes. I was stopped in my tracks by the attraction. It came as a complete shock, mainly because I'd always prided myself on the gift of self-control. You see, I had maintained it with great diligence, but that was before I'd met the tall, dark, and handsome Irish fisherman.

"Hey there, young lady," he said in a voice that could wake the dead.

I looked around to see who he was talking to.

"I mean you in the daffodil shirt," he shouted again.

He was talking to me, Ada Rose Pinkerton. My face must have turned three shades of red for the acknowledgment.

Up to that moment, I thought love at first sight was a myth. But when Daniel jumped down onto the docks and shook my hand, I was in love.

We were married six months later. Though ten years my senior, Daniel had never married. But I'd never met someone so young at heart in my life. That's why, despite our ages, we wanted a family. Several years went by, and we never conceived. Though disappointed, we adjusted.

Then a miracle happened. I got pregnant. It was our dream come true...every day, another wonder to behold. I'd been blessed and blessed some more with a new life growing inside me. Daniel treated me like a queen. He was downright silly at times, waiting on me hand and foot, which made me love him even more. He was a great husband, so I knew he'd be a great dad.

I still had more than two months to go before delivery when I woke up one morning with a nauseating headache. Thinking it was from hunger, I tried to eat but threw up violently. That's when I knew I was in trouble. Thank God, Dan was in port, because he called an ambulance.

I don't even remember Ada being born. . .I was that sick with pre-eclampsia. Took me out for days.

When I did get to see my baby girl, my heart nearly stopped. I'd never seen a human being so tiny. Dan's wedding ring fit over her hand, and she fit in his palm. Ada looked like a helpless little bird with parchment paper skin, and a full head of hair. Our daughter was a miracle of God's handiwork but from the beginning, doctors warned us she'd never make it.

Every breath was a life-and-death struggle. That's when we named her after me, figuring the doctors were right. Each day she lived we were told would be her last. Desperately, Daniel and I cried out to God, begging Him to save our precious girl. And He did. But not the way we thought.

She defied all the predictions for her survival, and after months in the hospital, her homecoming was a monumental celebration with bells and whistles. She slept, nursed well, and smiled when coaxed, yet in my heart of hearts I knew something was wrong. As a nurse, I well understood what the development of a newborn should be. Ada was expected to be behind schedule as a preemie, of course, but this was more than overcoming an early arrival.

The day I shared my concerns with Daniel, my perfect life began to crack at the foundations. Did God not realize that I had been His faithful servant all these years? Perfection deserved reward. Ada's imperfections seemed like punishment. Why would God punish me? And Daniel? Daniel was the last person to incur the wrath of God, for heaven's sake.

I was living under the assumption that as long as I kept the rules and loved God, nothing bad would happen to me. After a battery of tests confirmed what we already knew, Daniel sat me down with his worn-out Bible and took my hands in his.

"Jesus never said that His followers would have no pain, my girl. He said He'd be with us in the midst of life, which is full of pain, sorrow, and disappointments"—he was looking me right in the eyes—"and little children born too soon."

I refused to listen to what I didn't want to hear. That's when the enemy came into my life like a flood. Depression imprisoned my senses. I only got out of bed when my daughter needed me. When Daniel was home, which was a lot in the winter, he met her needs.

The quilt you found was one I made while pregnant. I'd wrap myself in it tight, trying to capture the dreams I'd had before Ada was born. I blamed myself for her early birth, thinking I should have taken better care of myself. Because I was a nurse, I could have done more.

That's when I wrote the letter. I didn't want to burden Dan with my deepest thoughts, so I put them on paper. I don't believe I was depressed enough to actually harm myself, but as I remember, those were very dark thoughts. I was drowning, spinning round and round in a huge whirlpool of sorrow, gasping for breath. I saw no way out. . . .

Rose paused and excused herself for a moment to check on Ada.

Jennifer leaned back and thought about what Rose had shared. She was a complete stranger to this woman, yet here she was, baring her soul. This had to be a "God" thing. Meetings like this didn't just "happen." They were ordained.

Rose returned and refreshed their teacups.

Jennifer thanked her and cleared her throat. "Rose, how did you come out of it? The depression, I mean."

So Rose told her the rest of the story.

One day, an older lady from church came over. I wasn't fit company, but Daniel let her in anyway. Margaret had snow-white hair and the face of an angel. She gave me a hug and wouldn't let go. I tried to pull away, but she held me fast. In that embrace, I experienced the love of Jesus, in a way I'd never felt before. It was as though God Himself was loving on me.

I started crying. Deep sobs racked my body until I shook from the effort. Margaret never said a word, just kept handing me tissue after tissue. When my sobbing stopped, she asked to see Ada.

Daniel brought our baby into the room. Margaret unwrapped her, looked her over from head to toe, and began to pray. Jennifer, I don't remember the exact words she said, but the whole prayer was a thank-You to the Lord.

She thanked Him for the divine appointment this child was in our lives. Thanked Him for her survival. She went on and finished with a prayer of blessing for Ada, Daniel, and me. Every word cut through to my soul.

When she'd finished, the last drop of my depression had been removed. Darkness had become light because of the faithful prayer of one of God's saints. I was speechless.

Before she left, Margaret took both my hands and looked deep into my eyes. "Rose," she said, "I'm eighty years old. God never blessed me with children, so believe me when I tell you this: despite her shortcomings, your daughter will always be a blessing to you and Daniel."

I believed her. And to this day, Margaret's proclamation has been true.

When my husband died five years ago, it was Ada who got me through. Even though she's like a little girl, God's given her a special wisdom.

One day, soon after Dan's death, she found me crying and came over to hug me. "Mama," she said with this big smile, "don't be sad. Daddy's with Jesus. We should be happy. . . ."

Jennifer removed a tissue from a pocket and blew her nose. "I'm so glad you're still here, Rose," she whispered. "You and Ada, both."

Rose set the cup on a side table. "Jennifer," she said hesitantly, "I'm a woman who knows when God's in a person's business and when He's not. Am I right to say the Lord brought you here for a reason?"

Jennifer was crying nonstop now, unable to control her emotions. She nodded yes.

"I don't know what your hurts are, dear, and I don't have to, but I can see that sorrow's been spinning you around in the same whirlpool I was in those years back."

Jennifer nodded again, searching for another tissue. "I'm a Christian, but I don't seem to have enough faith right now. My husband left me a year ago, and now my son's in Iraq, and I haven't heard from him in over two weeks. Christmas is three days away, and I could not care less."

Rose got up just as Ada walked back into the room.

"Movie's over, Mom." She stopped in her tracks when she saw Jennifer crying. "Ohhh, Mommy," she said as big tears welled up, "oh, Mommy, can we pray for her?"

"What do you say, Jennifer. How 'bout it?"

Before Jennifer had a chance to answer, they both had their arms around her.

Ada Rose prayed first. "Dear Jesus, please take our friend's tears. Put them in the special bottle You have. Make her feel better, 'cause she's got hurts. Amen." She was finished praying but not hugging. Her face was next to Jennifer's, and she found the heady tang of Ada's lemon-scented shampoo a rich comfort.

Rose was next. "Lord, You're the one who brought Jennifer to my door. Only You know the secret places of her heart. Only You know the depth of the hurt that lies there. Touch her please, Lord. Where there's been betrayal, bring trust. May she know the width and the depth of the love You have for her. Keep her child safe and give her peace in the waiting. Amen."

Jennifer felt completely changed when they finished. She blew her nose.

"She's smiling, Mom. See?" Ada Rose clapped her hands and gave Jennifer one more hug.

"I'm amazed," was all Jennifer could say.

"We love an amazing God, honey girl. An amazing God."

"You know what?"

"What?" the Adas asked in unison.

"I'm going to splurge and buy new decorations for Christmas."

"Jack's! Jack's!" Ada Rose squealed.

"It's the closest thing to a department store we have in Ocean Park," Rose explained.

"I came down here brokenhearted, and now I'm talking about Christmas decorations. This is unbelievable. How can I ever thank you two?"

"Well, you can come to church with us on Christmas Eve and then stay for dinner. I'll guarantee you'll love the people."

"I love the food!" Ada Rose threw her head back and laughed at her own enthusiasm.

Her laughter was so contagious, Rose and Jennifer joined in.

"Merry Christmas, Jennifer." Ada Rose's face glowed with the greeting.

"Merry Christmas, Ada Rose. Merry Christmas indeed."

Angel for Sale or Rent

SHARON BERNASH SMITH

Christmas has to be perfect for Leslie. It's how she makes up for all the holidays her father ruined by his drinking when she was a child. This year, Christmas could be more than perfect if only she could win the neighborhood lighting contest. Convinced a huge angel in the front yard would secure her first place, she's determined to find one.

Circumstances have eaten up her time, and it's only at the last minute that she's able to find one in an obscure little rental shop near the local shopping center.

A rather "different" kind of clerk helps her find exactly what she needs and promises to deliver it on time for the contest judging. Only what she discovers in her front yard on Christmas Eve far exceeds her dreams and expectations. . . .

"It has to be life-sized. . .and glowing. Glowing would be good, don't you think?" Leslie could tell her husband was not the least interested in what she was saying. "George, are you listening?"

"To every word, Leslie. . .to every word."

"Then what do you think?"

"About what?"

"George! Sometimes I think you don't care about Christmas at all."

"Leslie, if I didn't care, would I be up here on this ladder. . .when it's freezing?" He blew on his red hands for emphasis.

"No, of course not. I'm sorry." She fed him another string of lights. "Seriously, George, what do you think of my idea for an angel?"

They both knew exactly how this conversation would go. He'd give his honest opinion. . .the one about having enough decorations already. Then she'd remind him they had yet to win the neighborhood lighting contest, and he would remind her that he didn't care. She'd pout. He'd ignore her. But in the end, he'd give in. She knew it, and he knew it.

So George breathed deeply and expressed himself to the depth of his being. "Whatever."

"Oh, George, you are such a wonderful man."

"Thank you," he said. But he spoke to thin air, because she was already inside to phone around in search of the seasonal goal. He shook his head in surrender and hoped the life-sized being wouldn't have to go on top of the roof.

Leslie Crawford regretted that they were weeks late in getting the Christmas lights up and glowing, but with her mother's sudden illness, she couldn't help it. As a Christian, she knew where her priorities lay (or was it lie?). Regardless, now her mother was well enough for Leslie to be released from nursing duty, albeit late for Christmas decorating.

After an hour on the phone, she'd not found one place that sold a life-sized angel, glowing or otherwise. Not even Walmart had a reasonable facsimile. Positive she could win this year's competition if only she had one, Leslie was in tears. Theirs was the only house on the block that had never won.

God, You know how much this means to me, especially since we're practically the only Christians in all of Stony Brook. Don't we deserve a little break? She blew her nose and realized she'd be late for a dental cleaning if she didn't get going.

On the way, her mind was cluttered with thoughts of how gracious she'd be when accepting the award for "Best in Show." One thing was certain: she'd give God all the credit and glory. *What a witness that would be.*

After leaving the dental office, she caught sight of a business she'd never noticed before. . .a rental business. Funny how you could pass by something again and again without ever seeing it. She slowed a bit and immediately saw the sign.

Angel: For Sale Or Rent.

Her heart skipped. Amazing! Hope rose for a winning year as she searched for a place to park. *If only their stuff's not chintzy. . . .*

Outside, the tiny shop was nothing special, but inside, heady aromas of Christmas teased her senses. Fragrances of pine and cinnamon permeated every square inch. But there was something more: an elusive, butterflies-in-the-stomach kind of feeling. . .gentle, yet strong at the same time.

"May I help you?"

Leslie jumped at the sound of the man's voice behind her. Where had he been?

"Oh my, you startled me." She turned and looked into the face of one of the most handsome men she'd ever seen. Snow-white hair covered his head, though he was obviously not old. Opal eyes, clear and wise, stirred her spirit. She tried to recompose but found herself at a complete loss for words.

He spoke: "I'm sorry I startled you. What is it you need?"

Even his voice was handsome. Leslie rushed on with her tale of woe. "What I need is to win a lighting contest in my neighborhood." She paused for breath while the man waited patiently. "I believe a life-sized angel might just do the trick, if you know what I mean. One that lit up would make it perfect. I've called all over town, but I've waited too late to find one. I'm desperate."

"Yes, I see that."

She suddenly felt petty and wanted to explain herself, but there wasn't time. Instead, she asked to see what they had, and the man brought out a catalog. There were several pages with angel statues of various descriptions, all of them gorgeous. One had a flaming torch; another's hands were raised in a gesture of praise.

"My, these are wonderful," Leslie exclaimed. They were far beyond her last-minute expectations. "Are they weatherproof?"

"All of them, Leslie." The way he spoke her name created chills along her spine. Funny, she didn't remember introducing herself.

"I'm on a really tight budget, so. . .ummm. . .what's the cost?"

Her chin dropped when she heard his quote. "Oh, there's no way my husband would go for that. Is it possible to rent it for one night only?"

"If you reserved it, yes, that would work."

"You see, Christmas Eve is the night when the contest judging will be done, so I'd definitely need it there by dark."

"Very well, Leslie." He looked into her eyes, causing her heart to flutter. She felt so small and childlike in his presence that she nearly forgot about paying.

"Oh, I need to give you some money." Leslie reached for a credit card.

"That can be taken care of when the angel arrives."

"Wonderful," she said. For the first time all season, the Christmas spirit washed over her entire being. "Wonderful."

"Merry Christmas, Leslie," said the handsome man.

"Merry Christmas to you. . . ? I'm sorry, I didn't get your name."

"My name is Michael."

"Really! Your name is Michael?" She laughed out loud. "How appropriate. I mean, you renting angels and all."

Michael smiled and held the door open. She breezed by him with a wave, musing over his name all the way to the car.

Before Leslie knew it, Christmas Eve day had arrived. The weather forecast promised a snowfall.

"Snow for Christmas. How perfect." She'd taken care of every detail of the festivities, not trusting anyone else with the responsibility for good reason. Christmas was her "thing."

As a child, holidays had been ruined by her father, who managed to be drunk for each and every one. Making them flawless now somehow compensated for all those years of painful memories. Leslie often found her motives misunderstood, yet she was never deterred in the mission of maintaining absolute perfection for Christmas. For instance: though most of her friends found their children's homemade decorations with long strings of popcorn "charming," Leslie had better taste. Oh, she allowed the children "their" small tree in the corner of the family room, but the important decorating was all hers. . .for weeks.

She checked the front of the house frequently that day, in expectation of the angel's arrival. Her grandchildren would be thrilled with the lights and decorations just as they were, but the glowing heavenly being would be beyond "perfection." Leslie was still feeling grateful for her find.

The entire family arrived at dusk with kisses and hugs, full of their usual praise for the house decorations. Leslie beamed. Their traditional dinner of ham, walnut–blue cheese salad, homemade rolls, and at least a half-dozen other dishes was gala quality, with one exception. George's eggnog was not up to Leslie's standard. She regretted not making it herself.

When the time came to leave for Christmas Eve service, the angel was still missing, and with only hours to go before the judging, Leslie's stomach churned. She considered staying home to wait, but three of the grandkids were in the Nativity pageant, and she couldn't miss that.

Leslie felt blessed after the church service. The children were adorable, and now even the rented angel was temporarily forgotten. She hummed a chorus of "O Little Town of Bethlehem." A couple of blocks from home, a glowing radiance emanated into the cold sky.

"George, look! Pull over, quick!"

"Holy smokes," was all he could manage.

They were stuck behind a line of cars. . .all slowing to marvel at the light emerging from their very own front yard. It was more than Leslie could ever have imagined. It was downright, well. . .heavenly.

Right next to the manger crèche stood a magnificent angel, clothed in brilliant white layers of flowing robes. Its glimmering light danced across the entire street, melting upward to highlight steadily falling snow. It reminded Leslie of an enchanting snow globe she'd possessed as a child.

"Oh, George, how incredible. It's beyond my wildest expectations. Look, his wings are moving, aren't they? Am I just imagining that? No, they are! I'm going to win this year, I know it."

"I'm not going to like the electric bill for this, Leslie. I'm not going to like it at all."

"You are such a Scrooge sometimes, George Crawford."

It had been difficult to get the family inside, away from the spectacular display, but it was time for George's reading of the Christmas story. She at least gave that tradition over to him. His rich baritone voice lent itself well to the task, even if he was a bit melodramatic.

All the family had gathered around George's feet, when the light coming into the living room intensified, pulsating with life in imitation of a rising sun.

Must be the reflection off the white blanket of lawn, Leslie thought.

Normally by this time, the children were antsy and cranky, but here they were, already in PJs, eyes on Papa, mesmerized by every word. Tonight the familiar story was brand-new, alive with the sacrificial reality of Jesus leaving the opulence of heaven for the cruel place of earth. Tears flowed, and even George struggled to read beyond the emotion. Was she imagining the light outside getting even more luminous? It arched higher and higher with the passing evening.

Her daughter's crystal clear voice lifted into song: "O holy night, the stars are brightly shining; it is the night of dear Savior's birth."

Never had the meaning of "holy night" been so understood by Leslie. Was it the light? Jesus came to be the "Light of the world." She felt that truth deep within her inner spirit.

One by one, the children fell asleep right where they had sprawled, so they were given pillows, covered with blankets, and left for the night. The adults were too tired to move, or perhaps they didn't want the night to end. The crackling fire died to glowing embers close to midnight and the decision to stay at the Crawfords; was made, the snow-covered streets too risky for travel. They'd be braver in the morning. "Good nights" were whispered in hushed tones.

Leslie went to bed with complete peace for the first time in years. A scripture tugged at her mind, and she picked up the bedside Bible before turning out the light. She flipped to the book of Philippians:

Who, though he was in the form of God, did not count equality with God a thing to be grasped, but emptied himself, by taking the form of a servant, being born in the likeness of men. And being found in human form, he humbled himself by becoming obedient to the point of death, even death on the cross (ESV).

Tears filled her eyes. "Thank You, Lord, for coming to save me. I'm sorry for how I've set aside the truth of Christmas for so long." She meant to pray longer but drifted into deep sleep just before the clock struck midnight.

The children were up first, excited to get outside and play in the knee-deep snow. Leslie had rummaged in the basement and found galoshes and mittens enough for everyone, and they spent the entire morning in the backyard making a lopsided snow family. Not one of her grandkids mentioned the presents that were waiting under their own trees at their respective homes. The laughter and squeals of delight were the best present she could ever receive.

In the hustle of getting the children dressed and fed, Leslie hadn't had a moment to look in the front yard.

It was George who first noticed the angel was missing.

"What do you mean it's gone?"

"Leslie, look for yourself. I went out to check on things up and down the street, and it's just not there."

"Well, Michael must have come and picked it up already."

"Who works on Christmas Day?" George shrugged and reached for a cup of coffee.

"George, I never told you this." She paused to search for a word that would describe the angel renter. "Michael was a little 'different.'"

"Different how?"

"I don't know, just different." She walked to the front window and looked to where the magnificent statue had put on its heavenly display. "George, come here."

He came and stood beside her, looking to where she pointed. "Leslie, what am I looking for?"

"There are no footprints in the snow, George. If someone had come to pick up my angel, there would have to be footprints to and from. Right?"

"I'm sure it has probably snowed since then." He patted her shoulder and returned to the kitchen for more coffee.

"I don't know." *I'll never forget how I felt last night,* she thought. *It had something to do with that angel statue, I'm sure.*

The roads were still a mess three days after Christmas, but the mystery had to be solved. She didn't know what she'd say to Michael if the angel had been stolen. It would be costly to replace, but she'd pay up if she had to.

Thinking back to Christmas Eve put a smile on Leslie's face and renewed the wonder in her heart. She laughed out loud, recalling the absolute misery she'd experienced year after year over the neighborhood lighting contest. And then, when she'd actually had a chance to win, the record snowfall had wiped out the entire contest.

"Lord, You do have a sense of humor. Thanks for the lesson; help me not to forget it ever."

She was near the corner of Mill Plain and McGillvrey, slowing down to make the turn. Once around the corner, she looked for the driveway to the rental shop, turned in, but found. . .nothing.

"Wait a minute; this was the place!" She stopped the car, turned off the engine, and got out. This just couldn't be. She was standing in the middle of an empty cement slab. . .no sign, no building, no Michael.

Completely mystified, Leslie walked to a small kiosk next to where the rental shop once stood. Inside, a man was making keys. He looked up and came to the door.

"Can I help you?" he asked.

"I know this sounds strange, but I was wondering if you knew what happened to the business that was right there before Christmas?" She pointed to the empty lot for emphasis.

The man scratched his head. "Ma'am, I've been on this spot for going on five years, and I'm certain there's never been another business here. Are you sure you're on the right block?"

Leslie turned around, scanning the entire area. "I'm positive. The man who worked there was very distinguished looking. . .tall, with snow-white hair. Maybe you met him?"

"Funny, a man looking just like that came the day before Christmas. He left a note."

"Really?" Leslie got a familiar chill. "What kind of note?"

"I still have it. There's a name written on the front. . .I'll show you." He reached behind the register, picked up a small envelope, and handed it to her.

Leslie's hand went to her heart when she saw her name. "This is for me," she whispered. "I'm Leslie."

"No kidding?"

"Thank you," Leslie managed.

"No problem," the man answered before getting back to work.

Leslie returned to her car. She fumbled for the keys but had difficulty opening the door because her hands would not stop shaking. She got in and sat for several minutes, working to regain some composure before opening the special communiqué. Pulling out a piece of gold paper, she gasped when she read the single word written in a bold script: *Believe.*

The Star of Bethlehem Lecture

ROSANNE CROFT

When a cynical, unbelieving student at a crowded university meets the astronomy professor, he gives a lecture authenticating the Star of Bethlehem. What the student hears will forever change her beliefs in the reality of Christmas, God, and science, and will change her heart, too. . . .

This true story is a tribute to Dr. Karlis Kaufmanis, a great man who was kind to this lonely student. The compassion and godly example of this humble Christian man spurred her to follow the Star to Jesus.

I was a number, a nameless face in a long line behind the registrar's window. My student ID number felt tattooed to my forehead, because when I faced the clerk, she didn't see me at all. It was fall, the beginning of my junior year at the jam-packed University of Minnesota. I'd waited two hours in a line swarming with students, last names beginning A–C, only to be told that my science class was full.

"I need this science credit to graduate," I pleaded.

"Your only hope is to go to Professor Kaufmanis's office and ask to be allowed in," said the woman behind the window. "If he signs this paper, bring it back here. Next!"

I walked slowly to the building that housed the Physics Department. After spending summer break home in Wyoming, I steeled myself against the all-too-familiar homesickness. Depression followed me around like a hungry mongrel. Worse than ever, I'd abandoned my early religious training. I was a skeptic, bitterly searching for God and the meaning of life, and cynical about the truth of the Bible and Christianity.

But deep inside, I knew I couldn't figure it out myself. I began to read rebuttals against my doubts in books by C. S. Lewis, Leo Tolstoy, and

Alexander Solzhenitsyn. That fall day in 1976 I didn't realize I'd meet another great thinker, a scientist who studied black holes and calculated stellar magnitudes...and was a devout Christian.

And that's how a shy introvert, a rabid hater and flunker of math and science, found herself with pounding heart in the School of Physics, knocking on the astronomy professor's wide-open door.

"Come in," was the quick answer.

Professor Karlis Kaufmanis stood and shook my hand lightly like the European gentleman he was. Dressed in a warm brown suit, he was about my height, crowned with fuzzy white hair. *A little like Einstein,* I thought, *or Bilbo Baggins.* His smile was sincere, and his eyes twinkled like the stars he studied.

I introduced myself and, in a shaking voice, told him why I was there. I spoke like I felt: a generic student, jumping through hoops to get a degree, one of the minions at the huge university. To my surprise, Professor Kaufmanis began to chat with me as though I were a fascinating and remarkable person with ideas and dreams and a family.

"Where are you from, Miss Black?" he asked in his thick Latvian accent.

When I told him, he related how he'd crossed Wyoming on a journey to the Arizona meteorite crater that he took graduate students to visit one summer. Gracious and friendly, he acted like he cared about a confused young woman far from home. He seemed to know the gnawing of homesickness. He didn't know that my graduating schedule depended completely on him but cheerfully signed the request paper.

In turn, I faithfully attended every lecture, sitting in a back row of the crammed auditorium. I was one of over eight hundred students in the class that semester.

My eyes opened to a new world: the universe, with all of its mystery. I came to appreciate the complexity of the cosmos and the hopeful idea of infinity. Stars had names and properties that were unique to them. They even came in colors and twirled around each other in an unending dance to the music of the spheres.

Professor Kaufmanis revealed parts of his life during his lectures, always with a deprecating sense of humor. Later I found out the terrible facts of his background: that he had to go into hiding when the Soviets occupied Latvia in 1940; then, in 1944, the Nazis forced him to leave

Latvia and work for the German Fatherland. When Germany lost the war, he had nowhere to go. He couldn't return to his homeland because Stalin's Soviet troops had reoccupied it. From a displaced persons' camp in Germany, he sent out letters to American colleges and universities. That's how Karlis Kaufmanis came to America to teach astronomy. I also learned that he'd been widowed twice but was now married to a doctor.

Professor Kaufmanis was the first to show me Orion and the Pleiades. No matter where I go in the United States, my favorite constellation, Orion the Hunter, is there, too. An "old school" European-style teacher, Kaufmanis tailored his lectures with an orderly and polished technique. Even though the material was not new to him, he made it fresh to us. His accent was thick but pleasant to listen to. Often the whole auditorium of students stood and applauded him. It was the only class I ever attended where that occurred. Sometimes, if he was talking about an unknown, he'd say, "Only the good Lord knows."

By the time of his retirement a few years later, he'd guided 26,000 students through Introductory Astronomy at the University of Minnesota.

In early December, before I'd even thought that it would soon be Christmas, I saw a poster announcing the "Star of Bethlehem Lecture," to be delivered by Professor Karlis Kaufmanis the next afternoon. My Minnesotan friends said that he gave his famous lecture throughout the Twin Cities every December. I intensely wanted to know what the professor thought about this religious symbol of Christmas. I had come to respect him, and I knew that he would have a good answer for the appearance of this Star.

And that's how a semiagnostic, cynical, ex-religious student found herself sitting in an auditorium on a metal folding chair on a gray December afternoon. Christmas approached with all of my questions, the magic of it shattered by my unbelief. I teetered on the edge of losing faith in God. Was the Star of Bethlehem real? Was the story true? I was about to find out.

The floor in the auditorium wasn't sloped like the Astronomy classroom, and I watched dirty slush form puddles on the linoleum as people stamped the snow from their shoes. This time I didn't sit in the back row but as close as I could get to the front. Behind me, the lecture hall quickly filled with at least a thousand people talking and clanging chairs. Then I saw Professor Kaufmanis himself, up on the side of the stage.

Suddenly, he strode down the side stairs to floor level, looked around, and spotted me. Recognition passed over his face, then a confident smile. He astonished me by sitting on the empty chair beside me.

"Hello, Miss Black," he said. He'd remembered my name.

"Hello, Professor," I answered, "why are you sitting here? I mean, aren't you going up there?" I pointed to the stage.

"I like to find a friend in the audience," he said, "and sit next to them for a few minutes. That is how I get rid of my nervousness."

Incredibly, this great lecturer thought I could help him with his nervousness. At this kind remark, somewhere inside my icicle of a heart a God-flame flickered and Pluto's ice began to melt. The brilliant professor about to give the definitive Lecture on the mystery of the "Star of Bethlehem" had called me his friend. I wasn't nameless or a nobody. . .to him at least.

We sat quietly together. I didn't want to disturb his thoughts. In a few minutes, he stood to go onstage. Nervously, I mumbled something like, "Best of luck, sir," or "I'm sure you'll do very well, Professor."

The lecture was delivered with his famous accent and disclaimer: "When I came to the United States, I meant to learn your beautiful language. I have failed." Of course, he went on to give the lecture in perfectly acceptable English.

And that's how I learned that the Star was real. It was the conjunction of two planets, Jupiter and Saturn, a phenomenon that only happens about every eight hundred years. But since there is predictability in the clockwork of the heavens, Professor Kaufmanis had calculated the date as 7 BC The spectacular pairing was so bright that it was noticed by Jewish astronomers in Babylonia, longing for the Messiah. Since Jupiter and Saturn signified the planets of the Hebrews and the King, they set out to find the Messiah, knowing this to be a sign from God. They believed not that stars and planets caused earthly happenings, but that there were signs in the heavens of earthly happenings.

The planets passed very close to each other three times in 7 BC. When the Magi arrived in Jerusalem in November, the spectacle was no longer seen in the sky but conjoined again for the last time on December 1st. At that time, they saw the Star south of Jerusalem, followed the road until it forked, and took the road to the southwest, where the Star was, the road to Bethlehem. There they found Jesus.

Two years later, I found Jesus, too. Christmas renewed its magic in my heart, and I understood "Joy to the World" like never before. The "Star of Bethlehem Lecture" was part of God's plan to lead me to the truth of the Bible, through wise men like Professor Karlis Kaufmanis. As an unbeliever, my confusion had been melted by the scientific reality of that bright Star. Here was a scientist who could explain the supernatural events written in the Bible with confidence that they did happen, and he could explain exactly how they happened. God began to show me that His Word was true.

Professor Kaufmanis had suffered the loss of his homeland and two beloved wives during his lifetime, yet he still believed that God held the universe in His hand. He still reached out to others with kindness. He told a newspaper that he would give the lecture until his dying day. Through his lecture, he held out that bright Bethlehem star to an unbelieving universe, and some of us were changed by it forever.

> *. . .children of God. . .you shine like stars*
> *in the universe as you hold out the word of life.*
> PHILIPPIANS 2:15-16 NIV

A San Antonio Christmas

Sharon Bernash Smith

Remember your first Christmas away from home? Aubrey and his wife are newly married and living on an army base in San Antonio, Texas. She's seriously convinced they've made a huge mistake marrying when they hardly know each other. Her heart is broken, away from her childhood home on Christmas and living with a near stranger.

But Aubrey has a surprise, something to distract his wife from the chili-pepper Christmas lights he's hung on their aluminum tree. He might be a stranger to his bride, but he could become her hero with a simple knock on the door. . . .

It was the chili-pepper lights that put her over the edge. There was absolutely no way that she could celebrate a holy holiday with an aluminum Christmas tree lit up with dozens of images that imitated a food group. In Minnesota, you could step outside her childhood home and cut down one of a hundred evergreens.

Suddenly, she knew, beyond a shadow of a doubt, that her marriage to Lt. Aubrey M. Baker had been a huge mistake. What had she been thinking? They barely knew each other, after all. He'd swept her off her feet. Not only her, but the entire family fell in love with him when her brother brought his best friend home on leave over Labor Day weekend.

Aubrey loved the Lord, his country, and her mother's fried chicken. It didn't hurt that he was tall, dark, and handsome besides. What was there not to love? Nothing, absolutely nothing.

Then why was she so completely undone by the chili peppers? It was the homesickness. She tied her auburn hair into a ponytail, flipped on the ceiling fan, and plopped on the couch with her Bible.

"Oh, Lord, I'm sorry for being so infantile. I had no idea moving this far would bring me to an emotional breakdown. I need to grow up, I guess."

With their small but wonderful ceremony behind them, the car ride from Minnesota to San Antonio had been absolute magic. Then, she thought it all divine providence and terribly romantic.

Now, sitting in the middle of a rundown base housing, sweating profusely on Christmas Eve, she was miserable. The tree would have been comedic if she wasn't missing every single thing she remotely remembered about Minnesota.

She turned to the chapter of Luke and read the Christmas story. *Oh, Lord, I've been foolish. The real meaning of Christmas is You. . .it's not about me. Thanks for Your faithful reminder.*

Noises outside the front door caught her attention. She blew her nose, wiped swollen eyes, and made an effort to regain some composure.

"Susan, help. . .please!" Aubrey's voice was muffled.

Opening the door, her husband could not be seen behind a forest of lush green.

"Move aside, honey, this sucker's big." He stumbled inside, pushing and shoving a huge evergreen tree that took up half the living room and clearly was a foot taller than the ceiling.

His smile went from ear to ear. "Merry Christmas, Mrs. Baker," he said with a smart military salute.

Both hands flew to her mouth. "But. . .where. . . ?"

"Oh, now, ma'am, we have a don't ask, don't tell policy on this base." He winked.

"You're my hero. You know that, right, Aubrey?"

"Ah, but will you say that fifty years from now?"

"You betcha, Mr. Baker. Merry Christmas, my special army elf." She walked toward him, standing as close as she could get without getting stuck by the tree. "But there is just one thing."

"What's that, Mrs. Army Elf?"

"The chili peppers have to go."

He dropped the tree and grabbed her into a big hug, whispering into her hair, "Merry Christmas, sweetheart."

The Not-So-Ordinary Doll

LINDA J. REINHARDT

A little doll stood in her box on a shelf at the toy store. She had sparkly eyes, long hair, and was very squishy soft. She didn't eat, drink, talk, or any other special thing like the other dolls that Christmas season. She was just an ordinary doll. . .or so she thought.

But the discovery she made one Christmas Eve, when she met one little girl, would be a special memory to hug and hold forever. . . .

Based on Psalm 139.

O
ne Christmas not too long ago, a little doll stood in her box on a shelf at a toy store. She had sparkly eyes, long hair, and was very squishy soft. She didn't eat, drink, talk, or any other special thing like the other dolls that Christmas season. She was just an ordinary doll.

Each morning, soon after the lights turned on in the toy store and Christmas music began playing over the speakers, precious little girls showed up in the doll aisle. For hours a person could hear their oohing and aahing over the dolls that could eat, drink, talk, or do any other special thing.

This made the ordinary little doll feel like she wasn't very special. Day after day, she watched the other dolls be chosen by a little girl. Soon after, the dolls would leave in the arms of a mommy or daddy, to be brought home and loved by one of the little girls. The little doll became very sad. There was no one who chose her to be their baby doll, and Christmas was almost here. In fact, it was Christmas Eve.

"I don't want to be left here alone on Christmas Day. Isn't there any little girl who thinks I'm special?" A tear slid down her face.

Later that day, the ordinary little doll once again heard the words of a little girl say, "Mommy, mommy, please may I hold that special doll? Please?"

The ordinary little doll sighed and tried to look out her box to see which one was the chosen one. This time, much to her surprise, hands wrapped around the ordinary doll's box, and she was taken off the shelf. She could hardly believe it! The little girl had picked her. A smile crept on her face.

"Oh, Mommy, could you take her out of the box for me? I want to hold this doll. She looks so squishy."

But the mommy didn't take her out of the box. Instead, the mommy put the ordinary doll back on the shelf.

Oh no, I don't want to go back on the shelf. I want to go home with the little girl, the doll thought. She could hear the girl crying and begging to hold the special doll.

Soon the cries faded away when they left the store.

"Special? She thinks I'm special." The doll felt good inside for a minute. "If only I could go home with her."

Then she heard a man's voice talking loudly to someone. "She said the doll is down this aisle. Long hair and sparkly eyes, doesn't eat, drink, talk, or any other thing but is a very special doll. Oh good, it's still here."

Much to the doll's delight, she was carried from the shelf, and paper was wrapped all around her box. It was very dark in that box, but she was too excited to be scared.

The night seemed to go so slowly. . . .

Finally, Christmas morning arrived. The ordinary doll heard the sounds of paper ripping and squeals from the same little girl who thought she was special at the toy store. The doll was taken out of her box and put in arms that held her tightly.

And that's when the ordinary doll discovered she wasn't so ordinary after all. Instead, she was made special, just for this little girl to hug and hold day and night.

A Note to the Reader

Hi! I just wanted to say you are very special and loved by the Creator of everything. He made you to be very unique.

My prayer is that you would enjoy who you are and walk in the love that God has for you. You can check out how special you were created in Psalm 139.

Merry Christmas, and may God bless you in many incredible ways.

A Christmas Dream

SHARON BERNASH SMITH

Noelle knows in her heart that you can't have Christmas without Jesus, so when the figure of baby Jesus is missing from the family's small Nativity set, she goes to bed upset.

What she dreams that night will make you wonder: Are dreams ever real? Do they sometimes come true?

This story is meant to be read aloud.

$\approx$

Girls, hurry up. If you're not down here in five minutes, you can forget about any decorating."

It had been a long day for Nancy. "Boy, would I like to skip Christmas this year." *I don't like Christmas as a single mom.*

She wasn't *really* single; she loved being married. But this was Brian's second trip to Iraq, and the unfairness of it weighed heavily on her heart.

"Mom, I heard what you said about Christmas." Hayley plopped down on the couch. "That's depressing, you know."

"Sorry, you heard that. I'm just missing your dad, and I need a hug." She walked over and pulled her daughter to her feet. "Wow, Hayley! Dad would not believe how tall you are."

"Can we Skype him tonight?"

"Let's wait until all the decorations are finished. Where's your sister?"

"Noo-elle! Come down here." She put two fingers in her mouth and produced an ear-splitting whistle.

"Hayley, that's not very ladylike." She winked. "But your dad would be so proud." Nancy gave her daughter a high-five and laughed.

"What's so funny?" Noelle came down the stairs carrying her favorite doll of the week. "Are you having fun without me?" She walked over to her mom for a hug.

"No, we called you down to start the fun. I want to set up the Nativity scene in the Christmas village, and you guys are supposed to *want* to help, remember?" She set a plastic tub on the table in front of the girls.

"We do want to help, but I don't see how it will be fun without Daddy."

"Me neither," Hayley said.

"Look, I don't like him being gone any more than you guys do, but for his sake, we need to make the best of it. If he knows we're depressed, it will just make it harder on him. You know how much Dad loves Christmas."

"Yeah, and how much he loves to dress up like Santa." Hayley laughed.

"Dad is Santa?"

Both Nancy and Hayley looked at Noelle. "What? Noelle, don't tell me you still believe in. . ."

"Ha, ha, fooled you." She was jumping all around the living room, pointing her finger at them both. "I'm almost eight, you know. Only little kids believe in Santa. Besides, Dad says Jesus is the reason for the season. He always says that."

"Well, if you're such a big girl"—Hayley gestured wide— "then why do you still play with dolls?" She snatched the doll out of her sister's hand by its platinum blond hair and held it above her head out of reach.

"Give it back, Hayley. You're being mean. You know Daddy gave me that doll; it's special."

Hayley gave back the doll. "Here. . .you. . .big. . .baby."

"Mom!"

Nancy took a deep breath. "Girls, come on; I'm worn out, and I need your help. If we finish early enough, we'll have time to Skype Dad. We can take turns putting the pieces in the village."

The old-fashioned Christmas village had been handed down to Nancy from her Nana Winters, and every single house, little person, and snow scene brought a special joy each year it went up. Even though it took hours to assemble it all, Nancy never minded. . .except this year. She'd only taken the time because of the girls.

Her favorite out of the entire village was the skating pond. The "water" was an old mirror that reflected the surrounding lights. Each "skater," placed lovingly in the same spot, brought the frozen wonder to life. The mother helping a child had a nick or two, as did the couple ice-dancing, but she'd never minded. As a little girl, her grandmother let her play with them, and she'd named every one after a family member.

The Nativity set was small, but her grandmother never wavered in making it the center of the village, "because Jesus is the center of Christmas," she'd said.

Since having children, Nancy had made this part of their tradition, and even though her bones ached from tiredness, the ritual of adding the Nativity set felt good. Every piece lay nestled in its special place, wrapped and waiting in a gold box. She lifted the delicate, hand-carved figure of Mary. So exquisite was the detail that even a slight smile on her face could be detected. Just looking at her made Nancy feel good.

"Oooh, I love her." Noelle stepped closer to touch Mary. "She's so beautiful, Mommy. Can I put her down this time?"

"Sure."

Noelle walked over to the lit village and, with great care, set Mary in the proper spot. "How does she look?"

"Great, perfect, Noelle. Okay, Hayley, you're next." Nancy removed Joseph from the box. "Careful."

"I think Joseph is very handsome," Noelle said.

"That's what you said last year, Noelle."

"Well, he's *still* very good-looking."

Both Nancy and Hayley laughed.

After Mary and Joseph were in place, the various other characters— one camel, three wise men, and a shepherd boy carrying a lamb—took their spots. The actual manger piece was always last.

"Since Dad always places the manger, and he's not here, I'll do it this year." Nancy unwrapped a very small hay-filled trough and put it down on the table, stepping back to admire the entire scene. "There, what do you think?"

"Where's baby Jesus?"

"What? Oh, sorry, I almost forgot." She reached inside the box, moving the wrapping paper to the velvet-covered sides. Nothing. Even after removing all the paper, she didn't find the small baby Jesus figurine.

"Mom," wailed Noelle, "we can't have Christmas without Jesus!"

"Noelle, that little statue is not the *real* Jesus."

"I know, but look how empty the manger looks." She was ready to cry. "Daddy wouldn't like it."

Nancy couldn't imagine what had happened to baby Jesus. Maybe

He'd been lost in their move right after last Christmas. Regardless, she'd had enough drama for one night.

"Okay, girls, tomorrow I'll look around some more. We can call Dad then. . .when I find it. Right now, I want you in bed."

Both girls protested, but their mother didn't back down.

"Okay, but I still say it's just not right." Noelle grabbed her doll, blew her mother a kiss, and stomped her way up the stairs.

"Night, Mom. I'll help you look for Jesus tomorrow, 'kay?"

"Thanks, Hayley; love you."

"Love you, too."

Nancy breathed a big sigh, flipped off the lights, thinking she might have enough energy to grab a quick bit of reading, when she heard Noelle.

"Mommy! Mommy, I need you, please!"

Nancy took each step with a short prayer: *Lord, give me strength.*

Noelle was sitting on the edge of her bed, the doll clutched in one arm.

"Sweetheart, get under the covers and I'll tuck you in."

"Mommy, my heart hurts so bad."

"Is it because you miss Daddy?" She moved a strand of hair off her younger daughter's face.

Noelle nodded. "Yes, but that's not all." She paused. "What if we can't find baby Jesus? It's not right that He won't be in the manger. He's the most important part." She chewed on her lower lip.

"Noelle, you know that the entire Nativity set is just a reminder of Christmas, of Jesus. We know what Christmas is really all about."

"But what if somebody comes in our house, likes the village, but doesn't see Jesus? Then what will they think?"

"Noelle, I. . ."

"Mommy, will you promise me that if you can't find our old baby Jesus, you'll buy a new Jesus?" Her eyes were filling with tears, and she clung even tighter to the doll.

"Oh, Noelle, I'm sure I'll find our 'old' baby Jesus. Honey, would it make you feel better if we prayed about it?" She was tucking the covers in snug and tight.

Noelle nodded and closed her eyes.

"Dear Lord, thank You that You sent Jesus on Christmas. Thanks that You cared that much about all of us. Help us find our missing Nativity piece, and please help Noelle have a good night's rest."

She opened her eyes and saw that Noelle had already fallen asleep, the doll by her side.

As tired as she was, Nancy knew she had to find baby Jesus. She went back to the living room, flipped on the lights, and started searching in another box. . . .

Noelle woke up and looked around her room, blinking twice. Funny, parts of it still looked the same, but now the curtains were different, and the light fixture was not where she remembered it being when she'd gone to bed. She rubbed her eyes and looked again. Strange.

Getting out of bed felt different. The wall-to-wall carpeting in her room was gone.

Gone? Now she walked on bare, hard wood. Her heart pounded; she needed her sister.

She ran down the hall to Hayley's room. "Hayley, wake up!" No response. "Hayley, please; something's wrong!"

Hayley rolled over, stretched, and sat up. "Noelle, it's still nighttime. What are you doing?"

"Hayley, something really weird is going on."

"You mean more weird than you?" She lay back down and rolled to the wall.

"Look around your room, Hayley, and tell me what you see."

"Okay, if that will get you to leave me alone." She sat up, looked, and rubbed both eyes. "What?" Now she was out of bed and walking around in a room she barely recognized. "Noelle, what's your room like?"

"Different."

"What's going on?"

"Maybe we're dreaming?"

Hayley got right in her sister's face. "Noelle, two people cannot have the same dream at the same time. Let's go downstairs."

Nothing in their house looked the same. Every room seemed altered.

"This looks like our house, only maybe from a long time ago," said Hayley.

Noelle ran to the living room window. "Hayley, come quick."

The two of them looked, but neither could believe their eyes. The entire neighborhood was lit up, while just down the street, the town

127

square was bustling with people walking from shop to shop.

"Noelle, this isn't our regular neighborhood, but everything still looks familiar."

The two girls looked at one another and spoke in unison. "The Christmas village!"

"How'd this happen? How'd we end up in Grandma Winters's Christmas village?"

"We are dreaming," Noelle whispered.

"Maybe, but I'm going outside. I'm not going to miss this. Come on, let's get our coats."

"Okay, but Mom's not going to like this."

"Well, so far, she's not in our dream." Hayley helped with her sister's coat.

"Wait," Noelle shouted. "I'm taking my doll."

Hayley waited by the front door.

Noelle came down the stairs with the doll and announced, "Okay, now I'm ready."

They opened the door and stepped onto the front porch. It was snowing. Both girls made their way down the steps and out into the street. They stepped aside in surprise, just as a horse-drawn sleigh went by.

"Merry Christmas," the driver yelled. The bells on his horse jingled all the way down the street.

"This is the best dream I ever had," Noelle said. "Look, Hayley, there's the candy shop and the toy store. I wonder where the Nativity is?"

"Well, if this is really Grandma Winters's village, then we should know exactly where it is. Right?"

Noelle giggled. "Oh yeah, I forgot. Let's find the center of the square."

They held hands and made their way through the crowd. In the far distance they could hear laughter coming from the frozen pond filled with nighttime skaters.

"I see it, Noelle. It's right ahead. I don't believe it."

"Where? I can't see." She let go and stepped around a man carrying a little boy on his back. "Oh, there it is." She stopped in her tracks. It was more beautiful than the tiny one at home; and all the pieces were life-sized. "Hayley," she whispered, "they're alive."

They walked closer. There was Mary, kneeling before the manger, while Joseph stood behind her. The camel was chewing his cud to one side, while three grown men and a young boy carrying a lamb stood nearby watching.

"Amazing, isn't it, children?" An older woman with a small little girl in tow was admiring the scene. "I'm very impressed."

Hayley and Noelle could only nod. They moved closer, and Mary looked up to smile at them.

They inched a little closer. Noelle stretched her neck to look into the hay-filled manger.

It was empty.

She jumped back. "Hayley, there's no baby Jesus." Hayley walked closer to look for herself.

"You're right. He's gone all right. Just like at our house."

"It's not right, you know. There cannot be a Nativity scene without Jesus." Noelle walked up to the shepherd boy. "Hey, kid, where's baby Jesus?"

"Shhh, get out of here. You're not supposed to talk to me, or any of the others." He turned away from her.

"Listen, I'm telling you, it's not right. Not right."

"Little girl, nobody can see inside with all that hay, anyway. Go away, I said."

She went back to her sister's side. "Hayley, what can we do?"

"Noelle, this is just a dream, remember?" Hayley tried walking in another direction. "Let's see if we can buy some candy in the sweet shop."

"No, I'm going to find baby Jesus, Hayley."

"Are you kidding me? Where will you find one?" Hayley was losing patience.

"Let's ask someone in the candy store." They found the shop but discovered they had no money for treats.

"Sorry, girls, it's cash only, I'm afraid." The shop owner was polite but firm. "Christmas or not, business is business, you know." He ran his fingers down his beard.

"Mister, can I ask you something?" Noelle walked closer to the counter.

"Make it quick. I'm busy." He gave a scowling look.

"Can you help me find baby Jesus?"

"What? What'd you say? Baby Jesus, what baby Jesus?" He was drumming his fingers on the glass countertop.

Hayley spoke up. "See, mister, the Nativity set is supposed to have baby Jesus in it, and well. . .well, He's missing." She took Noelle's hand. "She, we, want to know if you'd help us find a baby for the manger."

The shopkeeper rolled his eyes at both girls and frowned again. "You two scoot on out of here; I don't have time to deal with the likes of you. . .I'm busy." He motioned for the next customer to come forward.

Outside, the girls were beginning to feel cold. "I guess we should go back home, Noelle; no one else seems to notice that baby Jesus is missing."

"I can't, Hayley, I just can't." Suddenly, Noelle's face brightened. "I've got an idea. Will you come with me?" Not waiting for an answer, she turned toward the living Nativity again.

When they got there, Noelle approached Mary and tugged on her sleeve.

"What is it, little girl? Are you lost?" She was much nicer than the shepherd boy had been.

"No, I'm not lost; I'm upset."

"Tell me," said the Mary person. "Maybe I could help."

"Well, I'm upset because there's no baby Jesus in the manger." She fought back tears.

"I know," said Mary, "but it's just too cold this year to have a real baby, and I guess we didn't think anyone would notice."

"I have an idea, if you don't mind."

Mary leaned down closer.

"Could I leave my doll to be baby Jesus? She's really a girl, but a baby's a baby, after all."

Mary straightened up and smiled. "I think leaving the doll is a very good idea."

"See, she's my favorite because my daddy bought her for me. I know he wouldn't mind if I left her, though, because he says Jesus is the center of Christmas." Noelle held up the doll, and Mary motioned for her to place it in the manger.

Very carefully, Noelle laid the new baby Jesus onto the hay. "There," she proclaimed. "Jesus is back." She smiled.

"Come on, Noelle, we need to get home. I'm freezing out here."

"Coming, Hayley, coming. . . ."

"Coming, Hayley, coming. . . ."

"Noelle, Noelle, wake up. You're dreaming. . .and what are you doing in my bed?"

Noelle opened both eyes and looked around. "Oh. Oh, I just had the most awesome dream, Hayley. We were in the Christmas village, and everything was for real. I mean, alive!" She was wide awake now.

Hayley said nothing.

"And, Hayley, you were in it, too. Remember?"

"I do. I do remember, Noelle." She scratched the side of her head. "I can't believe we had the same dream." She jumped out of bed. "Noelle, where's that doll?"

"What?"

"Where's the doll you had last night when you went to bed?"

"Uh, I don't know. Let's look in my room."

They looked everywhere. . .in the closet, under the bed, but the blond-haired doll was nowhere to be found.

"We've got to tell Mom about this."

But when they went downstairs they found a note:

Out jogging. Be back soon.
Love, Mom

"We'll tell her when she gets back, Noelle. Let's eat."

Noelle had her back turned, staring at the Christmas village.

"Noelle, did you hear me? I said, let's eat." Both hands were on Hayley's hips.

"Come here," Noelle whispered. "Come here, quick."

When Hayley got to the Christmas village, Noelle was pointing at something.

"What?"

"Look, Hayley, look at the manger." Noelle was smiling while big tears rolled down her face.

"I don't believe it."

Right in the middle of the Christmas village square, they saw all the figures that had been there last night. It looked the same all right, except for one thing. Now the manger that had been empty just hours before held a tiny little being. Baby Jesus had been found! Only, instead of the traditional figure they'd used from years past, this baby Jesus had bright blond hair.

"It's my doll," Noelle whispered. She turned to her sister. "It's the doll that Daddy bought me. Hayley, is this a miracle?" She looked at her sister. "Is it?"

Hayley hugged her sister as tightly as possible. But, for once, she had nothing to say.

A Note to the Reader

I believe in miracles. It's a miracle any time Jesus enters the heart of a person and changes them from the inside out. The Bible says, "If anyone is in Christ, he is a new creation; old things have passed away; behold, all things have become new" (NKJV) That's miraculous.

In this story, Jesus is missing from Christmas. Does that sound familiar to you? For millions, Jesus is missing from their Christmas every year. Please don't let this be the case for your own heart or your own home.

Merry Christmas, from my heart to yours.

Messages of Love

Linda J. Reinhardt

After many years of not celebrating Christmas at home, Dee hopes to find the perfect ornaments for her tree. But after searching the mall, she comes home empty-handed.

Then her fiancé, Buddy, pulls out her Christmas boxes from storage, and she discovers the gifts given to her through the years from God and those who love her. . . .

❧

It had been over two hours, and still Dee hadn't found the right Christmas ornaments for her tree. The mall was jam-packed with shoppers. Dee felt hot and tired. Fighting discouragement, she decided to leave the mall with a plan to entice her fiancé to return the next evening with her. Maybe the two of them would be able to find just the right ones to put on her tree.

Instead, Buddy suggested they spend the evening setting up the tree and for Dee to take a look at what she already had.

Buddy stood Dee's tree up in her living room right in front of the window. It was beautiful. Her heart skipped with excitement. Buddy went out to the garage to search for boxes marked CHRISTMAS.

This would be the first Christmas in what seemed eons that she would be able to decorate her home, *soon to be their home*, and have Christmas dinner. For many years she'd been in a relationship where her husband—now her ex—didn't believe in celebrating the season. He was against anything that had to do with her newfound faith. It had been very hard. One day he left a note, and she never saw him again. All communication came through his lawyer.

It had been a hard and painful journey for her, until she met Buddy. Whenever she looked his way, the memory of her first encounter with him would flash through her mind.

Buddy had his hand out to help someone. When he finished helping, he gave a nod at their thank-you, and went on his way as though it were as natural as breathing for him. Dee didn't know anything else about him, but it stirred her heart in such a way, she just had to meet him.

And she did. On a rare snowy day, her car had a flat tire in the church parking lot. Buddy pulled up next to her in an old Volkswagen Beetle, filled with a group of laughing friends. When he finished fixing her tire, Buddy said, "We have room for one more."

Dee didn't even have to think twice about it. She squeezed in, and they spent the day driving around town, visiting people who were housebound due to the snow. At the last stop, they ended up at an adult care facility, where they made snowmen outside some of the residents' windows.

Dee helped Buddy with his snowman. He asked if she would like to hang out with him again sometime.

Sometime? All the time, her heart said.

But she just nodded and smiled.

That marked the beginning of a wonderful two years. Now, here she stood with a ring on her finger and a date to forever be with this man.

The doorbell rang, interrupting her thoughts. Dee opened the door to her best friend, Laura. She had a present in her hand.

"I wanted to make sure you got this tonight since you were putting up your tree. Hope you like it. I have to go. See you."

And she was gone before Dee even had the opportunity to open it.

Cries of delight filled the room when the present was revealed. Dee loved snowman ornaments, and this one was a skiing snowman. Laura was an avid skier, so Dee would always be able to remember this gift was from her.

Buddy came in from the garage and dropped a box down in front of her. Dee moved quickly to open it and tore through the tissue. One by one, she pulled out ornaments given to her throughout the years.

"Buddy, I remember when I would get these ornaments and decorations. It would upset me so much because I didn't see the point. I couldn't use them, so I'd wonder why anyone would give me Christmas stuff for a gift."

She started placing them one by one on her tree. "I think I was actually offended by the gifts. I mean, I used to go to *other* people's homes to have

Christmas. Never did I have Christmas at my own. So what's the point, to rub it in?"

Dee continued decorating, pulling them out one by one. Buddy stood and watched her with a broad smile.

"One Christmas, I was a bit more sensitive than other years. The entire street seemed to be lit up with colorful lights. Every time I looked out my window, I was reminded of how I couldn't celebrate in my own home. It was a beautiful light show, right outside my door, every time I sat down in my favorite chair.

"Then one day I went to church in a sour mood to help set up for Sunday school. I complained to the most wonderful lady ever about my situation. I told her I really wanted to be able to participate since I loved Jesus so much. Christmas was a very special time for me.

"God gave her some wise words to say to me. 'Dee, maybe God put the Christmas lights right outside your window for you to enjoy since you can't put up your own.'

"I was stunned. I'd been so focused on what I couldn't do, I didn't even realize how God and people who loved me were helping me celebrate. When I returned home that evening, I sat in my chair and looked outside the window at the wonderful Christmas lights God had put up for me to see. It was wonderful. I had my Christmas at home."

Dee stepped back and looked at the tree. It was pretty full, with all of the ornaments given to her through the years. "Last night at the mall, I couldn't find the right things to put on this tree."

Buddy put his arm around her shoulder, giving her one of his handsome smiles. "You already had the perfect ornaments."

Dee reached over and touched a few of them, remembering who had given them to her. "I couldn't see back then what a gift each of these was. But they were messages of love."

"Dee, I know it was hard for you when you couldn't do all of the things that go with this holiday. And I love how God and everyone helped you. But you were able to celebrate the gift of love and salvation given to you through God's Son whenever you sang a song, said a prayer, and hung out with family and friends. No one can take that from you. And isn't that what Christmas is really all about?"

Dee looked up at this incredible man she planned to marry and nodded. "You're right! I did. The most important thing is the gift of Jesus.

I did get to celebrate Christmas after all."

"This tree is filled with gifts of love, which make it look incredible, but there is one thing missing from this tree." Buddy bent over and handed her a box.

Dee's eyes lit up.

"A gift of love from me. Merry Christmas, my Dee."

Merry Christmas, Darling

SHARON BERNASH SMITH

Michael has the fondest memories of Christmas because it's also his wedding anniversary. Even though he's in a nursing home now, he doesn't really mind because his loving wife is a frequent visitor, and their time together makes it all worthwhile. . . .

A reminder that sometimes Christmas, like love, is celebrated only in the heart. . .but that doesn't make it any less meaningful.

December 24

Michael Browning had been waiting for his wife's visit all day. He wasn't angry or even a little ruffled that she'd not arrived. Karen had a busy schedule with a myriad of Christmas preparations; he completely understood the delay. Passing the time meant studying his Bible, then visiting with staff and residents. Today he found everyone in a pleasant mood for the holiday.

Coming to Oak Glen had been a difficult transition for Michael, but he'd never wanted to be a burden to his family, especially not to Karen. It had taken time, but with the Lord's help, this place became "home," and he was making the most of it.

Oh, definitely there were things he still missed, including their dog of many origins, the ornery cat, and really good coffee made from freshly ground beans. Just as well, he told himself. It probably was too strong to be good for him, anyway.

"The steadfast love of the Lord never ceases; his mercies never come to an end; they are new every morning" (ESV). Deep within his spirit, Michael was satisfied, because of all men, he considered himself blessed beyond measure. With the Lord's goodness surrounding him, the memories he kept dear were sweet companions in the lonely times. His huge scrapbook, resting by the bed, was filled with family pictures old and new, as well as dozens of cheerful cards from friends.

He heard familiar footsteps in the hall. Karen!

She swept into the room, carrying a vivid, crimson poinsettia. "For you, darling husband!"

"You're a sight for sore eyes, Karen." He rose to gather her into his arms. She fit perfectly, as always. "You smell wonderful." He squeezed her for emphasis.

"I'm wearing your favorite, Shalimar. It's not too much, is it?" She returned his embrace, giving an affectionate kiss on the cheek. "You'd think you'd be tired of the same old scent."

"Well, I'm not tired of you, am I? Whenever I think of you, I'm reminded of that cologne, and vice versa." He laughed with the memory.

"Michael Browning, you are such a flirt after all these years."

"Fifty-two tomorrow, Karen. Where have they all gone?"

"Well, most of them have gone right to my hips, in case you haven't noticed."

They walked to the couch and sat close to one another. "You look the same to me, honey, exactly the same. Always have, always will."

"Michael, I hope you know that I think every year we've had was wonderful. Maybe not perfect, but perfectly wonderful." She inclined her head for a kiss.

The time he'd waited for her visit had been worth it. When she was in his arms, the world was exactly how it was supposed to be. How blessed he was indeed. He sighed and thanked the Lord out loud for His goodness.

"Merry Christmas, darling Karen."

"Merry Christmas, my Michael. And happy anniversary, too. . . ."

The door opened, letting in two of the night staff.

"How long has he been sitting there?"

"A couple hours. I checked on him right after dinner. Didn't look like he ate much. He's hardly eating at all now."

"Does he say anything?"

She walked over and began getting Michael ready for bed. "Not for weeks, except for a word or two. Maybe it's because his wife isn't able to visit anymore. I really miss him. Remember how he always had a joke ready on the good days?"

She turned down the bed and went to help the other attendant finish getting Michael undressed and into pajamas.

"Alzheimer's is a mean disease; I hate it."

Just as they settled him into bed, one of the staff said, "Maureen, look close. Do you see that? On his cheek?"

The younger woman stepped closer, bending over the withered shell of Michael Browning. A sigh escaped. "It's a tear. Oh, poor thing, could he be in pain?"

"Not physical. The doctor was here this morning. But seeing that tear makes me wonder. What goes on in his mind all day? Wish I knew."

"Do the doctors know?" Maureen tucked the covers around his shrunken shoulders, watching his eyes flutter closed. She stroked his face, running a caring hand down one cheek, then the other.

"I don't think anyone knows but the Lord."

Maureen leaned down close to his ear. "Good night, Mr. Browning. May God bless you as you sleep."

He sighed. They turned, switched off the light, and left, catching the door so it wouldn't slam and disturb his dreams.

The Longest Silence

ROSANNE CROFT

Working in an army hospital in Vietnam at Christmastime, a young medic is angry at the world. He just wants to go home. But a chance meeting with one of the guys and he finds himself in a Jeep going out of the compound to find a Christmas tree—in a war zone, no less!

In the long silence between life and death, he'll learn more than he could ever imagine about waiting and hoping for something, for anything. . .and maybe even for God.

❦

It was a good day. I had two letters at mail call—one from my mom and one from a guy who'd shipped out of Vietnam two months ago. I walked to my bunk and tore open the one from Charlie. *Peace on Earth—1968,* his card said.

But the picture had nothing to do with Christmas; it was a photo of an M48 tank. We'd given Charlie a celebration barbeque at our Quonset hut, our hooch. But his attitude had been so cynical and mean; I didn't see why we'd gone to any trouble for a selfish guy like him. Now he sends me a demoralizing Christmas photo card.

Merry Christmas to you, too, pal, I thought gloomily.

Charlie's sarcastic greeting threw me into a cranky mood of self-pity. *He* was home, far from the rocket attacks on our evacuation hospital. He'd never have to carry another gurney off a helicopter in the middle of the night, I thought bitterly. Charlie was spending the holiday at home with his family, complete with stockings on the fireplace and a decked-out Christmas tree. Oh sure, here the cooks at the mess would roast a big turkey dinner for us, I knew. But the turkey, and especially the potatoes and gravy, never tasted like home. Must have been all the insects buzzing around, ending up in the food. Extra protein, some guys said.

141

We medics were friends for life, *most* of us, locked together in mortal combat against wounds received by our fighting men in the rice patties and jungles of the Central Highlands of Vietnam. At the 71st Evacuation Hospital, our job was to save as many lives as we could, and we did it twelve hours every night shift and twelve hours every day shift. We stabilized them and sent them on.

But this December of 1968, when US casualties peaked at over 16,000 killed in one year, I felt the same hopelessness depicted on that card. There would never be peace on earth. I tucked the card into my pants pocket with dismay and walked out of the hooch.

I almost rammed straight into Phil, the chaplain's assistant, as he hurried back from the direction of the sergeant major's office. Poor Phil; he'd lost every hair on his twenty-year-old head from taking quinine to fight against malaria. We all took it, but some men had the bad luck to have side effects. Young guys look strange when they're *that* bald. Talk about nerdy. That'd be Phil.

"Hey, Sergeant," he said, "I have a surprise."

"Call me Ray," I replied. "I tell you guys that over and over. So what's your surprise?"

"I requisitioned a Jeep. The permission's right here!" The guy was happy.

"What're you, crazy? There's a war on. Why would you go out there joyriding?"

"Because"—he looked at me straight on—"we're going to get ourselves a Christmas tree!"

Two of our hooch mates resting on bunks behind me jumped up like shots from a double-barreled shotgun.

"Hey," Mack said, "when do we leave for this mission?"

"Count me in," said the other guy. We called him Spider on account of his long, skinny arms and legs. He was a walking daddy longlegs.

"You're insane," I said, "but heck, I might as well go to protect you loonies."

We borrowed a hacksaw and some rope from the quarter master's supply tent and drove out of the gate in our canvas-topped Jeep. After spotting a few water buffalo, we didn't see a thing for miles. Nothing but six-foot-high elephant grass swaying in the breeze and the dusty red road in front of us. No trees.

"Think there are Viet Cong in that grass?" Mack ventured to say.

It was what we'd all been thinking. An ambush would've been easy to spring on us. No one answered him. I just shrugged, but I don't think he saw me.

It had been cloudy all day, and now a light drizzle began. By the time we noticed the first stand of pine trees, we'd traveled twelve kilometers away from the safe gate of the hospital compound. Phil hummed Christmas carols under his breath. We didn't dare make too much noise as we jumped out of the Jeep and headed up the hill.

Looking for the perfect tree, we held our rifles more out of habit than because we were in a war zone. We'd temporarily forgotten that fact and were experiencing a little joy in the looking. The trees had long needles, eight or nine inches, like a ponderosa pine back home.

"Over here!" Phil said. It was a great tree, the perfect size and shape, so we cut it down, all six feet of it. We slung it over the top of the jeep and roped it down, just like any family in Oregon or Vermont would do.

We leapt back into the Jeep, excited, laughing. "Wait till the guys see this tree," Mack said.

Phil turned the key. There was no sound.

"Try it again, Phil," I said, my heart pumping fast.

It was no use. The Jeep was dead. I watched the blood drain from Phil's face. He shut his eyes and hunched over the steering wheel.

It was the longest silence of my life.

Raw fear flooded in and crushed me. I couldn't breathe or think, except about the enemy hiding in the elephant grass, ready to slaughter us. How stupid we'd been to risk our lives for a Christmas tree. My rifle went limp in my hands. Twin demons, Panic and Paralysis, screamed into my ears.

Spider reached his long arm over the seat to tap my shoulder. "Sarge," he whispered, "let's push it down that hill with the clutch down. It always worked with my old truck back in Wyoming."

I turned to him. "Uh, that just might work, cowboy," I said, pounding down my panic. "Phil, pop the clutch when you get some momentum, okay?"

Phil nodded as some of his color returned. His forehead wrinkled with hope.

Spider, me, and Mack got behind the Jeep and put every muscle we had into pushing it. I filled my lungs with the misty air. Action seemed to chase away the smothering fear. Red mud from the road spewed over our boots and pants as the Jeep began to roll down the hill, the spark ignited, and the engine roared. Relief flooded our souls. Exhaust never smelled so sweet!

We ran to catch up and slide into our seats, not wanting Phil to brake for anything.

There was a curious smile on Phil's face. "Way to go, you guys," he said.

Then he started to sing a Christmas carol, louder and louder. It was catchy. We all sang: "O come, all ye faithful, joyful and triumphant. . ."

We'd been rescued from that long, fearfully silent moment. We were *alive*. We wouldn't be a hash mark line on some North Vietnamese blackboard.

We drove through the gates past pointing guards, our tree sinking into the canvas top of the Jeep along with the rain. We found out that while we were gone, the other guys in the hooch retrieved a piece of cardboard from behind the central medical supplies Dumpster and painted it to look like a warm redbrick fireplace. They'd even hung army-green socks on it. After we'd built a tree stand, our Vietnamese ponderosa tree took on its new form; it sparkled with a string of lights someone had from a Christmas package. We added popcorn garlands and glittery paper decorations. If you narrowed your eyes just right, at the same time inhaling the intoxicating fresh-cut smell of pine, it transformed itself into a true Christmas tree just like back home.

At our party that night, I sidled next to Phil and handed him a glass of our special punch. "Enjoy," I said.

"Thanks," the poor guy said warily. Then I got out the smashed-up Christmas card from my pocket. "I got this greeting this morning. What d' you think?"

Phil unfolded it. Somehow I didn't want him to agree with the cynical message on the card. I didn't want him to say: "Ain't it the truth?" I wanted to believe in peace on earth. Mostly, I wanted some word of wisdom from this young, nerdy chaplain's assistant.

He came through. Sighing, he said, "No one wants peace more than a weary soldier. Or medics, in our case. But I think peace is more than the absence of war."

Now I wished I hadn't shown it to him. I knew he was going to say something about God, and I happened to want to be angry at God. 'Course it was Christmas Eve and I knew I should hear him out.

"You know I'm going to talk about God, right?" Phil smiled at me, looking remotely like the baby in the manger with his bald head.

"Yeah. Go ahead."

"Sarge, real peace comes from faith in God alone. We find peace with God first, then with ourselves and our fellow men. Peace comes when you trust in the One who made you." He sipped his punch. "Whew," he said, "what's in here?"

I drank a sip, too. "Our special mix. But seriously, Phil, I've read a little of the Bible, and I think that if everyone did what Jesus said, there wouldn't be any wars." I was a little drunk.

"You're getting there, friend," Phil said. He saw Mack and Spider across the room, filling their cups with more punch. "I'm glad I was with you guys today. Some guys would've panicked."

I coughed on my next sip. "Um, Phil, I want to know something. Did you *pray* out there when the Jeep wouldn't start?"

He just smiled a kind of Mona Lisa. "Not in so many words, but He heard me anyway. He hears us even in the longest silence."

Nana's Christmas Drive

Sharon Bernash Smith

Nana has a special surprise in store for her grandchild. Right before their eyes, the familiar representation of the first Christmas will come to life—even a for "reals" baby and a huge, furry animal. . . .

Read, and see through a child's eyes a first visit to a living Nativity scene. Snuggle down with a child or two, and read this story aloud. You'll find a great opportunity to share the "real" meaning of Christmas.

❦

I love Christmas! My mom bakes a million cookies, and I get to help. But we don't eat them all. Some of them we give to our neighbors, all wrapped up in red and green tissue paper. Baking and eating cookies makes me happy.

Another thing that makes me happy is to drive around and look at Christmas lights. I love that. This year, my Nana and I are going by ourselves while Mom and Dad wrap Christmas presents.

When Nana comes, she reminds me to get my warm jacket, the one with a hood. I'm so excited! First, we stop by Starbucks and get hot chocolate for our ride. It smells really good. So does Nana, but not in the same way.

"Where are we going next, Nana?" I ask.

"Some place different," she says.

"But, Nana, we always go to the big houses with all the zillions of lights." I was getting a little worried.

"I think you'll like where we're going, but there aren't any lights."

I didn't say anything because I was almost ready to cry. Good thing it didn't take long to get to the place with no lights. Well, there were some, only they were all shining on a really, really weird thing. I couldn't believe it. Standing right in the middle of this huge field was a donkey.

And that's not all. There were white sheep, two llamas, and something I'd never seen in person before. A camel. A living, breathing camel.

"Nana," I asked, "is this the zoo?"

"Oh no. For sure, this is not the zoo."

I was confused.

Nana parked the car, and I couldn't wait to get out. When we walked closer to the animals, I took Nana's hand because I wasn't sure what a living, breathing camel might do. I was so excited about seeing the animals I almost missed the people. There were people!

"Nana, where are we?"

"This is someone's farm, with a living Nativity!"

"No way. That's what my mom has on our fireplace mantel. I'm sure about that because I help her put it up there. Every year."

"Really." She smiled. "Tell me about it."

"Well," I say, "there's a donkey, some sheep, and. . .and. . .a camel!"

"And what about people, are there people?"

"Oh, right. There's Mary, Joseph, and of course, baby Jesus. Because it's His birthday on Christmas, huh, Nana?"

"You are absolutely right." She patted my shoulder. "Tell me, does your Nativity set have shepherds in it?"

"Yes. Yes, there are shepherds. The Bible says they were out in the fields, watching their sheep. Then a gigantic, huge angel came and told them to go to Bethlehem."

"Why?" Nana asked.

"Because that's where Jesus was having His birthday."

Nana laughed and then stopped.

I looked up. I had to blink three times to make sure I was seeing what I was seeing. My Nativity set was alive now! There was Mary, Jesus' mom, kneeling in yellow straw, and standing right beside her was Joseph, her husband. Behind him, some big boys were holding baby lambs.

But here is the part you won't believe. There was a baby! He was wrapped in lots of blankets with a hat on his little head.

"Nana," I asked, "is that baby Jesus? For *reals* baby Jesus?"

"No," Nana said, "he's only pretending to be baby Jesus. . .for a little while."

"But, Nana, he's sleeping in an animal feeder. That can't be right."

"Well, when Jesus was born, that's exactly where He slept. . .in an animal feeder, a trough."

That made me cry. "Oh, poor baby Jesus. Why did He do that?" I wanted to know.

"Jesus left heaven for earth to show people that He loves them. It's all part of God's plan."

"Nana," I whispered, "is the baby cold? Was baby Jesus cold?"

"This baby is nice and warm with blankets. Jesus' mother wrapped Him up tight, too, so He wouldn't be cold. Probably the stable they found was in a cave, so they had shelter from the wind and some of the cold."

"Oh." I can't take my eyes off that tiny baby asleep in the hay. "'Asleep in the hay!' Nana, that's the song we sing, right? 'Away in the manger, no crib for a bed.' That's the song, isn't it?"

"Yes, you are absolutely right. Now do you understand what the song means?"

"Yes I do," I said. When I turned around to smile at Nana, I got another surprise. The camel was standing right next to me.

"He's very friendly," Joseph whispered.

One of the shepherds put down his lamb and came to lead the camel away. I was glad because, up close, he was way bigger than he looked from the car. I shivered.

Nana said it was time to go. As we walked away, I kept looking over my shoulder. A live Nativity set was pretty special. And guess what? I didn't miss the bright Christmas lights at all.

All the way home, Nana and I sang:

"Away in the manger, no crib for a bed.
The little Lord Jesus lay down His sweet head.
The stars in the sky look down where He lay.
The little Lord Jesus, asleep in the hay."

I was glad I had a nice warm bed to sleep in. Nana said she was glad for her bed, too.

I told Nana "thank you."

I loved Christmas even more now.

"Jesus is the whole reason for Christmas," Nana said. "Amazing isn't it? The King of all kings came to earth and slept in a bed with hay, just for us. Merry Christmas!"

"Merry Christmas, Nana," I said. "And happy birthday, Jesus."

And she brought forth her firstborn son, and wrapped Him
in swaddling clothes, and laid Him in a manger,
because there was no room for them in the inn."
Luke 2:37 nkjv

What Do You Say to a King?

SHARON BERNASH SMITH

Jeremiah loves spending time with his shepherd brothers in the fields outside of Bethlehem. He loves their stories but is very afraid of the darkness just beyond the fire of their camp.

When a huge heavenly being makes a mighty declaration, Jeremiah is paralyzed with fear and loses his voice.

All the shepherds are praising God, and Jeremiah wants to do the same. It's only after encountering the baby King, lying in a manger, that the little shepherd boy gets more than his voice returned. . . .

This story is another chance to tell a child about the true meaning of Christmas. First published by Focus on the Family's Clubhouse Jr. *magazine; also previously published in the novel* Like a Bird Wanders *by Sharon Bernash Smith, Rosanne Croft, and Linda J. Reinhardt (OakTara).*

A long time ago in the hills of Judea, there lived a small shepherd boy named Jeremiah. Although he was very young, his older brothers would sometimes let him spend the night with them in the fields with glittering stars for company. This made Jeremiah very happy.

It was winter, and his brothers had built a huge fire to scare away wild animals from the sheep and also to keep themselves warm. They worshipped the God of Abraham, Isaac, and Joseph, their ancestors, and loved to sit around the flames talking of the promise the Lord had made to all the people of Israel. Jeremiah wanted to talk, but he was too shy.

"Someday God will send us a King," Jeremiah's oldest brother, David, shared.

"He will be our Messiah," Micah, another brother, added.

Jeremiah had never met a king but knew that Messiah would be mighty and powerful.

When Jeremiah began to get tired, he wrapped himself tightly in the blanket his mother had sent and snuggled close to David's side. His eyes became heavier and heavier, until he was sound asleep. . . .

Jeremiah woke suddenly to find the sky ablaze with the most brilliant light he'd ever seen. His mouth dropped open with wonder, and he was filled with fear. Right in the center of the dazzling display was a heavenly being who took up the entire night. An angel! Jeremiah's little body began to shake. What was happening? His brothers were on their feet now with other shepherds in the fields. All were shouting, pointing to what their eyes could not believe. Jeremiah was speechless.

Then the angel said to them, "Do not be afraid, for behold, I bring you good tidings of great joy which will be to all people. For there is born to you this day in the city of David a Savior, who is Christ the Lord. And this will be the sign to you: You will find a Babe wrapped in swaddling cloths, lying in a manger."

The angel's voice rolled like thunder across the hills. Only now there was no storm overhead. . .only more angels. Suddenly they were surrounded by a multitude of the heavenly host praising God and saying: "Glory to God in the highest, and on earth peace, goodwill toward men!" (NKJV).

Then, as quickly as they came, they vanished, with the sounds of their praise still echoing off the hillsides, fading away into velvet darkness.

David spoke first. "We have seen the heavens open up and speak to us. What do you make of this, my brothers?"

Filled with excitement, they all began to talk at once. "Glory to God! We join with the angels and say: Glory to God in the highest."

"And you, Jeremiah, what do you have to say?"

Jeremiah stood first on one foot and then the other, still wrapped in his blanket. He wanted to answer. He wanted to praise God with the others, but when he tried, nothing came out. He'd been so afraid, his voice had left him. His brothers patted him on the head to tease, which made him feel even worse. *Glory, glory, glory,* he practiced in his mind. Yet. . .no sound.

"Don't worry, Jeremiah. You've seen a miraculous thing tonight; your voice will return. But it's not over. Come. I'll carry you, and we'll go to Bethlehem, just as the angel said. A baby King should be quite a sight."

After putting Jeremiah onto his back, David and the others set off to see the Infant of promise.

Though the littlest shepherd felt safe with his brothers, secretly he hoped they'd not see another heavenly being for a long time. Jeremiah swallowed hard, trying one more time to speak a word of praise for all he'd seen. Nothing.

He had fallen back to sleep, despite the bumpy ride, when they arrived at Bethlehem. The manger wasn't hard to find, since a bright, shiny star gleamed and twinkled directly above the spot.

David woke Jeremiah, then put him on the ground, rushing ahead to enter an animal shelter carved in the hillside. Jeremiah stayed behind, feeling small and unsure that a real king would live in a cave.

Jeremiah's heart skipped a beat when a small beam of light near the entrance grew and grew until an angel almost like the one he'd seen earlier appeared. He wanted to run in fear, but the angel motioned for him to enter. With his heart still pounding, he moved closer.

Once inside, he walked to a bed overflowing with straw. It held the tiniest human being Jeremiah had ever seen. He was confused. Was this the King?

Just then the baby woke, stretched His little arms, then turned His head to look right into Jeremiah's face. Jeremiah reached out and touched the infant King's very small hand. When the baby took hold of one of his fingers, all fear left the shepherd boy, and he felt the most wonderful joy spread over him like warm honey.

He laughed out loud. His voice. . .he'd gotten his voice back!

"Jeremiah," David asked, "what do you say to a King?"

A huge smile spread across Jeremiah's face as he leaned down and placed his mouth right next to the baby's tiny ear. "Glory," he whispered. "Glory to God in the highest."

Always Home for Christmas

20 short stories to bring delight,
reverence, and meaning to the season

Reality Fiction™ *Faith Meets Imagination*

Sharon Bernash Smith, Rosanne Croft, Linda J. Reinhardt

Dedication

To my mother-in-law, Ovie Jewell Baker,
who has graced this earth for 91 years.
Mother, you are truly my own, and I'm grateful
for every minute you've been in my life.
I will always love you.
—Sharon Bernash Smith

To my mom, Monica Yvonne Black
(December 28, 1933–August 23, 2011)
She who first took my hand,
first made me smile,
first told me a story.
—Rosanne Croft

To everyone in my life:
You are beautiful packages
arranged in my heart.
I hope you are blessed
by reading all of these stories.
—Linda J. Reinhardt

Always Home for Christmas

Contents

The Wonder of Christmas

SHARON BERNASH SMITH

The wonder of Christmas is as old as the starry night God's own Son entered the world in a cold, dark stable. Did you ever wonder at the wonder of it all? Have you ever asked yourself why the King of kings and Lord of lords left the splendor of heaven to become mortal in such a humble manner?

I've asked that question a hundred times or more, even though I know the answer. It's Love. See, my finite mind cannot grasp it. It's that way with miracles.

In that love gift of Jesus rests the wonder of Christmas because "God so loved the world that He gave His only begotten Son, that whoever believes in Him should not perish but have everlasting life" (John 3:16 NKJV).

Rosanne, Linda, and I are excited to share another book of Christmas stories with you. You're invited to kick off your shoes, grab a cup of coffee or tea, and find a comfortable chair. Now you're ready to take the journey of Love with us.

Merry Christmas! May the miraculous Spirit of wonder transform each of you.

A Christmas Destiny

Sharon Bernash Smith

On Christmas Eve in 1905, a couple hears a faint cry, coming from underneath their home on the wharf in Astoria, Oregon. Is it an injured sea mammal or something else washed ashore?

What they find is shocking—and life-altering.

Based on a true story that happened in Astoria, Oregon, within the family of my friend Kim Upson.

The effective, fervent prayer of a righteous man avails much.
JAMES 5:16 NKJV

Port of Astoria, Oregon
December 24, 1905

I don't care what you say, Rebecca, I think it's going to snow." Eli stomped his feet just outside the door.

"Well, if you don't close that door, we'll freeze regardless."

"You're a little testy, seein' how it's Christmas Eve and all." He walked to the woodstove and held his hands close to the top.

She came up behind him and clasped both arms around his middle. "Sorry, Eli; I'm taking my frustration out on you." Even after forty years, she still received great comfort from his strength in times of disappointments. . .big or small.

He turned to face her. "I know you were countin' on the kids bein' here, but there'll be plenty of celebratin' with folks at church tomorrow, Becca." He brushed one cheek with a gentle kiss and went to light his pipe.

Rebecca Stenerson found the tangy aroma of her husband's pipe tobacco and his tenderness soothing, but her mother's heart longed for her children and grandchildren, nonetheless. When she'd received word they wouldn't be coming for Christmas, it felt like all the life had gone out of her holiday plans. Christmas was supposed to be all about family, and now. . .it felt nothing like she wanted it to be.

She poured herself a cup of tea and pulled a rocking chair closer to the stove. "You might be right about snow after all, Eli. My bones tell me the weather's changing."

"Yep, I feel it, too. Good thing I locked Bessie in for the night or we might have frozen milk in the mornin'." He laughed at his own joke. "Might you like me to read the Christmas story, Becca?"

She put down her knitting and smiled at her husband. "Right this minute, when you asked me that, I'm convicted over wanting my own way for Christmas, Eli."

He peered over the top of his glasses. "What?"

"Well, here I am, feeling so sorry for myself and all because the children aren't coming, when all along my focus should have been on the Lord. Makes me think I'll never get it right."

Eli got up to stoke the fire and added a few more logs. Just as he returned to sit back down, he froze. "Listen, Becca, did ya hear that?"

She stopped rocking a minute but heard nothing and picked up her knitting again. "Just the wind or something knocking against the pilings. Maybe a night critter searching for food."

Their house sat on acreage right on the edge of Young's Bay. Built up with pilings, the house was kept from wild waves that could wash them out to sea. Their living had come from the ocean's bounty and had blessed them abundantly from the beginning of their marriage.

"Dunno, I thought I heard something different. . .kind of a moaning sound almost." He shook his head. "Probably only the wind." He picked up the Bible and began to read from the Gospel of Luke.

Then, from underneath the house, the sound came again.

"That sounded human," Becca said.

"My thoughts exactly. You stay here, and I'll go check." Eli had his wool hat and coat on in a flash. Becca wrapped a neck scarf around his neck, while he slipped into a pair of worn boots.

"Be careful. It's bound to be extra slippery out there."

"Don't worry. I'll be right back." He lit a lantern before going out the door.

Grateful for the low tide, Eli held the light as high as he could, causing shadows to dance in front of him while making his way around the side of the house and down to the water.

"Hey there, hey!"

He listened, and heard nothing.

"Anyone there?" No answer but the night sounds of the bay. He was about to turn around when a horse whinnied. At once, he knew it wasn't his.

He squinted in the direction of the sound and saw the silhouette of a horse on the bank above the water. Someone must have tethered it there, but who would be out on a night like this? He was almost to the shoreline when he pivoted and swung the lantern so that its light was cast under the house. For an instant, Eli thought his eyes and the weak light were playing tricks on him. He'd never been more surprised.

There, near the middle, two people sat huddled together. One of them stood, and Eli's mouth dropped open with the shock of seeing a very tall man walking from beneath his home on Christmas Eve.

As the man got closer, Eli could make out his buckskins and braided hair. He extended his hand in greeting, and the young man shook it readily. Eli said a silent prayer that the man would be able to speak English.

He spoke it perfectly. "I am Running Elk. . .Christian name John. So sorry to upset your night."

"Goodness sakes, who's that with ya under there?" The lantern light didn't reach far enough to tell.

"My wife," he said. "She's having baby, and we tried to get to her mother's before, but baby not wanting to wait." His face showed the concern Eli heard in his voice.

"A baby?" Eli said, stunned. "Did you say 'baby'?"

John Running Elk nodded and pointed. "Yes, she could not go on, and your place was first we came to."

"You get her out from there and bring her to the front. I'll go inside and tell my wife you're here."

Well, Lord, looks like Becca's going to get company on Christmas Eve after all.

Becca didn't have the luxury of getting used to the idea of her "company," because by the time John made it inside the house with his wife, it was apparent that time was of the essence.

Unlike her husband, the young girl spoke little English, but Becca figured it really didn't matter because women had been able to communicate in these situations for eons anyway. Right away she went to work getting the girl settled in bed.

Becca had attended enough births—her own children included, of course—to know what to do. A quick look at the laboring girl revealed enough clues to realize that the baby's grand entrance was close. When she told the men, they both began to pace.

Becca had to laugh. "Eli, make you and our guest some coffee and see if he's hungry. And while you're at it, let's make this place warmer. The baby will need as much heat as possible." She turned to the expectant father. "Do you have blankets and clothes for the little one, by chance?"

Immediately, John went out the door and was back in a few minutes with a bundle of things wrapped in deer hide. "My wife has been getting ready for long time now. It's all in here." John handed the bundle to Becca, and his eyes met hers. "Thank you."

She winked and patted him on the back. "You're more than welcome. Now, why don't you put your horse in our barn and bring in some more wood from out there?"

Just a little while earlier, she'd been feeling sorry for herself, and now here she was, filled with energy and hopeful expectancies. *Thank You, Lord.*

An hour and a half passed, and John Running Elk's wife, whose name was Mary, had proved to be a trooper. In between contractions she smiled at Becca. She asked for nothing but water.

"You're a sweet girl, little one, and very brave. I know you'd like your own mama right now, but I'm happy to be here for ya."

Mary was no more than fifteen or sixteen, just like Jesus' mother, and the irony was not lost on Becca, not on Christmas Eve. Thoughts raced about that first Christmas and how scared Mary must have been. . .far from home and having a baby in a strange, cold place. *Lord, bless* this *Mary girl and her baby. Help me remember what to do when the time comes.*

Becca had taken out the scissors and a piece of heavy string to tie off the umbilical cord, as well as a large pan to catch the afterbirth. "All right, baby, we're ready for ya."

Mary indicated she wanted off the bed, and Becca helped her into a squatting position. "Good girl—had my babies the same way." Mary's focus was entirely on the task at hand, and she never cried out, just panted and pushed when a contraction overtook her.

Although in her sixties, Becca got down on the floor with the birthing girl to give whatever support was needed. After six or seven pushes, Mary reached down and pulled her own baby up into her arms with an expression of total wonder and surprise. She laughed out loud and sat down, leaning against the bed for support. Her eyes fluttered closed.

Becca helped Mary up and back onto the bed. Then, taking a soft cloth, Becca began rubbing the little perfect body with vigor until it gave a big, lusty cry.

Both men rushed to the bedroom door to listen to the baby's cry. John beamed with pride and relief, while Eli swiped at a tear or two.

"Congratulations to you." Eli pumped the young man's arm with enthusiasm.

Several minutes later, Becca emerged with a red-faced baby swaddled in a wool blanket. "Are you ready to greet your firstborn?"

John took the baby, held it close, and began whispering something. He considered the Stenersons with misty eyes. "I am asking God for long life for my. . .my. . ." He shrugged at Becca. "Mrs., do I have a son or daughter?" He laughed.

"I'm happy to tell you that God has blessed you with a son." She clapped her hands together.

The new father held his child close. "I am so grateful for this new life."

He looked up suddenly. "How is his mother?"

"She's resting now. What a marvelous young woman you married. You must be very proud."

John sat down. "Mary is young but very strong. She has strong faith as well. We met at the missionary school down the coast."

Eli spoke. "Tell us, John, do you have a name for this little Christmas bundle?"

"I will wait for Mary to wake, and then we will decide. In the Chinook tribe, naming a child is very important. We have talked about nothing else for months." John's entire countenance had changed from fear and anxiety to pure joy. He walked to the bedroom door. "I will see Mary now."

"John," Becca said, "you make yourself ta home in there. Eli and I will make us a nice cozy palette here on the floor in front of the fire. Come get me if ya need anything."

"You have been too generous already. How can we repay you?"

"Land sakes," Eli said. "For the rest of our days, young man, we will never forget you or what happened under our very roof tonight. We've been reminded of Christ's birthday in a way that'll stick with us until we take our last breath. We're grateful to be part of it."

"Seeing you with that healthy baby in your arms is all the payment we need," Becca added. "Now git on in there and share your son with his mother."

John nodded and entered the bedroom.

The fire crackled and popped while the Stenersons sat in wonder over what had happened in the last several hours.

"Eli, I know I should be worn-out, being how it's so late and all, but I feel like a little girl on Christmas morning. Is God good or what?" She covered her face with both hands.

"Are ya cryin', Becca?"

She sniffed. "Only tears of joy, Eli. I so wanted to have children in this house for Christmas, and now. . ."

". . .and now ya do!" He looked at their old clock on the wall. It said five after twelve. "Becca," he whispered.

She dried her eyes on a sleeve. "What is it, Eli?"

"I want you to know that I prayed you wouldn't be sad on Christmas." He threw his hands joyfully into the air. "And look how God answered!"

"I know." She couldn't stop smiling.

"Oh, and Becca?"

"Yes, Eli?"

"Merry Christmas."

The Keeper of the Bell

ROSANNE CROFT

How could a bell change a life forever? Just ask Joe Sunday, a hell-bent sailor. . .until his sea voyage where part of the cargo was a church bell, meant to be delivered in time for Christmas.

"For I am the LORD your God,
who churns up the sea so that its waves roar."
ISAIAH 51:15 NIV

On a gray Sunday afternoon in 1823, a baby boy was born in East London to a washerwoman. Without a father's surname to give him, his mother called him Joe Sunday. At age twelve, he ran away from the land of his birth for adventures on the high seas as a sailor. He'd known nothing but hunger, neglect, and scorn. What worse thing could befall him?

Joe grew into a man while mopping the decks of ships—ships that sailed to the West Indies, to the Americas, to Africa, and to Arabia. At twenty, he'd sailed around the Cape of Good Hope, the tail of the African continent, on a voyage to India. The crew had spotted ostriches on the coast and, when they landed, captured one to take to the ship. Joe knew it was sure to starve aboard, that large flightless bird lurching wildly on deck far from the grasses of South Africa. It left a huge egg near the foremast, big enough to feed several sailors a fresh omelet. Eventually, out of mercy, he killed it, and they all ate fresh meat for over a week.

Now, at thirty-one, Joe Sunday had toughened into a muscular, seasoned sailor. He was known as a rascal who could drink any other sailor under the table. He lived on the edge of survival, a dissipated life without sorrow or regret. Joe continued in this life because he knew no other.

But as first mate of the ship *Remembrance*, he found he had to step up to be the man in charge of the bill of lading for Captain George. It was a good day indeed that the woman he'd lived with in India had taught him to read! The bill of lading listed all the goods transported on this journey—their origin, condition, and destinations. It was a heavy responsibility for a man like Joe, this opportunity to advance himself as first mate. He began to take his duties seriously.

As he skimmed over the bill, he saw the list included a church bell, made in the foundry at Whitechapel, close to the place where he himself had been born. *I'd best have a good look at it,* he thought, since a bell would be one of the heaviest freight on the deck. The church bell was to be delivered to a place called Astoria, in Oregon on the western coast of North America. To get there, the *Remembrance* would have to fight her way around Cape Horn, the tip of South America, where two mighty oceans met, the Pacific and the Atlantic. A place Joe dreaded because he'd heard that many a ship larger than his clipper had sunk there.

But he didn't want to think about the Horn now, as he gazed at the bell carefully caged in its wooden crate. Between the boards, he could see that it was a gray bell, dull in color but gleaming in the lamplight in the predawn morning air. The waves and wind could damage it, he knew, but it was heavy enough to withstand most storms there at midship deck.

He wondered how it would sound when it rang, high in its steeple above the town of Astoria. Etched in his memory were the familiar sounds of London church bells, calling worshippers. After age seven or so, he'd never answered them. He'd lived on the streets of London, stealing and lying to survive. Churchgoers would not understand such a life. Even if he'd wanted to attend a church, he would be a laughingstock among his fellow sailors.

His stomach tensed from drunkenness the night before, and he spat, willing his nausea away. Wee morning hours were his enemy after an evening of carousing. The paper shook in his hand as he inspected the bell for dents and cracks, the bruises that cargo sometimes received as it was loaded onto the ship.

But the bell was unscathed, glowing in good health beneath his lantern, a thing of fluted beauty made by human hands yet with an ethereal quality, like an angel in disguise. This bell took up residence in his ship, a presence too large to be ignored, a being too beautiful to look upon casually.

He suddenly remembered all his sins the night before as he gazed at it, that pure bell, fresh from the foundry. It had been wrought in fire and cast out from molds, a creation shaped to ring out good news and peace on earth from a steeple. Joe had learned about Jesus and God the Father when he was little, but he'd forgotten so much. He scowled under the weight of those memories.

Why must this bell be on *his* ship? It would now be his responsibility to see that it arrived safely to the people who had paid for it in Astoria, and he was not anxious to enter into the world of churchgoers. *Maybe the bell's going to give us luck,* he thought, *luck to round the Horn.*

Shaking his head, he went below into the hold and stalked among the crates of other stuffs and goods, all listed in detail on the bill of lading.

Joe stood with Captain George as the *Remembrance* set off at noon that day, a clipper in full sail. It was his first time sailing to Tierra del Fuego, the Land of Fire, and he couldn't shake a bad feeling about it. If he made it, he'd be entitled to wear a gold earring in his left ear. Rounding the Horn had its privileges. Since he'd also sailed around the Cape of Good Hope, he'd be able to place both feet on the dining table without trouble from anybody. Then, in Mexico or San Francisco, he'd get a tattoo of a full-rigged clipper ship on his chest, because surviving the Horn was the extreme test of any sailor. He tried to think of these things instead of his fear.

Cape Horn. Try as he might to stifle it, dread surfaced in Joe's gut, his thoughts changing to the screaming winds and giant waves sure to be higher than he'd ever seen before. Drunken sailors everywhere talked of the Horn, either of surviving it or of shipmates who had sunk to the bottom. Ships were broken into matchsticks after hitting hidden icebergs if they went too far south. The strong eastward current would push the *Remembrance* with force, as she strove against it to reach the western coast of South America. He didn't want to think about the pristine bell, lying at the bottom of the sea with his own bones, on the edge of the world. It didn't belong there, and neither did he.

"Sinner though I be, I don't deserve that," he whispered, glancing up at the setting sun. He wondered if he'd live to see another Christmas. Every Christmas, his mother's kind master had given him a silver coin at the Christmas feast for the servants. He could see the master's Jesus-like eyes, loving and generous. At twelve, Joe had taken those silver coins with him when he'd run away and never looked back.

Joe's heart hardened as he was wont to do, and he shook himself free of worry and regret. *I won't be burdened by these thoughts of Jesus and Christmas.* Turning his back on the bell, he went below to get a swig of the whiskey flask hidden in his bunk.

Joe Sunday didn't visit the midship area again for weeks. He forgot the bell as it stood stoically on deck at the mizzenmast. Through fog and rain, the gray church bell in its wooden frame stood guard over the *Remembrance* during weeks of gambling card games and dice, of work and sweat, of rationed hardtack and kipper, of salty air and screeching gulls.

Now on this day, Captain George announced that they were below the 40th latitude and had entered the South Sea. A stop at the Falklands days earlier had proved a marvelous salve to the morale of the crew, with parties and drinking, merrymaking and women. They'd toasted the New Year of 1855, genially hiding fears of not living to see Christmas. The revelry was forgotten now, and the sailors set their faces to the wind, marveling already at the size of the waves. The rounding of the Horn had begun. As sailors readied lifeboats and oars for use if the clipper was broken by the waves, Joe Sunday once again remembered the bell and went to check that it would hold fast.

He noticed with chagrin that the bottom board of the crate had been chewed through by a rat, the kind of large pest that lived on every ship. The rat had gone up through the crate's bottom and taken residence inside the heavy bell, nested next to the metal. No one would be able to move the rat out until the bell was uncrated in Astoria, unless the waves on deck reached up and under and carried the vermin out to sea.

Joe shrugged and extended a rope, binding the bell in its crate to the mast. "Watch out there, Rat," he whispered. "Take cover, for we're in for a bad time of it."

The captain gave the "Get below!" signal, and most of the crew scrambled down inside the hull. Except for Joe and Deaf Charlie, the coxswain, who'd lost all control of the ship's wheel and staggered away, not knowing what to do next. He was caught by a wave on the aft deck, and Joe saw him, struggling against being washed out in the salty embroiled stew of the South Sea.

The waves covered the aft-castle as Joe grabbed Charlie by the shoulders and dragged him over to the mizzenmast. There was no time to go below as the ship pitched and swerved in the icy water. So Joe bound them both with strong rope to the same mast as the bell had been bound. He squinted up at the clipper's three proud masts, the spray hitting him hard in the face, and hoped that none would break, that the ship was quick enough and the wind would be right to round the Horn without disaster. Without control of the rudder, they'd need a miracle.

The deaf man shouted, and together they saw a wall of water so tall that he knew the *Remembrance* would be engulfed by it. And in that moment, as he stared at the death wave, a prayer he'd learned when he was four rose up in him. "Our Father who art in heaven, hallowed be Thy name," his voice cried inaudibly in the roar of the hundred-foot wave hovering above them, "Thy kingdom come, Thy will be done, on earth as it is in heaven!"

The memorized prayer somehow released his true heart's prayer. "Lord! Forgive me, a sinner! Save my life, and I'll be Yours." His anguished lament melted in the noise of the storm. The wall of water rose higher than the ship in a terrible swell. The *Remembrance* floated innocently below it, like a toy in bathwater. Joe closed his eyes and braced for a deathly crash, but there was none.

The wave let down gently, like a blanket covering a babe. Water filled his ears, eyes, and mouth. He thought drowning might come within seconds. Then he was sputtering, the wind chilling him to the bone. The ship kept right side up, bobbing from side to side. A strong wind caught her sails, and the fast clipper shot forward, out of the dangerous waters.

Two hours later, Joe released himself and his grateful shipmate, Charlie. He'd watched the bell the whole time, seeing the waves actually lift it once or twice. Peeking out from the bottom of the crate, the rat's black beady eyes watched him, too. The creature had survived. He was curiously relieved that it was alive and still under the bell. He and that filthy rat had rounded the Horn together, and the bell had been more than luck. It'd been a lightning rod for a miracle.

The seas calmed, and the *Remembrance* sped all the way to San Francisco. His escape from death forgotten in front of his shipmates, Joe went into town as the rascal he was known to be, a cussing, drinking sailor. But something had changed within.

What am I doing here, with hard liquor in my hand, my fists ready to fight, and a woman on my knee? he asked himself in the midst of the tavern.

Joe Sunday walked outside. His shipmates could never know what had happened to the hard-drinking first mate who'd saved Deaf Charlie's life going round the Horn.

When they found him the next morning sleeping not in his bunk, but next to the bell under the mizzenmast, they knew that Joe Sunday had changed into a different kind of man than the one who'd set out from England with them.

He allowed them to pierce his ear with an awl—not only because he'd rounded the Horn, but as a sign of gratefulness to God, who had saved him. He would forever be God's servant.

In December they neared the mouth of the mighty Columbia River, whose waters shot out into the ocean with great force. No slow-moving delta here, the "Graveyard of the Pacific" would have to be faced at the Columbia Bar. The Oregon coast had seen its share of shipwrecks. The weather held, and the crew of the *Remembrance* steered their clipper with caution, muscles tense as the ropes they knotted. Joe was reminded to pray by a still, small voice within.

They landed at last, right after noon of that day, weary after the long voyage from England. Every piece of freight intact, Joe greeted the waiting leaders of the city of Astoria on the pier with Captain George. There were several strong men with a sturdy wagon to move the bell with pulleys, lowering it for the journey up the steep hill toward the church.

Joe stood near the wagon, directing the men on his ship as they lowered the bell. Out of the corner of his eye, he saw a small blond girl approach him and bent down with a listening ear.

"We prayed for you," she said, "for one hundred days. We knew that God would help you get our bell to us before Christmas!"

"Aye, and He did, too. Thanks to you, we are here safely." He stood. "I'll help ye with the bell and see it through all the way to its steeple," he told the elders.

So the church leaders allowed him to accompany the bell, and on the way, he told them how he and the bell had rounded the Horn together, with God's help.

Up the steep hill was a white clapboard church, simple yet beautiful, like the bell. The congregation gathered round.

It was in that moment that he first saw his own pink-cheeked Diana holding a bunting of holly and berries, and if there ever was a stronger feeling of love in his heart, he had not known it. She stood near her father, Pastor McGinty, and smiled. She was a pure girl, and scarcely had he smiled back but that pangs of grief plagued him. Grief for his debauched life, grief for running away from God for most of it. Sorrow hit him like a wall of waves, and he turned his face down inside the wagon.

Splashed by his tears in the wagon was the rat. Smelling land, it had taken an opportunity to see its new surroundings and had come out from under the bell. Of course, several other people saw it, too, and a man riding a horse rode up to kill it with a heavy stick.

"Nay, nay," Joe shouted, "give the rat to me. For he and I survived the worst together in the Horn." They stared at him, and the rat tilted his little head and blinked his eyes.

"You see," he said, "I'm the worst creature here; I lived lower than this rat, but God loved me anyway. We lived through the storm by grace and were able to keep the bell safe, he and I."

Everyone calmed themselves at the sailor's plea. The little blond girl brought an old bird cage, and the rat climbed in to claim the cheese inside. The pastor asked him inside the parsonage for some figgy pudding and tea. Then the bell was lifted up, higher than any house in Astoria, into its steeple home.

When the sun set on that Christmas Eve, Joe gazed back at the western sky. Two sun dogs on either side of the bright sun made it appear as though three suns lay on the horizon in the pink-and-coral light. "Red sky at night," he murmured, "sailor's delight." He knew it meant that all storms were behind him. It confirmed from heaven what was in his heart.

Diana and the women finished festooning the church with holly and pine. Candles were lit, and a holy peace descended that night. Pastor led Joe Sunday to the pulpit, where he stood, sheepishly holding his worn hat, in his briny boots and looped earring.

"No more sailing and searching the world for what I couldn't find," said Joe. "I've found peace here with this bell. I didn't think I'd see another Christmas, but now I know God has more for me. I'm here to stay."

Deaf Charlie nodded in the corner pew, looking ever so happy and grunting affirmation. He, too, aimed to stay in Astoria.

So Joe and Charlie went into business together as fishermen and made an honest living with a small boat. The rat roamed freely on their boat, and they called him Quasimodo. During the next two years that the rat lived, he rode atop Joe's shoulder whenever he took his turn as bell ringer.

Joe married the rosy Diana after those two years, at the end of summer when he'd built a house for her. From that year on, every Christmas Eve, he walked with his children to hear the bell ring and told them the story of rounding Cape Horn. Then, looking into their eyes with love, he gave them each a silver coin he'd saved that year.

Joe Sunday may have grown from a boy to become a man at sea, but he grew to become a real man, solid and true as the mizzenmast, on land. He remained steady Joe Sunday, the Keeper of the Bell, until he was eighty-one years old and could ring it no more.

The Christmas Bonus

SHARON BERNASH SMITH

Thousands of homeless or neglected children left the streets of New York City in the middle 1800s until 1920. Intended for adoption by families in the Midwest, they were sent by rail on "Orphan Trains."

Right before Christmas 1907, the McFarlane family is traveling all the way from rural Washington to Troy, Missouri, to welcome siblings into their own family. They think they're prepared for the task. . .until they arrive.

The unexpected surprise might just overwhelm their good intentions.

Excerpted from the novel Old Sins, Long Shadows *by Sharon Bernash Smith, with minor changes for clarity.*

Troy, Missouri
December 24th, 1907

Shepard McFarlane stiffened upon entering the church sanctuary. It was filled with the saddest group of children he'd ever seen, ranging in age from infants to a few in their teens. A total of forty, perhaps. A heady buzz filled the space, along with air that reeked of sweaty children, dirty diapers, and something Shepard recognized as familiar. Fear. Raw and animallike in nature, it permeated every inch of the place.

His stomach churned with identity. *Oh, Lord, give us strength to make a difference.*

Some children wiped at red, bewildered eyes. Whether from lack of sleep or too many shed tears, he couldn't be sure. Others picked at fingernails and clothing in boredom, shyness, and that fear he'd recognized. They looked well fed and wore fairly clean clothing despite the distance they'd traveled. Each bore a number pinned to jacket and sweater fronts.

He scanned the room for a familiar face. She was walking toward him, arms outstretched, a huge smile lighting her face.

Shep ran to his sister, swept her up with a big hug, and spun her around twice. "Oh, lassie, how good to see yer smilin' face." He let her down to the floor, holding her at arm's length.

She blushed for all the attention. "Oh, Shep, this is a dream come true. It's been too long since I've seen you, and now you have a family." She peered over his shoulder. "And where might yer lovely bride be?"

Grace was still at the door, bewildered and overwhelmed, when she caught Shep's gesture to join him. He was holding hands with a young woman who shared the exact same eyes as his own. *Annabeth.* They'd been writing one another for years, waiting for this moment to meet. Annabeth broke away from her brother to greet Grace with a warm embrace.

"Annabeth. I would know you anywhere." She returned her sister-in-law's enthusiastic hug.

"Would you now?" Annabeth laughed out loud. "I didn't realize until moments ago how much Shep and I resemble each other." She took Grace's arm.

Annabeth wore an armband declaring her role as one of the "Guardians." Along with others, she was present to answer questions and facilitate the matching of families to their children from the "Orphan Trains."

"What in the world is an orphan train?" Grace had been shocked when her husband had broached the subject.

Shep wasn't surprised that Grace had never heard of the trains, nor its occupants, since most people in the far West were unfamiliar with few, if any, of the grim details.

"Grace, the whole thing began when people could no longer turn a blind eye to the terror of thousands of children roaming the filthy streets of New York City."

"You mean like dogs?" Grace had been astonished and grieved.

"Yes, maybe thirty thousand, or more. . .right along with stray dogs, pigs, and rats. Of course, not all them little ones were true orphans. Some had one parent or another, and truth be known, some had both."

Grace could not hold back the tears, shaking her head in disbelief. She thought of their own sweet Bonnie.

"When a family was dirt poor with too many *bairns*, often the children were left to the streets," Shep continued. "Some found their way to orphanages, but in time those walls were full. . .splittin' at the seams with human beings too little or too sick to fend for themselves."

"Oh, Shep! I had no idea. I mean, I saw a lot of sad things when I lived in Los Angeles, but nothing like what you're describing. It makes me sick."

"A couple of the institutions had the idea that people out West might be able to take a child or two, and when the word went out, many good people did say yes. It must have been around the middle 1800s when the first trainload of children left for somewhere in Missouri. That's how it all began, Grace. . .with those first dozen brave little bairns."

If Grace had been shocked over the fact there had been so many children left on the mean streets of New York in the 1800s, she was doubly upset to learn children by the thousands were still uncared for and still in need of homes at the turn of the twentieth century.

They had desperately wanted Bonnie to have brothers and sisters, but when that didn't happen biologically, Shep and Grace began to talk about adoption. After months of discussion and prayer, they finally made the decision to take a child or two from one of the orphan trains.

Their entire family and church had supported them from the start, so when they'd left their home town of Yacolt, Washington, right before Christmas, they were ready. Well, as ready as a couple could get before traveling deep into the emotional unknown.

Before leaving home, they'd spent many months of inquiry, obtaining enough information to form a plan. A lot of that plan was due to Annabeth. But still they were not sure of the children's health conditions, nor did they have any other pertinent information as to ages or gender. All they knew was that they would be picking up a family unit made up of three siblings.

The rest of the throng were potential parents like the McFarlanes, scanning the various groups of children, looking for their new child, or children, as the case might be.

Adoption, most of which was without legal bonds, was common even in the rural Yacolt valley. Sickness and accident often robbed children of one or both parents. So families taking in "other" children, blood related or not, was not unfamiliar. Posted on a pillar near the entrance was a copy of the notice Annabeth had sent the McFarlanes months before:

Wanted
HOMES for CHILDREN
A company of homeless children from the East
Will arrive at TROY, MO.
December 24, 1907

These children are of various ages and of both sexes, having been thrown friendless upon the world. They come under the auspices of the Orphan's Aid Society of New York. They are well disciplined, having come from the various orphanages. The citizens of this community are asked to assist the agent in finding good homes for them. Persons taking these children must be recommended by a local committee or pastor. They must treat these children in every way as a member of the family, sending them to school, church, Sabbath school, and properly clothe them until they are 17 years old. Applications must be made to, and endorsed by, the local committee.

 Distribution will take place beginning at 1:30.

"Annabeth." Shep's eyes swept the room. "This whole thing reminds me of something else."

"An animal auction?" She raised an eyebrow.

Shep wiped his hands on his coat front. "Yes."

"I know. Look at that." He turned to where she pointed.

A huge man dressed in mud-splattered bib overalls stood before a girl about ten and a boy around twelve. He stuck a filthy forefinger in the boy's mouth, moving it from side to side, with intense purpose and vigor.

"Shep," Grace asked, "what's he doing?"

"Checking the boy's teeth."

"You mean, like a horse or something?"

"Exactly, Grace." Shep shook his head in disgust and was about to say something to the man when the massive farmer let out a scream. The boy had clamped down hard on the invading finger in his mouth. When the man threatened retaliation, one of the facilitators intervened just in time.

Shep and Grace looked at Annabeth. "I know that was bad," she said, "but most people taking children from the orphan trains have the right heart, I assure you." Annabeth stood between Grace and Shepard, glancing back and forth. "I've met *your* children," she said, grinning from ear to ear. "They're lovely. The oldest two are scared as field mice, but they're just lovely. Come on. Let's meet your family."

The whole scene unnerved both the McFarlanes. They wanted to get their children and leave as soon as possible. Since they knew they'd miss Christmas at home, they'd brought some special things to celebrate their first holiday together as a new family.

Following Annabeth, Grace was glad they'd chosen to leave Bonnie behind, even though they'd miss Christmas with her. She'd have wanted to bring every last child in the room home with them, the exact desire that filled Grace's heart. *Lord, make me strong.*

The woodstove in the center of the sanctuary pumped out heat like the train locomotive. Grace and Shep scanned beet-red faces as they walked behind Annabeth. Their assigned number was 37.

"There." Annabeth pointed. "Look there!" In a corner stood a dark-haired boy with a thin face and wide, doe-brown eyes. Cowlicks had their errant way with the top of his head, while anger transformed his perfect features into a mask of feral proportions. Standing in front of three others in a protective big brother stance, his upper lip curled. Even so, he was still beguiling and handsome.

How pitifully small he looks, Grace thought.

Three others? "Annabeth, those could not be *our* children." Grace took Shep's arm. "See, there's four in that group. We were told there'd be just three, right? Just three." Grace's hands went to either side of her face in puzzlement.

"Well, the identification number's right, Grace." Shep looked at his sister for confirmation. She nodded.

They moved closer to where the rag-tag group huddled together like abandoned puppies. Cautious in their approach, Grace and Shep knelt before them. The small boy in front shook with fear and anticipation, though his thin arms were raised for battle in a street fighter's stance.

"Hello there. What's your name?" Shep held back any touch, but his voice was soft and caressing.

"Gerald." It was a raspy response from the next oldest child. "His name is Gerald."

Surprised, Grace asked, "And what might your name be?" Sheer will kept her from breaking down at his bravery. What nightmares disturbed his sleep at night? How many ways had their innocence been compromised by a life that should have been more fair?

"Dooley." The voice belonged to an only slightly smaller version of Gerald, still on vigilant guard duty.

"And how old are you, Dooley?"

"Tree." He held up three grubby fingers for emphasis.

"Three." Grace smiled and touched the top of his head. "Well, you're a mighty fine boy for three." She wanted to grab him up, kiss his face, and head for the train. This little boy, with rich chestnut-colored hair, was one of her sons. She now had three little men. Maybe four?

Dooley grinned from ear to ear and would have stepped forward, but Gerald held him back. "Stay," he snarled. His eyes darted between Grace, Shep, and Annabeth.

In defiance of sibling orders, the younger boy pushed forward to stand in front of his new mother.

When Dooley moved, Grace saw a one-year-old boy sitting on the wood floor. He idly stroked his face with a wet corner of an aged, swaddling cloth, eyes dazed. . .his complexion the color of pale oatmeal. Beside him lay another baby, perhaps a few months old. Gobs of dark ringlets pushed out of a crocheted bonnet. Wrapped in a threadbare quilt, long overdue for replacement, she. . .or. . .he. . .was sleeping in a woven basket lined with newspapers. No doubt the paper was an attempt to make restitution for the blanket's lack.

Grace took Dooley's offered hand while Shep unfolded an envelope, removed from the boy's pocket. Tears dropped onto the tattered paper, held so Grace and Annabeth could read with him.

Dear famly,

I'm a woman of lowly means, but I love my children. I cannot watch 'um suffer because of the great lack with which fate has seen fit to offer 'um and me self. They's good wee ones, and they love one another.

Becuz of being so young each might not remember me ever, but don't let 'um think I didn't want 'um. Most of my heart will be with 'um as long as I live. Baby Marnie Ann, of course, will not know nothin', so's she'll be the easiest, I'm thinkin'. I know you was not expecting the wee one, but I fear she'll die if she stays. My children be use ta my singin' to 'um nightly. . .so if it wouldn't be trouble for ya. . .coud ya sing 'um t'sleep?

Gerald wants ta protect Dooley and Andrew but doesn't like ta be bossed much. Truth is, he's but a wee boy himself beings only four years and six months.

Aeofi O'Connor

P.S. Gerald, 4, Dooley, 3, Andrew, 13 months, and Marnie Ann, 1 month. Could you keep their names, so's it be easier on 'um?

Trying to speak, Grace choked on the emotion of the letter's content. "Shep," she sobbed, "these are *our* children. God meant for them to be with us. I feel it in my soul."

Annabeth reached from behind to give Grace a hug.

Shep wiped at his face with the back of a hand. "You're dead center right, Grace, and now we've another daughter, as well as these fine sons."

"Marnie Ann," she whispered. "I love that name. . .it's beautiful. Wait until Bonnie finds out she has *two* babies to help take care of." She looked up into Shep's face. "My, my, *two* babies, Shep. How's this going to work?"

"I dunno Gracie, but God does. Did ya not just say they were meant for us?"

Grace chuckled at her instant lapse of faith and walked to where the basket lay. With one hand on the sleeping infant, she reached with the other to touch Andrew. He smiled, revealing two top teeth. At the same time he offered his special blanket in her direction. She leaned over so he could touch her face with the corner. Its dampness landed in the middle of one cheek. His generous version of a kiss.

In an instant, the bond between mother and child formed, and Grace knew she would love this boy with all of her heart for the rest of her days. *Thank You, Lord.*

There wasn't time to contemplate the miraculous moment, but there'd be other days for the remembering. She picked him up, and he gazed deeply into her eyes. His were old, a miniature sage. "You're light as a feather, Mister Andrew."

He gave another funny-toothed grin, then rested his head on her shoulder and closed his eyes with a long sigh. Grace had been offered this baby's two most prized possessions—his blankie and his trust. She looked over at Shep, who'd been watching, eyes brimming.

Rarely does one get the chance to witness the beginning of a brand-new family, Shep knew. *Would the tears never stop? How many had these children shed on their uninvited journey?* He wondered, too, how it would be with Gerald: scared and defiant Gerald, who squirmed to get free from the grip of his new father.

He caught Grace's eye. "You know, I was feeling bad about not havin' time to Christmas shop for you, lassie." He winked. "But God saw fit to give us both an extra gift with Marnie Ann."

Tears streamed down Grace's cheeks as she nodded in agreement.

Annabeth clapped her hands. "Well then, McFarlanes, all I can say is merry Christmas. Merry Christmas to you all."

Shep went with Annabeth to finish the paperwork and left Grace to wait. He was back in fifteen minutes. His heart stopped at what he saw.

Grace leaned against the back wall, fast asleep. Marnie Ann and Andrew were laid in her lap, with the older boys on either side, each lost in separate dreams.

Lord, he prayed, *thank Ya that we're in the palm of Yer hand every minute. Thank Ya for bringin' us this new family. Make me man enough to protect each one. Amen.*

And then he chuckled. *Now, how am I goin' to manage gettin' 'em all on the train?*

He knelt beside his wife, lifted Andrew to one shoulder, and waited for him to settle. The boy's breath was a sweet caress against Shep's stubbled cheek.

Shep smiled. Although the trip back home would be long and tiring, in his heart he knew this would be the most unforgettable Christmas of his life.

More Than the Shirt on My Back

Linda J. Reinhardt

Ginny's dad received a special pair of gloves for Christmas.
Much to Ginny's and her mom's surprise, he gave them away.
But who he gave them to is what makes this story heart-memorable.

To the memory of my grandpa...and to my aunt Ginny,
who shared a story of a sweet action of my grandpa's,
which I stretched an extra mile or two.

I'll never forget what happened the day after my eighteenth Christmas. 1969. It changed my parents and my life.

I was the youngest of eight children, the last one living at home. Well, sort of, because while school was in session, I lived in town to attend it. We lived on a farm in one of the small towns in North Dakota. Since it was Christmas break, I was home.

All of my brothers and my oldest sister had left after the festivities last night. My other sister had stayed over and was taking the train back to Minneapolis. She had to be at work the following day. When it was time to take my sister to town to catch her train, my dad, mom, and I donned our coats and made it out to the freezing cold.

I climbed into the backseat of the old blue Impala. Though Dad had let the car heat up a bit, I could still see my breath. It was so cold. Shivering, I pulled my scarf up around my face and gazed at all the new fresh snow while the Impala made its way down the long dirt driveway Dad had cleared early that morning. He always got up before the birds did.

"Looks like we got at least another foot of snow last night. It must feel like a waste of time to shovel the sidewalk all over again, huh, honey?" Mom asked Dad.

Dad gave a shrug along with that lazy smile he had. "I'll probably have to do it again when we get home. Weatherman threatened more snow this afternoon. Nothing like a Dakota winter. It's cold but beautiful." He met my eyes in the rearview mirror. "You two should use the blankets so you warm up faster. Me, I've got my new fur-lined leather gloves to help keep me warm." He gave my mom a wink.

My sister and I reached over to grab a blanket. I unfolded the blanket and wrapped it around me. It felt good. I don't know why, but I always waited until my dad told me to grab it. I leaned back against the seat, thinking about all of the extra piano lessons my mom had given and the extra hats and scarves she'd knitted for the bazaar to get those gloves for him. My mom had spent all of her piano teaching money on those gloves. I could tell from her expression that she was proud of the gift she'd given my dad.

We finally reached the nearest town of Larimore just as the train pulled in. Ever since I was little, I have loved to watch trains. To this day, I still try to count all the cars before the train completes its stop.

Just then I noticed that a man had jumped out of the number 10 boxcar. "Hey, look! A bum just jumped out of one of the boxcars."

"Ginny! We don't call people *bums*." That was my mom.

"What else do you call them, then?"

"I don't know, but don't call the poor guy a bum. You don't know what has happened in his life to make him have to steal a ride. . ."

My dad interrupted her. I could tell he had his eye on the guy. "He's going into the drugstore. . .oh, nope, he's just taking a rest on the bench in front of the store."

Dad parked the car close to where the guy sat. When we got out of the car to walk over to the station, Dad tipped his hat to the guy. That's something I admired about him—he always showed respect to everyone. He never judged them.

I soon forgot about the guy. My sister didn't live too far away, but I hated to see her go. It would be lonely without the rest of the family around. I wondered how my parents felt when they were in the house alone.

After my sister left on the train, we did a bit of exploring around town. We ate lunch and shopped a bit, then got back into the old blue Impala to head back home.

As we drove back to our farm, just over a hill we saw the top of a man's head bobbing. My eyes fixed on him, wondering who was walking in this cold weather. A person could die out in these elements.

I was startled to see it was the guy from the train. My dad pulled up ahead of him and parked the car on the side of the road.

"Oh, dear, you're not going to give him a ride, are you?" Mom asked.

My dad just got out of the car and walked over to the fellow.

"He's going to give him a ride," Mom muttered.

I stole a glance out the back window. My dad was having a conversation with the man and looking at a sheet of paper the guy held in his hand. Soon my dad put his arm around the fellow's shoulder, and they began walking in the direction of the car.

My dad got back in the driver's seat, and the guy hopped in the back. I didn't know what to expect. It scared me a little. I hoped he didn't stink. I held my breath for a minute before I dared to take a breath. Nope, he surprisingly smelled like fresh soap. That made me curious.

Dad turned the Impala around and headed back to town. Mom raised one eyebrow, which usually meant, "What in heaven's name are you doing now?"

My dad didn't offer any explanations. He pulled up in front of the only hotel in town and motioned for the guy to get out of the car. Dad led the way through the hotel entrance, and soon they disappeared behind the closed doors.

"I wonder what he's up to," Mom whispered.

I knew she already knew the answer to that question. My dad had come over from Denmark looking for his father, and many people had helped him along the way, so my dad was known to help anyone who crossed his path. Plus, he believed the good Lord had given him so many blessings in order for him to pass it on to others in need.

Soon Dad exited the hotel and headed next door to the restaurant. After a few minutes, he came back and got in our car. We drove in silence for several minutes.

"Honey, did you leave your gloves somewhere?" Mom asked suddenly.

My dad nodded.

"Did you honestly give your Christmas present to that stranger?"

"Poor guy didn't have any gloves or a coat. I asked Dean to go down to the store with him and purchase him a coat. Seems he got mugged on the train and lost his coat."

"Dear. . ." Mom frowned. "How do you know he's telling the truth? He could be making the whole thing up."

Dad shrugged. "It's not me he'll have to answer to."

"But dear, I worked hard to get those. . ." My mom stopped talking. I know she knew it was pointless. And I also knew she might make a fuss about it, but my dad's generosity was one of her favorite things about him, even though sometimes it cost the two of them to give.

"I know, and I loved them. I'm very grateful for those gloves, because I had a perfectly good pair to pass on to someone who needed them. I still have the pair you bought me last year."

"What's the use?" Mom threw up her hands.

We drove the rest of the way in silence. When we got to the house, I noticed my dad was more quiet than usual.

We took off our extra layers in the back porch. When Dad finished, he went to his room, and my mom followed. A couple minutes later, I made my way to the stairs to grab the new book I got for Christmas from my room.

I stopped at my parents' door before heading up. My dad's voice came through into the hallway.

"I wish I could've done more. I've been wondering if I really did all I could for that man, or did I just do enough to make me feel like I had done my Christian duty?"

"Well, you did more than most people do for anyone any given day of their life. You put him up in the hotel for a few days and bought him some meals. What more can a person expect?"

"I can't explain it, but I feel like I should have done more. I only got his first name. I don't even know why he is riding cars and walking on long, cold country roads. I only took him to the hotel."

"Well, he'll get a bath and food, along with a good night's sleep tonight."

"It's not enough."

I didn't know what to make of the conversation. I wanted to stay rooted to my spot at the door but feared they would open the door to find me eavesdropping. I continued on up to my room and plopped on my bed to start reading my book. I dozed off after about the fifth chapter.

When I awoke, it was dark. A little disoriented, I made my way to the bathroom and splashed some water on my face. A delicious aroma floated up the stairs. My mom had already started dinner without me. I moved quickly to do my chore of setting the table and putting the food in the appropriate dishes.

A stranger's voice coming from the dining room stopped me in my tracks. I smoothed down the front of my skirt and blouse before I entered. The man from the train was sitting at our table! I hoped my mouth wasn't hanging down to my shoes.

"Ginny! I hope you had a nice nap." My dad waved me over to him. When I stood by my dad, he put his arm around me. "Ginny, this is Dean. He's traveling through town and is going to stay with us for a few days instead of at the hotel."

"Nice to meet you." I held out my hand. Dean gave it a good shake. I excused myself to the kitchen. "Mom?" I whispered anxiously.

My mom shook her head. "Don't worry about it, Ginny. Can you get the plates down? I have all the food in bowls and platters."

"But, Mom, where is he staying? The thought of a stranger in the house is a little scary."

"He's staying out in the porch area where Vern stays when he's here helping your father. We can lock the door, and he still will have access to the basement bathroom. It was my stipulation while you were in the house."

That piece of news didn't sit very well with me. During dinner, I stayed pretty quiet. My dad had always done wonderful things for people in the past, and all of us kids followed his example. But we'd never had a stranger stay in our house.

"So, Dean, what brings you to our town?" Mom asked.

My ears perked up, waiting to hear what he had to say.

"Well, while I was in Vietnam, both of my parents died. Vietnam was a horrible place, and it was harder when I stopped getting letters from my parents. Soon after my parents died, I stopped getting letters from my fiancée. When I returned to the States, I discovered she had gone and married someone else. They even had a baby together."

"No! How terrible. You must have been heartbroken." My mom reached over and patted his arm.

"Still am. It wasn't that long ago. When I went to my home and my parents weren't there, it made me feel worse. So I packed up what I needed, got some money out of the bank, and started walking. I thought I'd try to see the entire country. I had nothing holding me back. But then yesterday I got jumped and lost my wallet with all my money, my ID, and my coat. They didn't take my bag, though. I need to get some ID and see if my bank is around here. I'd seen guys hopping off and on trains and thought I'd get a ride. My dad's brother lived around this area, but I found out he's moved to Illinois."

"Sounds like you've had it rough and need a break. I can help you get the stuff you need," Dad said, "but since you were traveling around anyway, how would you like to stay here for a bit and help out around the farm? My oldest son works half the farm, and I work the other. During the winter, it's a matter of taking care of the animals and snow. The job comes with room and board and a small salary. Give you a chance to have some people around you."

Dean's eyes were filled with admiration for my dad. It put a lump in my throat. I was proud of my dad.

We had a great time the rest of the night eating and playing games. Later that night, when we'd all retired to our bedrooms, Dad came upstairs to say good night.

"Dad?"

"Yeah, pumpkin?"

"Why did you go get Dean from the hotel?"

He sat on the edge of my bed. "After I set him up at the hotel, I didn't feel right. You know, at the Christmas service Pastor Ken talked about how much God sacrificed for us when He gave us the gift of His Son, Jesus. Jesus was His *only* Son. Well, this may sound silly, but I kept thinking I didn't even give away my only pair of gloves. I didn't give away all my money. I just gave the guy something and went on my way without even seeing if he needed anything else."

"So are you saying it's not good enough to do what you did?"

"No, I'm not saying that at all. There've been plenty of times I have done only a small act, and I knew it was enough. But for Dean, it was different. I felt like I was supposed to give him something of me—not what I had in means of material things. And now after hearing his story, I realize he needs some people around. He's a lonely guy."

"I think I get it, Dad. It's really cool what you are doing."

"You know what I think is really cool?"

"What?"

"Not what I'm doing, but that God knew Dean needed some TLC and didn't let me stay all comfortable about giving him the gloves Mom gave me for Christmas."

"Yeah, well, that was a risk in itself." I laughed.

"You're right about that. Although it was your mom who told me to go get him and bring him home for dinner. She acts tough, but she's the one who kicked me under the table before I offered him a job. I knew that's what she wanted."

"Really?"

"Yep, now you have a good night's sleep. Love you."

"Love you, too." I curled up in my blankets and smiled at the day's turn of events.

That year I learned the real lesson about sacrifice. Dean ended up staying with my parents for a year. When I came home on weekends, I spent a lot of time hanging out with my family and Dean. During the summer, we had really good times together. I told him one day I couldn't believe his fiancée let him get away. He winked and said it was the best thing that ever happened to him. Otherwise, how would he have met me?

The next Christmas Dean tried to return the pair of gloves to my dad. My dad refused to accept them. Plus, my mom got him a new pair. And Dean. . .he gave me something to wear on my hand. I didn't refuse to take it.

Along for the Ride

DARLENE P.
EDITED BY SHARON BERNASH SMITH

David is a very special boy who has faced some daunting challenges in his young life. Through his mother's own words, you'll discover that David embraces life with courage and stubborn determination, especially when it comes to his two favorite buddies—Smokey and Cash.

This is a true story.

Three days before Christmas
Little Acres Stable, Brush Prairie, Washington

I watched him ride. Round and round the dusty arena he loped, back straight, tears flying.

So much pain for him today, Lord.

My son was now one with the comfort horse. His yearning heart's desire was being played out in the hazy scene before me.

God, You are faithful.

When David was born, he had multiple health issues, but he was beautiful, and he was mine. From the beginning, I knew he was a fighter and, for sure, God had a plan for my son's life. Therefore, whatever it took to help David thrive, I would do it. His father was equally committed, and so our journey began.

At age four, we enrolled David in a riding program as therapy to help his cerebral palsy. His progress was amazing, and right from the beginning, it was obvious my son was meant to be on the back of a horse. Each lesson brought great improvement to his coordination, and more importantly, his confidence in his abilities grew as well.

David went from novice rider to experienced horseman by age eight, riding his own horse, a gentle POA (Pony of America) named Smokey. Quite a team, the two participated in competitions on a regular basis, even winning ribbons in jumping events.

Their camaraderie continued for several more years. Then it became apparent that Smokey's health was rapidly deteriorating. I guess, as David grew older, we failed to notice the horse's decline, but there came a day when we could no longer ignore the inevitable pain the animal suffered. Because we all loved him, we decided together that Smokey would have to be put down. We made the appointment with the vet to do just that. However, he couldn't get out to the stable for three days.

This, as it turned out, was a gift. It gave us time to talk with David, getting him used to the idea of what needed to be done for the sake of his pony. Life is hard, and as parents, we want to spare our children as much pain as possible. Yet we felt that David was old enough to say good-bye to his friend and companion when the time came.

Those days of waiting for the vet seemed overly long, but David wanted to spend as much time as possible with his faithful friend.

The very day we'd made the difficult decision about Smokey, someone brought out a roan quarter horse to the stable. When the owner stepped away from the tethered animal, I watched David walk over and touch the gelding's neck with no intimidation. The horse acknowledged the attention by rubbing his head against David's shoulder. I wondered what was going on, but soon I understood. At that very moment, an instant connection formed between a brokenhearted boy and a handsome, viral horse.

This was David's introduction to Cash.

David insisted on visiting Smokey each day before the vet appointment, and we did. Yet now there was another reason to drive to the stables. After David left the pony's stall, he'd make his way to the one that held the roan. Cash was big and strong, eager to greet my son with a nod and a nicker of recognition. During that hard time, I saw David's mood turn from misery over Smokey's demise toward a keen interest in the new horse at the stable.

"Mom," he asked after leaving, "do you think Cash is for sale?"

We had no way to know, but it was the first time I'd seen David smile since he knew Smokey's days were numbered. "I don't know, David, but we can find out."

Inquiries about Cash were postponed, because the next day was our appointment with the veterinarian. Cold morning mist hung over the entire landscape as we made the short drive from our house to the stables. David was silent, as were my husband and I, each of us lost in the sweet memories of Smokey. The gray tint of the weather matched our mood precisely. I wanted to turn around and change the plan, but it would have been cruel to make Smokey suffer because of our lack of courage.

The vet's SUV was already there when we pulled into the driveway. When he saw us, he got out, walked right over to David, and put a hand on one shoulder. "Sorry, bud."

David bit his lower lip. His chin quivered anyway. "I want to bring Smokey to the apple tree." He glanced at his dad and me. "He loved the apples on the ground 'cuz he's too short to reach the ones on the branches." He scooted some gravel around with the toe of one boot. "I really like the way he looks when he's chewing one," he whispered.

Then he walked toward the barn, head bent into winter's biting wind.

We waited in the cold, no one saying a word. Soon David reappeared, leading his pal, who followed just behind. Smokey's head was down as far as David's. Both were in obvious pain for different reasons.

"Okay, David, here's how this is going to work," the vet explained. "First, I'll insert a catheter."

"Will it hurt?" David interrupted.

"It will sting a little. After that, I'll give him a sedative that will make him want to lay down."

"And then?" David was shaking, his fists clenched.

"Then I'll give him medicine that will stop his heart. It's totally painless, David."

A short while later, Smokey's breathing slowed. With one long exhale he was gone.

David, who was still kneeling, bent over to hug the pony's neck one last time. He looked up at us, as if to say, "Now what?" I wanted to grab him in my arms until all the hurt was gone, but before I could even take a step, David got to his feet. I could tell he wanted an escape, his eyes searching for a way. But where would he go?

In a flash he took off for the riding arena as fast as possible.

There, tied up with a lead rope, was Cash. Someone had been grooming him. Before we could stop David, he'd unsnapped the rope, placed a step stool next to the calm roan, and jumped on the horse's back. Grabbing a hank of mane, he nudged him into a canter.

Cash wore no saddle or bridle, just a boy who was growing up with each pass around the arena. Who knew it was possible to watch such a thing?

Soon a dozen or so people had gathered to watch in silence. . .with tears.

Wow, I thought, *three days before Christmas. This could be a downer.*

I was wrong.

December 24, 9:00 a.m.

"Darlene, that money is for the future," my husband said.

"I know," I answered. "But the way I look at it, the future is now."

He gave me an understanding look. "Is the bank open this morning?"

"Until noon."

Little Acres Christmas Party, 4:00 p.m.

The barn was all decked out with white Christmas lights, several huge pine trees, and lots of people bundled up. Some huddled around space heaters, while traditional carols played in the background. Tables set up for the occasion were heavy with every sweet treat possible. Curious horses called out to one another from the perimeters.

The minute we walked in the door, David was looking for the owner. He found her sitting at one of the decorated tables placed near the food. He walked up and took an envelope from his jacket pocket.

"Hey, David, what's that you have?"

"Uh, I need to ask you something." I could see his hands were a little shaky.

"What's that, hon?"

"I, that is, we"—he cocked his head toward his dad and me—"heard that you now own Cash."

"That's right, I do."

"And you want to sell him, right?"

"Yes."

"I want him." He took his money out of the envelope and slapped it down in front of her. "Cash for Cash!" He looked her right in the eye.

"Well, David." Big pause. "He's all yours. Now come here and give me a hug."

"I brought Cash an apple for Christmas," David said. He was grinning from ear to ear.

Every day, I marvel at God's plans for my son, and as far as this one was concerned, it was certainly all Him, I can tell you for sure.

We were just along for the ride.

Who Cares?

LINDA J. REINHARDT

Holly is devastated. It's close to Christmas, and her husband just lost his job. Worse, his company doesn't even have the money to pay him for the work he has done. And her husband, Shawn, has been on unemployment for a year before this job.

Does anyone care? Holly wonders in desperation. Her family needs a miracle.

To my sister, Wanda,
who showed me one Christmas that God cares.
And to those at Living Hope Church
in Vancouver, who did, too.

The ringing alarm forced Holly out of her dark cave of oblivion. With a groan her fingers searched for the right button to shut it off before it woke up little Shannon, who had crawled into bed next to her sometime during the night. Once the alarm was off, she turned away, pulling her blanket up close around her chin. She had a strong desire to close her eyes and sink back into. . .

Butterflies in her stomach caused her to take a deep breath. Reality opened her eyes wide. Shawn's words from last night rang loud in her mind. . . .

"I got let go. The company's going under. They said my sign-on check is my payment for the month."

"Your sign-on check? That was months ago. We've been on unemployment for a year before this job. We don't have any money!"

"I know. I'm not sure if I can get back on unemployment or not." Her

husband had reached out his arms and Holly fell into them. The two clung to each other, Shawn whispering prayers of help. . . .

With a sigh, Holly kicked off her covers, then turned to make sure Shannon was still covered before she made her way out of the bedroom to the cold start of the day.

A couple of hours later, after dropping Shannon off at school and kissing her husband good-bye, Holly pulled into the parking lot of the welfare office. She parked her car and sat for a minute watching the people walking in and out of the door.

"I never thought I would see the inside of these walls." She pushed her door open and got out of the car. She felt self-conscious walking into the building and wondered what others were thinking of her. She made her way over to the appointment line to let them know she had arrived on time and was told to have a seat.

A quick scan of her surroundings made her want to keep herself from touching anything. All was very dreary, and the place needed a good scrubbing. *I'm glad I brought my sanitizer.* She pulled a book out of her purse and tried to hide behind it. After a frustrating several minutes of trying to read, she let the book fall to her lap. She wanted to people-watch but didn't want anyone to think she was staring. It surprised her how many of the people waiting were nicely dressed.

When Holly heard her name over the loudspeaker, she moved swiftly to the door the voice overhead told her to go to. A kind but tired-looking young lady motioned for her to follow. Holly kept her head down, embarrassed to meet anyone's eyes.

I can't believe I'm here, asking for a handout.

Finally, the lady stopped at a cubicle and sat at the desk. "Here—take one of these seats."

Holly sat, keeping her back straight, trying to hold her head high.

"I have a few questions," the lady said before turning to her computer and going over almost all of the questions Holly had already answered on paper, while the lady keyed the information into her computer. "So your income this month is. . . ?"

"At this time we don't have an income, and we are unsure if we can collect any unemployment. We were informed that our sign-on check a few months ago would be payment for this month before they shut the doors to the company."

"Wow, too bad. And so close to Christmas. I'm sorry."

Holly nodded and blinked hard, refusing to fall apart in this place.

"Well, everything looks good. Looks like $700 will go on a card for you, and then if nothing changes, $900 for next month. The only thing you do is swipe it at the checkout line just like a debit and then put your security code in. You will need to go to section C to get the card activated after they've set your code up."

"Thank you."

"I hope things go better for you. I'm really sorry this happened to you so close to Christmas."

Holly nodded and got up to leave, then followed the directions to section C. After waiting for what seemed like forever, she got her card activated and finally was able to leave the dreary building.

Thank You, Lord, that we will have food. I pray my husband can find work so we can pay our bills and maybe have a Christmas.

She needed a break before she picked up Shannon. She punched in her husband's number. "Honey, can you please pick up Shannon? I'm exhausted and need a break before I see her."

"I'm sorry, but I'm in the middle of putting in résumés. I really don't want to stop, because we need a job."

Holly sighed. Yes, they did need a job. She slid into her car and shut the door. *How can this be happening again? What will we do if we can't get back on unemployment? Why did they hire my husband if they knew the company was going under? I had such high hopes for this Christmas. I thought we'd be able to truly celebrate after over a year with no job.*

Tears streamed down Holly's face. *Lord, why? We finally got a job, only to have it taken away. I don't understand.*

Holly could no longer hold back her anger. Slamming her hand against the steering wheel, she screamed until she finally succumbed to the sobs that racked her body. She didn't know how long she sat in the parking lot.

After a while, she took a deep breath. *What am I crying for? It's not going to help me. And who cares if I cry, anyway? Who cares?*

"It's not going to change anything!" she yelled out.

She turned the key in the ignition and made her way out of the parking lot so she could get Shannon. *I just have to put one foot in front of the other. It doesn't matter how I feel, because everything has fallen apart, and I merely have to learn to deal with it.*

After she picked up Shannon, she tried hard to reply to her daughter's chatter in a pleasant manner, but she was exhausted.

When they finally arrived home, she convinced Shannon to sit and watch a movie with her.

When Shawn came home, she made a quick dinner and then put another movie in to watch. She had no energy to do anything. After tucking Shannon in bed, Holly crawled into her own and lay there in the dark, staring at the ceiling. She fought her tears, but they rolled down the sides of her face, soaking her hair and pillow.

What about Shannon's Christmas? How do I explain why Santa didn't bring her a present this year? Lord, what am I to do? I know so many children suffer this time of year, and it's always broken my heart. But now to know my own daughter may suffer breaks my heart more.

Holly clutched the pillow until eventually sleep took over and she drifted away from the pain for a while.

The next day Holly slept through the alarm and had to rush Shannon to school late. Shannon begged to be able to put up the Christmas tree when she got home from school, but Holly knew she had no energy. She put Shannon off with a "we'll see."

When they got to the school, Holly realized she had forgotten to pack a cold lunch. She knew Shannon wouldn't eat what the cafeteria had for hot lunch, so Holly ran home to get the lunch and rushed back to drop it off. In between, she got pulled over by a cop for rolling through a stop sign.

By the time she got home later in the morning, she was tired and frazzled. She sat on the couch and put her head in her hands. *Lord, I need You. I'm not coping very well.*

No answer.

She struggled to get up and make it the best she could through the day.

Her sister called just before lunch and told her she was coming to pick her up because she had to go shopping.

"I'm in no mood to go shopping. I don't want to hear Christmas music or see all of the things I could get for Shannon."

"Listen, I have gift cards, and you are coming with me."

"Hattie, no," Holly insisted.

"I'll be there in a minute or two. Quit arguing, and just get in the car." Hattie hung up.

A couple of minutes later, Holly heard a pounding at the door. She opened it to a smiling Hattie.

"Come on, Sister, let's go. You don't have much time until you have to pick up Shannon."

"Hattie. . . ," Holly started.

"I'm not listening. Now come on."

"Look at me—I'm a mess."

"I'll give you five minutes. Hurry."

Holly's cell phone rang on the way up the stairs. "Yes, Shawn," she answered.

"Honey, I need you to put our bills together. I told the pastor what happened, and they want to help. Can you get them together for me?"

Holly stopped on the stairs, remembering her screams in the car the day before. "Are you kidding? When do you need them? Hattie is here, and she's insisting I get in the car and go with her to the store."

"By Sunday."

"'Kay, I can do that." *What on earth is happening?*

Holly changed her clothes and brushed her hair. She grabbed some makeup to put on in the car.

The first stop they made was to get a cup of coffee and a cookie. "This is for you." Hattie handed Holly's coffee to her along with a coffee gift card.

"What?"

"Listen, don't argue. I feel like God told me I'm supposed to do this today. Please just go along with it."

"God told you?"

"Yep." Hattie led the way out the door of the coffee shop and across the parking lot to the toy store. "I have a bunch of gift cards, and I feel like God wants me to use them to buy Shannon's Christmas presents."

Holly stopped in her tracks. "Shannon's Christmas presents?"

"Yep, so we only have a couple hours and three stores to hit. Do you think we can do it?"

Holly couldn't answer. Tears rolled down her face.

Hattie gently nudged her to start walking. "We don't have time for tears. We have lots to do." Hattie gave her sister a hug.

And then they were off to shop.

The next couple of hours were spent putting together Shannon's Christmas morning. They happened to walk in on a great sale and got even more things than were on her list.

They finished in just enough time to pick up Shannon from school. Hattie hid the packages in the trunk and under coats in the car while Holly ran in and got her.

Shannon was exuberantly happy to see her special aunt. "Are you coming over to help decorate the tree?"

Holly shook her head, realizing "we'll see" must mean "yes" to Shannon.

"I'd love to, but I need to get back to work. I'll come look at it later, 'kay?"

"Sure." Shannon gave Hattie a hug and jumped out of the car. "Hey, Daddy's home." She ran into the house, giving Hattie and Holly an opportunity to rush the gifts into the garage. When the last bag was hidden, Hattie gave Holly a hug and left for work.

Holly decided that, since Shawn was home early, they could go and get the tree, so she better unpack the Christmas tree decorations.

She pulled the ladder down from the attic and stopped when a thought hit her: *Remember when you asked who cares if you cry?*

Holly knelt on the garage floor.

"I CARE!"

Holly knew beyond a shadow of a doubt that the quiet voice was God. "Oh, thank You. Thank You."

Holly stood with a new resolve. Things might be hard right now. But

God was with them, and she was going to celebrate because nothing could take that away from her.

Just like all those years ago, when God gave the miracle gift of His Son, Jesus, to take care of those He loved, He was still doing miracles today, to take care of those He loves.

He is the same yesterday, today, and forever.

A Battle Ground Christmas

Sharon Bernash Smith

Change is difficult, and with it comes all kinds of frustration. Just ask Amanda Brennan. Right before Christmas, she discovers that dealing with change has a lot to do with attitude. . .hers.

In the middle of a laundry "crisis" she meets a complete stranger, who is able to speak to her deepest need. Who knew such a thing could happen at a small Laundromat in rural Battle Ground, Washington?

Amanda might even have met an angel.

December 23

ATTENTION:
PLEASE DO NOT WASH
HORSE BLANKETS IN
THESE MACHINES!

Amanda kicked the door shut behind her as she read the sign, dropping the heavy laundry basket to the floor in disgust. "Well now, isn't that just perfect?" She thought she'd seen all the small-town idiosyncrasies that Battle Ground, Washington, had to offer, but the brown stained sign tacked over the washers took the prize.

In response to the comment meant for no one, an older lady reading a book lifted her head to nod and smile.

Ignoring the small greeting, Amanda dragged her basket to the first empty machine, only to find an OUT OF ORDER sign resting on top.

"Per-fect!" She sighed. Having her water pipes freeze was bad enough, but with Daniel out of town at a medical seminar, she had no clue on earth how to "unfreeze" them. Now dirty laundry was coming out her ears, and she had no choice but to come into town and find a

Laundromat. Battle Ground had *one.*

The other dozen machines were full, a testimony to the fact she was not alone in the two-days-before-Christmas-frozen-pipe fiasco. Alone or not, she felt the now-familiar anger rising from her gut. *Lord, I've given this over to You time after time, yet here I am, swimming in my own pity once again.*

Until six months ago, Amanda would have said her life was near perfect. A wonderful husband, two adorable, creative children, and a life that revolved around God, church, and family. Born and raised in Brooklyn, New York, she'd grown up in a loving Italian family. They were loud, loyal, and proud of their heritage and each other.

Her senior year of college, she'd met Daniel. He swept her off her Italian feet and introduced her to his Irish family. They were as loud as her bunch. . .just as loyal and just as loving. They married only six months after their first date.

Married life was a struggle with money issues and Daniel's demanding schedule as a med student. Though his grueling work assignments for residency training gave them little time for one another, it all worked out because they realized they were giving up the short term for the long term. Somehow, it made perfect sense.

Daniel had intended to go into pediatrics as a specialty, but in the midst of their "perfect" plan, Amanda began to feel sick. She told herself it was just because she was burning her candles at both ends, with working on her master's and teaching high school English at the same time. She'd made a valiant effort to ignore it. It was Daniel who suggested she might be pregnant.

"Don't be ridiculous," she said. "I've never missed a pill. . .ever."

Regardless, eight months and sixteen days later, they welcomed a big, robust boy they named Daniel Adam Brennan Jr. Shortly thereafter, he was dubbed JR.

Both Daniel and Amanda loved being parents but were shocked to find themselves pregnant again shortly before JR's first birthday. Amanda found it too difficult to juggle school, JR, and work with another pregnancy, so she quit school, promising herself she'd find an online course and finish her credentials.

But the "right" program never materialized, and a few months later she gave up the teaching career. . .if only temporarily. Money was tight, but Amanda found some afterschool tutoring, and it helped. Though they were as broke as they'd ever been, the joy of who they were with each other gave them strength and contentment.

Just before their daughter, Bella, was born, Daniel came home from the hospital in an unusually somber mood.

"Daniel, I know you—did something bad happen at work today?"

"Not something bad, Amanda, something good."

She was puzzled. Big as a house in the last month of pregnancy, she lowered herself to the couch and patted the cushion beside her. "Tell me."

Daniel sat and placed one of his hands on her belly. "You know that, growing up, I went to church every Sunday." He paused to make eye contact.

"Yeah, so did I, remember?"

"Of course, but somehow when I got out of high school, none of it stuck."

She laughed. "For me neither." She looked at him and frowned. "But what does that have to do with what happened at the hospital today?"

"I'm getting to that. Remember I told you we got a new boss last month?"

"Dr. Rafferty, right?"

"Mmm. Turns out he's not only a great doc, but he's an incredible man as well." He took her hand. "I've been watching him, Amanda, and he's not like anyone I've ever been around."

She tilted her head. "Like how?"

"There's something special about the way he works with the staff. The guy's brilliant, but not once has he been arrogant or cocky to anyone. Anyway, one day I said something to one of the nurses about his attitude. That's when she told me Rafferty's a Christian."

"You can talk about that stuff at work?"

"We did. I couldn't get over the way he seemed to be able to cope with all the junk around him, especially hospital politics, yet remain so peaceful."

"Peaceful, huh?"

"Right. Anyway, today we were in the break room together, and I asked him about his faith."

"And?"

"He told me he'd grown up on the streets because his dad drank and his mother died when he was seven. He said he was scared to death after that, but his older brothers taught him the ways of the street, and by age ten he was selling drugs. When a cop busted him, he went into foster care, but after running away a dozen times he landed in a Christian group home for boys, way upstate."

Amanda got up to get JR. "I'm listening. . .keep talking. . . ."

He followed her. "He said he lived there for over a year, playing by all the rules, but plotted his escape just the same. One day he realized he didn't want to leave. He told me God got ahold of his heart when he finally understood how much Jesus loved him."

He reached out and took the baby from Amanda, smiling at his son's lopsided grin. "Rafferty said that when he realized the truth, he couldn't help but want to be a Christian."

They walked back to the couch.

"I can tell there's more." Amanda smiled.

"I told him how I'd gone to church all those years, yet none of it seemed relevant now."

"Hmm, that's kind of harsh, don't you think?"

"I was merely being honest. Next thing I know, he's telling me that Jesus actually died just for *me*." Daniel wiped at his eyes. "Amanda, until that moment, I'd never put the whole idea of Jesus dying on the cross in that context." He coughed.

"What do you mean?" Something in her began to stir.

"Of course I've known Jesus died, but never once did I take it personally. It was like a light went off deep inside me today." He placed a hand over his heart. "When Doc Rafferty finished talking, all I knew is that I wanted what he had. I told him so and. . ."

". . .and?"

"And I prayed to become a born-again Christian."

"No kidding? So that's what happened to you today."

"Exactly." He took out a hanky and blew his nose.

A few weeks later, after going to a Bible study at the Raffertys', Amanda gave her life to Jesus Christ as well.

That had been ten years ago, and they'd never looked back. It was their faith that helped them make the decision to move cross country from all things familiar to the rural town of Battle Ground, in southwest Washington, where Daniel now worked in a small medical clinic as a general practitioner.

When he'd flown out for the interview, the staff welcomed him with open arms. His ensuing excitement is what convinced Amanda the move would be a good thing. However, she had no clue what she'd said yes to!

No clue to the size of the town, nor what living 3,000 miles from all their family would be like. Nor did she know that winters in the Pacific Norwest meant rain, rain, and more rain. Unless, of course, it was drizzling. Snow she could handle, but in New York that had been endured from the inside of an apartment building maintained by a superintendent who fixed anything that broke and/or froze.

And there'd been more. She was completely shocked to learn that Daniel's secret dream was to live in the country. . .with acreage. Who knew? The property was beautiful with amazing views of the Columbia River, but so was the Hudson in New York.

It wasn't all bad; she was grateful for their new church family at Hockinson Community Church. They fell in love with Pastor Mike White and his wife, Lara, the first Sunday they visited. Every week since had brought them closer to the body of Christ, which helped ease their homesickness, especially now that it was Christmas.

She even had a special friend, Cheryl, who prayed with her whenever Amanda felt overwhelmed, which was at least once a week. It was Cheryl who offered to take JR and Bella for a couple of hours while Amanda did laundry.

A thought struck like lightning. *What if it snows more and I'm stuck and can't get out to shop for Christmas dinner?*

A dark cloud followed her to a stack of old magazines, hanging over her head like an albatross as she dragged the overflowing basket to an empty seat in front of a window.

The lady who'd smiled at her before looked up. "Did your pipes freeze up?"

Amanda nodded. "Yes, unfortunately." She wasn't really in the mood for idle conversation, but the woman seemed sweet. "And you. . .how about you?"

The woman chuckled. "No, no, they didn't. I don't have a washer or dryer in my little place."

"Really? That must be inconvenient." Amanda felt a twinge of guilt about the big drama she'd made over the laundry situation.

"Oh, I don't mind, really." The woman flashed that incredible smile again and leaned forward like she was about to share the secret of the Universe. "See, I like talking with people, and I've met some really nice folks—like you—in here."

Amanda felt something shift within her spirit. She stuck out her hand. "I'm Amanda. So nice to meet you."

"Very nice to meet you, Amanda. I'm Dolores. Tell me where you're from; I don't recognize your accent."

Amanda laughed. "I'm from New York. . .born and raised."

"I'm not from around here, either," Dolores said, "but I've lived here for years. Twenty-five by now, I guess." She got a faraway look in her eyes.

"Do you have children here as well?" Amanda was surprised that she was really interested.

Dolores shifted in the hard plastic chair but said nothing for a minute. "Not now."

Amanda thought Dolores was going to cry, but she lifted her head before speaking. "My only child lives in Colorado. John's got a wonderful wife and two daughters. . .mostly grown now."

"Do you get to see them often?" She reached over and touched Dolores on the arm.

"Not as often as I'd like, of course, but we talk on the phone once a week. John would like me to come live there, but. . .I don't want to be a bother to them."

"But, Dolores, would they have asked if they thought you'd be a bother?" For some reason, she wanted this woman to be happy and not alone. "Aren't you lonely, living so far apart, I mean?"

Dolores thought a minute. "Mmm, sometimes I am, but I have friends here, and I love my church family." She took a deep breath and exhaled slowly. "God has taught me a wonderful secret."

"Really? Do you mind sharing the secret with a stranger?" Amanda laughed.

"Of course not." She leaned in closer. "He's taught me to be content," she whispered.

"That's your secret?" Amanda laughed again. "I've read that in the Bible a dozen times. I'm sure that's not a secret, Dolores."

Dolores beamed. "I'm glad you know the Bible, Amanda. I'd read that passage where Paul talks about learning to be content in all circumstances myself...dozens of times...and trust me, I thought I knew what it meant." She excused herself and got up to put more change in the dryer.

Amanda watched her new acquaintance. *God, I know You brought me to this place today. . .thank You.*

Dolores was back in a minute. "Recently I began to read my daily Bible passages out loud."

"Why out loud?"

"I'm not sure exactly, but there's something very special about *hearing* the Word, don't you think? For some reason, it's helped me find deeper contentment. Loneliness made me discontented, but reading out loud, for whatever reason, has helped. I'm amazed myself."

"I've enjoyed listening to others read it, but it's not something I do myself," Amanda said. "Tell me more."

"I love the psalms, and today's reading was the twenty-third." She closed her eyes and began to recite from memory: "The Lord is my shepherd; I shall not want. He makes me to lie down in green pastures; He leads me beside the still waters. He restores my soul" (NKJV).

Amanda placed a hand over her heart and struggled to hold back tears.

"Oh, Amanda, I didn't mean to upset you."

"No, no, it's all right. See, I've been struggling with our big move out here and being homesick and. . ." She took out a tissue and blew her nose. "When you started to recite that scripture, my heart was pierced with the truth of how God takes care of me, regardless of where I live." She gazed intently at Dolores. "I'm wondering, are you an angel?"

Dolores chuckled. "No, I'm not an angel. I'm merely a woman seeking to better know and understand my God." She started to laugh so hard that tears formed in her eyes. "Me, an angel!"

Dolores's reaction was contagious. Amanda began to laugh, too. "To tell you the truth, I've been so busy feeling sorry for myself that I've barely looked in the Word lately. And. . .well. . .I can't remember the last time I laughed this hard. Oh, I see an empty machine. I'll be right back."

When she returned, Dolores was folding laundry. "You know, Amanda, I think our meeting was a divine appointment today, don't you?"

"Absolutely. For sure. And you know what else? Battle Ground just got a whole lot more appealing, thanks to you."

Dolores paused folding and looked directly at Amanda. "That's the nicest thing anyone has said to me in a long while. Thank you."

"No, thank *you*." They were quiet for a moment, when Amanda had an idea. "Dolores, do you have plans for Christmas?"

"I always go to Christmas Eve church service and spend Christmas day with friends from there. Usually we have an early dinner," she said. "I guess we're pretty boring."

Amanda's heart pounded with. . .what was it. . . ? Excitement! "I know we've only met and all, but I feel like I've known you for a long time. How would you like to spend Christmas Day with my husband and I? We have two really wild little kids, but I know they'd love you."

Dolores's eyes filled. "One of the loneliest days for me is Christmas. I. . .I think it's because a holiday without children is way too quiet. When John was little and my husband was alive, I loved it all, you see. . .the mess, the chaos. . .all of it."

"If it's chaos you want, Miss Dolores, you'll love the Brennan home."

"Well then, I'll say yes to your sweet invitation."

They exchanged phone numbers.

When Dolores left, Amanda hummed a Christmas song while finishing her laundry.

When she stepped outside the Laundromat doors, the skies were darker than when she went in. She stopped and looked up before heading to her car. "Let it snow, let it snow, let it snow," she sang.

God, You are so good. Thank You for Dolores, and thank You for Battle Ground.

The first feathery flakes began to fall. "Yes indeed; let it snow."

Santa Works for Jesus?

Linda J. Reinhardt

There's one gift that eight-year-old Charley wants more than anything in the world. But then Grandma reads Charley and his twin sister, Emily, a story about a very naughty boy who didn't get any Christmas presents.

When Emily informs him that Charley is like that boy and insists he'll get nothing for Christmas, Charley can only hope it's not true.

&

I'm home!" Grandma called when she opened the door, disarming herself of a bundle of bags and her umbrella.

"Grandma, did you get my Christmas presents? Huh, did you?" Eight-year-old, rambunctious Charley charged toward her bags.

Grandma caught Charley around the waist and pulled him close. "Whoa ho, wait a minute, good buddy. That's a secret." She planted a big kiss on his cheek.

"Grandma!" Charley wiped at his face.

"Did you get anything for me?" Charley's twin sister, Emily, made her own attempt to peek in the bags.

"Okay, Emmers, the same goes for you." Grandma pulled Emily away and ruffled her hair. "Where's your mom and your little sisters?"

"Mom's putting them down for a nap before she leaves for work," Charley answered.

"If you help carry these bags to my room"—Charley and Emily ran for the bags—"without peeking, I will give you a surprise."

"Deal!" Charley and Emily's scramble to pick up bags soon evolved into a tussle between the two. "I get that one."

"No, I do."

Grandma shook her head. "You two. Can't you ever. . .never mind." She went over and divided the bags between the two and led them into her room. "Okay, here you go, kiddos." Grandma extracted a book out of a shopping bag. "An early Christmas present." She held the book up above their heads, and immediately the two started shouting.

"I get to read it first."

"No, I get to read it first."

"I knew I should have bought two," Grandma muttered. "How about I read the book to you, and then you can read it at the same time."

"Can you read it now, Grandma?"

Grandma sunk back on her bed, knowing it would be easier to give in. "Okay, you two sit on the floor."

"Will you sit down here with us?" Emily asked. "Then we can snuggle."

"Of course! Who can resist that invitation?" Grandma slid down onto the floor. "I may need help getting up, though." She chuckled before she started reading the story of a little boy who did lots of pranks and got in trouble all of the time, so he wasn't going to get anything for Christmas.

"Nothing for Christmas just 'cause he was a funny guy?" Charley asked.

"Charleeey—he isn't funny, he's naughty," Emily informed him.

"I don't think he's naughty; he's funny."

"That's because you do stuff like that."

"Yeah, 'cause I'm funny." Charley beamed.

"Ha! So you are getting nuthin' for Christmas, 'cause you are bad," Emily stated. "Right, Grandma?"

"I wouldn't say that. This is only a make-believe story, and we aren't..."

"What about the song, 'you better watch out, you better not pout, 'cause Santa Claus is coming to town,' huh?"

"Well..."

"Ha, ha, you are getting nothing for Christmas," Emily chanted.

"Not so," Charley argued.

"Is too so."

"Grandma?" Charley looked up at her with a pout. "That's a dumb book."

"You said dumb! See, you're getting nothing for Christmas," Emily teased.

"Okay, Emily, that's enough. Charley, this is just a story. Why don't you two calm down and let me finish?" Grandma continued with the story about the boy getting naughtier and naughtier until he went to see Santa at the mall and had to admit how naughty he had been. Santa told him to go home and try harder to be good.

"Charley, if Santa found out how naughty you were. . ." Emily started.

Grandma stopped her. "Emily, no one is perfect."

"Yeah, but most kids don't paint their parents' car with house paint or their dad's work shoes." Emily covered her mouth and giggled. As long as Charley's antics weren't directed at Emily, they amused her.

"That's 'cause most kids aren't as funny as I am." Charley stuck out his tongue.

"Knock, knock." Sarrah, their mom, peeked her head in the door. "I'm getting ready to leave for work now. Come give me a hug good-bye."

The two kids scrambled to their feet and raced to their mom.

"Charley, you're squishing me." Emily's voice was muffled.

"I'm just hugging you and Mom." Charley exerted a little more pressure.

"Ugh! You're squeezing a bit too hard," Sarrah grunted.

"Sorry, Mom."

Sarrah poked at his nose before she gave him a kiss. Charley swiped at his cheek. Sarrah laughed.

"Bye, kids. Go to bed tonight for Grandma with NOOOOO arguing, got it?" Sarrah put her coat on and waved before she went out the door.

Just as the door shut, Annabelle's cries drifted down the stairs. Grandma excused herself to go check on her and came back down in a short amount of time with Annabelle and Audrey in her arms. Grandma didn't have a chance to get back to the story the rest of the afternoon.

Every time Charley did something, Emily would remind him he wouldn't be getting anything for Christmas. He started to wonder if this could be true. That would be the worst thing ever, because there was a huge present he really wanted. He began to worry.

After dinner, Grandma called their dad, who was over in Afghanistan, to see if he was available to Skype. The kids sat around Grandma in nervous anticipation. When Grandma shook her head with a frown, all of their shoulders dropped, even Annabelle's. Still, they each got a minute to say hello. Charley quietly waited for his turn to talk.

That was Mom and Grandma's very strict rule. When Dad was on the phone, everyone had to be super quiet and wait their turn without arguing, or the consequence would be beyond their wildest imagination, Mom had added.

Finally, it was Charley's turn. "Hi, Dad!"

"Hey, sport." His dad always called him that. "How's your day been? Are you taking good care of my girls?"

"Sort of." Charley got sad remembering how bad he could be.

"Sort of? What do you mean by that?"

"Well, I can be naughty sometimes."

"Hmm, but are you still taking care of them? No harm has come to any of them, right?"

"Right."

"Good. Okay, I have two seconds left. So I'm going to make sure to tell you I love you and I am proud of you, Charley."

Instead of being happy, Charley felt sad, because he'd been extra naughty lately, and Santa might not be bringing him any presents.

"Even though I'm naughty?"

"No matter what, you are my special boy, and I love you. I need to hang up now. Can you give your mom a hug for me and tell her I love her?"

"Yes, sir." Charlie stood tall and gave a salute. "Bye, Dad."

After he handed the phone back to Grandma, Charley slipped out of the room and went upstairs to put on his pajamas. He decided to try hard to be good.

He got all ready for bed before the rest of the gang made their way up the stairs.

Grandma stopped in her tracks at the top of the landing. "Charley? Why, you're all ready for bed. Yay for you, buddy."

"He's only trying to get a Christmas present from Santa Claus," Emily teased as she skipped past Charley. Charley stuck his foot out in front of her. Emily didn't see it and went flat on her face.

Charley gave her a big smile. "You sure are klutzy."

"Grandma, Charley tripped me."

"Charley, really? Come on, you two. Let's get to bed without fighting tonight, okay?"

When Grandma turned her back, Emily stuck her tongue out at him, and he stuck his out right back. Then he dived into his bed and under the covers.

"I'm the first one in bed. I'm the first one in bed," Charley chanted.

"You still won't get nothing for Christmas," Emily insisted.

Charley stopped chanting and sunk under his covers to hide his face. He had to get his present for Christmas.

Grandma came into his room to say good night after she had gotten the girls all tucked in. "Charley, are you still awake?"

"Yeah," he answered in a sad voice.

"Is something wrong?"

"Yeah."

Grandma sat on the side of his bed and gently stroked his hair back from his face. "Can you talk about it?"

"Am I really so bad Santa won't leave me a present?"

Grandma let out a sigh. "Are you still thinking about that?"

"Yep. Emily has reminded me about it all day long."

"Charley, did you know you got a *huge* gift the day you started believing in Jesus? Bigger than any Christmas present?"

"I did? What is it?"

"Well, when you mess up and do something naughty. . ."

"Yeah. . ." Charley pulled himself up on his elbow.

"Whenever you tell Jesus what you did, He washes you clean."

"Washes me?"

"Yes, the sin will be all gone."

"So if I tell Him every bad thing I did today, I will be all clean?"

"Yep, so you won't have to worry about all the wrong you did."

"Wow. Okay, good night, Grandma." Charley gave her a hug and then fell back onto his pillow.

"Good night, Charley. Do you want your door open or shut?"

"Shut."

"Good night, sport."

"Good night." As soon as he heard the door click, Charley got into a serious discussion of listing off every bad thing he could remember he had ever done. It took awhile for him to finish because he had quite a sense of humor and his pranks didn't always turn out so good. He was polite enough to thank Jesus when he was done, then turned over for a good night's sleep.

The next morning he got up full of energy and ready to go to school. He even helped Emily with her backpack instead of hiding it. But when the teacher made the announcement there were only two more days left until school was out for Christmas break, it became hard for him to control his energy. *Oh, I hope I get my present. I really do.*

Charley had a hard time listening and a hard time not talking. His teacher finally had him go sit in the principal's office. While he sat on the time-out chair, he took time to tell Jesus what he had done. He felt confused that he still had to sit in the time-out chair because Jesus was supposed to wash him clean, but still he had to stay there for the full thirty minutes.

By the time he got home from school, he was in a foul mood and stomped up to his room.

His mom followed after him. "Charley, can I come in?"

"Yeah."

Sarrah came in the room and sat beside Charley on the floor. "I hope you will help me get up from here."

"Grandma always says that, but you get up just fine," Charley grumbled.

"I guess I do. I thought it would make you laugh."

"No."

"So. . .did something happen today at school?"

Charley shot his mom a look of impatience because he knew the principal had called her when he was in the office. "Don't you remember? I had time-out in the principal's office?"

"Yes, but you've been there before and didn't get this upset."

"Grandma told me that if I told Jesus what I did wrong, He would wash me clean. So I did, and I still had to sit in the time-out chair." Charley turned his back away from her. "Now I know I won't get my present for Christmas."

"Why won't you get your presents for Christmas?"

"Because Grandma read us a story about a naughty boy who didn't get anything for Christmas, so Emily said I was just like that boy and I wouldn't get anything for Christmas."

Sarrah gently touched Charley's shoulder. "I'm sorry. It's hard to explain, but even though He washes us clean, sometimes we still have to face the consequences. But your record is all clean."

"So then, how can my record with Santa Claus be clean? Don't I have to face the consequences with him?" Charley turned to his mom and crawled into her lap.

"That's a whole different story." Sarrah sat for a minute, as if thinking how to explain it. "You know how Santa Claus has lots of helpers in the malls?"

"Yeah, so?"

"Well, Christmas isn't about Santa Claus. Santa Claus is a helper to bring the message of Christmas to people."

"What? I've never heard that before."

"You're older now and can understand it better."

"How about Emily? I'm older than her by two minutes."

Sarrah ruffled Charley's hair. "Yes, you are."

"So how is Santa, the helper, supposed to bring the message of Christmas to people?"

"He gives gifts that bring hope and joy and show love to people, right?"

"Yeah. . ." Charley's eyes lit up. "Hey, it's like God gave us a gift in Jesus that brings hope and joy. Like the song 'Joy to the World.'" Charley started singing the song loud and off-key.

Sarrah nodded. "Right, Charley, just like that. So. . .do you know how God shows His love to us?"

"I know this, 'cause I had to memorize it. He gave His only Son because He loved the whole world so no one would pear."

"Perish."

"Yeah, something like that."

"Do we deserve the gift God gave us?"

"Umm, no. I remember that one, too. He died for us while we were still sinners."

"That's right. So if Santa helps bring the message of Christmas, do you think he would bring gifts to people who don't deserve gifts?"

"YES!!!!!" Charley jumped up in the air, then plunked back down. "But what about all those songs—you know, about being naughty and nice?"

Sarrah let out a long sigh. "When we love Jesus, we're supposed to love Him so much we *want* to be nice. But sometimes we mess up and aren't so nice. That's when you let Him know about your mistake, and then He washes you clean."

"Ohhh. Okay, so I'm still in the running for this present, right?"

"Charley, Charley, Charley, another thing I think you should learn is you shouldn't be nice only for a present."

"Okay, but it is something that comes with it, right?"

Sarrah laughed and pulled him close. "I love you, silly boy."

"But am I right?" Charley's voice was muffled against her shirt.

Sarrah just laughed.

"Mom?" Charley pulled away. "I'm right?" His eyes were serious.

"Yes, Charley, you are right."

"Yes!" Charley jumped up and ran to the door. "Do you want to play a game on the WII?"

Sarrah nodded and followed him out the door.

Several days later it was Christmas morning. Charley could hardly sleep all night in anticipation of his gift. There was nothing he wanted more, and only Santa and Jesus knew about it.

He crept carefully downstairs in the dark so he didn't wake anybody. There were lots of presents under the tree, and quite a few had his name on them. This would normally excite him, and he would run and wake up everyone. He looked carefully over each present, but none of the presents were the size of the one he wanted more than anything.

Charley sat in front of the tree, trying hard to swallow the lump in his throat. Tears rolled down his cheeks and dropped on the wrapping of one of the gifts. He sniffed and wiped his nose on his sleeve. Soon the tears fell so fast he had to put his shirt over his face.

"Hey, Charley, you okay?"

He hadn't heard his mom come down the stairs.

"Yeah, sport, you okay?"

Charley's eyes opened wide. He turned around really fast. His Dad was standing right there in the living room. He was home for Christmas! Santa did work for Jesus.

Charley got up and jumped, and his dad caught him midair. "Dad!

You're here." Charley squeezed his dad's neck as tight as he could. His dad had to pull Charley's arms free. "You're the only thing I wanted for Christmas."

"Being home is the only thing I wanted, too, Charley." His dad gave him a huge smile and then planted a big kiss on his cheek.

Charley didn't wipe it off.

Oak Leaves in the Past

SHARON BERNASH SMITH

Christmas is supposed to be about peace and goodwill, but one young mother struggles with both when her husband abruptly abandons the family. In her desire to teach her children that it's better to give than to receive at Christmas, she discovers that her own mourning is changed into dancing. And, in the process, others are blessed, too.

N ight, Mom."

"Good night, Joel."

"Love you, Mom."

"Love you, too, Michael."

"Night, Mommy."

"Go to sleep, Katie."

Lord, please give my children a restful night. Melinda sighed, leaning her head against the couch back, her gaze scanning the living room. The tree glowed with flashing lights, loaded with all the homemade ornaments and brightly colored paper chains the children had added over the years. On top was the lit angel Joe had given her their first Christmas together.

She felt her chest tighten and choked back a sob. *Why, Lord, why, why, why?* That one word was still driving her crazy. No matter how many times she asked the question, she was no closer to receiving an answer—not from God, not from anyone.

Exactly four weeks ago, her handsome, charming husband of fifteen years came back from an evening run and asked her to join him for a cup of coffee at their kitchen table. She thought he wanted to talk about some last-minute Christmas presents for the kids. Joe loved Christmas and rarely stayed within their planned budget.

She sat across from him and smiled. He was graying at the temples now, but at forty, still looked like the college kid she'd married. He placed a large manila envelope on the table.

"What's that?" she asked.

He dropped his eyes to the table. "Melinda, this isn't easy for me. . . ." He cleared his throat, still not making eye contact.

"What's not easy?" Her heart jumped.

"It isn't easy for me to say what I need to say." He looked right at her now.

Her mouth opened and closed, but no words would come. It was as if her internal MUTE button had been activated.

"I'm sure you've noticed how unhappy I've been this last year and. . ."

"What? What did you say, Joe?" Her jaw clenched. "You've been unhappy? What does that mean, 'unhappy'?"

"Come on, Melinda, you've had to notice."

She shook her head. "I don't know what you're talking about. You haven't said anything." She was fighting back hot tears.

He laughed. "Why do you think I spend so much time at work, Melinda? Haven't you noticed I'm rarely home for dinner?" He pushed the envelope in her direction.

Now her ears began to ring. "You told me you were working late because of the economy. I believed you, Joe." She didn't want to look inside the envelope.

"I just need some time to. . .you know. . ."

"No, I don't *know*. Tell me exactly why you need some time, please." She knew by now her face and neck was all blotchy red.

"I need some time for *myself*, Melinda. You and the kids will be okay. It's just that after all these years of taking care of you and them, I need some quality time for myself." He ran his fingers through his hair and, with one finger, nudged the envelope closer in her direction.

"Are you kidding me? I thought time with the family was quality time, Joe." She had trouble breathing, and her hands began to shake. "I feel like I've been dropped on another planet. Is this some kind of joke?"

His voice went flat and cold. "I'm not laughing. Open the envelope."

She'd hated his tone.

They'd been interrupted by one of the kids, and the conversation had been postponed until after all three children were in bed.

Joe's announcement had been no joke, and the reality of it was mind-numbing and life-shattering. He said there was no "other" woman, but she didn't trust him anymore now that he'd become a familiar stranger. He was the destroyer of all their family dreams. The loving husband and father she knew had disappeared and been replaced by a narcissistic man interested only in his own pursuit of happiness.

The kids were confused, but Joe's charming ways convinced them that time at his new place would be fun and interesting, especially since the apartment complex had a workout area replete with a lap pool.

Over the last weeks, many friends and family had come forward with advice, and though they all meant well, their input only left her more confused.

Now, with Christmas merely a week away, she felt like she was drowning in all that advice and her own emotions. *Lord, please help me figure this out.*

The phone rang. Her mother. She thought about ignoring it but answered on the third ring. "Hi, Mom."

"Hi, sweetheart. Kids in bed?"

"Hmm, just."

"Well, fix yourself some tea and relax."

Melinda could tell her mother had something else to say. She always had something else to say. She took a deep breath. "Sounds like a good idea, Mom. How's Dad?"

"Oh, fine; he's fine. Listen, Melinda, Dad and I have been talking. We've decided to give you your Christmas present early."

Melinda said nothing.

"Here's the thing. We wanted to give you and the children a little vacation. . .you know, during Christmas break. But we were talking a bit ago, and we wondered if you might want to go *before*. There'd be less people that way, we think."

"Mom, that's so generous of you guys." *But I'm so emotionally exhausted I don't have energy to brush my teeth.* "Where did you want us to go?"

"Skiing, of course. How does three days in Colorado sound?"

It was Joe's favorite place to take the kids. "I don't know, Mom. It's pretty short notice, and I'm worn-out."

"Melinda, if you don't want to ski, you could sit by the fire and do nothing. Or you could read a book on that fancy new thing you have. What's it called—the Thimble?"

"It's a Kindle, Mom. . .it's called a Kindle."

Her mother was a notorious "fixer," but her heart motives were pure, without a doubt. Maybe time away from home would be good for them all. The kids would be thrilled, since none of them had been skiing all season. They didn't have the money now.

"Whatever! Are you still there?"

Before answering, Melinda had another thought. Kind of an off-the-wall one, but she needed some time to think it over.

"Yes, I'm here." Pause. "Mom, could I call you back in the morning? Your offer is sweet, but I'd like to sleep on it, if that's okay with you."

"Well. . .I guess so. Sure, call me back ASAP, because I'll need to cancel the reservations, if you're not going."

Melinda winced. Of course her mom had already made the reservations. "Thanks, Mom. I really do appreciate you and Dad, you know."

"We love you, Melinda. You know we're always here for you, right?" She could tell her mother was crying.

"Of course I do, Mom. I promise to call you in the morning. Night."

Her mother blew her nose. "Talk to you then."

Melinda held the phone to her chest, leaning deeper into the couch. *Lord, You know I don't have the energy for skiing, but I don't want to disappoint my parents. I never wanted to disappoint Joe, either. Do I spend too much time trying to please others? Help me make a decision about this, please. Amen.*

She jerked awake. "Joe?" There'd been a noise in the kitchen. She threw back the covers and listened. It was just one of the kids.

Getting in the shower, thoughts drifted back to her mom's offer. Yes, the kids would love to go skiing, but her parents lavished expensive gifts on them all the time. Joe would probably do the same with Christmas—his way of soothing his guilty conscience, no doubt.

Melinda finished in the shower and began drying her long, dark hair.

The alternative she'd thought about the night before began to take shape in her mind. Forming her hair into a ponytail, she smiled at the reflection in the mirror.

When all the kids were up, Melinda called a family meeting at the dining room table.

"Mom, we're on Christmas vacation. Give us a break."

"That's what I want to talk about, Joel—your Christmas break, that is. . .about Christmas actually."

They looked at her with faces of disinterest, but none of them said a word. She imagined they thought she'd gone over the edge. She'd hardly been recognizable as their mother since Joe had left.

She cleared her throat. "Uh, your grandparents want to send us skiing in Colorado before Christmas."

Screams and high fives went all around the table.

"For how long?" Michael asked, clapping his hands.

"When do we leave?" asked Katie.

Melinda braced herself. "I've decided we're not going."

"You've got to be kidding," Joel cried. "Mom, this might be our only chance to go this season. You're ruining it for all of us!"

"That is so not fair!" Michael was all red in the face.

Melinda exhaled. "Look, I know how much you love to ski, but I want to make this Christmas special."

"How much more special could it get than going skiing?"

"Look, Mike, hear me out on this one." She could tell he was fighting tears. "Here's what I want. I've prayed about it, and I have a plan."

Joel started to interrupt, but Katie spoke up. "Wait—let's hear what she has to say."

"This house is full of stuff," Melinda said. "Don't get me wrong. I love my stuff as much as you guys like yours." She got up and started to heat milk for hot chocolate. "Not only do we have tons of possessions, but we also have some fabulous memories from skiing. Do we not?"

Each child shook their head in agreement, albeit reluctantly.

Melinda was working up courage to continue. She swallowed hard. "This year, everything is *different*." She looked at her children and saw sadness on their faces. "I have no control over what's going on with your dad, but like it or not, this is how it is." She set cups of steaming chocolate in front of each of them and got marshmallows for topping. "Because all of it is so painful, I thought it'd be good to start a *new* Christmas tradition."

"Define *new*."

Katie asked, "We're not going to have to give all our presents to the poor, are we?" She had marshmallow on her upper lip.

"Only one."

"Uh-oh, here's where turning down the ski trip comes in, right?"

"Right, Joel. But let me finish. That three-day trip to Colorado costs a lot of money."

"And. . . ?"

". . .and I have a plan to use it somewhere else."

"What if Grandma doesn't want to give you hard, cold cash?" Now Michael had a marshmallow mustache.

"Then she'll go to Grandpa," Katie offered.

This brought the whole kitchen alive with laughter.

"Look, here's my plan."

She spent the next twenty minutes going over her thoughts. To her surprise, the kids came on board with few complaints.

Now, to convince her mother.

"You want to do what? Melinda Rene, I swear, you've gone over the edge. Your father and I offered you a gift. . .a gift for you and the children. Why would you not want to accept it?" She sniffed loudly for the drama.

"Mom, we still want the gift, just in different form."

"Cash, you mean. You want the cash! I thought surely you had better manners than that."

"Look, Mother, if you don't want to participate, just say so. We'll find another way."

"Oh, and have you make me feel guilty?" More sniffing. "Your father wants to talk with you."

"Melinda, this is Dad."

"Hi, Dad."

"I'll bring the cash over this afternoon." There was a lot of yelling in the background before the phone clicked her mother off in a rant midsentence.

Poor Dad will never hear the end of this one. For the first time since Joe had moved out, Melinda felt a small seed of joy creep into her spirit. "Now to make a phone call."

Melinda's original idea had been to get a name from the giving tree at church, but when she'd called, all the names had been taken. It only took her a minute or two to come up with plan B. Years before, a few Christians from her church had started a small homeless shelter in the downtown area of the city. Over time Open House Ministries had grown and now housed dozens of families in a bright, beautiful building.

She talked to one of the case managers who'd told her about the latest family they were working with. The husband had been in a car accident but had no hospital insurance. He'd lost his job during the long recovery, and subsequently, the family lost their home as well. His wife, a stay-at-home mom, had her hands full taking care of six children, ranging in ages from six months to twelve-year-old twins. Right now, the dad was in jail for drunk driving. He'd been clean and sober for years, but all the stresses of the past few months had dragged him into relapse.

"How soon before the mom and kids can move in?" Melinda had asked.

"Even though they're on our docket already, it won't be until after Christmas, I'm afraid." The woman on the phone sounded frustrated.

"Where will they stay until then?"

"To tell you the truth, I don't have a clue. Maybe they could stay with family. I just don't know."

"But what if they don't have family?"

The woman on the phone said nothing.

"Hello?" Melinda thought she'd hung up.

"I'm here, ma'am." She paused again. "The only other option for them would be to stay in their van until our apartment is ready."

Melinda had been in shock. "Oh my, I can't even imagine that happening in *good* weather, but it's been freezing outside."

"Yes, ma'am, it has been."

"My family and I want to help as much as we can, but even if we bought them all presents, they'd have no place to put them."

"For sure, that's the reality."

"Tell you what," Melinda said. "I'm going to talk it over with my family and see what they have to say. I'll call you back this afternoon. Thank you very much."

"No, thank *you*."

When she hung up, Melinda noticed something. Before the phone call, her problems were mountain-sized, but her issues felt smaller, moved aside by the plight of this poor woman facing the possibility of living in her car with six kids. "No, no, no!"

"Mom, who are you talking to?"

"Oh, Katie, I've just heard the saddest thing." She went on to tell her daughter what she'd found out about the family from the shelter.

"What can we do, Mom? Even with Nana and Poppa's ski vacation money, there wouldn't be enough to get all those people a place to live."

"You're right, Miss Kathryn Elizabeth. Get your brothers in here. I have an idea, but we all need to be on the same page for this one."

It took only a few minutes of sharing the idea before all three of her children were on board. More of the burden from the last weeks lifted from Melinda's heart. Of course, sadness remained, but now? Not so much.

"Okay, people, we're going to need a big vehicle. I'll call Open House Ministries back and then call the church to use their van."

The phone was ringing. She'd never been more proud of her children than at this moment.

"Open House, Joanne speaking."

"Hi, Joanne, this is Melinda Stayton calling back."

When Melinda's dad brought the money over, the children were so excited about their special project, they all talked at once to share it.

He stared at Melinda with astonishment. "Well, Ms. Melinda, I have to say I'm not really surprised by any of this. If anyone can pull this off, it's you."

She laughed and gave her dad a big hug. "Thanks for the vote of confidence."

"How can I help?" he asked. "Just boss me around, however you want."

The children thought this was hilarious. Katie took his hand and led him downstairs. "Here's the plan so far, Papa."

Within forty-eight hours, most of the Staytons' family plan had been completed. All the ski trip money had been spent, plus what the children had kicked in from their own individual Christmas stashes. But when word went out among the church body, money, encouragement, and supplies flowed their way in abundance.

Melinda stood and surveyed their accomplishment. *Lord, I'm brought to my knees in humbleness at the power of Your grace and blessings.* "Thank You."

"Mom, you're talking to yourself again." Katie took her by the hand. "Come on, we're waiting." She gazed into her mother's face. "You look different, Mommy."

"I am different, Katie. . .from the inside out." She squeezed her daughter's hand.

It took twenty minutes to find the modest neighborhood on the other side of town. They turned on Adams Avenue. "Look for 8901," Melinda said. "It's a white house with blue trim."

"I see it," Michael said. "It's the one with the kids in front. Man, they look scared."

Melinda willed herself not to cry. "Anybody else nervous besides me?" She laughed.

"I'm just excited," Katie said.

The others agreed.

They pulled into the driveway as a young woman came out to stand on the porch. She was carrying a small baby wrapped in a pink blanket, while a boy about two clung to her legs, thumb in his mouth. The other four children were boys as well.

Melinda and the kids got out of the van and walked to the door. "I'm Melinda Stayton, and these are my children—Joel, Mike, and Katie."

The woman smiled. "I'm Suzanne Mitchel, and as you can guess, these are all *my* children." The corners of her mouth quivered. "I cannot thank you enough for all your help." She was fighting tears.

"Suzanne, we're here because we believe God directed us to you."

Now Suzanne was openly crying. "We've been praying and praying, Mrs. Stayton. Our lives seemed to spin out of control, and then when the shelter wasn't ready to take us, I..."

Melinda stepped forward to hug the younger woman. "First off, please call me Melinda. Trust me when I say this, Suzanne, I know exactly how life can change in an instant." She took the baby's outstretched hand. "Your children are beautiful, by the way."

"Oh, thank you. They've been wonderful, but they can be a handful, too. Especially since..." Her voice dropped to a whisper. "Especially since their dad's been in jail. He's a good man, Melinda, he really is."

Melinda patted Suzanne's shoulder. "I believe you. I also believe things will get better. I know it." She changed the subject. "Well, people, let's get this family to their new home."

Suzanne looked at Melinda. "You know, Joanne at the shelter didn't even tell us where we're going, and I didn't think to ask."

"Oh, I think you'll like the place," Katie chirped. "Yup, you're going to like it a lot." Her faced glowed with exuberance.

It was a tight squeeze getting all the family and their personal belongings into the van, but they managed. Melinda could hear Suzanne's children whispering to one another as they strained to see out the side windows. It tore at her mother's heart to see them upset one more time. "Hey, Joel, why don't you start a Christmas song?"

He led them in several, but the group's favorite was "Jingle Bells." They'd finished the third round when Melinda pulled the van onto a beautiful tree-lined street decorated with Christmas displays in almost every yard.

"Wow," Suzanne said, "how beautiful." She appeared puzzled and glanced at Melinda, who said nothing.

Melinda slowed down and turned into the driveway of a two-story brick home with a sign in the front yard that read WELCOME HOME AND MERRY CHRISTMAS.

Suzanne was staring at Melinda now. She whispered, "Are you kidding me? This is where we'll be living?"

"Not by yourselves," Melinda said.

Katie, Joel, and Michael all spoke at once. "Nope!" Then they laughed.

"I, I don't understand." Suzanne and the children piled out of the van.

"Suzanne, this is my home. . .our home, I mean. Come, let me show you."

Suzanne had one hand over her mouth while carrying the baby with the other. Michael opened the front door with a flair of drama. "Welcome," he declared, then bowed.

Once inside, Suzanne and her children were speechless for a minute. She looked all around the room and then at the striking woman before her. "How can I ever repay all this?"

Melinda shook her head. "Suzanne, you owe me nothing."

"Come on, guys," Katie said, "you have your own private part of the house." Like ducks in a row, everyone followed her through a side door, down a short hallway, and into a brightly lit kitchen. "We'll all share the kitchen, just so you know."

Melinda laughed. Her daughter sounded like a tour guide at Disneyland.

They left the kitchen and followed Katie down a flight of stairs and entered the daylight lower level. It was a spacious, well-decorated, cozy apartment. At one end an enormous sectional heaped with pillows faced a large, flat-screen TV. Above and around it were shelves stacked with DVDs, games, and books. A "mini" kitchen flanked the other end, complete with microwave, fridge, and a stacked washer-dryer set. Melinda flipped open a cupboard filled with snacks of every description.

"There's more," Joel said. "The last two rooms are bedrooms, and there's a bathroom after that."

Suzanne opened the first door and gasped. There were enough beds for all the boys. . .some bunks. The comforters matched the curtains, while the walls were covered with various sports graphics. Two oversized dressers stood at the end of each bed. An open walk-in closet was stuffed with clothes and assorted sizes of shoes alongside brightly colored towels, stacks of washcloths, and assorted bed linens. All five boys began claiming their "own" beds.

When Suzanne went into the last bedroom, she was in tears. A beautiful whitewashed crib stood next to a queen bed covered with a Battenberg lace comforter. Layered pillows to match took up half the bed and white wicker side tables flanked either side. A crystal chandelier lit the entire space, making it breathtaking. A changing table, with dozens of diapers, wipes, and brand-new baby clothes, stood inside another huge closet.

"I'm overwhelmed." Suzanne's children gathered around her for hugs. "Mama," one of the twins asked, "am I dreaming?"

Melinda stepped forward. "No, you're not dreaming. This place is yours for as long as you need it. We'd finished the basics down here last year, but people from my church came and made it cozy with new furniture and all the other stuff. Your daddy will be home soon, and he'll need a place, too." She turned to Suzanne. "The shelter told me if you want to stay here instead of moving yourselves over there, they'd still be willing to help your husband find another job and get him into their rehab program as well."

Suzanne collapsed onto one end of the sectional, setting the baby on the floor. The other children were still busy looking over their new room. "How can I ever thank you enough, Melinda?"

"Suzanne, you have no idea how much healing I've received from working on this and meeting you and your family. Just a short while ago, I was ready to skip Christmas altogether, but now. . .I can't wait." She smiled. "I just remembered something my grandmother used to say."

"What's that?" Suzanne asked.

"All the stuff that's happened to me and my family is now 'oak leaves in the past.'"

"I've never heard that expression before. . .what's it mean?"

"Oak leaves don't shed their leaves, until the new ones push them off. You know, the present replaces the past."

"I love that, Melinda. Your grandmother was a wise woman."

"Yes, she was, but I have to say, until this very moment, I never fully understood that saying." She winked and started to leave. "I know you and the kids didn't get to put up a tree, but the church gave you one— it's in the garage. Wait until you see all the decorations they brought, and gifts as well. Oh, one more thing: we have enough food to feed an army for a week, thanks to the wonderful cooks I know. We can eat separately or together. . .whatever you want. We even have a high chair for the baby."

"Would we all fit at one table?" Suzanne sounded skeptical.

"Hey, we can make it work. . .you get settled in, and I'll start laying out everything. The kids can be the cleanup committee."

"Sounds great." Suzanne picked up the sleeping baby and held her close. The tension in the young mother's face disappeared.

"What's her name?"

"Sophia. Her name is Sophia."

Melinda bent to kiss the top of the baby's head. "Merry Christmas, little Sophia."

Suzanne leaned back with a sigh.

Melinda sang "Jingle Bells" all the way up the stairs.

One Christmas Night

Rosanne Croft

A sixteen-year-old who visits her grandmother after school gets more than love and the cozy smell of baking on a chilly December evening.

The old woman can still see and hear the events of a snowy Christmas Eve night when she was four years old, when a tinkling sound outside her family's cabin door led to an experience she'd remember for a lifetime. . . .

I often visited my great-grandmother after school when I was a teenager, driving a blue Volkswagen bug to her apartment. In her nineties, Grandma Nellie was a feather of a woman, with thin gray braids tucked up on her head. I liked the cozy smell of baking in her apartment, and sometimes she even had cookies for me.

One afternoon in December, she blinked several times in her recliner and peered at the snow blowing past the windowsill laden with pots of fuzzy African violets.

"Looks like a blizzard's cookin' up," she said. Then, out of the blue, she added, "Did you know I was born in French Canada?"

"No, Grandma. Do you remember it?"

"I remember some. I must've been about four years old when a snowstorm like you've never seen settled in around our cabin. And it was Christmas Eve, too."

"Did you have much for Christmas back then?"

"I don't remember getting presents. Not like now. But we always had a roasted bird and sweets. Except that Christmas, we were snowed in. My daddy couldn't go out hunting for a bird for Christmas dinner."

Grandma sighed ferociously. "Lawsy may, it was cold and dark. My dad kept stoking the stove he'd built inside the cabin. It was a brick oven with a long chimney and warm mud walls all around. Looked like a kiln, so it did. It just radiated heat out of those walls. And I got to sleep right next to it every night."

She settled in her chair, sipped her tea, and went on.

"What I remember is that I knew my folks had sweets for us hidden somewhere. I was awake for a long time next to the oven wondering about that candy. My mama had made bread that day, and the smell of it filled the cabin. Now bread's enough for most people, all slathered with butter and honey. But I wanted candy."

"Grandma, *you* make the yummiest bread and cinnamon rolls ever. Did you learn it from *your* mother?"

Her eyes sparkled. "As you know, I made a living on my mother's dough recipe. I started by selling pies and doughnuts and such to the Plains Hotel downtown. Made enough to have a restaurant of my own."

"I'm proud of you for that, Grandma. But you were talking about French Canada."

"Oh, yes, we were in the far north on a winter night. The wind howled, and the windows completely frosted over on the inside. Drifts of snow covered them on the outside. I really did dream of sugar plums that night." She smiled. "I woke up and heard what sounded like tinkling coming from outside. Then someone stomped on the crunchy snow near the door."

"Don't tell me it was Santa and his reindeer."

She laughed that cluck of hers. "Someone knocked softly, like they were wearing gloves. My daddy got up. I followed him to the door. We weren't scared at all, but maybe we should've been."

"Why?"

"Because in walked the tallest Indian man you've ever seen! The snow swirled in around him, and a cold wind blasted right through my nightgown. I ran back to my place by the stove and watched him shake my daddy's hand."

"Did he say anything?"

"When he warmed up, he spoke Algonquin to Daddy, who understood some of it, even though he was from Scotland. The Indian took off about five or six furs and skins one by one, and he was wrapped in a red blanket underneath it all. His dark eyebrows and hair were completely iced up with icicles. His face was the color of bread crust. On his legs were buckskin leggings with teeny tiny bugle beads on 'em. I think that was the tinkling sound I heard. That, or the icicles falling off of him. Some tall feathers stuck up on top of his head, brushing up against the ceiling of our cabin."

"What did your mother do?"

"Why, she got up and made him some hot coffee. There was no going to sleep for any of us; our eyes were wide as saucers. We five kids all stood and stared at the big Indian man."

"Weren't you scared of him, Grandma? I mean, Indians and white people fought all the time."

"Well, I kept my eye on that Indian, and I could see that even though he didn't smile much, he had nice eyes. My daddy talked to him using a little French and some Algonquin. Pretty soon, my mother sliced a hunk of bread for him. I want to say us kids weren't scared, but we'd never seen an Indian. Margaret, my little sister, started to cry, and I tried to shush her."

"I think I would've been scared, too."

"My parents were friendly, so why shouldn't I be? He spoke slowly and looked my daddy in the eye when they shook hands. Mama knew we were a little timid, so she made us feel better by giving us our Christmas candy that very night. She reached up into the top cupboard where we were never allowed and handed us swirly candy sticks. Mine was butterscotch, all golden yellow—was it good! We lingered with our tongues on that candy, making sharp points of it, listening to the grown-ups go on and on. You know how they do."

Now it was my turn to laugh. "It was probably boring to a four-year-old."

"I may have been closer to five. Anyways, there wasn't a lot of room in the cabin, so after the other kids had been carried to their beds, my daddy looked at me. 'Nellie,' he said, 'sleep in Margaret's trundle tonight.' So I did. When I opened my eyes during the night, that Indian had spread his skins next to the mud walls where I always slept, and there he was, curled up like a deer under his red blanket."

"So you gave up your place for him."

"It wasn't much of a place to sleep, but it was warm. Christmas morning when I woke up, he was gone. There wasn't a trace left of him, but on the table, he'd left us a gift." She chuckled. "It wasn't wrapped, though!"

"What was it?"

"Somewhere under all his skins and such, he'd carried in a big wild turkey, shot clean through. He left it for our Christmas dinner. Because of the blizzard, my mama thought we'd only have bread and cheese for dinner. But we had the grandest roasted and stuffed turkey you ever did see. Then we played with those feathers like we were Indians all the rest of the day."

"Did you ever see him again, Grandma?"

"No. We left Canada as soon as spring came and ended up in Nebraska. We had more kids, ten altogether." She sighed. "But only eight lived to be adults. None have lived as long as I have, so maybe I'm the only one to ever tell about that Christmas in Canada. Maybe I'm the only one who remembers the Indian man who came to find shelter in our house that night."

It never occurred to me that Grandma was so old that she remembered Indians dressed in feathers and skins. They say old people can remember things that happened long ago better than short-term things. Grandma Nellie had a brain as sharp as a porcupine quill most of the time. I stood. "What else do you remember, Grandma?"

"Lawsy, honey, I remember so much that I could fill a book up with stories. I sit here, and sometimes, I can see the past so clearly. In the dying firelight, I can see Margaret's little face with the rag curls in her baby hair, next to me in the trundle. I'll bet she remembers that Algonquin. I ought to call her and ask. Oh, but. . ." Grandma hesitated. "Margaret's been gone these ten years. I forgot."

I shifted my feet. "Guess I better go, Grandma. Wish I could stay and hear more stories, but I've got homework to do."

"Wait, honey. I've got something for you." Standing on her tiptoes, she reached into an upper cupboard. She turned around slowly and drew something out from behind the skirt of her apron. She handed me a butterscotch stick. "I still love 'em."

I put my arms around her. At sixteen, I was almost a full head taller than my petite grandma. "Me, too," I said, "and I'll remember. I'll remember."

A Miracle for You, Too

Linda J. Reinhardt

More than anything, Darci wants to surprise her husband, Eldon, with the news she is carrying their child as his Christmas present. Instead, it looks like the baby is lost.

Then her friend Kimberly tells Darci her miracle baby story. Might Darci and Eldon have their own Christmas miracle after all?

To Deanne and her daughter, Sarah, who got their own miracle this year.

D arci, is that you?"

Darci tried to respond to her husband on the other end of the line. She breathed in deep and blinked her eyes. Her lips moved in that quirky way they did when she tried not to cry. She should have waited to call him. "I. . ." Another fit of sobs took over.

"What's wrong? Where are you?"

"I just came. . .from. . .the. . .doctor," Darci forced out.

"The doctor? I didn't know you had an appointment. What did you go there for?"

"I wanted to surprise you."

"Surprise me? What?"

"For Christmas. . .I was pregnant, but I lost the baby, and they want to do an ultrasound the beginning of next week." Darci was able to force the words out quickly before her face contorted into a wrinkled mess and tears rolled down her face.

"Pregnant? You lost our baby?" There was a dead silence on the phone. Darci filled it with the sounds of sobbing. "I'll meet you at home in a few minutes okay? Can you drive?"

Darci nodded, even though Eldon couldn't see her.

He clicked off the line.

Darci made her way to her car and made the short drive home. Somehow Eldon made it home before her. He waited outside, leaning against the back of his car. Before she turned the car off, Eldon had the door open and pulled her out of the car into his arms. Darci didn't know how long they stood there holding one another. After a while, they found their way into the house.

"Can I get you anything?" he asked when she sat down.

Darci shook her head.

Eldon sat next to her. "Honey, why didn't you tell me?"

"I wanted to surprise you. It was going to be your biggest Christmas present ever. I've been really excited since we waited so long and then finally. . ." Darci collapsed into a fit of tears again.

"That's so sweet, honey. It would have been great, but you went through a miscarriage without me being there for you?"

"I kept hoping everything would stop. . .I'm sorry."

"Nothing to be sorry for." He held her close and rubbed her arm.

Eventually Darci fell asleep nestled up against him.

Eldon carefully stood, laid Darci down on the couch, and covered her with a blanket. Then he phoned a few of their friends to ask for prayer.

The next days ticked by very slowly for Darci. Her heart felt like it had broken into a million pieces, and nothing would ever be able to repair it again. The Christmas tree stood in the living room waiting to be decorated, but she couldn't bring herself to do it. Christmas was only a few days away, and life looked so bleak.

Lord, I know You have a perfect plan for me, but this part of the plan hurts. You know how badly we've wanted to have a child. We've been trying for such a long time, and I had come to a point of giving up, only to find I didn't have to give up. You had given me a child. And now the baby is gone. I hurt, Lord, I really hurt.

The morning before the scheduled ultrasound, her good friend

Kimberly dropped by bearing gifts. "Every girl needs chocolate when times are tough. And, of course, your favorite coffee drink!" Kimberly handed the chocolate and warm paper cup from Darci's favorite coffee shop over to her. "And this"—Kimberly held out a box of tissues—"is for when we talk."

Tears sprang to Darci's eyes.

Kimberly enveloped her into one of her famous hugs. "Come on, my sweet friend, let's go sit and chat." Kimberly led the way into the family room and plopped down on their old couch that neither Eldon nor Darci could get rid of. It was way too comfortable, their friends and family agreed. Kimberly set the tissue box between them. "I know this is hard, Darci. I've been through this a few times myself. And there just aren't any words to make the situation better."

Darci nodded. She'd sat with Kimberly after her miscarriages. Kimberly and her husband, Matt, had tried for five years to have a baby. Kimberly miscarried twice in the middle of her pregnancy. It was the hardest thing to go through with a friend. Then Kimberly and Matt went on a mission trip for several years to Australia. One day Darci received an announcement in the mail about a little girl named Sasha. Kimberly had finally had a baby.

"Darci, there's something I didn't share with you about Sasha."

"Oh?"

"Early in my pregnancy, I thought I lost her. The doctors thought I lost her. I'd been through miscarriages before, and I knew beyond a shadow of a doubt I'd lost this baby. But Matt said I didn't. I thought he was in denial, but no matter how many times I told him what I was going through, Matt would say, 'I think the baby is fine.'"

"Really?"

"Yes, he even had me go to the prayer room and had me prayed over. I only went to appease him. I gave up trying to convince him the baby was gone, figuring when we had the ultrasound, he would have to accept it then."

"But, obviously, he was right." Darci smiled.

"Yeah, he was right. We went to the ultrasound, and there she was. Her little heart beat bright on the screen." Tears misted Kimberly's eyes. "I'll never forget how I felt at that moment. She was alive. Because of the previous miscarriages, we continued to have ultrasounds almost every month. The doctor wanted to keep a close eye on her development. We had a few scares even up to when she was born. They had to do an emergency procedure."

"And now you have your beautiful miracle girl—Sasha."

Kimberly swung her dark auburn hair from her face and reached over to hold Darci's hand. "I'm only telling you that because I feel like you aren't supposed to give up. Remember how long Matt and I struggled and what we went through before we had Sasha? And now. . ." Kimberly touched her stomach.

"What? You're pregnant again?"

Kimberly nodded.

"Are you excited and scared?"

Kimberly nodded again. "But it's a desire God has put on my heart, and even though it can be painful getting there, it's worth it. Every day I think of the children I lost. . .and I miss them. If I would have given up, though, I wouldn't have Sasha, and now, hopefully, whoever this is in my tummy. Only God knows, Darci. He writes our days, and I'm learning to trust Him with the amount of days He writes for the people in my life."

Darci nodded. "It hurts so much, though. I feel empty."

Kimberly moved over and held her friend. "Losing a baby is a great loss, Darci. It leaves a big hole. But please don't give up. Let there be a next time."

Darci nodded, leaving her head on her friend's shoulder. "I promise I won't give up, but I'm going to need time."

"Take the time, but don't give up. And hey, girlfriend, what about our coffee and chocolates? We can't let them go to waste."

Both girls smiled with delight after they took their first bite of rich, dark chocolate. While Darci enjoyed her coffee and chocolates, Kimberly persuaded Darci to let her decorate her tree and put other decorations out. Darci had to admit it made her feel good when Kimberly was finished.

Eldon came home soon after Kimberly left. He seemed impressed with the tree. Darci shared the conversation she'd had with Kimberly. "Oh, do you mind if she comes to the ultrasound with us?"

Eldon shook his head. "And I'm glad she encouraged you to not give up. I've been worried you'd want to stop trying."

"The loss hurts so deeply, though. It feels like I could fall into a big dark hole and not have energy to climb back out."

"I'm sorry, babe." Eldon held her close. "We'll get through this together. I was wondering if you just wanted to stay home this year for Christmas."

Darci thought for a minute. "I'm not sure."

"Well, think about it. So have you had time to do dinner?"

Darci shook her head.

"How about we make some fattening nachos and watch a movie, then?"

Darci smiled in agreement. It was one of their favorite things to do, especially after a hard or busy day.

The next day, Christmas Eve, the sun shone bright, and the air was cold. Eldon drove them to the hospital where the ultrasound would be performed. Darci had turned off the radio since it seemed strange to listen to Christmas music in light of where they were going and what they were doing.

Outside the hospital door, Kimberly waited for them, wrapped in a heavy coat, with a scarf around her neck. She waved as they drove by to the parking lot.

Kimberly is such a faithful friend. Lord, I pray You will bless her baby she is carrying with life. I pray You will go before me and hold me during this procedure.

When they met Kimberly out in front of the building, she grasped their hands and prayed for them. "Lord, I know the kind of pain my dear friends are feeling right now. Please go before them and give them peace as the technician checks to make sure everything is cleared. Give him wisdom. I ask for comfort for my friends." Kimberly ended the prayer by giving them both a hug.

Darci wiped at her eyes, and Eldon held her close as they made their way to the elevator. *Why couldn't I be coming here to see how far along the baby is instead of checking to make sure everything passed? I wanted a special Christmas celebrating not only the birth of Jesus, but the upcoming birth of our baby.*

She took the gown the nurse offered her and went into the side room and changed into it. Tears poured from her eyes. *I just want to go home.*

She couldn't meet Eldon's or Kimberly's eyes when she came into the room. She just climbed up on the bed and laid down. The technician gave her a gentle smile and then put some warm goo on her stomach. Then he took an instrument and started moving here and there on her tummy.

"Hmm. Looks like you are about ten weeks along." He smiled.

Darci gave a frown. *I was ten weeks? I didn't realize I was that far.*

"Everything looks good."

"So it passed okay?" Darci asked.

"Passed?" The tech looked at the file. "Oh! You're here because of a miscarriage." He took hold of the screen and turned it around. "Look here. See that little flashing light?"

"Oh!" Kimberly gasped and covered her face.

"What?" Eldon asked.

"It's your baby's heartbeat," the tech said with a big smile. "If you look close, it's not just one heartbeat but two."

"Two!" Darci sat up straight and looked closely at the screen. *Lord, am I dreaming? My baby's alive? I mean, babies?*

"Honey!" Eldon moved over to Darci and peered at the screen.

"Here—let me get some pictures for you," the tech said. "You'll have to lie back down."

Darci laid down and stared at the screen. *Really? Really, Lord, is it true? Oh, thank You, thank You!*

The technician finished with what he was doing. "That's it, and congratulations! I'll have the doctor check this out to confirm the two babies, but to me it looks clear as anything that there are two little heart-beats. I'm happy you got good news instead of what you thought you were going to hear. I bet you're going to have a merry Christmas!"

"Thank you." Darci beamed. She held on to her stomach.

"It's a miracle, just like Sasha," Kimberly said. "I guess I was right. You weren't supposed to give up, huh?" Her eyes twinkled.

Eldon, Darci, and Kimberly held on to each other tight.

"Lord, thank You," Eldon prayed. "Thank You that not only are we celebrating the gift of Your Son tomorrow, but the gift You have given us of children." Then he gazed at Darci tenderly. "I'd say this is the best Christmas present you could ever give me."

Darci gave him a bright smile. "Not me, honey. God is giving us both this Christmas present."

A Christmas Farewell

SHARON BERNASH SMITH

Marcus, a Marine Captain, is leaving for Iraq on Christmas Day. After moving his family to Portland, Oregon, for his deployment, he's ready for departure. He was hoping for a white Christmas, his lifelong dream, even if the weatherman says otherwise.

But God knows the heart of the faithful, and one special soldier finds that dreams really do come true, if only by mysterious intervention.

I'm sick you're leaving on Christmas Day, Marcus. Really! Christmas Day?" Her chin quivered, but she managed to hold back the tears.

"Em, if I had any part of when the government says I go or stay, don't you think I'd change things?" He walked over to sit by his wife on the couch.

She rested her head on his shoulder, taking in the comfort of his presence. Part of the comfort came from the familiar aromas of aftershave mingled with coffee.

"I wasn't blaming you, sweetheart. Guess I'm feeling sorry for myself." Looking up into his face, she saw disappointment written all over it.

He changed the subject. "What's the weather report for next week? Any chance of snow?"

Emily Rhoads squeezed her husband's arm and laughed. "You're just a big ol' kid, aren't you? A great big, US Marine-type kid."

"What—you don't want snow for Christmas?"

"Mmm, sure I do, but come on, Marcus. How many times has that ever happened in Portland, Oregon? In the hills maybe, but not down here in the lowlands."

"Well, at least you grew up in close proximity to the possibility. . .compared to San Diego, that is."

"Sorry, sweetheart." Sighing, she got up and stretched. "I'm beat. . .too much Christmas shopping. I'm heading to bed."

"Go ahead. I'll hide the presents and lock up." He stood and kissed her on the forehead.

Emily had to stand on tiptoes to kiss him back. *I'm going to miss this.* "Better stick that stuff in the garage; you know how sneaky your children are."

"Sure do—they take after their mother." He winked.

"Ha, ha, very funny! Would you let the dog out, too. . .please?"

Emily made her way up the stairs to the bedrooms, stopping by her kids' rooms on the way. *Lord, what will they do without Marcus? He's their hero.* Sweet little Willow was curled around a life-sized Scooby Doo, a thumb in her mouth. *He'll miss her birthday this year.*

In the next room, big boy Sam had kicked off his covers. She tiptoed in and drew the blankets back over him. He was a miniature version of his dad. Now she let the tears flow.

This would be Marcus's first deployment to Iraq. Even though they knew all along this was coming, nothing had prepared her for the desperateness she felt in her spirit this very moment. They'd been separated before in his Marine Corps career, but only for a few months. This time he was looking at a year's tour of duty. Just the thought of it made her depressed. *Father God, give me strength for this. Make me the woman I need to be.*

Crawling into bed, she couldn't help smiling at Marcus's unwavering desire to have snow for Christmas. He really *was* a big kid. Praying God would open the skies and grant her husband's white wish, Emily had an outlandish thought. She jumped out of bed, grabbed the phone, and punched in her sister's number.

A sleepy voice answered.

"Oh, sorry, Lainey, did I wake you?"

"Naw, I had to get up to answer the phone, anyway." Big yawn. "Your house better be on fire, Em. Just sayin'."

"Very funny, little sister. Listen, I have a brilliant idea, but I need your help."

"Tonight?"

"No, silly, just listen and tell me what you think."

"Morning, Marcus." Emily hugged her husband, who looked like he'd been up for hours. "I didn't even hear you get out of bed."

"Couldn't sleep."

"Oh?"

He looked up and she saw tears. "Em, I'm sorry I have to leave you and the kids. For sure, it's not fair to any of you." His head dropped, and her heart melted for him.

"Look, Marcus, I knew when I married a Marine, my life was going to be full of unknowns. None of us knows the future but the Lord." She sat next to him and spoke words of encouragement. "My parents are close by, honey. Besides, I've got Lainey and our entire church family for support. Moving back here while you're gone is a good thing, Marcus. We'll be fine."

"And don't forget, we'll be able to Skype almost every day."

"The kids will love it." *But, oh, it will not be the same, my darling. My empty bed will feel so cold without you.* She smiled and kissed him. "I love you."

"Do you guys have to be doing that before breakfast?" Their eight-year-old son, Sam, stood in the doorway rubbing his eyes.

"What's it to you, bud? Come over here and give your dad a hug." Marcus opened his arms and Sam ran into them, burying his head on Marcus's shoulder.

"I'm going to miss you, Daddy," Sam whispered.

"Me, too, Sammie boy, me, too."

Emily left the room and dried her eyes. Picking up the phone, she dialed her sister's number again. "Sorry for that late call, Sis, but have you had a chance to think about my idea?"

"Hey, I love it; count me in. And get this—when I shared it with Mike, he got on the phone right away with some of his buddies."

"Really? Oh, I think I'm going to cry. As soon as I get my act together, I'll be over."

"What are you going to tell Marcus?"

"Oh, I'll just say I'm going shopping. That's not really a lie." She laughed like a little girl. "See ya."

Three days later

"Mommy, when's it going to be Christmas Eve?" Willow was hopping around the kitchen like an overwound toy. "Is it one minute or two?"

"Willow, I just told you, it's only morning. When it gets dark, it will be Christmas Eve."

"Oh, Mommy, I love Christmas." She grabbed her mother around the legs and hugged tight.

"So do I, pumpkin." She so wanted to give the children a little hint about her plans for the day, but she thought it'd be good if everyone was equally surprised.

It had taken three days of surreptitious planning, but if all came off, the "great reveal" should happen around noon. Now, if she could maintain her composure until then...

Her thoughts were interrupted by Marcus. "You look like the cat who ate the canary."

"What?" She smiled at him coyly. "Well, Mr. Man, it is Christmas Eve. I've just got a surprise, that's all."

"You can't surprise me, Emily. It'll never happen, and you know it."

"Is that so?"

"Yup, pretty sure I know what's up your sleeve."

Emily's heart skipped a beat. Marcus *was* hard to surprise. "Okay, what is it?"

"That new fly-fishing rod I've been hinting about for weeks."

She breathed a big sigh of relief. "Marcus Rhoads, don't spoil things...stop guessing."

He pointed at her and laughed. "See, I told you I'd find out. I always find out." He picked her up into a big hug.

Willow ran over to them. "Daddy, don't drop Mommy; she's still got to fix lunch."

At precisely twelve noon, a van pulled up and parked down the street from the Rhoads' home. Over the next few minutes, six more vehicles did the same. In all, twenty people of various ages and sizes gathered with shovels and wheelbarrows. They waited!

Inside, everyone but Emily remained oblivious to the outside activities. Glancing at the kitchen clock, it was all she could do to stay away from the living room window. When the clock chimed 12:15, she heard the first truck.

The noise of the brakes brought Sammy from his room. He shouted, "Hey, Mom, Dad, look out in our driveway. Quick, hurry!" He bounded down the stairs and was at the front door, where he met Marcus carrying Willow.

Marcus stood on the front porch, shaking his head. He turned to Emily. "What's going on here, Em?"

While he waited for an answer, three more Mac trucks made their way to where the first one was now dumping a full load of pure, white snow into their front yard.

Sammy was beside himself, and Marcus had to set Willow down before she jumped from his arms. Emily hugged her husband, looking up into his face. "Merry Christmas, Marine."

"But how. . . ?" His eyes filled with tears as friends and family walked toward them to stand in front of him.

"Merry Christmas, Marcus," they shouted in unison.

His brother-in-law, Mike, stepped forward. "Marcus, this is our gift to you for serving our country and being the godly man you are." Mike choked up and could barely continue. "We, all of us, want to say thank you, Brother." He ran to the porch and gave Marcus a big embrace and kissed Emily on the check. "Okay, enough sentiment, I've got to get to work. You guys better get changed into some warm clothes, 'cuz things are about to get real chilly out here."

After bundling up with hats, boots, and gloves, the Rhoads family exited to a winter wonderland created by at least a foot of snow lying across their lawn. By now the street was filled with laughing neighbors as well. A local TV station had arrived and began dragging equipment out of their van.

Marcus took Emily's hand. "I owe you an apology, Em." He was fighting deep emotion. "I, I said you could never surprise me."

"Marcus Rhoads, you're going to have to eat your words now, aren't you?" She poked him in the ribs. "Well, admit it, Mr. Marine, you got blindsided." She couldn't stop laughing. It was all pure joy.

"Emily, I've never been speechless in my life, you know that. I cannot believe you did all this. And how?"

"I didn't do it by myself, for sure. Once I shared the idea with Lainey and Mike, they made phone calls, and then more phone calls." She made a wide gesture toward the snow piled before them. "Ta-da! All the way from Mount Hood to you, my husband-kid."

Marcus suddenly grabbed her up into his arms and deftly stepped off the porch. "Hey, Sammy and Willow, come quick and watch me dump Mommy into the snow."

"Yippee," Sammy cried.

"Careful, Daddy. She *still* hasn't made lunch."

"Yeah, don't hurt me, Daddy," Emily said right before Marcus dropped her.

December 30

Marcus took off his helmet and wiped the sweat from his forehead. He'd only been gone from home five days, and already homesickness clung to him like the desert heat. He took the lid off a bottled water, drained it, then popped a CD into the DVD player in the mess hall. "Got to love this new technology."

He watched the screen come alive with what the media had dubbed "Iraqi Snow Day." He'd never get tired of seeing his childhood fantasy unfold in front of him. The camera had caught the exact moment he'd dropped Emily into the snow. Her expression was priceless. He reached out and touched the image on the screen. *Thank You, Lord, for all my blessings.*

In rare moments of complete unity, Willow and Sam had made a lopsided snowman, complete with a carrot nose and button eyes. They waved to the camera with pride written all over their faces. He and Emily were applauding in the background.

The next scene cut to him talking to the camera about his deployment and how much he'd always wanted a "white" Christmas. Tears streamed down his face.

"And," the newscaster said, "this ends the story of one Marine's Christmas surprise. From all of us here at Channel 12 news, thank you, Captain Marcus Rhoads, for serving your country. Now, ladies and gentlemen, this reporter has a snowball fight to attend."

Ready to get to work, Marcus punched the EJECT button and sighed. Despite being thousands of miles from home and family, and despite the misery of war all around him, Marcus Rhoads felt the seed of pure joy growing within his spirit.

But I Remember

LINDA J. REINHARDT

Shelly's car breaks down on an errand to drop off gifts to a family on Christmas Eve day. When she asks them for help, she meets Sue, who faithfully visits her husband, Jay, every day at the Alzheimer's unit. . .and discovers a fresh, new meaning to Christmas.

To Sue Balfour, who shows the faithful love of Jesus every day when she goes to see Jay and hold his hand.

Shelly turned the key in the ignition again. Nothing. Her SUV was dead. *What am I going to do? It's snowing out. I have Kari with me, and we have one more stop to make for the Christmas deliveries.* An exasperated groan escaped her lips when she realized her cell phone was sitting on the counter at home. "Great!" she muttered.

"Mommy, what are we doing?" five-year-old Kari asked from the backseat.

Shelly reached over to the passenger seat and grabbed her gloves and scarf. "Honey, the car isn't working. We're going to have to walk. You get out, and I'll come around and join you on the sidewalk. Be careful—the snowbanks are kind of high. And don't forget your gloves and scarf. It's pretty cold out there."

Shelly picked up her purse and notebook, then slid out of the stalled SUV. She walked cautiously around the front of the vehicle and made her way over to Kari, who was fumbling to pull her scarf up to cover her nose but her mittens made it difficult.

Shelly helped adjust Kari's scarf and then peered at the notebook in her hand. "I think the house is just down this block. Oh, I can't believe I forgot my cell phone at home." She grabbed Kari's gloved hand before they turned to make their way to their destination on foot. Most of the sidewalk had been cleared, making the journey easy. "I sure hope the Gartleys are home. I wonder what they're going to think when they hear we've come to deliver Christmas, but first we need them to help us."

"Are we going to be home in time for Santa Claus to come?" Kari asked.

"Of course, honey. I just need to call a tow truck."

It was starting to get dark, and the wind bit at them while they walked. A few minutes later, Shelly let go of Kari's hand. "Here we are. It looks like we're in luck; they're home."

An older, petite woman stepped out the front door and busied herself searching for something on the porch.

"Hello, ma'am," Shelly called out as she started up the cleared rock steps. Everything else was covered with snow until they reached the covered porch.

"Huh? Oh, hello," the lady answered in a friendly voice. She peered at them over wire-rimmed glasses. "Do I know you?"

"No, but your family's name was given to our organization to deliver food and Christmas presents."

The woman put her hand on the knob of the front door. "What? How sweet. How did that happen?"

"I don't know, but this is the Gartley residence, correct?"

"Yes, it is. Here, why don't you come in? I can't seem to find the paper. Our paperboy throws it from his bike, and it lands in a different place every day." The lady chuckled as she opened the door to a dimly lit room. A bare Christmas tree stood in the corner. "Here—you can put your coats right here on this coat rack."

"Umm. . .actually, we weren't planning on staying, but I would like to use your phone, if you don't mind. My vehicle broke down a couple of blocks from here."

"Oh, dear, of course you can use the phone. It's too bad my son wasn't able to make it over today. He could take a look at it. He's very good with cars."

Shelly smiled. "Thank you, Mrs. Gartley."

"Oh, goodness, call me Sue. My name is Sue. Now follow me." Sue led them through a short hallway to a small kitchen area. "The last time I used my phone, I think I was in here. I forget where I put it, and I'm constantly searching for it." Sue glanced around the clean counter spaces and then lifted up some papers from a pile in a basket. "Oh my, here it is." She handed Shelly the phone. "You can call your husband now."

Shelly took the phone while thanking her and stepped out of the kitchen, leaving Kari with Sue. She overheard Kari inform Sue, "My mommy is calling a tow truck, not my daddy."

"Ah, I see. Your daddy must be busy at work."

"Yep, he's working hard today so he can be home for Christmas tomorrow."

"Your daddy sounds like a good man. Well, young lady, do you think it would be okay with your mom if I gave you a cookie?"

"I don't think she'd mind at all."

Of course I wouldn't mind. What else would I say? Shelly could hear Sue take a lid off of a jar. She made a few calls, then headed back into the kitchen. "Thank you for the use of your phone. I guess the tow trucks are behind today. It'll be two hours or more before they can arrive. I called my husband, and he's stuck in a meeting."

"Hmm, my son put chains on my car last week in case it snowed and I had an emergency. I promised him that's the only time I would drive. Although I almost did today so I could go see my husband. Normally my son comes over sometime during the day and drops me off over where my husband lives now and then comes back later and picks me up. He couldn't come today, though, even though it's Christmas Eve." Sue gave a small frown. "I do miss Jay."

"Jay is your husband?" Shelly asked.

"Yes, he is. I had to move him to an Alzheimer's facility a couple months ago. It was a hard decision, but I had to do it."

"I'm sorry to hear that. Listen, I don't want to take up much more of your time. My daughter and I will just go and wait in our vehicle for the tow truck."

"Nonsense. I'd feel horrible knowing you're sitting out there in a cold vehicle. As I was going to say earlier, why don't we hop in my car and go get the things you were delivering and bring them back here? I was about to decorate my tree but didn't want to do it alone. Would you two like to help?"

"I don't know. . ."

"Mom, that would be so much fun. Please can we, please?" Kari begged. Shelly hesitated for a minute, then shrugged. "I guess."

"Oh good, we'll have so much fun." Sue scurried off and came back with her coat and scarf on. She grabbed a set of keys off a hook attached to one of the kitchen cupboards. "Here you go."

Shelly took the keys from her and followed the two of them out to the garage. Sue pushed a button to open up the big door and then moved with surprising speed to get into the passenger side of the car. Shelly and Kari followed suit.

After Shelly got adjusted, she backed the car out and pulled it out of the driveway. It was pretty easy to maneuver through the snow, and it was only a short distance, so she didn't get too nervous about possibly wrecking a total stranger's car.

"Here we are. I'll open your trunk and quickly transfer the items over, okay?"

"How about I help you? I'm pretty strong for an old lady." Sue chuckled and got out of the car before Shelly could protest.

"Kari, stay in the car. We'll be back in a second." Kari nodded and strained to look out the side window to see what Sue was doing.

Shelly was pretty impressed by how strong Sue actually was at her age. She was able to help Shelly with most of the boxes. Finally, they put the last box in the trunk.

"Wow, this sure is a generous gift for one little old lady," Sue said.

"Our organization wants everyone to be provided for at Christmas."

"I wish Jay could experience this. He loved Christmas. I'm not sure whether he'll realize it's Christmas or not this year. Last year I had to keep reminding him why people were at our house."

"I'm so sorry, Sue."

"Yeah, so am I. He is such an intelligent man. He was an admiral in the navy until he retired."

"That's impressive."

"Yes, I think so. He was gone quite a bit, but when he came home, it was so wonderful. We had two children far apart in age. So during the toddler years, I only had one at a time to handle on my own."

"It didn't wear you out being alone all the time? Didn't you feel like a single mom?"

"Oh, I suppose, but when I married him, I knew his dream was to be active in the navy, and I had committed to that. So I made the best of it while he was gone, and when he came home, I really made the best of it."

"My husband travels a lot."

"Oh."

"Yeah, he's gone most of the time. His job provides for us really well, but he's so busy traveling, I hardly see him and I feel like I'm raising Kari on my own. When he's in town, he's busy with meetings most of the time."

"It can get lonely."

"Yep." Shelly brushed at her eye.

"When Jay was gone, I wrote him letters. We didn't have computers like they do now, or I would have been emailing him all day. But I would write him letters throughout the day. And then I'd either talk to him about everything on the letter when he called or I would mail them. He kept them all."

"That's romantic."

"I would also spend time letting my daughter know how valuable his time away from us was and how hard he worked to provide for us. We'd prepare for him to come home. I also got involved in different charities and the church while he was gone, so I kept busy."

"That sounds healthy."

"Yes, well, I loved Jay so much. I had to find a way to keep that love alive through the years. I didn't want to lose him. He was too good of a catch."

Shelly threw back her head and laughed.

Sue gave a chuckle. "Well, he was. He still is. Every day I go see him. He doesn't recognize me at first, but then eventually he lets me hold his sweet hand. I sit there with him until my son comes and picks me up. One day someone said to me, 'Jay wouldn't even notice if you didn't come. He doesn't remember anymore.'"

"Ouch, that must have hurt."

"Yes, it did. But you know what? Whether he remembers or not, I remember. I hope I never forget all of those wonderful years we had together."

Kari opened the door of the car. "Are you two almost done?"

"Yes, honey, we're done. Come on, Sue. Let's get these things back to your house." Shelly shut the trunk, got back in the car, and drove the short distance to Sue's house, contemplating what she had said about Jay still being a good catch and what she did to keep the love alive between them.

Sue opened the garage door with the automatic door opener. Shelly pulled in carefully and turned off the engine.

"You know, you could drive my car home and return it in the morning after church, if you don't want to stay and decorate the tree," Sue offered.

"Oh no, we could never take your car. You don't even know us."

"I know you well enough. Besides, I just have to call the number of the organization if you don't come back tomorrow with it."

"But I want to decorate the tree with you," Kari cried out.

"Kari could help me with the tree while you unload my car. And then if the tow truck hasn't arrived yet, you can drive home and come back tomorrow."

"I guess," Shelly said carefully. "I feel a little strange about it, though."

"Nonsense, it's just a car."

"Thank you for your generous offer, but could I make some phone calls first?" Shelly asked.

"Sure! Whatever you want to do, know my offer is on the table." Sue got out of the car, and Kari followed excitedly behind her.

Shelly popped the trunk open before she made her way back to get the items. *If only I had some of the energy Sue has. Wow, must be nice.* It was slow bringing the boxes into the house. Shelly stopped to take her coat off when beads of sweat started dripping down her back. Finally, she dropped the last box onto the only space left in the kitchen. Heaving a sigh of relief, she bent her neck to the right and then the left to stretch it out.

Kari's and Sue's voices could be heard from the living room. Shelly took light steps to peek around the doorway to watch undetected. Kari took a decoration out of the box and brought it over to Sue. She couldn't hear what Sue said, but it brought a big smile to Kari's face.

She went back to the kitchen and called the tow company. They were still a couple of hours out. Her shoulders dropped. She tried Brent's office again. Brent was stuck in meetings and wouldn't be home until late that night. He did promise he'd be fully available the next day for Christmas. Shelly thought of calling a few of her friends, but with the roads in such bad condition in certain areas she didn't want any of them to have to bundle kids up and then battle the snow.

Shelly went to join Sue and Kari. The tree looked pretty much decorated. Kari would be a little easier to get out the door.

"You two did a beautiful job."

Kari turned and gave a big smile. "Mom, you should hear all the stories about each of these decorations. Sue's husband, Jay, used to bring them whenever he came back to town. And Sue would buy one for Jay every year in return."

"Oh, that's so nice."

"We tried. Having a husband who travels as much as he did isn't easy. But we found our ways to stay connected." Sue stood back and gazed at the tree. "I'd say this is the best-looking tree I've had in years. You are a good helper, Miss Kari."

Kari beamed in response and touched a decoration. "See this one, Mom? Sue bought this pretty one with the little kids and mommy praying to tell Jay they prayed for him every night together." Kari looked up at her mom. "We could do that for Daddy when he is out of town."

Shelly reached out to touch the decoration but didn't answer Kari. Instead, she put her arms around Kari and drew her close. "Listen, honey, we're going to need to get going."

Kari groaned in response.

"Sue, would it really be okay if I drove your car home?"

"Sure. Do you still have the keys?" Sue asked.

"Yes, I do. And thank you so much. I put the boxes in the kitchen. Do you think you need help emptying them?"

"Naw." Sue waved her hand. "It will give me something to do."

"Well, thank you again. I can't tell you how much I appreciate your kind offer."

"No problem. Just bring the car back sometime tomorrow. My son promised he'd try hard to make it over so I can go see Jay."

"What time do you normally go and see him?"

"Around one. . .unless my son is busy with meetings. Then I go before dinner. But today is Christmas Eve, and I was hoping to be there all day and stay for the Christmas Eve celebration. The Sunday school teacher is coming today instead of tomorrow so he can be with his family."

"A Sunday school teacher comes to the Alzheimer's unit? That's incredible."

"It's an amazing thing to be a part of," Sue said. "When the leader starts to sing a hymn, they all join in and they remember Jesus. Oh boy, do they remember Him and all that He has done for them. They may not remember what room number they're in, but they haven't forgotten Jesus."

Shelly nodded, not sure what to say.

"Since your car is stuck, you could come join us for Christmas Eve service, if you like," Sue offered.

"Uh, no, thank you," Shelly hedged. "We don't normally go to church much anymore. And it's so busy at Christmastime. It's not worth getting all dressed up only to face the crowds."

"Oh. What do you do on Christmas?"

"We normally have dinner and, in the morning, open presents and then head over to either my or my husband's parents' place for dinner."

"That sounds like a nice way to celebrate Jesus' birth."

Shelly paused again. "We don't get into all of that. I mean, they can't prove that was His birthday and well. . .we just do presents and family."

"I see. It would be strange for me to not celebrate the whole reason we have Christmas. Times have changed so much." Sue pulled a star out from a box and moved over to put it on the top of the tree. "Jay had been gone longer than normal one year, and I missed him like crazy. It was close to Christmas, and I had finished reading about the birth of Jesus in the Bible. It struck me that night how a star led the people to the baby. I went and stood outside to gaze at all the stars God had created. It was a clear winter night, cold and brisk."

Sue adjusted the star until it stood straight. "Out of all those stars He picked one to lead people to the gift He had given to them—His Son." Sue stepped back to admire the tree. "And then I realized how both Jay and I were covered by the lights that sparkled in the sky. It brought me great comfort to know we shared a faith in the God who created those lights. So that year I gave him this star."

"That's a beautiful story," Shelly said. She was feeling anxious to get home.

"No matter how much Jay has forgotten, he hasn't forgotten the gift given to him through God's Son, Jesus, and I know it's because God promises to never let us go." Sue gave Kari and Shelly a smile.

"Well. . ." Shelly didn't know how to leave without being rude.

"Oh, listen to me babble on. I know you need to leave. Just bring the car back tomorrow."

"Thank you for everything, Sue. It's been a delight getting to know you."

"Oh yes, I loved meeting you two and hope I can get to know you even better." Sue gave Kari a hug.

Shelly glanced at the clock. *Brent isn't going to be home until late. What would it hurt if I brought Sue to see her husband? She's so generous and sweet. Then she could spend Christmas Eve with him. I can endure hearing some old Christmas hymns for a little bit.*

"Sue, my husband's not going to be home until late. So why don't I drive you over for the Christmas Eve service? So you can see Jay tonight?" Shelly offered.

"Really?" Sue's eyes were bright.

"Yes." Shelly nodded.

"Okay, if you're sure, let's go." Sue once again grabbed her coat and made a beeline to the garage door.

Shelly stood and watched her. *After all these years, she's still excited to see her husband, and he doesn't even remember her.*

"Come on, Mommy." Kari pulled at her hand.

Shelly gave her head a shake and followed her out the door.

The facility Jay stayed at was only about three blocks from where Sue lived.

"As spunky as you are, I'm surprised you didn't walk here earlier," Shelly commented.

"I wanted to, but I had surgery on my hip earlier this year, and I didn't want to risk slipping and falling again. I can't wait until you two meet Jay."

Kari climbed out of the car and waited beside Shelly's door. *How am I supposed to keep up with these two?*

The three of them entered through the automatic doors into a spacious foyer with a tall, beautifully decorated Christmas tree that stood beside a grand receptionist desk. Two ladies stood behind the desk. They called out a Christmas greeting to Sue.

"Merry Christmas to you, too!" Sue walked over to the counter. "These are my two new friends, Shelly and Kari. They were nice enough to drive me over to see my Jay."

"Nice to meet you. You're here just in time for the celebration. Did your son have trouble coming over the bridge because of the snow?" one of the ladies asked.

Sue nodded. "I'm so grateful these two volunteered to bring me. I missed Jay. Come on, girls."

Sue led them down a hallway that ended with double doors. She pushed some numbers in a keypad and the doors opened. "They have good security here," Sue commented before she made her way through the doors. They walked into what looked like a recreation room decorated for Christmas. Quite a few people sat around in a circle in regular chairs and some in wheelchairs. A young guy stood in the middle of the circle shaking hands with each person.

Sue took a quick look around and then pointed to a tall, bald man. He sat on a couch positioned on the outside of the circle facing a big window with a view of a beautiful garden bright with colored Christmas lights. "There he is."

It was obvious this man had been very handsome in his youth.

"Jay?"

The man continued to gaze at the view.

Sue sat down next to him on the couch and tapped his arm. "Jay?"

"Huh? Me?" Jay looked at her. He had beautiful big blue eyes.

"Yes, you. I'm Sue, your wife. Do you remember me today?"

"My wife?"

"Yes."

Shelly and Kari stood, watching the scene unfold.

"I wondered where my wife went. You're my wife?"

Sue chuckled. "Yes, I'm Sue. I've missed you today."

"You did?"

"Yes. I prayed and asked Jesus if He would make a way for me to visit you."

"Well, here you are." Jay said and glanced back out the window. "Is it Christmas?"

"Yes, it's Christmas Eve."

"Pretty decorations out there on those trees," Jay said.

Sue didn't answer but reached over and took hold of his hand. Jay looked down but didn't seem to mind and went back to admiring the scenery. Sue sat back on the couch and nodded at Shelly and Kari. She patted the space next to her, inviting them to come and sit.

Kari ran over and snuggled up to Sue. Shelly shook her head and found a comfortable chair to sit in. Tears made their way down her face. Sue seemed so content just sitting next to Jay holding his hand.

Music started playing. Shelly recognized the song from when she used to go to Christmas services. It brought a warm glow to her heart. *That's strange.*

Suddenly, Jay sat up straight and sang in a strong baritone voice word for word.

Shelly regarded him in surprise. *He remembers almost every word. And he has a beautiful voice. How does he remember?*

Sue's eyes were closed, and she was smiling.

Look at her appreciating this moment with him. Such a brief moment, but still. . .

Shelly watched the two. The love between them was something she rarely saw. But it was the joy she witnessed as they sang to their God, their Savior, that Shelly wanted—to be a part of that joy. She decided to join in the singing. Soon a smile played on her own lips.

I can feel the joy. I remember how it used to be when I worshipped Jesus. I remember. Why did we stop going to church to worship?

The songs were over, and a prayer was said. Shelly said a prayer of her own. *Lord, I never want to forget again about You. I want You to be a part of my life, my family's life. If there comes a day I don't remember those I love, please, let me always remember You.*

Shelly opened her eyes.

Jay looked over at Sue. "Hello, what's your name?"

"My name is Sue. I'm your wife."

"My wife? I wondered if I had a wife and where she went."

"I'm right here."

"Is it Christmas?"

"Yes, dear, it's Christmas."

Shelly gave a sad smile over the interaction between them. *Even though he doesn't remember, Lord, he taught me to remember. He taught me to remember You.*

Shelly stood and walked over to Jay. "Hi, Jay!" She held out her hand.

"Huh? Me?"

"Yep, you."

"Do I know you?"

"Nope. I'm Shelly, and I'm so glad to meet you. I will never forget you."

"Oh."

"You reminded me about the joy of worshipping Jesus."

"I did?"

"Yep, you did."

"What did I do?"

Shelly looked over at Sue and saw the twinkle in her eye. Kari climbed off the couch and moved over to Shelly, giving her a hug.

"I liked singing about baby Jesus," Kari said.

"So did I, honey. So did I." Shelly held her close.

Montana Starlight

SHARON BERNASH SMITH

Born to ride, Mackenzie Runyon loves all things on the ranch where she lives below the Bitterroot Mountains of Montana. Youngest in a family of four children, and the only girl, Mackenzie feels she never measures up to the boys—at least in her father's eyes.

Then, during a Christmas Eve snowstorm, she and her father share an event that draws them together and changes both.

Mackenzie, I've told you a hundred times to leave my stuff alone. What is it about the word *no* that you simply cannot understand?"

"I was just sitting on it for a minute. . .one stinkin' minute."

"I don't care how *long* you sat on it. The point is, I told you to stay *off* it entirely."

"Know what, Joel? You're the most selfish, meanest brother anybody could ever have. And so you know. . .I wish you *weren't* my brother." Ready to go into a big cry, she refused to let him see her do it.

"Just so *you* know, you little brat, I wish I wasn't your brother, either." He slammed his bedroom door.

"Fine!" she screamed and gave the door a hard kick with one boot. When her mother walked up, she could tell the entire fight had been overheard.

"Tell me, Mac, what were you and Joel fighting about this time?"

Mackenzie stared at the floor and said nothing.

"Were you sitting on his saddle again?" Her mother had a hold on one arm.

"Mom, I was on it for maybe fifteen seconds. He's so selfish." She was still fighting back tears.

Abby Runyon looked at her youngest offspring and sighed. "Mackenzie, in case you forgot, Joel gave you the very saddle you use every day."

"Yeah, only because he outgrew it." She chewed on her lower lip.

"He saved up all year to buy this roping saddle, and he's asked you to respect the fact that it's new. It's more the principle of the thing. Know what I'm saying?" Abby tugged her only daughter into a hug.

"Mom, but it's so beautiful, I only wanted to see what it felt like." Finally the tears flowed, and she let her mother console her.

"All you kids need to show each other more respect. Understand?"

"Yes," Mackenzie whispered.

"What was that?"

Mackenzie lifted her head and sniffed. "I said, yes, ma'am, I understand."

"Good—go wash your face. You'll feel better." Abby gave her another hug. "Love you, kid."

"Love you, too, Mom."

She did love her mother, and though she hated being the only girl in the family, she loved her older three brothers, as well. But being a girl *and* the baby was beyond cruel fate in her eight-year-old mind. Still upset, she walked into the bathroom, careful not to slam the door and risk more trouble.

Life on the Rocking R was good, but cattle ranching in Montana was not easy. Keeping the thousand-head herd alive and healthy this winter was turning out to be especially difficult. Beginning way back in October, one railing storm after another had swept down off the Bitterroot Mountains and into the valley where the Rocking R had stood for three generations. The hay supply from last season was being eaten faster than anticipated, which meant they'd most likely have to buy from someone else, cutting into their profit for the year.

This meant that everyone in the family, from the patriarch Tucker Runyon all the way down to Mackenzie, was needed to keep the family business going. Though the work was long and hard, cattle ranching was in their blood, and Mackenzie Runyon savored it all. . .*especially* the horses. . .and one favorite cattle dog named Chase.

The working dogs weren't supposed to be pets, but someone forgot to tell that to Chase, who'd adopted Mackenzie as his own the minute they laid eyes on each other.

Even though she could ride as well as any of her brothers, the recognition she craved from her dad, Jack, and Tucker Runyon, her grandpa, never seemed to come her way often enough. Oh, Grandma Runyon and her mom were more than enthusiastic for sure, but Mackenzie often felt she never measured up to the Runyon males.

In her quest for attention, more than once she'd done things that put her in harm's way. Last branding season, she'd cut a calf away from its mother, corralling it with the others waiting to be branded. She'd been really proud of the team she, the horse, and Chase had made, and dismounted to shut the gate. In that thirty seconds, she'd totally forgotten about the calf's mother. When it came charging, Mackenzie would have been crushed against the corral if Chase had not intervened, nipping the bovine's heels just in time to turn it away.

When it happened, Mackenzie thought no one saw, but her dad had seen it all. When he'd scolded her in front of the entire crew, her cheeks burned hot like the branding fire. Why couldn't he see how hard she tried? Why didn't he love her as much as the boys?

If the other females on the ranch ever felt slighted by the men who surrounded them, Mackenzie never heard it, so she kept her feelings of rejection inside. Occasionally, when things got really tough, she'd take a long ride around the land. It was in those quiet times she'd pray; for as deep as cattle ranching ran in the Runyons' blood, so did a profound faith.

"Lord, let my daddy see how hard I try."

The whole family was dressed and ready to go into town for Christmas Eve services at Bitterroot Baptist Church. The boys had helped the pastor build an elaborate Bethlehem "city" for the pageant this year and needed to be there early to finish setting up.

"Boys," Abby said, "we're running late, so grab those roast beef sandwiches I made. You can eat in the truck." She looked around. "Where's your sister?"

"Here, Mom, but I'm riding with Dad. He's still checkin' Miss Molly. Thinks she might foal tonight."

"It's about time. She's overdue, right?" Abby slid her wool coat on. "Okay, Mac, there's food here and hot coffee in that thermos near the stove for Dad." She kissed her daughter on the cheek, patting the top of her head. "See you later, kiddo. Is Dad going to let you name this one?"

"Yup."

"That's an honor."

Just then they heard the truck horn. Abby gave Mackenzie one last hug and opened the back door. "Well, well, it's snowing. . .sideways. Tell Dad to drive carefully." The door slammed behind her.

Mackenzie shivered from the cold blast but loaded up the sandwiches, coffee, and two cups into a plastic grocery bag before shrugging into her coat, hat, and barn boots.

She found her dad in the barn, hat off, scratching his head. "Dunno what's wrong with her this time, Mac. She should have foaled three days ago unless I've got the time wrong."

"Doc Adams said the same thing, Dad, remember?" Mackenzie walked over to the mare's stall and took in the sweet smell of fresh straw and alfalfa hay. "How ya doin', Miss Molly?" she whispered. Her heart skipped a beat every time she looked at her prized horse.

The mare turned her head at the sound of Mackenzie's voice and nickered low in response. Their special connection ran both directions. When Mackenzie could barely walk, this quarter horse mare followed her around like a pup. From the moment she sat on Miss Molly's back, Mackenzie claimed the chestnut beauty as her own.

She entered the stall and began running her hands down the horse's neck with a gentle touch, then moved back to stroke her straining belly. She frowned. "Dad, maybe this foal is just too big for Miss Molly to push out."

Jack Runyon stepped inside with his daughter. "I was thinking the same thing, Mac. Might have to get the doc out here."

"Just so you know, it's snowing like crazy."

"Better get him on the phone right now, then." He left the stall to use a wall phone near the barn door. After punching in the numbers, he waited and then left a message when the answering machine picked up at the other end.

He winked at his daughter. "No telling when he'll be home. For sure, I'm going to need some help if he can't get here in time."

Mackenzie felt her heart quicken at the thought of being able to assist in a foaling. Until her dad said something else.

"Hope Joel and the others get back here in time in case I have to pull the foal."

Miss Molly whinnied loudly. Several other horses answered back.

Jack went back into the stall. "What are you trying to tell me, girl?" He rubbed the blaze on her forehead. "I'll do my best to help. . .I promise. Mac, get some oats, and let's see if she'll eat some. She needs the energy."

Mackenzie did what she was told, but the laboring mare wouldn't eat a thing.

"Looks like we're in for a long night," Jack said, giving the horse a couple of reassuring pats as he left the stall. "Do you mind missing the Christmas pageant, Mac?"

"Naw. I'm kind of old for that anyway, Dad."

"Oh, 'cuz now you're eight, you mean?" He laughed and grabbed a sandwich from the bag. Pouring the steaming coffee into one of the mugs, he looked at his daughter. When she met his gaze with tears, he winced. "Come on, Mac, I was only teasing."

"Daddy, I *am* eight, so that for sure means I'm not a baby."

Jack shoved the last bite of dinner in his mouth and pulled Mackenzie into his lap on top of a straw bale. "Come on now, sweetheart. You'll always be my baby." He kissed the top of her head.

"Daddy, you don't get it."

She had more to say, but a loud noise from Miss Molly's stall brought both of them to their feet and running.

The mare was trying to stand, struggling in obvious distress.

"Mackenzie, grab a lead rope, and let's see if we can get her up. Walking around will help move things along."

They'd been walking for nearly two hours when the phone rang. "Get that, will you, Mac?"

She ran, grabbing it on the third ring. It was Doc Adams. "Tell your dad I was on my way but slid into a ditch on Gray Stone Road, a little past the Simpsons' place. Lucky I made it to their house. Sorry about this, Mac, but Jack knows what to do. Remind him to keep the foal warm, 'cuz it's sure cold enough to freeze anything. Okay?"

Mackenzie began to shake. . .and not from the cold. "Okay." She stretched to hang up the phone.

"Who was it?" Jack asked.

"Doc Adams."

"And?"

"He ran off the road by the Simpsons' place on the way over here."

"Rats!"

"He said it's snowing so hard he can't make it. Said you'd know what to do, though, Daddy." She started to move away from the phone when it rang again. "Maybe that's Doc sayin' he's found a way to make it through. Hello?"

"Mackenzie, it's Mom."

"Mom, where are you?"

"Still in town. . .at the church. Looks like we're stuck until this blizzard lets up. Tell Dad, would you?"

"Yeah. We're in the barn with Miss Molly." She exhaled a deep breath. "She's in a bad way."

There was a pause, then Abby said, "Oh, Mac, try not to worry. Dad's been through this before. . .lots of times. You know that."

Silence.

"Mackenzie, are you there. . .hello?"

"I'm here, Mom, but Dad was counting on the boys to help him in case he has to pull the baby." She was choking back tears of fright.

"I know how much that little mare means to you, Mackenzie. Be brave now. There are lots of people stuck here at the church with us, so we'll all be praying. Okay?"

"Sure, Mom, I'll be fine. It's just. . ." She sighed. "I love her so much."

"I know, baby; she's your first horse. Listen, Mac, God gave you that sweet thing; He knows how much you love her. You can do this, Mackenzie. . .you're a Runyon. Remember that!"

"I know, Mom. . .love you."

"Love you, too, Mac. Oh, and merry Christmas."

"Bye, Mom." Mackenzie turned from the phone, trying to be brave. She walked back to her dad. "Mom and the boys are stuck in town."

"Looks like it's just you and me, kid."

She swallowed hard, her voice barely a whisper. "I'm really scared, Dad. Miss Molly is so special. What if something bad happens to her?"

"Mackenzie Runyon, have you no confidence in me?" He looked in her direction.

"I do, but—"

"Then let's keep walking."

They took a couple of more turns around the barn before the mare refused to budge. They had to pull and coax her into the closest stall. Immediately she strained while a huge contraction racked her body from head to toe, her eyes bulging with the effort. When the contraction passed, she laid down with a loud grunt.

Jack checked to see if she was making any progress for delivery. "Mac, I don't see any sign of the baby. I need to check her. . .get me a glove."

"'Kay." She ran across the barn, got an examination glove from a cupboard, and hurried back.

Jack slipped his arm into the vinyl and waited while another pain racked the mare's tiring body stretched out on the floor. "Come on, little girl, you can do this," he crooned.

Miss Molly lifted her head in response and gave a pathetic nicker.

Jack's eyes were soft as he looked at the horse, then Mackenzie. "Let's pray, Mac. Lord, give me wisdom to help Miss Molly. You gave her to us; You know how much she means to this family. . .especially Mac."

The prayer was broken by Mackenzie's sobs. "God, please don't let Miss Molly die. . .'cuz. . ." Her voice cracked. ". . .'cuz I love her so much." She bent down and whispered something into the mare's right ear, causing her to relax.

"Mac, I don't know what you said, but when she relaxed, something shifted. I can actually see two feet now." He quickly looped a rope around both of them and made a knot. "I couldn't do this without you, Mac. . .keep talking." He looked up. "By the way, what are you saying anyway?"

"I'm singing, actually."

"What'd you say?"

"I said, I'm singing."

Jack smiled, waiting for the next contraction. "And what are you singing?"

"The same song I always sing when I'm with her. 'Twinkle, Twinkle, Little Star.'" She glanced at her dad. "She loves it."

Just then Miss Molly began to strain. While she pushed, he pulled. In a few seconds, he saw a dark muzzle. "Okay, Mac, keep on singing. I can see the baby's head now."

She began to sing louder. "Twinkle, twinkle, little star, how I wonder what you are."

"Good job, good job, Mac. Keep singing." He pulled as hard as he could, straining against the weight and size of the foal.

"Up above the world so high, like a diamond in the sky. . ." Her voice went higher with each word, quavering with emotion as she watched her dad trying to deliver Miss Molly's oversized baby. "Daddy, can I come down where you are?"

"Yup, get down here and help me pull. . .hurry."

She ran to join her dad, placing both hands above his, and pulled with all her might. Miss Molly grunted and groaned with the strain. "That's my good girl," Jack crooned. "Atta girl. . .keep pulling, Mac."

In a big whoosh of water, Miss Molly's very large foal slipped out and hit the ground, creating a misty steam.

It didn't move.

"Daddy!" Mac moaned. "Daddy, it's dead. I know it's dead." Her face went pale, and she shook all over.

Jack jumped into action. Removing his coat, he began to rub the newborn vigorously. No response.

Mac was still kneeling beside her dad, silent tears flowing down both cheeks. She turned her eyes away. Without a word, she moved to squat next to Miss Molly's head. She stroked the lathered horse's neck, while watching her dad trying to breathe life into the baby's nostrils. She was about to look away again when a slight flicker of movement caught her eye.

She stood, breathless. "Daddy, tell me. . .is it alive?" The mare was struggling to stand, and Mac jumped out of her way. Once on her feet, Miss Molly shook herself and whinnied.

The animal on the ground sneezed. "She's breathing, Mac!" Jack shouted. "She's breathing."

"She? Miss Molly has a filly?"

"Yup, and she's a beauty. Come look."

Mackenzie was in awe. She couldn't believe it. The filly was the exact image of its mother, even down to the white blaze splotch in the middle of her forehead. Miss Molly was nuzzling the newborn, seeming none the worse for wear.

Mackenzie smiled with pride and relief. "Look, Miss Molly, you have a sweet little filly. Do you love her, do ya?" She was grinning from ear to ear.

Jack Runyon, a rough, tough cowboy, was moved to tears. Stepping closer to Mackenzie, he lifted her chin. He put out his arms, and she jumped into them with a squeal.

"Thank you, Daddy, thank you, thank you. I love you so much." She squeezed her dad's neck as hard as she could.

"Thank *you*, Mackenzie Jane. I couldn't have done it without you."

"Really?" She pulled back to gaze in his eyes.

"Absolutely. You stayed focused and kept Miss Molly calm. That was key for sure."

"And. . .don't forget I helped you pull."

He chuckled. "No way will I forget, Mac. Don't worry."

"Daddy?"

"Mmm?" Jack was enjoying the sweetness of holding Mackenzie in his arms. *When did she get so big?*

"Nothing."

Jack knew she had more to say. He set her on the floor. "Tell me, sweetheart, what is it?"

She looked down at the floor and moved some straw around with the toe of one boot. "Well, sometimes. . .sometimes I think the boys are more important."

"More important than who?"

She gazed up into his face, and he saw tears forming. Mac's voice lowered to a whisper. "More important than me."

Jack was stunned. A lump formed in his throat. "Mackenzie." He reached for his daughter's hand. "When your mom and I found out we were having a girl after three boys, we were thrilled."

"Both of you?"

"Especially *me*." He pulled her next to him on another straw bale. "See, you know I had two little sisters, right?"

"Aunt Cathy and Aunt Julie, right?"

"Right. I loved being their protector. . .made me feel special, I guess. When your brothers were born, your mom and I celebrated each of them. But we were so ready for a girl the fourth time. When God gave us you, we were over-the-mountain happy." He bent to kiss the top of her head.

She was silent a moment. "Sometimes it feels you think more of them because they're tougher than me...you know, better at doing stuff around here."

Jack threw back his head and laughed. "Mac, that's just because they're older and bigger than you. But, truth is, you're about the toughest Runyon on this ranch. Even your granddad thinks so."

Mac blinked, as if startled.

"I guess I'm so busy all the time, Mackenzie, that I don't take the time to tell you how valuable you are."

"Daddy, I never knew you felt that way." She scooted closer and laid her head against him.

"I promise from now on, I'm going to take the time to make sure you know exactly how I feel about you. How's that?"

"That'd be fine with me," she said. "Let's check on Miss Molly."

They found the mare busy nuzzling her offspring, inspecting every inch of her.

"Look, Dad, the filly's on her feet. That means she's a strong one. Wow, she's big. Oh, I love her already...she's so precious."

Jack checked both horses from head to stern. "Looks like they'll both be fine." He left after checking their water supply.

Mac blew them a kiss.

"Hey, little missy, do you realize it's after midnight?" Jack smiled.

"Really? Boy, and I'm not even tired."

"Well then, how about you and I go back to the house and have us a little *Christmas* snack?"

"Christmas! Wow, it's Christmas. I forgot." She laughed out loud. "Oh, Daddy, this is the best day of my life...ever."

Jack rolled back the huge barn door and whistled. "It looks like a Christmas card out here, Mac."

The snowstorm was over and all the clouds had passed, revealing the night sky dancing with the brilliance of winter's moon, surrounded by millions of stars. The snow-covered ground was alive with undulating light.

"It's all so beautiful, isn't it, Daddy?" she whispered. "Do you think this is how the sky looked when Jesus was born?"

"Could have been, Mac, could have been."

Mackenzie fell onto her back and made a snow angel, laughing the entire time. "I feel like I could actually walk *between* the stars." She whispered, "Sure wish I could count them all. Don't you, Daddy?"

"I wonder how long that would take? Guess only God knows," he said, then fell down beside his daughter and made his own angel. They lay there in silence for a minute.

Lord, help me to be the father this little girl needs. . .forever.

He stood and helped Mac to her feet. "Remember, Mackenzie, you get to name Miss Molly's foal. Got any ideas yet?"

She peered up into the midnight sky, then at him. "Well, I'm thinking Montana Starlight would be good. I could call her Starlight for short, or maybe even just Star."

Jack took her hand, gave it a squeeze, and headed for the house. "I think Montana Starlight is perfect. . .just like you, cowgirl."

Though snow had sneaked down into both barn boots and she couldn't feel her face in the cold, Mackenzie Runyon's heart was filled with warmth and absolute comfort. It was good to be a Runyon. "Daddy?"

"Yeah, Mac?"

"I'm glad to be your daughter."

"And I'm glad to be your dad, Mackenzie." He gave her hand another squeeze. "Oh, and merry Christmas."

She looked up at him again and smiled. "Merry Christmas, Daddy."

Is It True?

Linda J. Reinhardt

When young Ashley is told by someone at school that there is no Santa Claus, she insists this cannot be true.

To Ashley Jacobsen, who graduated to Santa's assistant.

December 1

D*ear Diary,*

Santa is real, isn't he?

Abigail can be so mean and say such nasty things! Today at recess she told me Santa Claus wasn't real! She laughed at me when I said, "Nu-ah!"

How can she say something like that?

Ashley closed her diary when she heard her little sister, Lindsey, coming down the hallway to their bedroom. Lindsey was just learning to read and liked to look over Ashley's shoulder to try to read what Ashley had written—out loud! *Annoying.* Ashley scrambled to tuck the journal underneath her mattress, then grabbed her library book and sat back against her pillows before Lindsey entered the room.

"Whatcha doin'?" Lindsey climbed onto Ashley's bed. Ashley scooted over, knowing it was no use telling her to get down until she had a chance to try to read from the library book. Ashley put the book in front of Lindsey and tried not to be impatient while she struggled over words that Ashley found simple.

After a few sentences, Ashley had enough of being patient and pulled the book back.

"Hey, I'm not done," Lindsey complained.

"Sorry, but I have to turn this in tomorrow, and I want to finish it." Ashley buried her nose back in the book. Lindsey scooted off the bed to go find her own book to read. Ashley found herself struggling even to read one sentence.

Santa Claus isn't real. The words went through her head over and over again. Tears came to her eyes. *How can Santa not be real? Who reads my letters? And hello. . .why would there be so many helpers every Christmas at the mall getting kids' Christmas orders? Of course Santa Claus is real.*

"Girls! It's time for dinner," her mom called from the other room. "Wash your hands and come to the table."

During dinner, Ashley didn't feel like eating much or being a part of the conversation. Her mom and dad asked if she was feeling well. She only nodded.

As soon as she cleared the table, Ashley went back to her room to get her pajamas on before watching the movie her dad had brought home.

A gentle knock sounded at her door. "Ashley?" It was her mom.

"Yeah," Ashley answered as she pulled her pajama top over her head.

"Can I come in?" Her mom opened the door a bit and peeked into the room.

"Yeah." Ashley shrugged.

"Hey, is something wrong?" Her mom sat on her bed and patted the spot next to her for Ashley to join her.

Ashley sat and scooted close to her mom.

"Do you want to talk about it?"

"I'm just upset at Abigail."

"Abigail? What did she do?"

"She said there is no such thing as Santa Claus, and when I said there is too, she laughed at me." Ashley focused on her mom's face. "Why would she say something like that about Santa Claus?"

"Not everyone believes in Santa Claus, honey. . ." her mom started.

"You do, right?" Ashley asked.

Her mom took a deep breath and blew it out very slowly.

"Mom, you believe in him, right? Santa Claus is real, right?"

"Ashley, Santa Claus is real in a sense."

"Huh?"

Her mom closed her eyes.

"Mom, is he real or not?"

Her mom shook her head and then put her arm around Ashley's shoulder.

Ashley jumped off the bed. "What? Santa Claus isn't real?" Her mom put her finger to her lips with a *shhh*. "Mom, how can he *not* be real? What do you mean he isn't real? Who reads my letters? And who brings me toys on Christmas Day?" Tears poured from Ashley's eyes. She loved Santa Claus.

"Santa Claus is your daddy and me."

"You and Dad are Santa Claus?!"

Her mom nodded.

"Why would you do that? Why pretend like that? I love Santa Claus." Ashley collapsed in a heap on the floor, unable to hold back tears. "I can't believe Santa Claus isn't real."

"I'm so sorry, Ashley. It's not that he isn't real. It's that he is me and your dad. Every parent is a Santa Claus to their children, ever since this man who lived a long time ago named Saint Nicholas died. Parents took over the job for him."

"But what about the elves and going to bed early so Santa Claus will come and how I have to be nice? And why did I have to visit those Santas at the mall and tell them what I wanted for Christmas?" Ashley wiped at her nose with her sleeve.

Her mom frowned and pulled a tissue from the box on her nightstand. "It's all part of the fun, honey. You had a great time doing all those things, didn't you?"

"Yeah, I guess, except going to bed early on Christmas Eve and trying to go to sleep so he would come to our house. That was hard because I was so excited about him coming." Ashley tucked her knees up under her chin to her chest and laid her head down on them.

Her mom scooted off the bed and onto the floor next to Ashley.

"Ashley, everyone discovers there isn't a Santa Claus who flies around the world in a sleigh and delivers toys to every boy and girl on Christmas Eve."

"I can't believe it's not true," Ashley wailed.

"Yes, but in a sense it is true. See, long, long ago. . ."

Ashley's dad popped his head in the door. "Honey, are you two coming to watch the movie?" He gave a questioning look when he saw Ashley crying. "Hey, what's going on in here?"

"Mom told me there isn't a Santa Claus." Ashley sniffed.

"Ohhh." Her dad nodded. "Lindsey and I will watch the movie, and you two can keep talking." He disappeared, then popped his head back in the door. "I love you, Ashley."

Ashley gave him a half smile, and he left quickly to rejoin Lindsey in the living room.

"As I was saying, there was a man who lived a long time ago. We call him Saint Nicholas. He was a toymaker. There was an orphanage in the town where he lived, and the children were very poor. Christmas was very important to the toymaker, because he appreciated the gift God had given him through Jesus and how much God had blessed his life. He wanted to be an example to others of how good God is. So he went over to the orphanage and talked to the director of the place. He got permission to talk to each of the boys and girls. He made a note of what each child really wanted. Then he went back to his toy factory and, during the month of December, made toys for each of the boys and girls."

"Mom, is this really a true story, or are you making this up?" Ashley's lips pouted.

Her mom squeezed her close and continued with her story. "On Christmas Eve, Nicholas, the toymaker, went to the orphanage after all the kids were asleep. The director let him in, and they put presents for each of the boys and girls under the Christmas tree. The director was sworn to secrecy about who brought the presents.

"The next morning the children awoke to a wonderful surprise. News traveled about this wonderful thing that had happened at the orphanage. The next year he did the same thing, but not to just one orphanage. Each year he added more and more to his list. Each person who ran the orphanages kept his secret. They'd help him by getting a list of what each child wanted for Christmas, and then he would make the toys and drop them off at the orphanages. He also talked to parents of families who weren't very well off, and he would drop presents off at their doorsteps, too. Soon people all around the area, and later all around the world, were leaving gifts for children after they fell asleep at night on Christmas Eve.

"After he died, those who had helped him give gifts to the children kept up the tradition each year so no one would be disappointed. When your daddy and I were young, there came a day we learned about Santa, and we graduated to be Santa's assistant. And now your daddy and I keep up the tradition so our own children won't be disappointed. Just think—it all started because Santa Claus was grateful for the gift God had given through His Son, Jesus. He wanted to bless others, and it just went on and on from there."

"So does that mean I graduated?"

"Yep, you have now graduated to be Santa's assistant. You get to keep the tradition going and bless someone else."

"But who does your Santa Claus presents? You and Dad still get them on Christmas morning."

"Your dad and I buy each other a special Santa present each year. Just like we will continue to buy yours, because you are so special to us and we want to continue to bless you."

"Mom, since you take care of me and Lindsey, can I pick anyone I want to be a Santa Claus to?"

"Yeah, I suppose." Her mom gave her a big hug. "Are you okay now?"

"Well, sort of. I have to get used to the idea that Santa isn't who I thought he was. But yeah, I think I'll be okay." Ashley stood and stretched. "I'm tired now. I think I'll go to bed."

"Oh. Okay." Her mom stood and gave her another hug. "Don't forget to brush your teeth. Sweet dreams. I'll see you in the morning."

After Ashley brushed her teeth, she made sure Lindsey was still involved in the movie before she pulled her diary out from underneath her mattress. She clicked her lamp on and plopped herself onto her bed.

Dear Diary,

It's true! I mean, it's not true. Santa isn't true. It's all just a tradition because of some guy who made toys years and years ago then gave them to an orphanage after the children went to sleep at night. But now that I know the truth, the tradition is that I am now Santa's helper and I'm supposed to pass the tradition on. I want to find the perfect person to sneak a gift to on Christmas Eve. Not sure who it will be, but I want to make the person super happy because the toymaker did all this over being grateful for God's gift to us through Jesus. Well, I'm grateful for Jesus, so I'm gonna pass it on. Cool, huh? It will take awhile for me to get used to the idea that Santa is all make-believe, but I think I kind of like the real story better. It makes more sense, and now. . .I get to pass it on.

This might be the best Christmas ever. I wonder if Abigail knows all of this information?

Maybe we can find someone to give gifts to TOGETHER. That would be so much fun. Just like God gave us the best gift ever, I'm gonna pass it on.

Night.

Ashley tucked her diary under her pillow, clicked off her lamp, and rolled over to sleep.

Every Living Creature

ROSANNE CROFT

Some people just care more than others. Eve and Marie care about the lowest of the low, creatures scorned and forgotten. . .perhaps because they feel the same way themselves. Along the way, miracles occur, and kindness and goodness reign on a little porch, where the lost are found and loved.

Compassion is the closest you'll ever come to perfection in this world.
—Pastor Steve McPherson

Eve lifted the artificial Christmas tree from its box and put it in the familiar corner of the living room where she'd always had it. Sifting through tissue-wrapped ornaments, she came upon her favorite cat-themed decorations. Her daughters had bought them for her, the ultimate cat lover. She sighed. At least her family understood her. Some of her neighbors and many longtime friends thought she was a peculiar eccentric, feeding feral cats. She didn't care; she was far too concerned with the needs of those wild cats.

It was Eve's privilege to love the unloved, the wild, stray felines on the edge of despair. She provided a place they could eat for free. Over the years, she'd tamed several cats and taken them in as family, paying vet bills and setting up a hotel of sorts in her garage. One of these was a cat named Penny, a black-and-white longhaired grimalkin who, though once feral herself, now ruled as Queen of the House and Garage.

Like Adam in Genesis, she loved to name animals. She named each of the wild ones and knew their personalities. Last night, she'd seen the scruffy Maximillian, with his distinctive swagger and confident manner of eating. He knew he was the King Alley Cat. Then there was Ollie, a marmalade stripe. Tux always showed up last, looking for dinner at midnight in his black-and-white tuxedo. Each night, the drama unfolded and Eve stepped in, hoping and praying for each and every living creature she came to know.

Her daughter Marie called from the front door, "She's here today again, Mom. Remember that little gray cat from last week? She's hanging around the front yard in broad daylight!"

Eve rushed to the door in time to see a silvery cat flit between the bushes and the front porch. Opening the screen door and holding it with her foot, Eve set a bowl of food down on the porch. She closed the door and watched as the gray cat stared from the bushes. Finally, it crept over and began to eat, crunching the dry chow noisily.

"She has to belong to someone, Marie. Look at that collar. They must've really loved her to give her that."

A red velvet collar shook on the cat's skinny neck like a hula hoop with room to spare. Hanging from it was a brass tag, with engraved information to return the cat to her home. But trying to capture this wild thing to read the tag was impossible. She ran and hid every time they moved.

"We need to lure her inside so we can look at that tag," Marie mused. "She's so skinny that the collar might come off before we can read it."

"I can try it," her mother said.

Marie looked at the clock. "I'd help you, but I have to get to work. I've got poinsettias to pick up and deliver all over town by tonight. Can you believe it's the day before Christmas Eve?" She owned a plant business, and December added more deliveries to her already busy schedule.

Marie left through the side door to the garage so she wouldn't disturb the tiny cat but forgot her keys. Going all the way back in to get them, Marie left the door to the garage slightly open. It took only that split second for their cat, Penny, to glide mischievously into the house.

Eve didn't notice Queen Penny. She gazed lovingly at the cat on her porch. Blasts of wind the day before had blown in masses of cold air, stirring up the two-month-old leaves around the porch. Snow was imminent; the sky shone white and heavy with still air. At least it would come and cover the ugly brown deadness of early winter.

A white Christmas would be wonderful. But what would this young cat do? As thin as she was, a snowstorm could be her death. Eve knew she must catch her today. She knelt and opened the door a crack. Her arthritic knees complained, but Eve hardly felt the pain.

"Come on inside," coaxed Eve. "We'll help you find your home. You've been lost for a long time, haven't you?"

The cat's eyes locked on to Eve's. In those green eyes she saw a reflection of the labyrinth the gangly kitten had been lost in, a tangle of pain, loss, and hunger. Constant fear had changed her from a pampered princess to a homeless wreck. "It could happen to anybody," Eve told the cat, "being homeless."

A burning question hovered in the air between them. "Can I trust you?" the cat seemed to ask.

Eve understood cats in an uncanny way. "You can trust us. We love cats like you. You need to come inside."

With slow motion steps, moving each paw gingerly, the cat came nearer. Eve spoke to her softly. She hoped her knees wouldn't freeze in this position and she'd be able to hold the door steady until the cat was all the way inside. The scrawny skin-and-bones with a fancy collar crept forward until she was inside the warm house. Eve closed the door softly with a triumphant smile.

Suddenly, there was a caterwaul equal only to the Queen herself, Penny. Her tail making switchbacks in the air, Penny hissed and growled at the gray cat. Startled, and seeing no way out now that the door was shut, the new cat zigzagged from the kitchen into the family room. She disappeared between a bookcase and the wall, pinching herself to get through. Penny followed, meowing wildly, her eyes flashing with jealousy.

"Penny!" Eve scolded. "What an ungrateful cat you are! You were a stray once. How dare you act like this?"

Penny looked at her with a guilty eye, the other on the bookcase. Then she licked her paws nonchalantly, as if she was innocent of any wrongdoing. Eve picked her up and put her into the garage, locking the door behind her. "You need to stay out here until you learn some manners." But the damage was done.

A whimpering came from behind the bookcase. "I'm sorry, little one," Eve soothed. "It's only Penny. She's jealous. We're going to find your owner. You're going home! But you'll have to come out of there first."

This time, no amount of encouragement could entice the cat to come out. Eve prayed as she knelt to remove the heavy books from the bookcase. "Lord, You care about every living creature. This little cat needs to find her home. Please help me get her out." Eve's knees hurt worse than ever, and she despaired of getting back up off the ground a second time.

Just then Marie popped back inside the house. "I forgot my lunch. . ." she started to say, then saw her mother peering behind the bookcase from the floor. "Mom? What're you doing?"

Eve just pointed, and Marie squinted behind the bookcase at two almond eyes, glinting in the semidarkness. "How'd you get her in the house so fast?"

"She *longed* to come inside. I just talked her into trusting us. "

"You sure can speak their language, Mom."

"If I really could, I would've had her out of there by now." Eve laughed. "Penny chased her off, and she was so scared, she hid back here!"

"Sorry. Penny must've come inside when I left."

"Do you have enough time to help me?"

Marie nodded, and the two of them removed a set of 1965 Britannicas, several years' worth of *National Geographic* magazines, and a shelf of old nursing books from Eve's college days. They moved the bookcase out, making some room to retrieve the cat, who remained in a squished position at the back wall.

"I'll get her out." Marie took garden gloves out of her bag. "Protection against those little needle claws." Reaching her hand in, she scooped up the shaking cat, who cried pitifully.

"Write this down, Mom!" Marie said as she held on to the struggling cat.

Eve grabbed the first piece of paper and pencil she could find as the cat began to fight against the gloved hands that held her.

"Louise Brewer, 246-0122. The cat's name is Peanut. Ow!" Marie dropped Peanut and looked at her scratched arm. Peanut leaped toward the Christmas tree.

"No! Not there!" Eve shouted, but it was too late. The cat squeezed herself in the corner behind the tree, trying to hide behind the boxes of ornaments and the few wrapped presents there.

"Hope we find her home. She's too wild for us to keep!" said Marie.

Eve nodded. "Put something on those scratches, and I'll call the owner."

The doorbell rang, and there stood Louise Brewer, who they guessed was about Eve's age. She was taller, though, and elegantly dressed in flowing clothes. Her hair was arranged neatly, and she wore high heels.

"Where is she? Where's Peanut?" Louise clucked like a mother hen. "She ran away when my husband and I moved here four months ago. I thought I'd never see her again."

"Don't worry. Peanut's fine. She's right over here," Eve said calmly.

The woman continued, "We're retired. My husband was in the air force, and we came from France. We brought our cat, Peanut's mama. Zella and Peanut were playing on the balcony of our new apartment. I looked out a minute later, and Peanut was gone."

Marie pointed. "She's behind the Christmas tree."

Louise smiled when she spotted the green eyes gazing at her. "It's you, Peanut! I can't believe you survived. I'm here to take you home, little Peanut. Come out now."

Upon hearing the voice of her master, Peanut rushed out, scattering ornaments. She sprang into the waiting arms of her owner, the one she'd known since birth, before she'd jumped from the balcony into a cruel, confusing world. Eve and Marie noticed that her tiny face looked completely relieved. All previous despair was gone. Peanut would be home for Christmas!

"Kettle's ready. Would you like a cup of Christmas tea?" Eve asked Louise as she cradled Peanut.

"That would be wonderful! I can't tell you how grateful I am," Louise began, "for your kindness to my lost kitty. She's so thin. I'm sure she would've starved soon. But now she's going home, and it's all because you stopped your busy lives and took time out to save her."

Eve laughed as she poured the hot water into mugs for tea. "I don't have a busy life, dear. But my daughter does, and she was a lot of help."

"What can I do to repay you?" Louise asked.

Eve and Marie looked at each other. "It's a way of life for us. You don't need to thank us. We take care of cats because we love them."

Louise glanced at the unopened mail on the table. "I see you give to a lot of charities."

Eve smiled. "I have special causes that I give to. Mostly veterans and poor children. And animals, of course."

"Well, I'm sure glad you cared about Peanut."

"We fed her off and on for a few months, I guess," Eve said.

"You feed wild cats?"

Eve nodded. "Every living creature is a miracle."

Louise opened her purse. "For your miracles!" She drew out a hundred-dollar bill.

Eve, a pensioner on a budget, looked aghast. "Don't be silly. We can't take that."

Louise cuddled Peanut. "It's worth every cent to have Peanut back. I hope it makes your Christmas a little brighter, too." She sipped the rest of her tea and stood. "You two are angels. My husband and Zella will be so happy! Good-bye—and thanks again."

Even now, each night a trickle of lost cats approachs the house on Brittany Drive. The wild ones know that goodness reigns on that porch.

Until the day Eve died of cancer, she fed them faithfully. Marie continues in her sad absence. And at least one small cat found her way back home at Christmas, because of kindness wrought in the heart of God.

Santa Saves Christmas

Yasuko Hirata
Edited by Sharon Bernash Smith

The possibility of having a merry Christmas looks impossible to a nine-year-old girl living in the desert of California. But, after sharing her heart's desire with a visiting "Santa" at school, her faith in the kindness of strangers is renewed and strengthened for a lifetime.

This is a true story.

❧

I grew up in what was considered a low-income family, yet we managed to get by. My mother, for most of my childhood, worked as a server at a local Denny's, often the graveyard shift. Sometimes she pulled double shifts to support her four children.

Although we never had the latest fashion trends or fancy playthings, we did have knock-off toys and food to eat.

The Christmas I was in the third grade, I asked my mother when we'd be picking up the Christmas tree. After all, Santa would need a place to put presents, I reminded her. My clearly stressed mother simply said we weren't having a tree because there wasn't money for one.

I wondered how, without a tree, would we have Christmas? We already didn't have a chimney, no snow because we lived in the desert, and to make it worse, no holiday lights. I felt in my heart as if Christmas would never happen that year.

A few days later at the school Christmas party, Santa Claus stopped by and asked everyone to write down on a piece of paper what they wanted for Christmas.

I'm sure plenty of children asked for dolls and trucks. Me? I only wanted a Christmas tree. To make sure that Santa knew where I lived, I even wrote down my address.

When I got home, my older sister asked me who I'd met that day. *Hmm*, I thought, *that's a funny question*. But once inside, I knew why she'd asked it. I was speechless!

There, in the corner of our living room, stood the most beautiful Christmas tree I'd ever seen. Lush and green, it filled the entire house with its tangy fragrance. It was the smell of a real holiday. At the age when most children stopped believing in a jolly old elf and started wishing on stars, I was overwhelmed by the kindness of my own special Santa.

Now, with children of my own, my eyes still fill with tears at the sweet memory of how a total stranger made the wishes of one little girl come true, restoring the marvelous wonder of Christmas forever. (It's my favorite holiday.) I would love to know if *he* remembers, because, thanks to him, I learned to pass it forward.

I'd like to thank all those who make a difference by sacrificing their time and resources to give others a chance to have a memory like mine. Merry Christmas, everyone!

Rose Chintz Reveries

SHARON BERNASH SMITH

Sarah finds grieving hard work when dealing with the loss of a lifelong friend shortly before Christmas. Her memories are both sweet. . .and haunting.

But a dusty attic, laden with the lingering aromas of the sea, will soon become a place of healing when it reveals an unexpected treasure.

Based on true happenings from a special friend, and elegant memories of rose chintz.

❧

Maybe if we got out of town for a couple of days, you'd feel better, Sarah." Ian Carmichael took his wife's hand and pressed it to his chest. "She wouldn't want you moping around, you know."

His wife looked up at him, then turned her head to the window. It was raining. "Mary Ellen loved the rain. Did I ever tell you that? Said it reminded her of Ireland." Walking closer to the window, Sarah traced a raindrop down the glass pane until it disappeared into the puddle on the outside sill.

She whispered to the glass, "I know she wouldn't want me to be this sad, Ian, but my heart won't listen to reason. I can't seem to give up one moment of it." Taking a hanky from a sweater pocket, she wiped at both eyes, turning to smile at her husband. "You're so sweet to think of getting away. I'm thinking the beach might be good. We could check out some shops in Seaside and have clam chowder at that place on the corner you love so much."

"Seaside—are you sure?" He peered at her over his glasses. "What about all the memories?"

"You mean, because Mary Ellen used to live there? I'm finding the idea comforting right now, actually."

"Okay, Seaside it is."

"Let's just plan on spending one night, though; I've got so much Christmas stuff left to do. Would that be all right with you?"

"Perfect. Let me call the kids and see if they can keep the dog. You go pack."

They left early the next morning for the drive to the Oregon coast. It rained early on, but as they left the outskirts of Portland on Highway 30, the sun came out. When they were in sight of the Columbia River, dancing highlights sparkled across it like Christmas lights. Sarah found it uplifting.

"I never get tired of this drive," Ian said. "Makes me feel like a kid."

"Me, too." *Mary Ellen used to make me feel like that. . .a very special kid.* They'd met right before Sarah started seventh grade. . . .

Word spread quickly around the neighborhood that a new family had moved into the Lamonts' old place. "Some girl and two littler brothers," the news was.

Since the entire block was filled with boys, Sarah was really interested in that *one* girl. "How old does she look?"

"'Bout your age, I guess." Sarah's brother, James, kept good tabs on the neighborhood's comings and goings. "And guess what, Sarah?"

"What?"

"She's got the same wild red hair you do."

"Really?"

"Yeah, now there'll be two of you to make fun of." He laughed like only an irritating older brother could.

"Shut up, you big fat"—she tried to think of something really mean—"butter squash."

James threw himself on the ground, laughing. "Sarah, no matter how hard you try, you can't say anything bad. Gotta love a kid like you, even if you are my little sister."

James always made her laugh. . .and she joined him. She couldn't wait to meet the new girl.

It happened the next day. Sarah was riding her bike up and down the street, back and forth to Carter Park on the corner. Stopping to take a spin on the merry-go-round, she saw her. It was the red hair.

The girl's name was Kathleen. That summer, Kathleen taught Sarah to dance, to do a back bend, and to make a bed properly. Who knew that even mattered?

Sarah's mother worked nights and slept a lot during the day. Since she was afraid of her dad who drank too much, she and James stayed away from home as much as possible. That's how she ended up spending so much time at Kathleen's.

Kathleen's mother was the complete opposite of Sarah's, who looked good, smelled of Wind Song and cigarettes, but never cleaned house or washed clothes. Though Sarah loved her, her mother's lack of domestic abilities was embarrassing on a daily basis.

The first time Sarah was invited for lunch at Kathleen's, she thought she'd died and gone to heaven. They ate on china plates with cloth napkins that matched the tablecloth. The best part was the fresh flowers in the center, nestled like a present in a cut-glass vase. Refracted light from its sides spun off the walls like magic ping-pong balls.

For dessert, Kathleen's mother served homemade applesauce with cinnamon. It was manna from heaven. When Sarah couldn't stop raving about it, Kathleen's mother sent some home with her. Sarah hid it in her room so she wouldn't have to share any of it and ate it all after she was supposed to be in bed.

That summer began a relationship that continued through grade school, into high school, and beyond. Though Kathleen and Sarah still maintained a friendship, Sarah and Kathleen's mother, who could now be called Mary Ellen, transitioned into a new relationship. Whereas before, Mary Ellen had been *Kathleen's* mother, she and Sarah became friends on an adult level. It was lovely.

Sarah could always count on Mary Ellen's sage advice when it came to raising her own two children. "Sarah," she'd say, when Sarah was in a parenting quandary, "you cannot put an old head on young shoulders."

Shortly after Kathleen's father had died, she and Sarah noticed how little energy Mary Ellen had. Chalking it up to grief, Kathleen let it slide for a while, but after taking her mother to a doctor, the news was grim. . .Mary Ellen had cancer.

Typical of her Irish heritage, she refused to give in to any dire predictions and planned a trip to Ireland. She went but returned extremely weak. It was then that Sarah made sure they had weekly visits, and that's when Mary Ellen, or Mère, as she liked to sign her name, brought out the rose chintz.

Delicate patterns of roses enveloped the outside of each cup, while a small bud clung to the inside well. Though the beauty of the cups was breathtaking, the loveliest of all was the teapot. Tall and gracefully curved in it Lipton never tasted so good. In the beginning, it was Mère who made the tea, but as the year progressed and her body failed to sustain her, it was Sarah who maintained the ritual.

Such an ordinary task, yet somehow, every time tea was sipped from the rose chintz, the mundane magically transformed into something that whispered of time suspended. The warmth of the beverage, sweetened with honey's nectar, transported them both from the reality of human mortality into a place of sustained joy. How like God to change something ordinary into the extraordinary, where in the midst of their intimate camaraderie, time itself was savored with as much or more delight than the elixir sipped from perfectly painted china cups.

In these moments of suspended animation, they spoke of heavenly things and heart longings that rang as God's promises to those who called Him Lord.

Earthly time for Mary Ellen, Sarah's surrogate mother, friend, and mentor, had ended just two months ago. The void left by her death was shocking—too deep, wide, and gaping to fill. Turning to the Lord for comfort, Sarah found it, but the approaching Christmas holiday brought the sorrow back like a tidal wave. The last week had been especially difficult.

"Hey, hon, we're almost there."

"Oh, good." She'd been so lost in thought she hadn't noticed where they were. "That was quick. Thanks for driving."

"How about some clam chowder, and then we can hit the antique shops?"

"Sounds like a plan; I'm starving."

The second they met the city limits of Seaside, Oregon, it felt like entering a time warp. One filled with delicious sights and the ever-present ocean's symphony. Sarah rolled down the window and took it all in.

Though the tangy salt breeze was chilly, it was nonetheless comforting. Kind of like a very familiar quilt, one you want to wrap yourself in regardless of how many times before you'd done the very same thing.

She inhaled deeply. *Thank You, Lord, for Your presence. I see You. . .hear You. . .feel You everywhere.*

They lingered over lunch with freshly brewed coffee. "Which side of the street should we take?" Ian asked.

"Doesn't matter to me. But we'd better get started, 'cuz it looks like rain."

They entered the third shop, which was really an old Victorian house. It held onto a faded sign that read ANTIQUES AND UNK, the *J* having worn off some decade before. "I'm going upstairs first, Sarah."

"'Kay," she responded. A lot of the shop was dusty, but a crackling blaze in an ancient woodstove made the entire place warm and inviting. "Linger here awhile," it seemed to whisper. As she walked around, Sarah felt a quietness reenter her soul. She exhaled and turned just in time to see Ian coming down the stairs.

"There's a surprise up there you won't want." He winked.

"Oh yeah, how so?"

"Go see for yourself." He took Sarah's hand and led her to the stairway. "I'll wait here." He smiled.

Curiosity aroused, her heart skipped a beat. She loved surprises. How grateful she was for a husband who knew her so well.

Winding stairs led to a part of the store that had once been the attic. Sloping sides and twelve-paned windows at either end testified to the age of the house. Each step on the creaky floor forced dust motes to rise from their rest. Walking around the perimeter, Sarah's eyes scanned every nook and cranny looking for the "surprise" she was not supposed to want.

Nothing.

Then she turned.

She found it. No, it had found her. . .sitting in the middle of a lace-covered oak table. One hand went to her throat, eyes brimming with emotion. She didn't move. Surrounded by odds and ends of someone else's must-have treasures, a rose chintz teapot beckoned. Was she dreaming?

Stepping forward, a shaft of soft sunlight pushed itself over one shoulder and onto the table. The roses on the pot pulsated with life in the muted glow. She picked it up, examining all the smooth surfaces, cradling it like a firstborn. Not a nick or ding. Could an object hold the past? In an instant, a flood of healing memories rushed over her soul, filling the longing place whose depths had been ravaged by grief.

At the precise moment her soul let go of the loss, Sarah's mind turned to thoughts of Christmas. Christmas joy! Joy had returned to its rightful place; Christmas would be exactly as it should be. . .centered on Christ and not her emotions.

Sarah's fingers caressed the sides of the memory keeper, lifting its lid with care. Pungent remnants of long-ago tea times wafted from within. With the release of the memory fragrance, Sarah would always believe she heard a lilting voice speak.

"Are you ready for tea, Sarah?"

Without You

Linda J. Reinhardt

Dee has spent the last two Christmases alone after a tragedy happened to her boyfriend, Doug. Could a simple prayer to the God Doug had told her about bring healing and a relief from her pain?

T he fire popped when Dee dropped another log onto it. She sat back on her couch and pulled her favorite fuzzy blanket up close around her chin. The warmth and crackling of the fire made her feel drowsy.

Only a few hours and one day left, and life will go on as usual. I'm doing pretty well, if I may say so myself. I'm actually enjoying the solitude. And I've made it without my old buddy.

Dee closed her eyes to fight the temptation to pick up the bottle of bourbon that sat on the end table beside her. She had decided several hours ago that she wouldn't drink this Christmas. She hoped she would drift off to sleep to help the time go faster.

Sometime later, Dee woke up, shivering, to a cold, dark room. Her blanket had fallen to the floor. She put another log on the fire and tried lighting it in her half-asleep state. "Oh, come on, start burning."

Dee sat back on her heels and rested her elbow on the table, tipping over her nemesis. *Bang!* The bottle hit the table, rolling its way to the floor. Dee grabbed it quickly before it fell and broke.

"I don't know why I saved you." She held it up close to her face. "It would have been better if you had broken. Then you wouldn't be sitting here, tempting me to have a drink before I go back to sleep. This year, I'm doing Christmas without you."

Just like I've done Christmas without Dana and Doug, for the last three years.

A lump formed in her throat. Dee bit at her fingernail and got back on the couch, clutching her blanket. "I'm not going to let it get to me. I'm not. What's the big deal about Christmas, anyway? So what if I'm here alone and have no presents? Day after tomorrow, I'll be at the stores to shop all the deals. I just have to get through this night and tomorrow," Dee said out loud.

She stared at the burning log, wishing for sleep to take her away from this lonely place. *Why is it such a big deal to be alone on Christmas Eve? And why do people make such an issue about it, anyway? It's just another day of the week.*

Her stomach knotted up when she remembered how much Dana and Doug had made a big deal out of it every year. And they used to make a big deal out of it with her. Dee glanced over at her bottle of bourbon, until...

Dee reached over and held the bottle close to her. "Now they're gone, and you turned into my best friend."

Dee sunk down into the cushions and forced herself to go to sleep. The long night was almost over.

The sun shone bright through her windows. Dee squinted. It hurt to open her eyes. Relief filled her when she realized it was morning. *Yes, just one more day and life is back to normal. Hmmm, it snowed a bit. I wonder if everyone is going to be able to make it over to Mom's house today. Oh well, it doesn't matter. I won't know if they do or not. I'm not going.*

After a quick shower, Dee made herself breakfast and some coffee, then bundled up and went for a walk. She wasn't sure which direction she wanted to take, so she decided to start by strolling through the neighborhood. She waved at a couple of neighbors who had stepped outside in their yards.

The street is already beginning to look like a parking lot. Guests are arriving early this year. Dee ignored the gnawing inside her. A smile escaped when she remembered how she, Dana, and Doug were always late arriving at her parents because they spent so much time opening presents and playing with the gifts. Dee pushed that thought away. That was before, when Doug and Dana were with her.

Now Dana lives on the other side of town with her mom. And Doug...

Dee pushed thoughts of Doug out of her mind. *I wonder if Dana is even close to opening all of her presents yet?* Doug had loved Christmas. He started shopping for the next Christmas the day after Christmas.

Dee shook her head. *He was such a nut. I miss him.* Tears filled her eyes. She knew better than to think about Doug today or any day.

But Dee couldn't stop the flood of memories of the first time she saw him at her friend's party. He was on leave from the military and about to be shipped out to Iraq. Dee and Doug wrote to each other almost every day and decided when he returned, they would pursue a serious relationship. He had a daughter but didn't introduce the two of them right away.

When he came back to the States, Dee fell hopelessly in love. Right before Christmas, Doug finally introduced her to his teenage daughter. That Christmas was crazy fun, and the next one after that was even better.

Dee stopped walking and closed her eyes. She tried with all her might to fight memories of Doug and Dana, but she couldn't. Tears began to pour from her eyes. Dee started to run toward her home before she ended up an emotional mess in the street.

Her hand shook, making it hard to put her key in the lock. Finally she got it, pushed the door open hard, then slammed it behind her. She fell onto the couch and put her head in her hands. She had been unable to run from...the last Christmas...

Dee sobbed into a couch pillow.

The scene played before her eyes as though it were yesterday. She sat up and stared at the bourbon bottle on the coffee table. It called to her, *"Take just one drink. It will numb the pain. . . ."*

It was Christmas Eve, three years ago. Doug was scheduled to leave again for Iraq the day after Christmas. Doug and Dana had gone to church while Dee stayed home, busy preparing for the evening ahead. She didn't like church. She'd had to go as a child, and it bored her. As soon as she was on her own, she decided to never go to another boring church service again. It bothered her that they were wasting time there instead of being home with her.

When she first met Doug, he had felt the same way, until something happened one Christmas. Doug and Dana had gone to church with *her parents,* of all people, and life was never the same again. Not only did they go on Christmas Eve, but they started going on Sundays. Dana joined the youth group and even started going on mission trips. Doug started reading his Bible and hung out with people who seemed to live to talk about the Bible.

It drove Dee crazy. She had no intentions of joining them at church or anywhere else that resembled church.

So that last Christmas, while Dee waited for Doug and Dana to come over, Dee busied herself around the house with hopes this would be the year Doug asked her to marry him. As had become her habit, she carried a glass of bourbon with her throughout the house, sipping on it as she kept busy and then refilling the glass whenever she passed by the bottle.

When Doug and Dana arrived later that evening, Dee realized she'd almost finished off the bottle. "Oh well." Dee walked into the living room with a slight swagger and plopped down on the couch next to Dana.

Dana grimaced. "Dee, you smell funny."

"Dana!" Doug had said.

"What do I smell like?" Dee asked.

"I don't know, but your breath. . ."

"I better get some gum." Dee struggled to get up from the couch. "Could you do me a favor, honey, and get me some gum out of my purse?"

Dana was quick to do as she was asked; obviously the smell really bothered her. Doug stood watching with a sad expression.

"What's the matter? Let's get going with some nice Christmas fun," Dee said. "Could you get me another drink before you come in and sit down?"

Doug shook his head.

"No? Why not? You old. . ." Dee caught the warning look from Doug and stopped before she said something wrong in front of Dana. "Then I'll get it myself." She walked by Doug and attempted to give him a kiss; she missed tripping over his feet and knocked decorations off of a ledge by the kitchen door. "Oopsie," she said with a giggle.

Doug and Dana moved quickly to make sure there weren't any broken pieces and to clean up the mess. Dee had continued into the kitchen and poured herself another drink.

Doug had followed her. When she turned around, she ran into him, spilling some of her drink. "Oh. . .look what you did, silly boy." Dee turned to refill her drink, but Doug's hand stopped her.

"Please don't, Dee. I think you've had enough to drink tonight. We really would like to just hang out with you and celebrate."

"I'm fine, Doug. Don't worry about me. Besides, it's time to party." Dee tried to pick up the bottle. Doug was quick to pick it up first.

"Dee, lately whenever we come over, you're filling up your glass. Do you think we could just. . . ?"

"Listen, don't preach at me, 'kay? I'm only having a drink or two. Now give me the bottle."

Doug closed his eyes for a minute before speaking. "Dee, I really don't want Dana to see you drunk again. Please, it's Christmas."

"I'm not drunk!" Dee's voice filled the kitchen. "Now, give me the bottle."

"Dee, please, it's Christmas. It's a time to celebrate the birth of Jesus and give gifts. We really want to enjoy this time with you."

"So do I, honey, just let me. . ." Dee tried to get the bottle from him but couldn't. It made her mad, so she finally gave him an ultimatum. "You either give me that bottle—or leave. If I want to drink, I will drink. Got it?"

"You don't. . ."

"Mean it? Yes, I do. Now give me the bottle."

"Fine—have it your way. Dana and I will come back in the morning. We can do our Christmas then." Doug walked into the living room and motioned for Dana to follow.

"If you leave now, don't bother coming back tomorrow, preacher boy. You can't tell me when to drink and when not to." Dee picked up her glass and drank it all in one gulp.

Doug and Dana stared at her with sad expressions. She didn't care. She poured herself another glass and gulped that one down, too. "There—now what are you going to do? Go to church and pray for me?" Dee had fallen back against the kitchen table laughing.

She heard the door shut. She slid into a chair by the table and poured herself another glass. "They really left," she said to the empty room.

She staggered back into the living room and fell onto the couch. The tree lights glowed, and presents filled in the bottom of the tree. Dee still couldn't believe they had really left.

The next morning they called. But when they came over, things had changed. Their time together that Christmas morning wasn't as fun and easy as all the other Christmases.

Dee apologized and promised to stop drinking so heavily when they had plans to do something together. Still. . .something had changed, and Dee didn't get a ring for Christmas.

The next day, Doug left for Iraq, and Dana went and stayed with her mom. Two weeks later, Dana called, crying. Dee couldn't understand her at first and then. . .she didn't want to understand her. Doug was gone, killed by an IED.

The next days were a fog.

How she made it to the memorial service she'd never know. She went over and sat with Dana and her mom. Afterward, Dana turned and gave her a hug. "Dee, my dad loved you. He prayed for you every night and hoped someday you'd come to believe in Jesus the way we had. That's my hope for you, too."

Dee didn't know how to reply, since she thought it wasn't an appropriate time for a conversation like this.

"And I have to tell you, I have been so angry at you for hurting him the way you did on Christmas Eve. I've had to pray and pray to forgive you. Now he's gone, and it makes me even angrier that you hurt him on his last Christmas. How could you do that to him?" Tears rolled down Dana's face.

"Dana!" Dana's mom put her arm around her. "I'm so sorry, Dee. She's upset."

"I am upset, and I don't want you to call me for a while until I can deal with how I feel about our last Christmas together. It should have been so special, but you ruined it!" Dana turned and ran out of the sanctuary. . . .

Dee held the pillow tight. It had been three Christmases since Dana had said those words. Dee had never seen her again. How would she ever forget those words? She *had* ruined Doug's last Christmas. He loved Christmas.

Dee started to open the bottle. *No! I'm not going to drink this time away. It's just another day religious people make a big deal out of.*

And Doug.

Dee leaned her head back against the couch. "Okay, if You really are real, God, then please, please help me with this pain. Please."

Dee spent the day alone. The loneliness hurt, and she struggled to get through it. Finally, it was time to turn on some lights. It was almost over. The pain was still there.

She put her pajamas on and then popped herself some popcorn. The doorbell rang while she was trying to decide on a movie to watch. Dee peeked out her living room window. A girl stood on her porch. *Dana?*

Dee moved fast to the door, smoothing her bathrobe, her heart pounding. *What is Dana doing here?* She opened the door to the most precious face she had ever seen. How she missed Dana and her dad.

"Dana?"

"Hi." Dana looked a bit shy. "Uh, I. . ." Dana looked away from Dee.

"Would you like to come in?"

"Sure." Dana followed her into the room. Dee was quick to offer her some pop. "I can't stay that long. I just had to come and see you for a minute."

"I'm glad you did. How have you been?"

"Okay."

"Dana, I'm so glad you came over, really I am. I am so sorry for hurting you and your dad." Dee sucked in some air and blinked her eyes hard to fight her emotions. "I love you two so much, and I was such a fool. . .please. . ."

"That's why I came over. I've been so angry and, today, well, you know how much my dad. . ."

Dee bit at her lip.

"How much he loved Christmas."

Dee nodded.

"He loved it so much. And when he discovered what it was really all about, Christmas took on a new meaning." Dana's voice lowered. "Christmas is so hard without him. I was in my room reading the Christmas story in my Bible. He used to love to do that with me. And then I skimmed through some pages, and something caught my eye."

Dee didn't care what it was. She was just thankful that Dana had come to her house. It was devastating to lose Doug, but she had also lost Dana three years ago.

"It said I need to forgive as Jesus forgave me. And you came to my mind. Dee, I'm truly sorry, and please know I forgive you. Will you forgive me?"

"Forgive you?"

"Yes, for how I acted that day and for. . ." Dee reached into her pocket and pulled out a small package. "I've kept something from you." Dana handed the package to Dee.

Dee ripped the package open, curious as to what it could be.

"He really loved you. He was going to give this to you that last Christmas Eve. He let me keep it in my pocket for safekeeping. The next morning I refused to give it to him or tell him where it was, because I was so mad at you for hurting him and ruining our Christmas Eve. So you weren't the only one to mess up his last Christmas. I did a really good job at it, too."

Tears rolled down Dee's face as she stared at the precious engagement ring in the box.

"Can you forgive me, Dee? You would've been my stepmom, and to tell you the truth, I really wanted you to be."

Dee opened up her arms with a nod. Dana stepped right into them. Dee held her close. "Dana, I sort of said a prayer today. I said, if You're really real, God, please take away this pain." Dee stepped away from Dana but still held on to her to look her in the eye. "Nothing could ever take away the pain of losing your dad, but being free from the guilt of ruining his Christmas and losing you eases the pain so much. I can begin to live again, not consumed by it. I love you, Dana. I never stopped. Now I know God is real, and I think I want to get to know this God your dad was so excited about celebrating Christmas over."

"Really?"

"Really. I think it's time we forgive ourselves because I think your dad forgave both of us even before he left for Iraq, don't you?"

Dana nodded. "I think you're right. Hey, were you going to watch a movie?"

"Yeah, too bad you have to go."

"I think I could stay for a movie as long as you have some pop and popcorn."

"I do. Want to go in my room and grab a baggy T-shirt and pajama bottoms to get comfortable?"

"Yeah." Dana gave Dee a big smile. "I missed you, Dee."

"I missed you." Dee gave Dana a big squeeze. "I'm going to say something I haven't said since your dad died."

"Since my dad died?"

"Yep." Dee smiled. "Merry Christmas, hon."

Dana laughed. "Merry Christmas to you, too, Dee."

A Tree at Heart Mountain

ROSANNE CROFT

Sometimes trials and pain cause the soil of hearts to become hard. True selves wither and die. But sometimes, those same trials stir up the soil just enough to grow love inside the heart.

And that's what happened with Jack Yamamori, who met Tamiko and gave her an unforgettable gift.

⁂

The first year I worked as the Yamamoris' housekeeper, I often stared at their wedding picture as I dusted. As a young divorcée, I delighted in their obvious love for each other and dreamed of some-day standing next to my own true love. The photo was framed in sil-ver, an extraordinary portrait with a snow-filled background, stark in black and white. How young and good-looking they once were! They stood in front of a plain wooden building with a Christmas wreath hung on it, their faces reddened by the cold. Mrs. Y wore a simple 1940s polka dot dress, and her groom looked athletic in spite of an ill-fitting borrowed dark suit and tie. Their smiles matched the puff of snow on the windowsill.

As sand in an hourglass relentlessly pours, within two years, housekeeping changed into caregiving as the couple crossed into old age. They moved into an ocean-view condo in Santa Monica, and I gave up my lonely rental and went with them. The memories of my bitter divorce and emotionally abusive marriage went underground as I worked hard to rid myself of any memories at all. But, at times, a bitter taste rose in my mouth when I remembered my short marriage, with all of its sorrows.

Now my daily rituals included giving new medications for a myriad of elderly health problems. I stayed busy so that my buried emotions

313

wouldn't surface. I wanted God back in my life, and Mrs. Y encouraged me to return to church. But on a sad Sunday in May, while I attended church for the first time in ages, Mr. Y died, a sudden massive stroke bringing him down. I returned to find a forlorn widow, unconsolable for months.

Her husband gone, Mrs. Yamamori fondly gazed at the wedding picture every day, took it down from the wall, and stroked it with her gnarled hands, thinking thoughts she rarely spoke about. Her habit was to sit on the balcony as I vacuumed the carpet. She lingered there a long time, watching palm trees sway in the breeze and waves crash on the beach. In her mid-80s, Tamiko Yamamori became a mother to me, and I loved her like a daughter. She'd borne three sons, all busy executives now in Simi Valley, and she needed a daughter like me to tend to her. I didn't mind. It filled the void in my heart.

Today she stroked the photo with devotion in her eyes, her lap covered by a silk Japanese quilt, her magazine abandoned beside her. Every day, even in her grieving, she cultivated the bonsai tree on the side porch. Mr. Y had always tended the curled and twisted tree while he was alive, and it seemed he had passed the task to his wife. She arranged the tiny pebbles with tweezers and watered carefully once a week. She wouldn't allow me near it, which was probably a good thing as sometimes I could be clumsy. But today I noticed debris had blown into the planter that held the gracefully twisted tree.

I brought it to her in its tray. "Mrs. Y, do you want to tend your tree today?"

"I'm so tired, Peggy," she answered. "Put it here on the table and I'll try. Do you know about this tree? Did I ever tell you?"

I sensed a story coming in gentle and wise Japanese style. "No, Mrs. Y."

She smiled, her eyes crinkling in her wrinkled face. Her hair was thick and white now, not at all like the shiny black hair in the picture.

"We were at Heart Mountain, my Jack and I," she said, holding the photo up. "That's where we met and married."

"Heart Mountain?"

"An internment camp in northern Wyoming." She sighed.

"A camp? You mean the kind they sent Japanese people to during World War II? I thought it was a mountain cabin in the photo."

She chuckled. "It was a mountain, sure enough. Roughly shaped like a heart. But all 10,000 of us Japanese lived in the camp below that mountain."

"That's a lot of people!" I was silent a moment, then, indicating the photo. "Was this your house there?"

She laughed again. "Not a house. This was the dormitory where my family stayed. There were 468 buildings like these."

"It must have been awful. I never thought that you and Mr. Y had to go to those camps."

She didn't answer but looked back at the photo. "We didn't speak of it much, but now that I'm old and Jack's in heaven, memories float back to me, Peggy, steady and strong, like flotsam down there on the beach. I can smell the food in the mess hall. I see frost on the windows and feel the warmth of the woodstoves. But mainly, I remember people. I can see their faces as clearly as yours."

"Tell me."

She smiled, her eyes gazing upward. "Every day, snow or not, the boys in high school played baseball. Jack was such a good hitter that the ball would fly all the way to the barbed-wire perimeter. They called a home run without even getting the ball back. Everyone was too afraid of the guards. Everyone except Jack."

She looked at the photo. "He didn't want the game to end for lack of a ball, so he ran over to the barbed-wire fence. He was a tall eighteen-year-old. He's only a year older in this picture. The guards saw him running and aimed their rifles at him. But he didn't notice, he was so intent on retrieving the ball. Not until he got right up to the fence and swooped up the ball did he see what everyone else saw— those guns trained on him."

"He wasn't hurt, then?"

"They didn't shoot. They scolded him for a long time and warned the other teenagers. You would think that Jack would never have approached the fence again. But he did." Her eyes smiled into a sparkly crinkle.

"Why?"

"While we were dating, we held hands and strolled around the camp. One spring afternoon, he told me to wait at the building on the very end row near the fence. I watched as he went right for forbidden territory! He bent down on both knees and pulled this juniper up by its scrawny roots. No guard saw him that time. 'Needs me to help it grow,' he told me. I laughed at him. 'It will never make it, Jack. It's too weak.'

"'There's something you don't know about me, Tamiko-san,' he said to me. 'I'm going to master the art of gardening. You'll see.'

"And he was right. Jack could make anything grow. Even a tiny juniper wrapping its roots around the rocks of its own destruction."

"And this bonsai is the same little juniper? How old is it?"

"Hmm. That was 1942, so it's about 68 or 69. Some bonsai can live to be 200 years old!"

"I hope this one does," I said quietly.

Her eyes watched a moving picture that I could only see in her words.

"That spring," she said, "Jack helped his father and other men on an irrigation project to grow vegetables. They were so successful that we had good eating that summer! Do you know that the irrigation we Japanese dug out helped present-day ranchers to raise crops on that desert land? We turned the desert into an oasis."

"You mean Mr. Y and the men dug ditches?" I couldn't believe that the wealthy man I had known would ever dig a ditch.

"All the way from the Shoshoni River to our gardens."

"So when did you marry?"

"I'm getting to that," she said with a coy smile. "First, Peggy, let's make some green tea, in the little blue cups in memory of Jack."

When I came back with the Japanese tea tray, her wizened head was back on the pillow, her eyes closed. My heart rose up. "Mrs. Y?"

She woke, her eyes fluttering like butterflies flying on their last day. I could see the pulse in her neck rapidly beating.

"I'm so tired, dear."

"Have some tea. We don't have to talk anymore about that terrible place if you don't want to."

"It wasn't so terrible. Just think, but for that place, I never would've met Jack. And his family! Do you know—they celebrated every birthday, every single holiday in their warm barracks space with a huge party. Such a bright place for me! I had only my mother, who was sad all the time, and a younger sister. My brother became a soldier in Europe. I lost him recently. He lived near Santa Barbara."

"I'm sorry."

She tried to sit up a bit. "His war picture is in my cedar chest. He served with the 522nd Field Artillery Battalion who liberated the prisoners at Dachau concentration camp in Germany. Those soldiers were Nisei Japanese."

"Nisei are American-born Japanese, right?"

"Yes. My brother had to shoot off the locks on the gates of Dachau. They thought everyone would be dead inside, but then skeletal people began to walk slowly up to the gates, like ghosts in striped clothes. My brother never forgot it. It was April of 1945."

"How odd."

"What's odd, Peggy?"

"Mrs. Y, you spent time in an internment camp in America, and your brother freed people from a camp in Germany."

"Life is strange. My brother helped us move to Heart Mountain and then joined the 522nd!"

It was hard for me to reflect on the sad irony of this, so I attempted to lighten the subject. "You look so happy in the photo, so in love."

"We were. But when I first arrived at camp, I wasn't happy, believe me. My mother said it was a 'God-forsaken place' as soon as she saw it. We had only the possessions that we could carry. We left our homes for wire fences and armed guards."

"It must have been a shock."

She nodded. "I was angry and asked God: Why did I have to be born Japanese? And the wind! You could never be rid of it. It filled our nostrils with dirt, as well as our food."

"Where did you eat?"

"There was a mess hall where we had three meals a day. Mostly good food, too. Our living quarters were tight, with army cots to sleep in. We had a potbellied stove and one bare light bulb. And we had a hospital!" She shivered a little as the red quilt slipped off of her shoulders.

I rearranged the quilt. Mrs. Yamamori showed signs of swelling in her ankles, and the skin on her legs was mottled. Her heart was working too hard. Taking her to doctor's appointments was part of my job, and I knew more than her sons about the state of her health.

"I visited Jack's grandmother at that hospital." She laughed at the memory. "Jack's grandmother must've been about as old as I am now! She wore a Japanese silk kimono with blue mums on it. By this time, Jack and

I were engaged. Do you know what she said to me?"

"What?"

"She asked me if I *liked* Heart Mountain! I was stunned, Peggy. No one *liked* Heart Mountain. It was a place to jail people the government didn't trust. So I told her how much I missed fresh blueberries and the smell of the rain on the fir trees in Oregon."

"What did she say?"

"She told me she missed California, too. I still remember how sparkly her black eyes were. Then she said: 'But we are the lucky ones.' Before I knew it, I'd shouted at her: 'Lucky? How are we so lucky?' I was angry and full of grief. But she was calm and said, 'Yes, we are lucky ones to be in this prison camp. We do not have prison in our hearts.'"

"What did she mean?"

"Jack asked that same question. He told her it would be better to be free. She said: 'We are free in our hearts. It's true freedom to forgive others and what they do to us and go forward with our lives.'"

I frowned. I didn't like that idea much. "That's easier said than done." Mrs. Y knew about my messy divorce. It had been three years ago but still hurt like an aching bruise.

"Peggy, after that Jack's grandmother died, and the two of us began to change our attitudes. We chose to appreciate just being alive, you know? We even got used to the wind at Heart Mountain and hung wind chimes from the eaves."

I glanced up at the wind chimes decorating her entire balcony. "You still like them, don't you? But it's lunchtime, Mrs. Y. What would you like to eat?"

She waved her hand dismissively. "I'm not hungry. You must hear the rest, Peggy." Her voice was weak.

"I'll make you some soup, Mrs. Y. You can eat it out here, and I'll listen to the rest of the story when I come back."

"Hurry, dear girl."

Her words worried me as I heated up my special clam chowder. I put two crackers beside it on the tray and went out to the veranda where she sat, eyes closed, humming to herself.

"Mrs. Y, it's ready."

"Set it down on the table," she said, "and hear how Jack and I got married."

"It must've been romantic," I said. "He was such a gentleman."

"Jack was my best friend, always looking out for me and my feelings before his own."

"He was like that to the end, Mrs. Y."

She chuckled in small breaths. "That Christmas Day, as we stood before our pastor during the ceremony, Jack presented me with that scrawny juniper as a wedding gift. Only it had been transformed! It was green and thriving under Jack's love and care, and I knew I would grow under his love and care, too. It's my wedding Christmas tree, reminding me of what I lost, but more of what I gained. In the midst of hardship, there was great joy."

"And to still have your wedding tree!" I sighed.

"Peggy, we were blessed! The mess hall served a huge turkey dinner. Even my mother made small cakes for everyone in our dormitories. It was a celebration we would never forget! That Christmas was by far the best I've ever had. God's holy light glistened on the moonlit snow at Heart Mountain that December 25th in 1943."

I sighed out of sheer joy for her.

"Peggy, I don't know if I ever told you, but sometimes trials are blessings in disguise. You see, we were in the palm of His hand all along. You are never so free, never so loved as when you look back and see God's goodness in your life, even in the trials."

I hardly knew what to say. Tears welled up in my eyes. "Where did you go after that? I mean, you were married!"

"One of the dormitories had room for a newly married couple, but after only two months, we were released from the camp. We took the train back to California so Jack could go to UCLA. You can only imagine our joy to be free."

The tears in my eyes finally splashed down on my shirt. "So you lived happily ever after."

She smiled. "We lived with the image of Heart Mountain etched into our souls our entire lives. But Jack's grandmother was right. With forgiveness, a bitter root cannot grow. Your life changes, and you become a nurturer of struggling hearts, like Jack did for me. You're able to love and spread mercy. In your soul, you nurture gratitude for every small thing."

"I think I understand, Mrs. Y."

She nodded wearily. "Now I will eat my soup and take a little nap. Can you hang our picture back on the wall?" She handed me the wedding photo, but her gnarled hand still held the graceful bonsai tree in her lap.

"Of course, Mrs. Y. Thanks for telling me your story. I loved hearing it."

I went into the kitchen to clean up. Twenty minutes passed, and I checked on Mrs. Yamamori. She had slumped over in her chair, still clinging to the tree. I knew she had quietly passed from this life to the next. God held her in His hands now, just as sure as she held the Christmas wedding tree in hers. I knew it as a solid fact.

I made the dreaded calls to her sons, and only afterward did wild tears stray from my eyes. I took away her cold soup and sat with her there, holding her hand on the veranda, thinking about Heart Mountain and the bonsai.

But what was this? An envelope perched in its branches. In shaky letters, it was addressed to me. I opened it.

My dearest Peggy,
Please take this bonsai and keep it for as long as it will live. It survived with grace. It overcame great adversity and grew. Like the bonsai, place your roots in good soil and grow forever. I love you, dear daughter.
Mrs. Y.

Later, I found out that Mrs. Yamamori left me enough money to buy a small house of my own. God came back into my life, swept it clean, and stayed at my invitation.

A mere six months later, I met my own Jack, only his name was David, and when we stood at the altar on December 25th, we held between us the Christmas wedding bonsai tree.

Starry, Starry Christmas Night

15 stories to prepare your heart for the King

Reality Fiction™ Faith Meets Imagination

Sharon Bernash Smith and Linda J. Reinhardt

Dedication

To the newest additions in our family:
Welcome, Sophia Kikumi, January Rose, and Jaxson Tyler (JT).
Jesus came as one of you.
—Sharon Bernash Smith

To those who hold on to the hope
of that starry, starry night so many years ago.
May God's light shine on you and through you
and draw others to His light.
—Linda J. Reinhardt

Starry, Starry, Christmas Night

CONTENTS

Starry, Starry, Christmas Night

SHARON BERNASH SMITH

Christmas seems to be most people's favorite holiday. I know it's mine. But last year, after perusing our local mall, I was sorely disappointed to see not one reference to the *real* meaning of Christmas except at the Christian bookstore. I wasn't surprised, just sad. Then, as I started down the escalator, music began to pour out of loudspeakers everywhere: *"Joy to the world, the Lord has come. Let earth receive her King. Let every heart prepare Him room. Let heaven and nature sing. Let heaven and nature sing. . . ."* The busy, uncaring, unadoring mall now pulsated with holy truth.

Even now, remembering those words and my feelings brings me to tears. As people rushed around—some in despair, many in debt, and others not caring—the truth rang out. Joy is possible, even in a world of chaos. *Let every heart prepare Him room.* Yes! Prepare, and He will come: He wants to abide with us. . .make His home in the place He created just for Himself. *Let earth receive her King:* the King of heaven came to be King of every living heart. Ah yes, *let heaven and nature sing:* sing of the greatness of a God who sent the Breath of Heaven for our salvation.

Dear friend, if this Christmas season finds you down, remember this: you're supernaturally loved. If heartaches threaten to consume you until your very soul feels empty, do not despair. Why? Because the Lord God of the Universe wants to give you life—abundant life. This life is an eternal gift, one He gives freely to those who ask. The celebration of Christmas, and each one of our stories, is meant to remind you of that precious, irrevocable life. We invite you to grab a cup of tea, coffee, or maybe sweet hot chocolate and enjoy our special way of saying, "Merry Christmas," to you.

The Night Sky of Orion

SHARON BERNASH SMITH

Harper Wilson is constantly coming under unwanted scrutiny from Mrs. Collins, her teacher. The fact that Harper's horse follows her to school on a regular basis only adds to the young girl's constant humiliation. Under a star-filled sky on Christmas Eve, this thirteen-year-old will learn something she'll never forget: everyone has a story.

Funny how time can be a shape-shifting magician, playing tricks on my mind, moving memories in and out of reference like free-flowing bubbles in the surf. Yet remarkably, others stay caught with absolute precision, creating an indelible and forever imprint.

It's with that kind of clarity, I'm able to recall the Christmas I was thirteen, in 1943. . . .

My classroom was opossum-dead quiet except for the crackle and hiss of the potbellied woodstove in the corner. That was because all eyes were riveted on Mrs. Collins, standing before us with a wooden ruler in hand. *Tap, tap, tap,* it went, snapping against the side of her wool tweed skirt. She cleared her throat before speaking. "Harper Wilson, please stand."

The very second my name was uttered, my thirteen-year-old insides began to stir like the winter storm brewing outside. Obediently, I pushed myself out of the wooden desk. "Yes, Mrs. Collins," I croaked, me wondering if anybody could hear my knees knocking.

"Walk up here this minute."

Every step forward added more to the fire going on in the center of my gut. I clutched it in nervous response. There was no way I didn't know

327

with all my being what was coming. How could I not? See, the evidence against me was waiting just outside the school room door.

I was standing right in front of Mrs. Collins when she grabbed one arm and half dragged me to the window. "What do you see out there, Miss Wilson?" Her voice intensity exactly matched the pressure she was putting on my arm. "What do you see?"

"My horse," I said in a wobbly voice. I could feel the crimson blush creeping from my neck to my face like a sneaky enemy.

"Of course that's *your* horse. It's always *your* horse, is that not right, Miss Wilson?"

"Yes, ma'am," I said again. Of course there could be no doubt it was him, waiting, head hanging over the fence, like an innocent bystander...a huge, innocent bystander, that is.

"How many times do you suppose this has happened, Miss Wilson?" She went on without giving me a chance to answer. "Too many to be tolerated." She tapped that dreaded ruler of hers right on my shoulder for emphasis. "Too. . .many. . .times. You've been told over and over again that a horse on the school ground is simply not acceptable; maybe in the old days, when there were facilities to accommodate such things, but certainly not today. Not in 1943."

My head hung low, but I managed to sneak a peek out the window. No matter how many times I double-checked the gate to Shadow's pasture, somehow he always got out. And, once he was out, the only place he wanted to be was with me. I had suspicions that somehow he'd found a way to unlock it himself. I looked again, noting how his fine ebony coat made a sharp contrast to the falling snow. *He'd be looking in the window if he had the chance*, I thought.

"Take your seat, Miss Wilson, but let this be a warning to your parents. The next time that animal shows up outside our door, I will not hesitate to call the sheriff. Understood?"

"Yes, ma'am," I said, trying to sound as sorry as I could. It seemed every chance she got, Mrs. Collins called me on some picayune offense in front of the whole classroom. For instance, whenever it was my turn to clean the blackboard, never did my efforts measure up to her standards. And real regular-like, my schoolwork seemed to be studied over and beyond any of the other twenty-one kids in the one-room school. Shadow's errant ways merely added to the scorn that came my way.

Shortly after that twenty-seventh-hundred scolding, Mrs. Collins made a declaration to the entire class. "Children, I'm dismissing you early due to the amount of snow that's falling. Since it's our last day before Christmas vacation, I'm sure you can make good use of the rest of your day."

The entire room erupted into shouts and whoops, followed by a mad dash to the cloakroom for coats, hats, and galoshes. I was absolutely beyond happy, my heart soaring with the possibilities that lay ahead in the days before my favorite holiday. I quickly pulled on my boots, coat, and wool hat. It would be a cold ride home. As I grabbed my gloves, I happened to glance at Mrs. Collins. Funny, she looked kind of sad. I can't say why exactly, but I walked back into the classroom.

Mrs. Collins glanced up from her desk. "Yes, Miss Wilson, what is it? Did you forget something?" She almost smiled.

"I...that is...no, I didn't forget anything, uh, just wanted to say merry Christmas."

Mrs. Collins seemed at a loss for words. "Oh, why thank you, Miss... Harper. Merry Christmas to you, as well." She rearranged some of the pencils and erasers on her desktop. "I suppose you'll have a houseful, with the size of your family and all."

I wasn't sure, but was she looking a little misty eyed behind her glasses?

"Oh yes, ma'am, even my grandma Wilson from Ohio's here...came all the way on a train. Took her two days and two nights." I could feel the sweat building up under all the clothes I'd just put on, but I was having a hard time leaving, since this was the nicest Mrs. Collins had been to me since school started. For some reason known only to God and the saints in heaven, I kind of enjoyed it.

The moment was broken by a sharp whinny from outside. Shadow was prancing back and forth in front of the gate. "Well, Mrs. Collins, I sure do gotta go. Do you mind giving me a leg up on Shadow, though?"

"Oh, of course. Just let me grab my jacket and boots." That time, she actually did smile. I have to say, I found it puzzling.

Outside, the wind blew snow hard, stinging my face with each mean gust. "Thanks for helping, Mrs. Collins," I shouted above the wind.

"You're welcome, Harper," she shouted back. Next, she turned and ran back into the building. Just as Shadow and me took off, I happened to notice that snow was piling up mighty fast on her old Ford car parked on the side.

"I'd rather ride on you than get in any ol' car, big boy," I said to Shadow. And that was the plain truth. Even though his back was real wide for a skinny girl like me, I loved being on him just the same.

The ride home was as cold as I'd thought, but Mama had some sweet treats ready that she and Grandma had baked. . .sugar cookies with frosting. Every morsel that melted in my mouth tasted like a gift all in itself. For sure, our family didn't have a lot, but "we always had food on the table and love in our hearts." That's what Daddy always said every time he gave thanks before a meal.

After the special treat, all us kids had chores. Since I was the oldest, I got handed the out-of-doors ones, which meant I put hay out for our cattle while Daddy milked. However, when I opened the kitchen door, the wind blew me clean back inside, nearly knocking me into a tumble. Good thing Grandma was there, 'cuz I could've never got the door closed by myself.

The little kids spent the rest of the afternoon oohing and aahing over the amount of snow that kept drifting in huge cloud-like pillows all around our farm. When Daddy came in from milking, his face was beet red, and we had to help him off with his boots 'cuz his hands were stiff from the cold.

"Harper, what happened to you, girl? Me and the ladies missed you in the barn." He winked, so I knew he wasn't mad.

"Well, I really tried. Grandma and the good Lord can witness to that fact. But, Daddy, it was so windy, the door kicked me right back inside. Just ask her."

"Hey, I believe you," Daddy said. "I tied a rope from the barn to here, so I can find my way back and forth. This weather's not fit for man nor beast. . .for sure."

That mean old blizzard kept blowing like crazy for two more days, until finally on Christmas Eve morning, it stopped. Though the sun came out full, the bone-chilling freeze never let up one little bit. Hardly ever did I think it was too cold to play outside, but this time even sticking my head out the door made me ever more thankful for our warm fire.

When the phone rang right after breakfast, I heard my mama say, "Hello," and then take in her breath, sharp-like. "Sure, sure, Hazel, I'll tell him. Yes, I'll do that." She hung up and turned to me. "Harper, you need to get to your daddy, quick. Somebody needs help on account of the snow, and we're the closest ones with a sleigh."

I wondered who would be so dumb as to be unprepared for a pretty much typical Iowa winter. Then I felt guilty, 'cuz maybe that person was really old and got sick or something and couldn't get into town for the Doc's help. I wouldn't have guessed in a hundred years who needed Daddy's help. Well, as it turned out, *our* help.

As I said before, the cold was beyond what a kid ought to have to endure, but Daddy said Shadow behaved better for me than him when it came time to pulling our big red sleigh. All my protesting would not change my father's mind. Therefore, I dressed with two layers of everything, including doubling up the long johns. I had on so many clothes that I could barely waddle around, let alone pull myself up onto the driver's seat. If it wasn't for Daddy pushing from behind, I'd a never made it. Mama packed us some hot cocoa in our biggest thermos, "just in case," she said, and we tucked it under the seat.

For some reason, when Shadow got himself all hooked up to that sleigh, he turned into something kin to a circus horse, shaking his head and dancing around. It took some sweet talk and coaxing to get him onto the road, but in a few minutes we were headed toward town, using the power and telephone poles as our guide since the actual road was three feet beneath the iced-over snow.

Despite the cold, being with my dad all alone was special, and singing "Jingle Bells" together made it all the more fun. Up to that point, I hadn't even thought to ask about who needed our help.

"Daddy, who we picking up, anyways?"

"Oh, I thought Mama told you. It's your teacher, Mrs. Collins."

My heart skipped a beat. "Mrs. Collins?"

"Yes, seems she's been at the schoolhouse since the storm started. At first, she thought she'd wait it out, since she had a fire going and some food. Guess she had a cot there, too. Anyway, the wood played out with the food, and by that time, the snow was way too high to drive herself anywhere."

"So, are we taking her home, then?"

"Heavens no, Harper. What kind of family would we be to let a helpless woman spend Christmas alone?" I could feel his eyes bearing into me. "We're bringin' her home with us, of course."

My mind whirled with the possibility of having every last drop of Christmas joy sucked right out of my body by a woman who obviously couldn't stand me. "But, Daddy," I protested, "Mrs. Collins doesn't much care for my company. . .at all."

"Sooner than later, I wish you'd remember that life is not all about you, Miss Harper Eileen Wilson."

Suddenly, I felt even colder. When my father called me by my entire birth name, I knew for sure that the conversation, any conversation, was finished. Period. . .end of story.

We neared the schoolhouse about the time my face had gone completely numb. Mrs. Collins was standing on the porch, waving. That old fire in my belly began its slow burn.

Since the snow was past knee-high, Daddy had to practically carry Mrs. Collins through the drifts and ice out to the sleigh. She had a small black satchel in one hand. He helped her into the back, handing her the quilt Mama had sent.

"Oh, thank you, Mr. Wilson; I'm ever so grateful to you for the gallantry. Indeed I am." She leaned forward to pat my back. "Thank you too, Harper, for rescuing me from the disaster I allowed myself. I've never seen snow accumulate so quickly. I made a foolish mistake by not leaving sooner."

I wanted to ask her if she was grateful to Shadow, the horse she hated even more than me, but I said nothing. While I turned the sleigh around, Daddy poured each of us a nice hot cup of cocoa. I loved that it tasted exactly like it smelled. When we headed back to our place, Mrs. Collins seemed perplexed.

"Oh, Mr. Wilson, I thought you knew. I live in the opposite direction." She was balancing herself on the backseat that had no springs. I couldn't help but enjoy—for a minute—the fact that she probably wasn't very comfortable. Then my conscience got the best of me, and I asked the Lord's forgiveness for my wicked thoughts.

"I *know* you don't live in this direction, Mrs. Collins, but our family doesn't want you to be alone on Christmas."

"Oh, goodness," she said, "I'm overwhelmed by your generosity, Mr.

Wilson. How lovely of you. But I surely do not want to be a burden."

I wanted to speak up and say I wouldn't mind a bit if we took her home, but I knew the invitation was settled. It dawned on me that I knew absolutely nothing of Mrs. Collins's life outside our classroom. Where was the "Mr." part of her "Mrs.," anyway? She must not have any other family close by, so where did she come from before here? She didn't quite talk like the rest of the folks around here, neither.

Daddy unhooked Shadow while I escorted Mrs. Collins into the house. You'd of thought the queen of England had walked through our back door, the way Mama fussed over our unexpected guest.

"Mrs. Collins, I'm so happy to have you. Please come in out of the cold and sit by the fire." Now, my mother said not one word to me, her very own daughter, the one who was now frozen solid like the ice outside our house.

She introduced my grandmother, then my brothers and sisters. They all thought she was royalty as well. I sat at the kitchen table, making some new observations about Mrs. Collins. Outside the classroom, she seemed smaller somehow. Yes, smaller and younger. As a matter of fact, she might have been even younger than my mother. There was something else about her I was trying to figure out when my father came in from the back porch.

"Well, ladies, you all look nice and cozy. Hope you're thawed out a little, Mrs. Collins."

She rubbed her hands together. "Yes, I am, Mr. Wilson, thanks to you. I need to tell you again how grateful I am for your rescue. And please, call me Alice."

Mrs. Collins's name was Alice? I could not stop staring at her. Here was my teacher, the one who seemed to take deep delight in highlighting my lowest virtues, sitting in *our* family's kitchen, warming herself by *our* fire, and asking *my* father to call her by her first name. Puzzling.

"You're unusually quiet, Harper. Cat got your tongue?" my grandma asked.

"No, ma'am, just thinking about Christmas is all."

"Well, speaking of Christmas," Mama said, "I've got all our decorations in the other room ready to put on our tree."

The little kids started jumping all around the kitchen, begging to help.

"Everyone gets to help, remember?" Daddy said. "How about you, Alice?"

"Why sure, I'd love to," Alice said. "I didn't even put up a tree this year since my husband is gone." Her face got all clouded over, and I could tell she wanted to cry. And she did. "I'm so sorry," she said, "it's just this time of year makes him being overseas so much harder." She wiped at both eyes.

"Where is he?" Mama asked.

"Right now, I don't actually know, which makes it even worse." Both my mama and grandma walked over and gave her a good hug. "Thank you so much. Your kindness is really sweet, and I think you should know that I—that is, we—are going to have a baby." She smiled through her tears.

"Oh my," Grandma and Mama said at once. They clapped their hands and gave Mrs. Collins another big hug.

I could feel my heart stir with each tear that trickled down her pale cheeks. I was beginning to think that her being all alone without a husband *and* having a baby might have something to do with how she treated me. Or maybe she'd always been on the mean side. Right then, I was real grateful nobody could read my un-Christian-like thoughts.

"One, two, three," we all counted before Daddy plugged in the tree. It was beautiful, filling my heart with a sweet, lovely emotion I'm sure was the Christmas "spirit," while all the bright lights bounced off the hanging tinsel and cast shadows that danced around like specks of glass in a gigantic kaleidoscope. As was our tradition, we toasted one another with hot, tangy apple cider and pigged out on homemade cookies.

I went to bed that night in my usual place with two of my sisters in the same bed, wondering how Mrs. Collins was doing on our living room couch with the poking springs. I was too excited to sleep, so I got up to get me one more cookie. I tried to be as quiet as possible, tiptoeing right in front of Mrs. Collins.

"You can't sleep either, Harper?" she whispered.

I jumped at the sound of her voice. "Naw, too excited," I whispered back.

"Where are you going?"

"To the kitchen."

Mrs. Collins pushed herself off the couch. "I'll come with you."

I poured us a glass of milk and got out two cookies each from Mama's cookie jar. Neither of us said a word, but I snuck a glance at her across the table. This was the very last place on the face of God's green earth I ever thought my teacher would be sitting.

She must have sensed me looking at her, 'cuz she looked up slow-like and smiled. I couldn't help myself right then, so I smiled back.

"Harper, do you know anything about the stars?"

"Whaddyamean?" I said with my mouth full of cookie.

"You know, the stars? Like the Milky Way or any of the constellations?"

"Well, for sure I know what the Milky Way is, but I'm not so sure about constellations." It wasn't like I really needed to know those things. Was this some kind of test she thought up in the middle of the night?

She got up from the table, took our glasses to the sink, and motioned me to follow her back into the living room, then walked me to the big window. The sky was filled with more stars than I ever remembered seeing. Starlight reflected off the icy snow, like a million tiny mirrors. It was dazzling.

Mrs. Collins sighed. "Amazing, isn't it? My husband knows all about the stars, and even though I'm the teacher, he taught me some of the constellations. Tonight, you can see all of Orion."

"Orion?"

"Yes, Orion is from Greek mythology. He's also called the Mighty Hunter."

"I don't see anything but a zillion stars," I said.

"Let me see your hand, and I'll show you some of the main stars. Point your index finger."

She took my hand and guided it from place to place and star to star. "See, there's his raised arm, and right there is the club he holds."

"Wow, I think I see it now." I couldn't believe how the whole thing came alive right there above us. I was mesmerized. "How come you know so much, Mrs. Collins?" I turned to gaze up into her face.

She looked down at me, and even in the half light of midnight I could see her eyes. "Well, Harper, I had to study very, very hard. See, I'm not nearly as smart as you are."

What? Did Mrs. Collins say she thought I was "smart"? I couldn't believe my ears. She was still looking at me.

"That's why I'm so hard on you. Of all the children in our class, you might be the brightest. I want you to do your best, and so I push you more than the others."

I could not believe what my ears were hearing. "But. . . ," I started to protest.

"I know sometimes my pushing is a little too strong, but just the same, please know I mean it all for your good."

I was left speechless. This had been quite the conversation. For sure, I needed some time to think about what I'd heard. . .to process it all and let the meaning soak into my puzzled mind. I decided to change the subject after a few minutes of silence.

"So, Mrs. Collins, what are you going to name your baby?" I was back to staring out the window into the holy light of the Christmas sky.

"If it's a boy, I'll name him Andrew, after my husband."

"What if it's a girl?"

She took a side step in my direction and laid a soft hand on one shoulder. "If it's a girl, I'll name her Harper."

It's been a long time since that Christmas in 1943, but like I said, I've never forgotten it. As it turned out, Mrs. Collins had a boy and, like she planned, named him Andrew. His father never came back from the war, and eventually mother and son moved away from our little town in Iowa. But we kept in touch, remaining friends for years after, until her death in 2001. She never remarried but continued teaching well past mandatory retirement.

One of my favorite memories of her is when she traveled halfway across the continent to attend my college graduation. I was beyond happy she was able to see me walk across the stage and receive my degree in teaching.

The Sage Brush Symphony Orchestra

SHARON BERNASH SMITH

In 1910, a woman named Mary V. Dodge moved to the homesteading town of Burns in the high desert of Oregon State. A gifted musician, Mary had a deep love for children and a strong desire for them to be educated in the finer points of music, like she'd been.

When Marlene Cooper* meets Mary, all the yearnings of a young girl's heart come to fruition in ways the child had only imagined. Based on historical facts about the beginning of the Sage Brush Symphony Orchestra, this story shows that God is in the details of dreams because, after all, He is the dream maker.

*A fictitious character

October, 1912
Outside Burns, Oregon

Hot, swirling winds blew acrid dust all over the fresh laundry she'd just hung on the line. Stooping over for more clothes, fourteen-year-old Marlene Cooper refused to be deterred. Instead, she filled her mind with plans, wonderful creative ideas that spun dreams in her head. . .lovely rescue dreams.

She cherished the rescue dreams. They were the ones that transported her from the wide stretches of prairie in Southeastern Oregon to a tree-lined street where lovely melodies drifted from open windows on the front of white gabled houses, carried on lavender scented breezes that. . .

"Mar-leeen? Stop dawdlin', and finish that laundry."

"Yes, ma'am," she shouted back over the howl of relentless wind.

"If you're not finished, there'll be no violin for you today."

Marlene's back stiffened with the warning, and she began working quickly to finish the basket.

Music and the violin had become Marlene's passion two years ago after visiting her father's sister in Portland. Both her cousins were taking violin lessons in their home.

It was the teacher's habit to play first—mostly scales, but once Auntie Ann made a request to hear "Amazing Grace." Marlene sat mesmerized while music flowed like gentle waves from the instrument to her heart, vibrating with something she'd never experienced and couldn't name. The tugging at the very center of her being left her in tears without explanation. Once home, she tried and tried to explain her desperate need to play, but the right words to describe what consumed her never seemed adequate.

"Marlene, music is a lovely idea," her father had said, "but where would you find a violin and learn to play out here?" She was helping him feed the beef cattle they raised while their conversation shot bursts of steam into the numbing cold.

"But, Papa, couldn't we order one from the catalog? That's where Auntie Ann got the two her kids play." She was tossing hay with a pitchfork from a moving wagon, so she couldn't read Papa's face to see if he was warming up to the idea or not. "I think I could teach myself," she'd added.

He was silent for a while before speaking. "You know how tight money is these days, girl. Every cent we make goes back into this ranch, all of it for pure necessities. I'd love to give you the moon, Marlene, I really would, but truth is, any way you look at it, a violin's not a necessity. Sorry."

"Sorry" had been the end of the conversation but certainly not the end of the young girl's precious dream. That's when she began to pray. . .every day. Without fail, pretty much the same words went out of her mouth to God's ears.

"Dear God, You know how much music means to me. . .You're probably the only one, in fact. It might sound foolish to everyone else, I guess, but I believe with my whole heart that music and my love for it comes from You. I absolutely believe in miracles, too, so I'm asking for a violin *and* someone to teach me. Please. In Jesus' name, amen."

All that winter, she'd prayed faithfully without response. But, when winter finally let go of its grip, Marlene's spirit had grown cold, discouragement taking its mean toll. School and never-ending ranch work kept her occupied, yet wherever she went, the lilting sounds of a violin drifted in and out of the mundane life she lived.

In early March, Papa returned from a trip into Burns. Mama was going over the kitchen supplies she'd requested, when Marlene heard her name called.

"Here, Papa."

Wearing an oddly suppressed smile, he stood near the kitchen table with a newspaper in hand. Unfolding the paper, he laid it on the table. Was she in trouble for something?

"Have a seat, Marlene," he said, pulling the chair out for her.

I must have done something awful, even though Papa doesn't look mad. She swallowed hard.

He pushed the paper closer in her direction and pointed at an advertisement in the middle of the page.

Attention!

Mrs. Mott Dodge, violinist and music teacher, will be teaching various classes for children beginning Saturday, April 2, 1911, in the old Burns Photography Building. Lessons will commence promptly at 10:00 a.m. Instruments provided free of charge. Bring a lunch.

Speechless, Marlene's eyes filled with tears.

Mama laughed. "Cat got your tongue, Mar?"

Papa walked around the table and drew his youngest daughter to her feet. "God's been listening, little girl. He's heard your prayers."

"But how did *you* know I pra—"

He tapped the paper. "Marlene, your ma and me have known all along how much this means to you." He looked at his wife. "We been praying right along with you." His voice choked with emotion. "Heard some mighty good things in town about this Mrs. Dodge. . .Mary's her name. Yes sir, everyone says she loves children and wants them to have some real opportunities even away out here."

Tears streamed down the stunned girl's face as she stared at the ad, reading it over and over like the ink might suddenly disappear off the page. "I—I can hardly believe this." She squealed. "I'm really going to learn to play. . .for real." Suddenly a thought gripped, causing a big knot in the middle of her stomach. She clutched her belly.

"What's wrong, girl?" Mama hurried over to the table and put a hand to her daughter's forehead. "Aren't gettin' sick, are you?"

Marlene wiped both eyes. "No, it's not that."

"Then why you bawlin'?"

"I just thought of something horrible." She sat down hard in a chair. "What if, after all this prayer and God bringin' Mrs. Dodge way out here, it turns out I'm no good at playing the violin?"

The question hung in the air for a second or two before both adults began laughing, startling Marlene.

"Mar, I have not a doubt in the world that whatever it takes for you to play a violin, God will give it, and then some."

Their confidence gave Marlene confidence. She could barely stand the wait until April 2nd.

Though the day broke sunny, vicious morning winds pushed the thirty-degree weather against her back all the way into town. She rode their oldest workhorse, grateful for the warmth of his broad, bare back. Still, both legs were numb before she'd passed the halfway mark.

"You're going to have to be a patient boy while I'm at my lesson, Toby. Hear me?" The horse nickered. "I'm not sure how long it will be, but you'll be just fine." The closer they got to town, the more her stomach was aflutter with butterflies of anticipation. Giving the big horse a few nudges put him into a bumpy trot.

Someone had washed the windows in the old photography building until they reflected the broad eastern sky like a mirror. Marlene slid off of Toby's back, standing for a minute to release the numbness in her legs before tying him to a hitching post where water buckets had been placed at equal intervals. Walking up the stairs felt unreal. She paused at the door, one hand on the knob, the other on her still-fluttering stomach. *It's*

not every day a girl gets to walk into her very own dream wide awake. Thank You, God.

Even before entering, Marlene heard the chattering of excited voices. She tried to slip in unnoticed, but the one adult in the room quickly came over to greet her. "I'm Mary Dodge," the woman said, extending a hand. "Welcome! Please tell me your name."

Marlene felt the blush start in her neck, spreading upward, but she reached out. "I'm Marlene Cooper, ma'am. Nice to meet ya."

"Oh, please, call me Miss Mary. I'm so happy to have you, Marlene. Tell me, do you live close by?"

"No, ma'am, uh, Miss Mary. We live about an hour and a half ride out of town."

"Goodness, you're a dedicated girl." She leaned forward. "That's the kind of grit it takes to learn the violin. I'm sure you'll do just fine."

There were an even dozen children that day—ten girls and two boys, who were twins. Marlene only recognized one girl from church, and they greeted one another with a nervous wave. A large table in the center of the room held a grand selection of violins.

Just then the door opened, and two men of about the same age entered carrying more instruments.

Mrs. Dodge spoke. "Children, I'd like to have your attention, please." A pin falling could have been heard. She walked over to the tallest man. "This is my husband, *Mr.* Dodge." She smiled up at the balding man beside her and winked. He returned the smile and the wink. Next, she introduced the dark-haired man sporting a huge black mustache. "This, children, is Mr. Corlini." The shorter man bowed and smiled, revealing the whitest teeth Marlene had ever seen. "My husband is quite the teacher and will, along with myself, instruct you in how to read music. And Mr. Corlini, all the way from Italy and now living here, is. . .that is, was. . .a professional flautist."

A humming undercurrent like bees in a hive vibrated around the room as the children looked at each other in bewilderment. What in the world was a flautist?

Every Saturday, Mary Dodge added new "recruits" to the initial group. It continued to grow, despite the many naysayers who thought the task of forming a cohesive group of performers from the likes of untrained children was a daunting, if not impossible, task. However, they'd never met Mary Dodge.

Music and children were her passion, and all the energy spent on those two things made her happy and successful. Marlene loved her.

"Marlene, dear, please don't cry all over the instrument. It's detrimental to the wood."

Marlene had tried her best to read the notes in front of her half a dozen times with no success and had been brought to tears for the second time that morning. She mumbled something under her breath, bringing Mrs. Dodge closer.

"Please don't mumble, dear. Speak up."

"I said, I don't think I'm cut out to play the violin." Crushing as the words sounded to her own ears, she believed them to be true.

Mrs. Dodge threw her head back in a raucous laugh, walking around to stand directly in front of Marlene. "Look at me, please."

Marlene looked up.

"I believe with all my heart that you belong in this place, in this classroom, at this very moment. I have a sense about people, you see. I know when there's passion in a person's heart for music. So remember this: you *will* learn to play. And I believe you will learn to be better than just *good.*" She stepped closer, causing Marlene to sit up straighter. "Do you wonder why I know these things about you?"

Marlene nodded, drying the tears with the back of one hand.

"Because," she whispered, "I *was* you."

Marlene gasped. "I—I don't understand."

"I was just like you in the beginning. I had passion and desire, but when I first started playing, I let doubts about my ability crowd out those things. I almost gave up." She smiled and folded her hands.

Marlene smiled back into the face of her teacher. "What can I do?"

"Each and every day I want you to find a quiet place and practice only the scales."

"What?" Marlene was puzzled.

"You heard me." She placed both hands on either side of the girl's face. "I promise if you will do that for thirty minutes before trying to play anything else, eventually you will have success. Play those scales like you were playing for an audience, Marlene, and you will see the results you want. See, right now, you and the violin do not know each other very well. By playing those simple notes, you'll begin to understand the ins and outs of your instrument." She removed her hands. "You love this violin already, am I right?"

"Oh yes, Mrs. Dodge, uh, Miss Mary."

"I knew it. I can see it in your eyes, my precious girl. It's right there, for sure. Let me give you another word of encouragement. There will always be people who are better and brighter than you. But if it takes one person one year to play the violin, or it takes you five, in the end, you will both know how to play. Does that make sense?"

Marlene nodded and couldn't stop smiling.

Mrs. Dodge had been right. Every night, after school and chores were finished, Marlene practiced and practiced those scales. In time, they became like a special friend. She let her imagination surround her with an appreciative audience who applauded for more whenever she'd finished. Always she remembered to bow.

The entire class had improved as the summer of 1912 came to a close and school started again. A few students dropped out, three moved to Portland, and one broke his arm. Despite this, their little group had grown to thirty students.

Mr. Dodge's and Mr. Corlini's students were as eager as the children tutored by Mrs. Dodge, and every other week the three classes got together. At first they played simple melodies, mostly children's songs or old hymns, but soon Mrs. Dodge was introducing classical pieces. Her enthusiasm and trust brought about intense loyalty from every one of the students.

On the first Saturday in August, Mrs. Dodge was standing by the door, giving each child a pat on the head as they entered. While everyone got their instruments tuned and ready, Mrs. Dodge paced the floor and hummed a Christmas carol. It was nearly ninety degrees outside in the high desert air, so the children were perplexed.

Marlene leaned over to the red-headed girl sitting next to her. "Maybe we're going to practice Christmas songs."

"Now?" the girl asked.

Mrs. Dodge stomped the floor, as was her habit. "Attention, class!" Her arms were full of books—shiny new ones with bright red-and-green covers. "I'm so very excited this morning." She giggled like a schoolgirl. "Truthfully, I'm excited whenever we get together, but this morning is very, very special." The children glanced at one another, each with the same "why" question on their minds.

She walked around handing out the books. "Two to a book, please. There are more on the way."

Marlene and the red-headed girl looked at theirs. "I told you," Marlene whispered.

"Aren't the books lovely?" Mrs. Dodge asked. She didn't wait for a response but began thumbing through the one in her hand. "Just look at these wonderful old tunes. There's 'Away in a Manger.' And oh, on page twenty-seven, you'll love this arrangement of 'Silent Night.'" She cleared her throat. "Now, I'd be excited just about the books, but I'm eager to tell you this: there's more."

October 1912

It was the "more" part that was on Marlene's mind as she finished hanging out the wash. There was going to be a concert for Christmas in Burns, and they'd been practicing every week since it had been announced.

Mrs. Dodge had been dead-on in her observation of Marlene's heart's desire and passion for music and the violin. Although at times it had taken her longer than some to play a piece, diligence paid off in the end, and she became an excellent violinist as predicted.

But, as the concert grew closer, she began to have serious doubts about her ability to play before others, regardless of her skill. Merely thinking about it made her stomach queasy, like now, finishing up chores.

Her mother was sitting at the kitchen table shucking corn when Marlene brought the empty wash basket inside. "I thought you'd never finish, Mar. What in the world took you so long out there?"

Marlene shrugged. "Thinking about the Christmas concert." She sat down across the table.

"You're not worried, are you?"

Marlene's head dropped to her chest before speaking. "Yes."

"But why, Mar? You're so good. How many times has Mrs. Dodge told you that?"

Marlene looked up. "I know, Mama, but when I think about playing in front of people, my head gets all fuzzy and something goes off in my stomach like a cannon ball." She picked up an ear of corn and started peeling off husks.

Mrs. Cooper reached across the table and took the half-shucked ear of corn from her daughter. "Look at it this way, Mar. You're kind of like this corn here...there are layers and layers to be pulled away, and that takes some time. But look what a wonderful thing awaits down underneath."

Marlene smiled a little and tilted her head.

"See, Marlene, we're all the time being peeled back by the good Lord in some fashion or another. It's not just you and music—pretty much all of life is like that." She patted her hand. "Is this making any sense?"

"Yes." Big pause. "But tell that to my stomach."

October's end brought a high-desert snowstorm, pushing winds down upon them like a giant thrashing machine. Residents in and out of town were forced to hunker down and wait it out. Most were not at all surprised and had been adequately prepared, able to take it all in stride. All except Marlene, who protested loudly during the entire duration. One evening she paced for over an hour in front of the woodstove.

"Marlene, you're wearing out the floor," her mother scolded. "Come sit with me a spell."

"I can't, Ma. I keep thinking about how bad the Christmas concert will be because we can't all get together and practice." She wrung her hands in frustration.

"I'm sure everyone is practicing at home just like you've been. Relax a little...please."

"That reminds me...I'm going to my room and practice scales."

Mrs. Cooper sighed. "Lord, help that girl."

Despite the storm in October, another in November, and the usual numbing cold of December, the musical group still managed to have very productive sessions that left them all encouraged and excited. December 17th was their last practice, with energy and tension filling every nook and cranny of the room.

"Children, may I have your attention?" Mrs. Dodge tapped her baton several times on a music stand. When all was quiet, she smiled. "I first want to tell you how proud I am of each and every one of you." She swept the baton around the room. "You have all worked as hard as any students I've ever taught, yet all this time we've been together, we've not had a 'formal' title to call ourselves." She leaned forward into a little bow. "Until now, that is."

"What is it?"

"Oh, please tell us."

"Very well." She laid down the baton and reached for a rolled-up piece of paper. Carefully she unfurled it, turning it around for all to see. There was an audible gasp.

THE SAGE BRUSH SYMPHONY ORCHESTRA PRESENTS

A CELEBRATION OF CHRISTMAS
FEATURING THE CHILDREN OF
BURNS, OREGON

DIRECTED BY MRS. MARY DODGE
DECEMBER 23RD, 1912

"You, my musical geniuses, are now officially called 'The Sage Brush Symphony Orchestra.'" Mrs. Dodge was beaming.

One boy raised his hand. "What if people laugh at the name Sage Brush?"

Mrs. Dodge took her time while rolling up the scroll before speaking. "Let them."

December 23, 1912

Marlene pulled back the window curtain and felt her stomach begin to churn. "Mama," she shouted, "it looks like snow. It can't snow today. . .not today. Please, God."

Her mother looked out the glass. "Hmm, I don't think so, Marlene. There's not a cloud in the sky. Where's your faith?" She gave her daughter a hug. "Stop worrying and get your dress on."

Marlene climbed the stairs in twos.

They left in plenty of time, singing Christmas songs along the way. The closer they got to town, the more fear poured into Marlene, causing her mind to reel with all the what-ifs. *What if I forget my solo? What if I mess up and disappoint Mrs. Dodge?* She hid her face in both gloved hands.

When they got to town, it wasn't hard to spot the huge tent Mr. Dodge had erected for the occasion. Rising smoke from a roaring woodstove gave testimony that it was even heated. Immediately, Marlene jumped down from the wagon, picked up the violin, and dashed for the tent opening. Her mother called to her back, "Marlene, I know you're nervous, but don't let fear steal your joy today. Just remember how far God has brought you. What a gift."

Marlene smiled, feeling herself relax. . .a little. Once inside, the canvas walls vibrated with excitement and the tuning of instruments. Bright lights hung along the sides and over the center aisle, while dozens of long wood benches were already full of chattering families. A huge pine tree in one corner exuded a heady, spicy fragrance.

Marlene's face burned with anticipation the minute she focused on the stage. *Oh, God, I do believe it was You who brought this whole thing about. I'm so sorry I'm such a baby sometimes. Please help me not to be afraid and to play good today. Amen.*

Within the half hour, all the benches had been filled and each musician was lined up behind their director, ready to take the stage. Mrs. Dodge turned toward them and mouthed the word *smile*. She nodded, did an about-face, and walked briskly toward the stage.

The instant the orchestra arrived on stage the entire place went quiet.

All that could be heard was the crackle of the fire and a whimpering child in the back.

Mrs. Dodge walked to center stage. "Good afternoon, everyone. I'm Mary Dodge, and I'd like to welcome you to the first ever concert from The Sage Brush Symphony Orchestra." The crowd went wild with applause; some even whistled.

Marlene felt the familiar tightening in her stomach, but before it could erupt into something more, she prayed, *God, thank You for sending Jesus. I just want to honor Him. Amen.* In an instant, the fluttering was gone, and all her attention was on her mentor.

"The children have worked long and hard over the last months to present you with this gift, and it has been my supreme honor to get to know each and every one of them. You as parents can be very proud of the job you've done raising such amazing, talented young people." She took a little bow. "I—that is, *we*—hope you enjoy the fruits of our labor. It's been one of love and devotion. Thank you."

She turned and walked to a small podium that held a music stand in the middle of the stage. All eyes were on her as she raised the baton.

Softly, almost like a whisper, the Sage Brush flautists began to play "Silent Night." The violinists joined them one by one until a crescendo of sound filled the walls of the tent with the purest of melody. The audience was swept along to another place, another time. Each note brought them all, performer and listener alike, to the Bethlehem stable where a tiny Savior King had been born.

In that moment, Marlene felt her soul rise with the notes floating around her and realized a truth that would last a lifetime: dreams really do come true because God is the dream giver.

When they'd finished, there was a brief silence. . .then the crowd erupted with applause and a standing ovation. And that was only song number one!

Marlene could not stop smiling. *Merry Christmas, Jesus,* she thought, *and thank You for everything.*

A Note to the Reader

By 1915, the orchestra was touring Eastern Oregon on a Chautauque circuit, and in September 1916, they traveled to the west side of the state. They even won one hundred dollars at the state fair in Salem and played several concerts in Portland. One included a performance for the famous opera star Madame Ernestine Schumann-Heink, who was so impressed with the talent that she helped the group continue touring.

When America became involved in World War I, plans for further tours ended, and the children disbanded. Mrs. Dodge moved to Portland. She led the Irvington School—the founding group for the Portland Junior Symphony, known today as the Portland Junior Philharmonic. It was the first organization of its kind in the entire United States.

A Little Bit of Home

LINDA J. REINHARDT

Matthew can't help but miss his oldest daughter, Meg, who moved with her husband and kids far from her childhood home. Meg had always hated the cold and snow, and now she's in a much warmer place. Yet this Christmas she's in for the surprise of her life. . .and a connection with home she hadn't bargained for.

Matthew kicked the snow off before entering the enclosed back porch. He sat on the old rocker and tugged his boots off, along with his wool socks. The smell of roasting turkey teased his growling stomach.

Last night had brought in another three inches of snow, so he had spent the morning, with help from his oldest son and grandsons, clearing the driveway. Soon the children who still lived in the area would arrive for Christmas dinner.

He hoped his other children—Dot, Matt, and Meg—had a nice Christmas together. This would be the first time he hadn't celebrated Christmas with his oldest daughter, Meg. She'd moved with her husband, Kelly, and two kids out West after visiting her sister and brother during the summer.

She had fallen in love with the area, and Matthew couldn't blame her. Beautiful majestic mountains, waterfalls, and the scene in the gorge were absolutely spectacular. The winters were much milder.

Her husband had walked in the snow around here for years delivering mail. Now he'd no longer have to do that. And if there was one thing Meg didn't like, it was snow. She couldn't stand the temperatures and having to bundle up all the time, not to mention all of the work it caused people to have to do.

Still, he'd have to deal with his emotions. He missed her and her family. Christmas wouldn't be the same without them.

"I see you got the drive clear," his wife, Alma, said. "Did Vern and the boys go home? I made a plate for all of you."

"No, they're still out in the barn. They'll be here in just a moment." Matthew stood up tall and patted his trim stomach. "I'll take my plate now, though. I see no reason to wait."

Alma laughed. "I'm sure you don't. Well, come in when you're ready. I just put it on the table."

Matthew moved quickly to wash his hands, then sat down to enjoy his lunch. The house was quiet now but would soon be filled with the sounds of laughter and little kids squealing. He could hardly wait.

Maybe he'd give Meg a call before all of the craziness started. Finishing up his meal, he brought his dishes to the sink, then headed for the phone.

Meg woke with a big smile on Christmas morning. *This is the life. For once, no snow to battle. Kelly doesn't have to shovel the sidewalks or the drive and. . .*

Her smile turned to a frown as she drew back her bedroom curtain. Snow covered the ground.

"What? When did this happen?" she mumbled to herself. "Kelly. . .Kelly," she called as she walked down the hallway of the rental home where they were staying while their house was being built. They had hoped the house would be done for the holidays, but now it looked like it wouldn't get finished until the end of January, maybe even February.

She searched around the house and couldn't find her husband. The kids were surprisingly asleep, or so she thought, until she opened up the front door and discovered her family dressed in snowsuits playing in the snow.

She groaned. *I thought we were done with snow.*

Just then the phone rang, and she ran to answer it. "Hi, Dad, you aren't going to believe this, but I woke up this morning to snow."

"Snow?" There was surprise in his voice. "I know it snows sometimes where your sister lives, but usually it's only a slight covering in the other areas."

"No, Dad, it's snow-snow. I'm talking at least a foot, and it's weird looking. . .kind of icy."

"Hmmm. . ." There was a smothered chuckle, then her dad said, "I'm sorry you got snow on your first Christmas away from home."

"Dad. . ."

"Well, it is your first Christmas away from home in almost thirty years. I'm going to miss you being here."

"I miss you, too, Dad, but you do understand this is a good move for me and my family, right?"

"Yeah, I guess. Can I say merry Christmas to the kids?"

"They're outside right now, but I'll have them call you when they come in, after they open their Santa Claus presents. I can't believe they're playing outside with presents sitting under the tree."

"Maybe it's their way of connecting with their home back here."

"Yeah, Dad. . .maybe." Meg felt uncomfortable. She knew the move was hard on her dad. "Can I talk to Mom?"

"Of course! Merry Christmas; I love you. And, Meg. . .I'm glad the kids got a touch of home today." She could hear the catch in her dad's voice, and she was barely able to tell him she loved him back.

After she talked to her mom, she swiftly got herself ready for the day. By the time she'd finished, the kids and Kelly were coming in from the garage, rosy cheeked, with big smiles.

"Merry Christmas, Mommy," Lynn and Allen chimed together in their young voices.

"Merry Christmas, kids." She gave them each a hug. "I can't believe you went outside before you opened your Santa presents."

They all piped up with responses, including Kelly.

"But it's snowing!"

"Like back home!"

"It's awesome. Wetter than the snow from back home, though."

"I got to build a snowman. I think Santa brought the snow."

"I think Jesus gave us snow today, because He knew what all of our hearts needed." Kelly put his arm around Meg's shoulder. "A little touch of our old home."

"Yeah!" The kids clapped and cheered.

"That's what my dad said." Meg rolled her eyes.

She watched as the kids unwrapped their gifts from Santa and enjoyed their excited responses. Kelly handed Meg a gift that her dad had sent. A lump formed in her throat. She didn't miss the snow, but she did miss her family. Tearing open the present, she discovered a nice pair of leather gloves. Every year her dad gave her a good, sensible pair of gloves to deal with the elements. But this pair wasn't the type a person wore on a snowy day but rather the type that just kept your hands warm when the temperature dropped and looked nice. Tears filled her eyes. *You're so sweet, Dad.*

Meg stood with sudden determination. She went over to the coat closet, got out her parka, and found the gloves her dad had given her the Christmas before. Then she called her dad.

After three rings, he picked up. "Dad, thanks for the gloves. I'm really going to love wearing them, but. . .I found my gloves from last year, and you know what?"

"No, what?"

"I'm putting them on, and I'm going to go build a snowman in your honor. I think Kelly is right: Jesus sent the snow so we can have a touch of home. And I don't want to miss out on anything from home."

"Well. . ." Her dad chuckled. "That's something I'd love to see. You playing in the snow."

"You will. I'll have Kelly take lots of pictures with his new camera, and then I'll send them to you, because even though I live here now, my heart is still with you at home."

Her dad was quiet for a moment, then cleared his throat.

"And, Dad, please take pictures for me so I don't miss out on anything. After all, it's the first Christmas I've been away in thirty years."

"I'll do that. Have a merry Christmas now, dear!" Meg felt good to hear a smile in his voice.

"I will. And, Dad. . .I do miss you."

"I miss you, too. Now go get some pictures taken of that family of yours before the snow melts. I heard it doesn't stay around too long where you're at."

Meg laughed. "Okay. Dad, tell everyone merry Christmas."

Donning her parka, she called for the rest of her family to join her. They played and posed for pictures until her sister and brother arrived. They joined in the fun, too.

Meg laughed as her brother threw a packed snowball at her just like when they were young.

She may have moved away from home, but Jesus was faithful to bring a part of home to her on this wonderful Christmas Day.

Weary Christmas Star

Linda J. Reinhardt

Zetty loved to volunteer at her church, but her family always wanted her home with them. Caught in her heart's tug-of-war, Zetty felt very weary one Christmas Eve day. . .until the greatest of all miracles happened.

Zetty blew at the curly tendril of hair that stuck to her damp forehead and groaned inwardly. *I'm so hot and tired I can hardly stand it.* Zetty quickly pushed the cart of food to the next station at church. This year the church had decided to do a Christmas carnival to draw more people in for the Christmas Eve service. Zetty had readily volunteered, thinking it would be fun. But she had discovered it to be far from fun. She ran one errand after another the last month in preparation, and today she hadn't sat down since she woke up at 6:00 a.m.

Instead of fun, it was exhausting. On top of preparing for the carnival, she had pressure from her family to spend more time with them this Christmas season. She had been to the zoo-lights, dinners, shopping, all in between work and helping to set up for this carnival.

Just last night her mom had said, "Now, Zetty, you will promise to be here early for our festivities, right?"

"Yes, Mom, I'll be home as soon as I'm done at the church. But I'm not sure what time that will be."

"You can explain to all of those people there at the church that you have a prior commitment."

"Mom, I have a commitment there, not just to the people, but also to Jesus. I love to serve Him."

"Well, coming home and making your family happy will be a good enough way to serve Him."

Zetty shook her head. She could never get her family to understand

357

how important her faith was to her.

This morning she had been put in charge of food for all of the volunteers. It had sounded easy, but Zetty was tired, so instead of enjoying the fun of serving, she felt overwhelmed. Along with passing out the food came the responsibility of making sure everything was set up and passed out for breaks and lunch and an early dinner for the volunteers, who planned on helping through the Christmas Eve service. A lot of the earlier volunteers had gone home to get ready for the Christmas Eve service, leaving her with the responsibility of not only packaging up the meal, but getting it passed out to everyone. Normally, she could handle things like this. She loved to serve Jesus, but with the busyness of the month and her family pulling her from what she loved to do instead of joining her, she was frustrated.

Carefully she pushed the cart through the throngs of children and their parents, being careful not to hit any of them. Pasting a smile on her face, she stopped close by the elf assisting Santa with pictures and counted the helpers. *The elf, Santa, photographer, two sign-up ladies, and. . .I think that's it.* She grabbed five bags off of the cart and placed them on the sign-up table.

"Here you go, ladies! It's time to eat. I believe someone will be coming around soon to take over for you on your break. What would you like to drink? I have soda or water." The ladies gave their orders along with the three others at the station. As soon as she passed out their drinks, she started to make a beeline for the manger station.

One of the ladies stopped her. "Zetty? Is that your name?"

"Yes," she replied.

"Do you think you could sit here for a minute? At least until someone else arrives to take my place? I had planned on leaving an hour ago to pick up my granddaughters, and well. . ."

Zetty looked around to see if anyone else could help instead of her.

"Zetty! Have you made it over to the cakewalk yet? I think they were supposed to have a break five minutes ago. And most of them over at the cakewalk are staying right through the service," Doreen called from over at the "Dunk Your Pastor" booth.

"I'm sorry," Zetty said to the volunteer she didn't recognize, which wasn't odd considering the size of the church she attended and the number of volunteers that usually signed up for events. "I have to run food over to the cakewalk."

"Oh, I could do that for you. No problem." The lady stood from her chair and proceeded to the food cart. "Don't worry. I'll put the cart back when I'm finished." And off she went.

Zetty felt as though she had no choice but to sit down and start signing up people for pictures.

"Oh, there you are. I've been looking all over for you. Did you finish passing out the dinners?" Marsha, the head of the volunteers, stood in front of Zetty's table with a friendly but tired smile.

"Well, sort of. . ." Zetty started to explain but was interrupted by a lady with a question about pictures.

"Marsha! Hey, the crew over at the cakewalk and the manger are starving. Do we have some food for them?" Pastor Don asked as he rubbed his hair with a towel. He'd obviously been dunked in the tank.

Marsha gave Zetty a questioning look. Zetty's eyes grew big. She stood and ran over to find the food cart. She found it abandoned close to the cakewalk station. For some reason, it hadn't made it the entire distance, and there were only three bags left on the cart. *Oh no! Now I have to run and make some more really quick.*

Zetty moved swiftly and was able to get the rest of the food passed out without any further complaints. She rallied a few volunteers to help her clean up and was finally finished for the day.

She desperately wanted to go home and shower instead of simply changing into her clothes in the bathroom. A glance at the clock told her she'd have to make do with using a few damp paper towels to freshen up if she didn't want to miss the early service.

Zetty cleaned up and changed her clothes, then made her way to the chapel. It felt good to sit down and relax. The pressure of her parents wanting her home tonight with the family for Christmas made her just sink down in a pew, instead of looking around to see if anyone needed help. She didn't want to listen to her family complain about how she spent more time with the people at church than her own family.

Zetty bit her tongue. Everyone in her family worked and had lots of outside interests, but none were interested in gracing the doors of a church. They thought she was nuts. So she'd given up inviting them a long time ago.

Soon the chapel filled and she found herself squished in between families as they tried to make room for everyone. Although she had a lot of friends at church, it was times like this, when families piled in together, when she would find herself feeling lonely. How she wished her family would join her, at least for Christmas.

But no. . .

Zetty decided to go sit in the back since it was so uncomfortable being squished in between everyone.

"Oh, there you are, Zetty!" Marsha exclaimed as she walked down the center aisle.

"Hi, Marsha!" Secretly Zetty hoped she didn't need her for anything, because she only wanted to enjoy the service and then leave to go be with her family.

"I have a couple out front, and I was wondering, if you aren't already sitting with somebody. . .if you could help them feel comfortable."

Zetty took in a deep breath. "I'd love to, Marsha, but I'm exhausted, and my family wants me home tonight. I've decided not to disappoint them by getting busy here."

"Oh, don't you worry. I'll be sure you leave right after the service. Just do this favor for me?" Marsha smiled.

Zetty shrugged. "Fine." She followed Marsha out to the fellowship hall until she stopped in front of. . .her parents? "Mom. . .Dad?" Marsha turned and gave her a hug before she left Zetty alone with her parents. "What on earth are you doing here? I thought you were getting ready for tonight's festivities."

"Well, we wanted to come here with you this year, but you didn't ask, so. . .we hope you don't mind."

"Mind? No, not at all. The reason I didn't ask is because you always say no."

Her dad gave a smile. "Tonight we're saying yes. Do you have anything you need help with before we sit down? We know you like to help out here."

"No, I finished everything and was taking a break."

"Well then, that lady, Marsha, said she had some seats set up for us. Let's go see where they are." Her mom took her arm. "This is a great way to start the holidays. Next year we'll have to get your brothers and sisters to come."

Zetty nodded. *Whatever you say, Mom!* One thing Zetty knew for sure was that she was going to ask them as soon as they were all together. She wasn't going to give up so easily.

Suddenly, all the weariness of the day left her and she was bursting with a joy that comes from a long-awaited answer to prayer.

The Tablecloth Freedom Flag

Sharon Bernash Smith

Why do people keep old things. . .things that have outlived their usefulness? Carol Ann Matthews wants to know after finding a very worn table-cloth tucked away in her mother's home. After declaring she's going to skip Christmas, a sweet journey back in time might just persuade Carol Ann to recant.

Although we can never change what's happened in the past, sometimes, every once in a while, looking back can give us a push forward just when we need it.

Placquemine, Louisiana
December 20, 1981

O nly one box left."

"One of twenty-seven hundred," she said under her breath.

"Carol Ann!"

"Merry Christmas to you, too, Ruthie." She sighed and plopped onto a sturdy box.

"Look, I was just trying to encourage y'all, Carol Ann. Excuse me!"

Carol Ann Matthews smiled at her sister, swallowing the anger. "Ruthie, I'm sorry, okay? I'm so wiped out right now. Please forgive me." She stood, walking over to the beautiful, blond creature she loved beyond measure. "I'm glad y'all are my sister, Ruthie. . .even if you are bossy." She laughed out loud.

Ruthie hugged her sister, planting a quick kiss on her forehead. "That's the first time I've heard you laugh since Mama died, Carol Ann. Even when you were little, I loved that laugh." Tears streaked down one cheek.

"Hey, where is ever'body?" A booming voice from the front door startled them both.

"Up here," shouted Carol Ann. "In the neverland of forgotten boxes."

They could hear him stomping up the stairs two at a time. "I thought y'all would be finished with this by now," he said at the doorway. Their little brother, Robert Lee, was never one to beat around the bush.

"Well, we're paid little, so we take our old sweet time," Ruthie teased. She greeted him with a fierce hug.

"Sorry I wasn't here sooner, but I had to work late." His eyes swept the room. "Seriously, you two are amazin'. Who knew Mom had so much stuff?"

"We did," his sisters said in unison.

Rob shook his head. "How we gonna handle all this?"

"Glad you asked," Carol Ann answered. "They're all marked, so when you and your band of brothers from church come on over Saturday, there'll be no doubt as to the destination of fifty years of. . .let's see, how can I put this kindly? Oh yeah, fifty years of junk." She took a big swig of cold coffee, swallowing in disgust.

Rob winked at Ruthie. "Uh-oh, one sister woke up on the wrong side of the world, I see."

"Lay off me, Robert Lee Sparks. This grievin' stuff's way harder than I thought, is all. And don't tell me you're cruising right through it either." She turned away, trying to hide the big ugly cry she'd been fighting off all day.

"Hey, big sister number two, sorry, okay? Really, Carol Ann, I *am* sorry." He walked over and tapped her on the shoulder. She turned and faced him.

"I'm sorry, too, Robbie. I thought I couldn't cry anymore, even after these weeks since the memorial service. Guess I'm not finished missin' my mama." She took a tissue from her jeans and blew into it hard. "And, in case y'all are interested, I'm skippin' Christmas."

"Carol Ann, I don't think anybody would expect to be over the death of their mother so soon. I don't feel much like celebrating Christmas either. Let's you and me just forget it, then," Rob said.

Ruthie's muffled voice came from the closet where she was dusting the top shelf. "Hey y'all, look what I found." She stepped out, holding a muted yellow cloth in both hands. "How'd we miss this?"

"What's that?"

"It's the old tablecloth Mama loved so much." She stepped out of the closet, rubbing a hand over the top. "I never did understand why. Did she ever tell either of you?"

Carol Ann and Rob both shook their heads.

"Let me see that." Carol Ann stretched it at arm's length. "My, oh my, look how many patches there are on this raggedy old thing." Held up to the light, it was easy to see the hand-sewn repairs. "It must have meant somethin' real special for her to keep it so long. You know, right up ta this very minute, I never thought of my mother as a woman of mystery, but now I wonder." She ran her fingers all along the embroidered edges. "Hey, these flowers are magnolias, right?"

"Yup, Mama's favorite. . .maybe *that's* why she kept it." Ruthie shrugged.

"Wait a minute. Look close here." Carol Ann pointed to one corner.

"What?"

"A name, I think."

"Let me look," Rob said. "You're right. But the stitchin's so old now, I can't quite make it out without a magnifying glass."

"Oh, I saw one in the kitchen. . .on the windowsill. Let me get it."

Carol Ann was back in a minute. "Now, let's see that name. Okay, there's an *A* for sure, then maybe a *b*. . .then there's nothin' but empty spots." She held the glass closer. "Ah, the last three letters are *ssa*." She looked up, disappointed.

Ruthie's face lit up. "I know—it's Abbalyssa! Abbalyssa Brown! Y'all must remember Mama's friend Pirti, right? Abbalyssa was Pirti's mama. I wonder how *our* mother got a tablecloth from *her?*"

"All I remember is, since I was a little boy, that cloth covered the old buffet in the dining room."

"Me, too. Only time it wasn't being used was when Mama washed it. But she had so many other coverin's, I wonder what made this one so special." Carol Ann folded it back up.

"Carol Ann, you have a funny look in your eye. What are you thinkin'?"

"That there's some kind of story about this little piece of cloth, and I'm aimin' to find out what it is."

"Well, in case you do go snoopin' around, I know for sure that Pirti's married name is Stone. She married Abraham Stone."

"Oh sure, I remember him. Didn't he go to jail for marchin' in one of those freedom demonstrations in the '60s?"

Ruthie smiled. "Bet neither of you knew our mama was marchin' right along beside that colored man."

"What?" Rob said. "How come I never heard this?" He shook his head in wonder.

"See what I mean?" Carol Ann said. "Our mother's a woman of mystery." She draped the tablecloth over one arm. "I'm not gonna wait."

"Carol Ann, you can't just go bargin' around town, stirring up dust."

"Ruthie, let me remind you this is the '80s and not the '60s."

"Well, let me remind *you* that some people don't know the difference. If"—she peered over the top of her glasses—"you know what I mean."

Rob spoke up. "Ruthie's right, Carol Ann. Don't be stirrin' up no hornet's nest around here, or you might be sorry."

"Look, I do so appreciate y'all giving me such sage advice, but I'm gonna find out about this little piece of cloth, hornet's nest or not, so help me, God."

"Well, Sister, you might need Him if any of those hornets come chasing you down the street after pounding on their little abode."

"Very funny, Rob." She rolled her eyes. "We're done here for today, anyway." She grabbed her purse, car keys, and the tablecloth. "See ya."

After leaving, Carol Ann couldn't shake the feeling that something really significant had happened in her mother's life and somehow the old tablecloth was connected. She'd planned on waiting until she got home to look through the phone book, but instead she pulled over to a Winn Dixie with a telephone booth out front.

Maybe Pirti didn't even live in Plaquemine anymore, but she had to find out. Despite the calendar date, it was muggy outside, and the inside of the booth smelled like a good-sized fish had died in it. Propping the door open with one foot, she combed through the white pages, careful not to touch anything else.

"Bingo!" There were only three *Stones* listed, and one of them was Abraham Jr. She rummaged through her purse and found a dime. "Please be home, please be home."

Someone answered on the third ring. "Hello?" It was a woman's voice.

"Uh, yes, I'm looking for Pirti Stone, please."

Nothing.

"Hello?"

"I'm still here. Who's this?"

"This is Carol Ann Matthews, uh, Sparks, Mrs. Stone. I'm Noonie's youngest daughter."

Another pause. "Well, land sakes, little Carol Ann. I read 'bout your sweet mama's passin', and I'd a been at the services but didn't have me no way to get there." Her voice broke. "Your mama and I was real close back in the day, Carol Ann. . .real close."

"You know, Mrs. Stone, I remember, and that's why I'm calling you outta the blue like this. I'm wonderin', do you have a minute to talk if I come over?"

"Right now?"

"Would that be all right?"

"Well sure, guess so. Y'all know where I live?"

"Sure, I have your address right in front of me. . .on Nat's Alley."

"Yes, that's right. Sure am excited to be seein' y'all, Carol Ann."

"Me, too, Mrs. Stone."

The drive took ten minutes. Pirti's house was bright yellow with crisp white trim, even on the wide shutters flanking both front windows. A huge laurel oak stood dead center in the yard, giving the small ranch a stately feel.

Carol Ann rang the doorbell and immediately heard footsteps. The door opened wide, revealing a tiny woman with snow-white hair. She was grinning from ear to ear.

"Carol Ann, I'd a known you anywhere, girl. You for sure do favor your mama." She took Carol Ann by both hands and led her inside. "I made us coffee. Do y'all want a cup?"

"Sounds good, but please don't go botherin' just for me, Mrs. Stone."

Carol Ann shut the door behind herself.

"I don't be havin' much company, so y'all stopping by is a special treat." The smell of freshly perked coffee filled the cozy house with a hospitality fragrance.

"Take a seat there at the dining table now, and I'll bring the coffee over."

From where she sat, Carol Ann had full view of the living room walls filled with family pictures all the way around. A small Christmas tree stood in one corner with the lights on. "How many children do you have, Mrs. Stone?"

"Oh, please call me Pirti. I had me six, but I lost Lizbeth, my only little girl, just days after she was born." Her voice dropped. "Somehow that seems almost like yesterday. My, my."

"I'm so sorry, Pirti. You must have been devastated."

"Tell you true, Carol Ann, it like ta kilt me. Worse even than when my daddy died. Laid my body in bed for nearly a month before I roused around enough to move on. Hadn't been for the good Lord Hisself, and my sweet husband, I'd never gotten back on my feet."

She limped to the table and set a tray with two cups and fixings in front of Carol Ann. "How you takes y'all's coffee?"

"Just a little milk is fine, thank you."

Pirti doctored her own cup with generous amounts of milk and sugar. "Your mama used ta tease me 'bout puttin' so much additions to my coffee. Said I liked a little coffee with my fixin's." She stirred the steaming liquid slowly. "I miss her, Carol Ann. Even though we didn't talk reglar-like, just knowin' I could if I had a mind to gave me comfort. You know what I'm sayin'?"

"I most certainly do, Pirti. At least once a day I pick up the phone to call her—hits me hard every time I remember I can't."

"Well, I'm happy to at least sit with y'all a spell." She took a sip of coffee and smacked her lips. "Mm, perfect," she said, smiling big and settling the cup back onto the saucer.

Carol Ann cleared her throat before speaking what was on her mind. "Uh, I'm sure you must be wonderin' why I called you out of the blue. . . ."

"Well, I am a mite curious." One hand went up. "Not that it ain't wonderful to see you. Nothin' like that, for sure."

Carol Ann reached into her purse and pulled out the tablecloth. "This is the reason I'm here," she said and unfolded it across her lap.

Pirti's right hand flew to her mouth as big tears flowed down copper-colored cheeks. "Oh," she whispered. "Oh my, oh my."

"I'm sorry, Pirti. I didn't mean to upset you. Are you all right?" She touched her on the arm.

Pirti drew in a big breath. "Sorry, I didn't mean to break down. It's jest I haven't seen that in a long, long time." She pulled a hankie out of her sweater pocket and wiped her face. "Oh, if that piece of cloth could talk." She shook her head. "What stories they'd be."

"That's exactly why I'm here. Somehow I just *knew* there was something special about this table covering." She handed it to Pirti.

"Do y'all mind if we move to the livin' room? I'm jest needin' ta put my feet up." She stood and Carol Ann did as well, helping her onto the worn sofa. Pirti opened the material and ran a hand over the entire thing, then touched it to her face. "Oh," she said in a low voice, and her eyes misted again as she began to tell the story. . . .

Noonie and I met on about as hot a day ever there was in the month of August. We was maybe ten or eleven. Jest girls, for sure. The air felt heavy, like it could suffocate the life outta any livin' thing that had breath. That's what drove us to that bitty stream a water oozing by the end of the block where I lived.

I was sittin' in the deepest spot I could find, which was no more than two feet at the most, eyes shut, thinkin' how I wished a cool breeze might come up and be friends with the parts of my body not underwater. That's when I heard someone singin' round the bend.

They was loud and kinda out of tune, but I was pretty sure it sounded like a girl. I stood up real slow-like, so's not to give myself away. I wanted to make sure it weren't no white girl. For if it was, one of us was in the wrong place. . . .

Carol Ann raised an eyebrow.

"Remember now, Carol Ann, this was 1920 or '21," Pirti said. "In those days, there was no minglin' of coloreds and whites. . .no sirree. Not only was it not allowed, it could be out-n-out dangerous."

"Even for children?" Carol Ann asked.

"Didn't make no difference, child. Not one iota did it matter how old ya was. Well, anyways. . ."

I snuck out, and I creeps myself up into the bushes 'longside ta gets me a better look. And. . .there she was, sittin' in the water same as me, eyes closed, still singin' some ol' song I guessed she'd heard off the radio. That's when I axdently steps on a dry twig.

Her head whips around in my direction, and she squints her eyes real tight-like. "I see you up there spying on me," she says, all grown up–like. "I say, that's mighty rude *of anyone* to be spyin' on another human being."

When she stood up, I could see she'd be no taller than me and prob'ly the same age. Scrawny as she was, I told myself I could outrun her skinny self for sure.

"I said," she yelled, "what y'all doin' up there in them bushes?" She started wading closer to my side of the bank.

That's when I made me an instant decision. I wasn't goin' to let no snot-nosed white girl chase me off from the only cool spot in the whole entire state of Louisiana. Right off, I stepped out in the open.

Her jaw dropped real low when she saws I was a colored girl. Chances are, she'd never been that close to one her entire white-girl life.

When she bent over, I thought for sure she'd be pickin' up a rock from the water to toss at me. But she just sat back down, saying nothin', like a cat got her tongue or somethin'.

Finally, she looks up at me. "Well," she said real slow and drawn out, "are y'all gonna stand up there gittin' all the more sweaty, or are y'all comin' in?"

For a moment I thought about runnin' off for safety's sake, but sweat had come back on me like before, and I couldn't resist the thought of gittin' me some relief, so I started toward the creek again. I never took my eyes off the girl in the water, thinkin' that maybe she really did have a big ol' rock she was fixin' ta throw at my head when I got closer.

I creeped back down the bank and plopped into that little bit of coolness once more.

"Now ain't that better?"

I said nothin' 'cuz I was still trying to figger her out, so I jest nodded instead.

"How come you ain't talkin'?" she said. "Why you actin' so uppity?"

"I ain't uppity," I answered kinda sassy-like. "I jest never been this close to a white girl, that's all."

"Well, I never been this close to no colored neither, but you don't see me bein' all uppity."

"That's *you*," I said, "that ain't me."

"Yep, that's me, all right, Armontine Marie." Then she laughs this big old laugh. "But I'm better known as Noonie." She kicked her feet, sendin' a little spray my way.

"Hey," I say, "aren't you afraid of gittin' in trouble for hanging out here so close to me and all?"

She sent more water in my direction before going quiet for a minute. "Tell you the truth, ain't nobody carin' much for what I do right now."

I thought I saw tears in her eyes, but she turned her head so's I couldn't rightly tell.

"See, my mama died just before school let out, and my daddy's been every day kind of whacked, if you know what I mean?"

"Well, not sure I do," I said. "Ain't never had me a daddy, 'cuz he got kilt right after I was born."

"Got you a mama?" the white girl asked.

"Yup."

"Then you got way more'n me. See, I'm staying down the road a piece with my daddy's sister. He brought me and my brother here and then left ta work in the Gulf shrimpin'. Haven't seen him since, not even no note. Not one. Auntie says he's all tore up over losing my mama."

"Oh," was all I said. But I felt sad, for sure. See, whole time I was growin' up I'd always thought all white people were happy. . .livin' in big houses sittin' on lots and lots of land they'd owned outright.

We two jest sat like that in the water for the longest time, enjoyin' what little pleasure we could git out of life.

But soon my stomach started ta growl like a lion.

"Hey," Noonie said, "is that y'all's belly I hear?"

I started laughing and then she started laughing, and then. . .we couldn't stop. Finally, I took a big breath and told her I lived just a wish down the block and asked her would she like ta come over and sip ice-tea and maybe eat my mama's buttermilk biscuits.

"She got jam for them biscuits?"

"Plum."

"Sounds good to me, but you know I can't be visitin' no colored girl's house. Ain't safe for me and even less for you."

"My mama ain't like that," I said. "I'll show you a way to come round the back at my house so's nobody will see ya."

"Okay," Noonie says with a big grin on her freckled white face. "I'll risk it if y'all are so willin' to die for my visit." Right off, her drama was able to make me laugh like nobody else.

I led her through the scrubby bushes right ta my back door. I needed to make sure no neighbors or family was a-visitin', so I went inside first.

"When I told my mama that a white girl was waitin' outside, her face turned real serious. "Pirti," she said, "what's a white girl doing in this neighborhood? Y'all know this could go bad."

"I know, Mama," I said, "but she's feelin' real bad. Seems like nobody cares 'bout her. And sides, she's real funny for a white girl."

Mama opened the door a crack ta see if Noonie was still there. She was. Mama stepped out, looked all round, and then pulled her through quick as bayou lightin'. . . .

"Your mother was Abbalyssa, right?" Carol Ann said.

"Yes, ma'am. She never did meet a human being she didn't think had some worth. *'God don't make nobody who don't need His lovin',* she used to say. *'And we be the human arms He uses to show it.'*"

"From that day on, Noonie and I was like two peas in a pod, 'cept one pea was black and the other white."

Carol Ann poured herself more coffee. "What about the tablecloth, Pirti? What did that have to do with you and Mama?"

Pirti rested her head against the back of the sofa. "It was our freedom flag, Carol Ann."

"Freedom flag? I don't understand."

"Like I told ya, those was different times, but my mama couldn't let Noonie be sad with no Mama or Daddy, so she'd do anything to make her feel better. Regardless of how dangerous it might turn out be, soon Noonie had a lovin' *new* mama. . .mine. And"—she sat up on the edge of her seat—"here's where the cloth part comes in.

"See, though I be havin' no brothers nor sisters, I did have me bushels of aunties and uncles along with all the chil'ren and their chil'ren. Since it be summer and all, Mama couldn't be knowin' when one of them might be walkin' through our front door unannounced-like. So, before Noonie could comes through the back door, she was to check an' see if there be this here tablecloth hanging over the railin' on our *front* porch."

"Oh, Pirti, I get it now. That was the sign to Mama. . .whether or not she had the freedom to come inside." She couldn't stop smiling. "I'd say Abbalyssa was one smart woman."

Pirti shook her head in agreement. "And never was allowed to step through the door of a school neither, Carol Ann."

Pirti got up to reheat their coffee. While Carol Ann waited, the Christmas lights seemed to beam brighter in the cozy space. With each word of Pirti's story, a fragment of grief had been lifted from Carol Ann's spirit. She smiled to herself. *Lord, You knew exactly what I needed today.*

Pirti returned and refilled their cups. "Now, where was I?" She paused. "Oh, now I remember. See, Carol Ann, most our kinfolk didn't have no use for whites, even if they was little girls. Noonie always came through the brush in back, but there was one spot where she could sees the front of the house, too."

"What if someone came to the door while Mama was already there?"

"That's when my mama started lockin' the front door. Oh, and doncha know a few times that stirred up some kinda talk in the family. But Mama would laugh it off, sayin' she was jest being careful s'all. Mor'n once, Noonie had to scoot real fast-like under my bed. Never got caught neither." Pirti chuckled out loud.

Carol Ann wiped at both eyes with the heels of her hands. "Oh, Pirti, I wish I could have met your sweet mama."

Pirti looked puzzled. "Honey, my mama's still livin'."

"What? Oh, wow! Do you think I could meet her? I mean, would it be all right?"

Another big smile crossed Piti's face. "Carol Ann, I think y'all might be a real good medicine for her." She stood slowly. "How's about today?"

"You mean right now?"

Pirti shook her head. "She's still livin' in that house by the woods. My cousin Della stays with her now so's she don't have to go to a nursin' home. Jest let me gets my hat and coat."

Carol Ann couldn't believe it. What had started out to be a difficult and depressing day was turning into a Christmas adventure she'd never imagined. *Lord, this could only have come from You.* She folded the precious tablecloth and put it back into her purse.

They pulled into the driveway of an old house that clearly had known better days. But, although it needed a facelift and some paint, the yard was mowed and a welcoming Christmas wreath hung on the door.

"See there, Carol Ann? There's that front porch I told y'all 'bout."

Carol Ann choked back tears, thinking about her mother finding such kindness within the confines of this very place. She felt glad and sad at the same time, able to picture two little giggling girls playing inside. "Oh, Pirti, I'm so grateful to your sweet mama." She reached over and patted the older woman's hand. "Just how old is Abbalyssa now?"

"Ninety-seven last September. Most days she's spry as a chicken, but lately her memory's been a-lackin' some."

Carol Ann helped Pirti out of the car and lent her an arm up the sidewalk leading to the porch. She let her hand rest on the railing, imagining the spot where the freedom cloth had often been placed.

A lady with snow-white hair answered the door and immediately ushered them inside. "Land sakes, Pirti, y'all should have called. I'm quite the mess now, it bein' bakin' day and all." She brushed flour onto the front of her apron and then turned to Carol Ann.

"I knows we never met, but y'all look so familiar somehow." Her eyes sparkled with curiosity.

"I'm Carol Ann Sparks, but y'all might be rememberin' my mama, Noonie?"

"Why, shore, that's why I knows ya. My, my, Abbalyssa will be delightin' herself with seein' y'all today, I can guarantee that."

"How's she doin' today, Reenie?" Pirti asked.

"Oh, today's a good one, Pirti. She's herself and then some." Just then a bell rang in the kitchen. "That be my bread. Y'all go on in and surprise Abbalyssa. She's sittin' in her room."

Carol Ann thought her heart might beat out of her chest walking down the narrow hallway. Pirti knocked on the door before entering.

The woman sitting in the chair didn't look anywhere near the age Pirti had mentioned. She hadn't taken her eyes off of Carol Ann since she'd walked in. One hand went to her throat, and then a beautiful smile spread across her ebony face. "Come closer," she said.

Carol Ann walked over and knelt beside the rocker. "I'm Noonie's daughter," she whispered.

"Oh, my heavens. I would have known y'alls anywhere, girl." She placed both hands on each side of Carol Ann's tear-stained face. "Your mama was a special person to me, do y'all know that?" Now Abbalyssa was crying.

"I sure do. Pirti's been tellin' me stories all afternoon. It's why I just had to come over." She stood while Pirti gave her mother a peck on the cheek. "Carol Ann's found somethin' Noonie kept. I think y'all will remember it, Mama."

The old woman's face lit up with expectation.

"Well, it once belonged to you, Abbalyssa," Carol Ann said. She reached inside her purse and brought out the tablecloth to lay in the lap of its creator.

Abbalyssa's eyes went wide with surprise before reaching out to run bent fingers over the flowers younger hands had stitched all those years before. "Mm, mm, oh my...if this cloth could talk..." She placed it to her face and rubbed one cheek. "Takes me back..."

Her eyes closed and she began rocking, whispering something into the cloth that Carol Ann couldn't quite make out.

Moving closer, she bent down. With every rocking motion of the chair Abbalyssa was saying, "Free...dom, free...dom, free...dom." Carol Ann eyed Pirti. Neither could contain their weeping. Neither of them cared.

"Hey," they heard from the other room, "bring Auntie out with y'all and let's have us a Christmas treat. Hurry now, before it all cools down."

Carol Ann helped Abbalyssa to her feet, offering support all the way to the kitchen table. When they were settled, Reenie brought out the source of what filled their senses with heady aromas. . .a huge plate of steaming yeasty biscuits, smothered with butter.

"These be the same biscuits Mama used to make me and Noonie," Pirti said. "And," she added with enthusiasm, "this be the same plum jam from the same tree."

"I cannot believe this day," Carol Ann said awhile later. "Earlier, I was ready to skip Christmas altogether, but now, my heart's as full as my belly, thanks to y'all." She hoisted her dripping biscuit in a kind of toast. "Merry Christmas, y'all."

All three of the older women giggled in response.

Taking up the tablecloth, Carol Ann laid it in Abbalyssa's lap once more. "I'd like you to have this."

Abbalyssa started to protest, but Carol Ann said, "I believe my mama would want *you* to have it." Their eyes met and a knowing passed in silence between them. Abbalyssa smiled.

"I want you to know that all the years I was growing up," Carol Ann said, "that tablecloth graced our home. My mother never forgot your kindness, and I won't, either. Merry Christmas, Abbalyssa."

Abbalyssa's voice was strong and vigorous when she spoke. "Merry Christmas to you, too. . .little Noonie."

Charley and Prankster Paul's Christmas

Linda J. Reinhardt

Charley is tired of getting in trouble for Prankster Paul's antics. Getting blamed for turning on the sprinklers at a wedding reception was bad enough. But now Prankster Paul has ruined his sister Emily's night at the Christmas concert. To top it off, to be nice, his mom has invited Paul and his mom over for cookies afterward. Charley's determined to have a talk with Paul, but it doesn't quite turn out the way he thought it would.

Charley and Emily sat in excited anticipation waiting for the Christmas concert to begin. For once they weren't fighting and squirming around. Neither wanted to miss a thing. They loved anything to do with Christmas and were so proud to be a part of the production.

Charley glanced around to locate his parents. He waved at them and got a wave back. His younger sisters, Annabelle and Audrey, waved, too. He was so glad his dad was home now from the war. He thanked God quite a few times a day for bringing his daddy home safe. A couple of his daddy's friends didn't make it back. Charley was sad for the boys and girls who had lost their daddies. And then some of Daddy's friends who did come home had got hurt really bad in the war.

His dad, though, only needed time to get used to being home again. Sometimes he needed to be by himself. There was also a really nice doctor who would let his daddy just talk and talk to him.

"Ow!" Emily cried out. Then she turned to Charley with a scowl and gave him a good hard elbow in the rib.

"Hey, what did you do that for?" Charley tried to elbow her back, but Emily pushed against him with her arm. Soon the two of them were tussling.

"Charley and Emily, stop that right now!" their mom, Sarrah, whispered sternly, close to their ears. They felt her hands on their shoulders. "This is unacceptable behavior in church."

Charley and Emily sat up, frowning at each other.

"He pulled my hair," Emily whined.

"I did not. She elbowed me!" Charley gave her arm a nudge. The two of them would have started wrestling again if their mom wouldn't have grabbed their arms and held on tight.

"I said. . ." Her expression told them that, no matter what they thought, they'd better behave.

So Charley and Emily sat up straight. Both crossed their arms and pouted.

"Try to fix your hair. It's all messy. And smile—you've been waiting for this night for weeks." Sarrah gave them both a squeeze and then made her way back out to the aisle.

"If you wouldn't have pulled my hair, we. . . ," Emily started.

"I didn't pull your hair," Charley growled.

"Yeah. . .then who did?" Emily asked.

"I don't know, but it wasn't me." Charley stuck his lip out and glared at Emily. Then something very interesting happened. A few girls down from Emily started crying because someone had pulled their hair. "Hey, someone pulled those girls' hair down there."

"You're just saying that. . ." Emily turned her head to look anyway and saw that Charley was right.

Charley looked around to see who did it. A couple of girls had been sitting behind Emily, but he doubted it was one of them. Then he saw the back of that prankster, Paul. Charley had always been the king of pranks at home and school, but he had to admit he was nothing next to Paul.

Paul used to be a super-quiet kid who no one paid attention to except Charley. Well, only because Paul would appreciate Charley's antics. Then soon after Paul's dad went away to the war, he started doing some funny things himself. Charley had to shake his head with a laugh and admit how funny *Paul* was.

Lately, though, Paul's pranks weren't funny anymore. They started annoying and hurting people, or they caused trouble, especially for Charley.

The last one he did caused lots of trouble. He set the fire sprinklers off and it ruined the decorations, cake, and food at a wedding reception.

The bride started crying. Charley had caught Paul right afterward with the lighter and took it from him; then a grown-up came in and saw Charley with the lighter. Paul had backed out of the room. Even though Charley tried to defend himself, the man wouldn't believe him. His mom finally believed him but wanted to know who really did do it and Charley wouldn't tell. . .even after his mom explained how expensive the reception was and that the parents should compensate the bride. Charley still didn't tell and then felt horrible when he saw his own mom give the bride a check to pay for the damages.

He'd been wondering if he should tell on Paul or not. He wanted to talk to Paul first, though. Paul needed to stop doing mean things because things like that aren't funny.

Charley could appreciate a good joke. He loved to put things in his three sisters' beds, so that Emily, Annabelle, and Audrey would think it was a bug. Or he'd wad up a small piece of dark paper, stick it up on the ceiling, and then scream for his mom to get the spider. His mom would come and be completely grossed out and nervous because she hated spiders. Charley would be in the other room laughing while she got the courage up to squish the spider in the corner. His mom was always afraid of the spider falling or jumping on her. So, just as she would be about to get the fake spider, Charley would come up behind her and say, "Watch out!" His mom would scream, and Charley would fall down in a fit of laughter.

His mom usually didn't appreciate his jokes, but it was good for a laugh. At least it was nothing mean like Paul had been doing lately.

Charley watched Paul and noticed that he passed through the pews one by one and pulled the girls' hair. Then he moved quickly so he couldn't be seen as the one who did it. Lots of kids were arguing and pushing each other because of it, just like him and Emily.

"Emily, watch Paul." Even though she was still pouting, she did as he asked.

"Oh! Paul is pulling the girls' hair. That no good. . ."

Emily stood and moved past Charley. He tried to grab her arm to stop her but failed. Charley sunk low in his seat. He felt sorry for Paul. When Emily got mad like that, watch out. Charley's mouth fell open as he watched Emily walk up to Paul, grab his curly hair, and yank on it hard. A big "yeow" sounded through the church. Emily then proceeded to tell Paul a thing or two.

Charley saw his mom get up from her seat and, boy, did she move fast. She took hold of Emily and pulled her away. Emily was still mouthing something as she was hurried down the aisle.

Charley was shocked when Paul sat on a pew and put his head in his hands. *Is he crying?* Soon Paul's mother and one of the teachers sat by Paul. It looked like they were trying to console him. Then, much to Charley's amazement, his mom brought Emily back over to Paul. Emily said something to Paul. Paul nodded. Then their mom gave Emily a hug before Emily came back over to sit by Charley.

Her lip stuck out, and she held her arms tight in front of her.

"Are you okay, Emily?" Emily turned her head and gave him the meanest scowl in sister history. He gulped. "Maybe I'll just sit here and not say a word."

"Mom made me apologize," Emily growled.

"What?!"

"And she invited him and his mom over for cookies afterward." Emily's lip went out farther.

"Uh..."

"Mom said I need to be nice to him. That it wasn't right for me to pull his hair just because he pulled mine. And I should be nice. It's Christmas, after all."

Charley gave Emily a sad smile. "Sorry, Sis." Emily shrugged and went back to pouting. Charley thought it was a bummer that Emily was so sad, because now the entire concert was ruined. She barely broke a smile the rest of the night, even when they were singing, "Joy to the World," which was Charley's favorite song.

Later that evening, after the program, and after they'd eaten some Christmas cookies, Charley had Paul come up to his room. He needed to talk to him. As soon as he shut his bedroom door, he started. "Paul, lately you've been causing me and my sister a lot of trouble with your pranks."

Paul just shrugged and turned to check out some of Charley's toys.

"Don't you care that I got in trouble for your prank at the reception *and* my mom paid for everything that got ruined? Don't you care that my sister Emily has been looking forward to this Christmas concert for forever and she didn't even smile during it?"

Paul turned in Charley's direction. Surprisingly, tears were running down his face.

"Are you really crying?"

Paul nodded as he used his sleeve to wipe at his face.

"What's wrong, Paul?"

"I...I..." Paul hiccupped and sniffed. "I'm sorry, but I'm just so angry inside, and the pranks make me feel better. I don't know why, but it makes me feel good when someone else gets in trouble."

"What? Uh, Paul, that's kind of weird." Charley frowned. "And why are you so mad?"

"My dad...at least you got your dad back. Mine's stuck in some place where he can't come back yet."

Charley lifted his eyebrows. His heart felt sad for Paul. He remembered what it was like not to have his dad around. "I was sad like that last year. And I was kind of naughty, but then I can be that way," he admitted. "I was so naughty I didn't know if I would get anything for Christmas from Santa Claus. But I prayed to Jesus, and I got my dad back for my Christmas present."

"Do you think if I pray, Jesus would bring my dad back to me?"

Charley bit at his lip. "I'm not sure. My mom said Jesus answers prayers in lots of different ways. So who knows *how* He will answer it, but it's worth a try."

Paul gave a small smile. He bowed his head, folded his hands, and together the boys said a prayer. Charley added, "And if You don't bring him back at Christmas, would You please keep Paul's dad safe?"

When they finished, Charley gave Paul a shove and got one back from Paul. "So does this mean you'll quit doing those naughty pranks?"

"Not sure," Paul said. "But I will tell my mom it was me who made the water go off at the reception."

"And you might think of apologizing to Emily," Charley added as they walked out of his bedroom. He only got a grunt in reply, but Paul did end up apologizing. After a few minutes, Emily forgave him.

Several days later it was Christmas Eve. Charley hadn't heard anything from Paul about his dad. His own dad, Cade, found him moping around.

"Hey, Charley, why the long, sad face?"

"Aww. . .just thinking about Paul." Charley told him about Paul's dad.

"That is a sad situation. I'm not sure how Jesus is going to answer that prayer, but how about we go and invite them to Christmas dinner?"

That perked Charley up a bit. When they arrived at Paul's, he and Charley played Wii games, while Charley's dad talked in hushed tones to Paul's mom. They left after only a short time, with the promise that Paul and his mom would be over for dinner the next day.

"What were you talking with Paul's mom about?" Charley asked when they got in the car.

"Oh. . .I wanted to find out some information about his dad."

"So when is he coming home?"

Charley's dad frowned. "Well, Son, he's not coming home. Ever."

"Ever?" Charley said in a small voice.

His dad shook his head. "No, that sometimes happens when daddies go off to war."

"Why did his dad have to go off to that stupid war, anyway?" Charley complained. He swiped at the tears that ran down his cheeks.

Charley's dad pulled over the car and pulled him into his arms.

"What is he going to do without his daddy?"

"I don't know, Son, I don't know."

Charley gazed at his dad. "Why doesn't Paul know?"

"His mom asked for it to be kept quiet until after the holidays. She didn't know how to tell Paul."

Charley clung tight to his dad, happy that Jesus had brought him back, yet sad that Paul didn't get to have his daddy back.

"Let's go home, sport."

The rest of the day, Charley didn't leave his dad's side. He was also on his very best behavior. He really wanted to show Jesus how much he appreciated his dad being home with him.

The next day, when Paul and his mother arrived for dinner, Charley could tell she had been crying, because her eyes were red and swollen. She kept clearing her throat and would talk about having a cold. But Charley knew better. Paul stayed close to his mom most of the afternoon.

They ate dinner, read the story about Jesus coming to earth as a baby, and sang some songs. It would have been a fabulous Christmas day if Charley didn't know the truth about Paul's dad.

While everyone was singing songs, Paul motioned to Charley to go upstairs. Charley reluctantly followed him to his bedroom. He hoped he didn't accidentally tell the truth.

"I wanted to tell you, Jesus answered my prayer about my dad."

Charley quirked an eyebrow. "How did Jesus do that?"

Paul took a folded wad of paper from his pocket. "I got this letter from him."

Charley's heart raced. *How did his dad send him a letter?*

"Can I read it to you?"

Charley nodded.

"'To my wonderful son, who I adore more than anything in the entire world, along with your mom, I will let you know the truth about this letter. I'm crying while I'm writing it, because if you are reading it, well. . .I'm no longer here. Something has happened to me, and I'm with Jesus. I hope you never, ever have to read this letter.'" Paul started to sniff.

Charley stared at him with shock.

Paul read on. "'I love you so much, I really do, and there is never enough time in the world to tell someone you love how much you love them. I love you, I love you. . . .'" Paul said about a million I love yous through his hiccups and then the letter fell from his hands onto the floor. He sat down cross-legged and put his face in his hands.

Charley didn't care if it was not a boy thing. He put his arm around Paul and held his friend as hard as he could and cried with him.

"Where did you get this letter?" Charley finally asked.

"My mom has been crying all day. She was going in and out of her room. She doesn't think I know about her crying, but. . ." He picked up the letter and stared at it for a minute. "But I went into her room and found it on her bed while she was in the bathroom."

"Did you tell her you found the letter?" Charley asked.

Paul shook his head.

"I think you should."

"But she might get mad."

Charley shook his head. "I doubt it."

"Charley, Jesus does answer prayers, even if the answer is awful."

Charley hugged his friend. "I'm going to go get my dad. He can help you tell your mom."

Paul only nodded and put his head back in his hands. Charley was nervous to leave his friend alone. He knew how it felt to be sad, but not that sad.

He brought his dad upstairs and showed him the letter. Paul sat in silence with his head down. Charley's dad went over and sat down by Paul and put his arm around him. "Come here, buddy." Charley's dad held him while he cried. After what seemed an uncomfortably long time, Charley's dad spoke while he rubbed Paul's back. "I talked to your dad before we both went to war. We agreed to watch out for each other's families if anything should happen to either one of us. I will never be able to replace your dad, but I want you to know, I will always be here for you. Understand, Paul?"

Paul's face was still hidden in Charley's dad's shirt, but he nodded.

"Your dad loved you so much. And no matter what, you can come to me about anything."

Paul nodded again. Soon after, with Paul holding tightly to Charley's dad's hand, they went down and let his mom know he knew the truth. Everyone in the room was in tears for quite a long time.

Charley felt very tired. Emily sat next to him and leaned her head on his shoulder.

Sarrah went into the kitchen and put together some snacks for everyone, and they all ate quietly, deep in their own thoughts. It was pretty late when Charley's dad walked Paul and his mom to their car. Charley's younger sisters, Audrey and Annabelle, were already in bed, along with Grandma. Emily and Charley were curled up on the sofa, fighting sleep.

"Okay, kids, let's get you up to your rooms," his dad said when he came back in the house.

"Dad, this was the saddest and weirdest Christmas ever."

"Yes, I agree, but we did something that was more important than presents and the whole fun stuff about Christmas. We opened our home to a family who needed love and encouragement. And really, Charley, isn't that what Jesus did?"

"Huh?"

"When He came down to earth as a baby, it was with the intent to help every person in the whole entire world. And He opened up the door to His home in heaven for us. See, at Christmas, sure it's fun to celebrate, but it's even better to do what Jesus would have us do. And that's what we did today. Especially. . .you." His dad poked at Charley's nose after he pulled the covers up around him.

"Me?"

"Yep, you really were a friend to Paul today, sport. You showed him so much love. I could see the love of Jesus pouring out of you and spilling onto your friend."

"Wow. I felt so sad for him, and I remember how bad I felt without you. It's so awful he'll never get his daddy back."

"Yes, Son, it is."

"It's okay if you want to be his daddy, too," Charley said seriously.

His dad grinned and ruffled Charley's hair. "I love you, Son."

"I love you, too, Dad." Charley closed his eyes when his dad turned off the light. "Jesus, thank You for answering prayer. It was an awful answer, but thank You that my dad was able to be there for Paul. I pray for him and all the other kids whose daddies aren't coming home and who are having very sad Christmases, too. Can you bring a bunch of people to give those kids love and to pray for them? Thank You, Jesus, for letting us share our Christmas. In Your name, amen."

When Christmas Came to the Dog-Trot

Sylvia Stewart

In the tropics of Africa, a young girl learns that God's truth has no geographic boundaries. This true story has been graciously shared by our dear friend, who not only grew up in Africa, but also served as a missionary there for decades.

T he Christmas Eve sun beat down on the grassless yard of our temporary home in the (then) Belgian Congo. Mother and Dad were trying to find a location for a new mission station, and we lived in a government rest house. Our "home" consisted of two dog-trot buildings, with a bridge over the deep drainage ditch that separated them. Our living room and my parents' bedroom took up one building. Each night, my brother and I walked across the bridge by lantern light. And, because the dog-trot was open to possible wildlife, or worse, we securely locked our bedroom doors behind us.

My first thought on that Christmas Eve morning was, *What are we going to do for a Christmas tree?* Later, sitting at breakfast in the dog-trot of the first building, I asked Dad.

His hearty laugh rang out. "Don't you worry, we'll find us one." Our glass ornaments languished in their tattered boxes in the living room. Would we really have a tree to make it a *real* Christmas? I had my doubts.

Jim and I, newly home from boarding school, moped around, remembering the small gifts we had managed to buy for our parents out of our snack money. Had Mom and Dad been able to find presents for us from our storage barrels, or perhaps from the few stores nearby? What would Christmas be like without presents and a tree?

Right after breakfast, Mom and Dad's daily schedule occupied them, while my thoughts continued. I knew evergreens didn't grow in the tropical environs of our home. Where would Dad find a tree? Jim and I whispered about it as we explored the acacia tree grove that surrounded our place. Chameleons and grasshoppers soon lost their fascination, and I couldn't blot out my troubling question.

By supper time, no tree had appeared, and the glass ornaments still lay forlornly in their sad little resting place. "Daddy, what about the tree?" I persisted at the supper table.

Dad smiled under the hissing pressure of the lantern hanging from rafters overhead.

"Will we have presents?"

"Don't you worry," he said, patting my back. "We'll have presents *and* a tree. Now, you kids go to your rooms and go to sleep."

Jim took our lantern, and we walked across the bridge side-by-side, casting guardian shadows as we went.

"Good night and merry Christmas," our parents called from the other side. "Lock your doors."

"Merry Christmas!" we called back.

The next morning after breakfast, Dad wandered away, whistling "Jingle Bells" all the way into the acacia grove. He soon returned with a dozen acacia tree branches. "It's our Christmas tree!" He tied the stems together and buried the ends in a bucket of sand. "It doesn't look much like a tree, I know, but it will do." Dad's face showed his obvious delight in the accomplishment.

Disappointed, Jim and I hung the glass balls on the branches and draped some tinsel around. But our hearts were heavy. We each unearthed our few presents from their hiding places, yet even then, it still didn't feel like Christmas.

By noon the dog's swishing tail had broken several ornaments. One by one, others had fallen from the now wilting branches, crashing to the cement floor in pitiful shards of red and green.

"Let's open our gifts before all the decorations break," Mama said.

"No snow, no evergreen, and few presents," I whispered to Jim as Dad opened his Bible to read the Christmas story. I shook my head in protest and crossed my arms across my chest. "This is not Christmas."

"'And she brought forth her firstborn son, and wrapped him in swaddling clothes, and laid him in a manger. . . . Glory to God in the highest'" (KJV).

My heart began to flutter, and I breathed deep. The truth of God's miraculous arrival spun around in my mind like fine strands of gold. There, in the scorching heat of a tropical day, without the worldly trappings I so craved, the love story of Christmas became real. I'd yearned for reality, and here it was. I looked at my dad and mother and smiled. They already knew what I'd only just discovered. . .Christmas had come to the dog-trot.

A Note to the Reader

Sylvia Stewart is the author of *Kondi's Quest*, a remarkable coming-of-age story, set in the red-dust of the African nation of Malawi.

The Humble Barber

SHARON BERNASH SMITH

Everyone likes to be remembered, especially during the holidays, and John Robinson is no exception. Except this year, he'll be alone. When he's asked to come to a local Christmas Eve church service, he has no idea that saying yes to an invitation will alter his life. This humble barber will never forget this Christmas. . .not ever.

J ohn Robinson let down the blind on his shop window even though it was only four thirty. Usually open until six, he figured that on Christmas Eve, his day was over.

The blond cocker spaniel stretched in the corner, wagging her tail in expectation.

"Seems everyone out there is busy tonight but you and me, girl." He bent and patted the dog on her golden head. "No use having a pity party; it is what it is, I guess."

He walked around the barber chair to flip off the overhead lights, giving the place an eye sweep before heading to the door. The dog came to his side.

Outside, the shop owner next door walked by. "Hey, John, merry Christmas."

"Same to you, Chuck. Got plans tonight?" The two men shook hands.

"Yup, headed to church for a candlelight service and then to the in-laws for dinner. Kind of hectic, but I have to admit I like it all. How 'bout you?"

"Well, both my kids are busy with college friends out of town, so. . ." He shrugged.

"Why don't you come to church with me, then? The service is short and maybe a little corny with the kids' Christmas play, but you might enjoy it."

John hesitated. "What about Daisy?" He was warming up to the invitation.

"Pretty sure we could set her up in the church basement during the service. You can follow me there if you want. What do you say?"

He smiled. "You know, I'm going to take you up on it." He looked down at the dog. "So, Daisy, want to go to church?"

She barked in response, making him laugh.

"Looks like a unanimous decision, Chuck. We'll follow you, then."

"Good. Be careful, though; things look real icy. Even our parking lot has spots of black ice."

John's mood lifted as he thought about not being alone. After his wife died several years ago, it was the children who really held their family together, but now that they were both in college out of state, the nagging loneliness had taken a huge chunk out of his morale.

Maybe it was just the holidays, but lately he'd even been questioning his purpose in life. Oh, sure, he had grateful customers, but they were in and out and not seen again for weeks at a time. Anyway, what real impact could a barber possibly have in the twenty minutes or so he was with any one of them?

From the day the shop opened for business, he'd always tried to share his Christian faith with every person who walked through the door, but now that faith seemed to be waning in the depth of his lonely heart's depression.

The parking lot was as icy as Chuck had said. He made his way slowly to the car and had one hand on the door when his feet began to slide. Hitting the ground, his head took the brunt of the fall. The bright overhead lights began to fade, and darkness closed in like a shroud.

"Mr. Robinson? Mr. Robinson, can you hear me?"

He tried to focus, but his mind was filled with fog and something else. Pain throbbed through his entire body, steady and strong like an electrical current. Who was calling his name?

"Mr. Robinson, can you open your eyes for me?"

He tried, but his body would not cooperate to the command.

Someone pried first one eyelid and then the other. "Try again to open your eyes. . .please."

Once more he made a supreme effort. This time he was able to respond, but where was he? Slowly, the parking lot memory flowed into his mind. He must be in the hospital.

A smiling woman wearing scrubs and a Santa hat stood over the bed. "You took quite a fall, Mr. Robinson." She picked up his wrist. "How's your pain level on a scale of one to ten. . .ten being the worst you've ever had?"

"Ten," he whispered.

"Well, the doctor has ordered more medication that will help a lot. Head injuries are very painful." She stuck a thermometer in his mouth until it beeped. "Do you remember any of what happened?"

"Some," he said, "but just thinking hurts."

The nurse injected something into his IV, and he soon drifted off. . . .

In a few minutes, he sensed someone had entered the room.

"John?" The voice seemed somewhat familiar.

He opened both eyes and squinted against the sunlight streaming through the window. "Morgan?" Wow—he hadn't seen her in years.

"Hi, John. I heard you were in the hospital, so I came by to tell you merry Christmas."

She took a step closer.

He was more awake now. "I haven't seen you since the boys and you moved. How are they, anyway?"

"Well, they're both in high school and doing very well. They're really good kids." She touched his shoulder.

"I can't believe you came all the way here just to see me. Thank you." His smile was weak.

"Well, I can't stay long, but I wanted you to know how much I appreciated all you did for me and the boys."

"What do you mean? I just cut their hair, as I recall." *Isn't that what a barber's supposed to do?*

She laughed softly. "But, John, you never charged me. Those were lean days for us, and for sure, haircuts weren't in our budget. Once you heard how hard I struggled, you never let me pay you. . .not once, even though I tried every time."

John smiled. "I knew you didn't have the money."

"Well, my friend, that's why I came by today. It would have been hard on them to be at school with scruffy-looking hair." Leaning over the bed rail, she patted his hand. "Merry Christmas, John. Thanks again."

His eyes drifted shut. . . .

When he opened them again, someone else was coming into the room. A young man walked to the end of the bed holding a sleeping toddler. "Hi, John, remember me?"

"I don't think so." He squinted, trying to focus, his vision still blurry.

"I'm not surprised; I've changed a lot." The man moved to the side, shifting the child to one shoulder. "I'm Bobby, Bob Forde, and this is my son, Greg. I think I was ten or eleven when you started cutting my hair."

John lifted one finger. "Oh sure; now I remember. You didn't like me much back then."

Bob laughed. "As I recall, I didn't like anyone much, and it only got worse as I got older. Things really went south for me, when I became a teenager." His face was somber. "But for some reason, you always treated me like I was a long-lost son whenever my mom brought me to your shop. One time, you told me that, no matter what, God loved me and had a plan for my life. You said it was all laid out in the Bible."

He shifted his child to the other shoulder. "You did a real special thing that day. . .just reached over and grabbed your own Bible and handed it to me. I probably laughed in your face, but I never forgot what you said, and I never threw that book away."

"Really?" John noticed his pain was all but gone now.

"Yup. I know it sounds strange, but those words echoed in my mind for years, until one day I finally believed them. About ten years ago, I took a long, hard look at my life and decided I didn't like what I saw. I finally started to read that old Bible of yours, especially all the underlined places. Some of them jumped off the pages like flashes of lightning. To make a long story short, one day I finally asked Jesus into my life."

John beamed. "I've often wondered what happened to you, Bob."

"Well, now you know. I can't stay long, but when I heard about your accident, I had to come and let you know 'the rest of the story,' as they say." He laughed.

The boy on his shoulder stirred, peered into his dad's face with a beguiling smile, and settled again.

Bob stepped toward the bed. "Merry Christmas, John, and God bless you." Before he walked away, he laid something on the side table.

John lifted his hand in response. Despite the accident, Christmas was looking up. Exhaustion pushed against his tired body, but voices from the hallway pushed back. Was that singing? It sounded like children. He liked it and smiled.

"O come, O come, Emanuel, and ransom captive Israel. . . ."

The nurse who'd been in earlier came through the door humming. "Want me to leave it open for you?"

He nodded yes. "Who are those kids?"

"From the church down the street, the high school group. Sound good, don't they?" She started to leave. "Oh, I almost forgot. One of them says she knows you. Feel like seeing her?"

"Please." *I wonder who it could be?*

In a few minutes, a tall red-headed girl slipped in, smiling from ear to ear. "Hi, Mr. Robinson, remember me?"

"Well, I think you were a whole lot shorter, last time I saw you. But come closer, Janie; let me look at you."

She laughed. "Yeah, my mom said if she knew I was going to be this tall, she would have put a brick on my head or something. She's the one who told me about your fall. Looks like you're doing better."

"Pretty sure I'll live," he said. "I don't think I've seen you since your junior high days."

"I know. When I moved out of your neighborhood, I lost touch with your family. But I came in to tell you I never forgot any of you." She flipped her ponytail over one shoulder. "I'm going to be a hair dresser, and it's all because of you."

John was puzzled. "Why's that?" He really didn't know.

"Well, when I was friends with your daughter, she used to ask me over to your house all the time."

"Hmm, sure I remember."

"Did you realize I lived in a foster home then?"

He shook his head. "I don't think I did."

"My foster parents were really nice people, but they weren't like *your* family. You always said grace before meals, and whenever I spent the night, you prayed with us kids before bed." She paused to wipe at her face. "No one I knew ever prayed." Another pause. "I never forgot that. Never."

"Thank you for telling me, Janie. It means a lot, more than you know."

"Hey, I've got to catch up with the kids from church. Don't we sound awesome?" She blew him a kiss and left the room. In a flash, she stepped back inside. "Look for me on Facebook. . .if you want to, that is. Bye."

When she was gone, the room felt quiet and empty. Maybe it'd be good to rest.

"Mr. Robinson? Mr. Robinson, can you hear me?"

"Yes," he whispered, "yes, I hear you." He opened his eyes. "How long have I slept?"

"Mr. Robinson, you've been unconscious since they brought you into the hospital about twelve hours ago." She straightened his covers. "What's your pain level on a scale of. . ."

"Wait a minute. I couldn't have been unconscious. I've had several visitors."

She smiled. "I've been on duty for six hours now, and no one but the man who found you in the parking lot has been here."

"Surely you must have seen them." Totally puzzled, he tried to sit up. "Uh. . .there was a woman, a man, and a young girl."

"Head injuries can cause the mind to play some strange tricks, Mr. Robinson. You must have dreamt your visitors," the nurse said with a wave of her hand. She checked the IV line before leaving.

Well, Lord, if my visitors weren't real, the dream was wonderful, just the same. His mind felt unfettered and full of honest joy. He reached for the water glass beside his bed, when something caught his eye. "What?" He picked up a falling-apart Bible. "Wow!"

John Robinson smiled. *Thank You, Lord, for this special Christmas gift.* His fingers wrapped around the Bible he'd given away so many years ago. . .to a special young boy named Bobby Forde.

A Place to Lay Her Head

LINDA J. REINHARDT

Keri can never understand why her fiancé, Roland, has such a heart for the homeless—why he makes lunches for them and freely gives his money to them—until a startling encounter one Christmas changes her perspective.

Keri held on to Roland's arm as she admired the city's display of Christmas lights. Lampposts had been turned into candy canes, and the lights were different colors. All of the stores showed off their creativity, and a tall tree stood in the downtown square, waiting to have its lights turned on.

Keri flashed Roland a bright smile as he gazed down at her and patted her hand that held on to his arm. "This has really been a good year, hasn't it, Roland?"

He nodded, his smile shining in his deep brown eyes. "It certainly has. And knowing you'll someday be my wife makes it an even more incredible year."

"I'd say you are right about that." Keri giggled, giving his arm a squeeze.

Just then an older man with baggy pants and a filthy red jacket held out a disgusting old hat in Keri and Roland's direction. Keri cringed inside and held her breath as they got closer to him. She hated the smell of the drunks and drug addicts who begged for money downtown. Worse, she hated it when they bumped into her and touched her clean clothes with their filth.

But not so for Roland. Even now he was reaching into his pocket to pull out some change and checking to see if he had any gift cards left over. Normally, he didn't just pass out a few dollars. To him it was ridiculous to take the time to give money to someone, if it wasn't enough to help them.

At the very least, he would give a five and a gift card, sometimes even more. He'd even gone so far as to make a bunch of lunches so he could pass out food to the homeless, all on his own time.

This was something the two of them disagreed on. Keri believed there were plenty of organizations in the city that could help the poor, including their own church. And there was government assistance. The problem, in her opinion, was they drank the money away or used it on drugs. So she didn't want to give them any money to go spend on whatever addiction they might have. Nor did she see it worth her time to give them money for food when there were food kitchens every few blocks or so.

Besides, she couldn't stand it when their dirt-embedded nails came near her. She'd pull out her sanitizer whether they touched her hand or not. Even right now, as Roland put money and a gift card in the hat, Keri was pulling out the sanitizer to put in his hands. He'd only shake his head and use the sanitizer to appease her.

"Roland, look—there's the food kitchen, and it's still open. Just tell him to go eat there," she whispered impatiently.

"Keri. . ." Roland warned.

Keri knew better than to try to make him see how senseless it was to reach out to these people, but she couldn't stop herself. "Do you really think you are making a difference giving them money for their addiction? I mean, at least if you direct them to the food kitchen, they get to hear the Gospel."

"There's a difference between hearing the Gospel and seeing the Gospel in action," Roland answered.

Keri shook her head and rolled her eyes. *What's the use? At least he has plenty of money to spare.*

"No person is immune to being homeless. When my grandfather found himself out on the street, someone was nice enough to take him in and give him a low-paying job. He worked hard, and look where it got my family."

"Yes, but he didn't spend his money on drugs or alcohol."

Roland stopped and regarded her quizzically. "Didn't I tell you that my grandfather was an alcoholic? He lost everything, even his family for a while. It was a kindhearted person who helped get him on his feet."

Keri's shoulders fell. "No. . .you never said anything about that. I suppose I just need to get used to you throwing our hard-earned money away."

And for Keri it was hard-earned. She'd started a business a few years ago and barely made it until this last year. Now her company was doing fantastic. She was even able to put a large chunk down on a house and paid cash for her car. She was hoping to have the house paid off before she and Roland got married. Then it would act as an investment for them.

"Well, I don't think of it as throwing it away. I think of it as dropping seeds. I pray over the money and cards and then let God do with it what He wants to do with it. I also pray for each person. When I'm down here alone, I spend time talking with the people. They have some very interesting stories. And just so you know, they aren't all drunks and addicts. Some of them have lost everything through bad investments, stocks falling, you name it. Times are different now."

Keri shut her eyes and took in a deep, calming breath. "Whatever. . .let's go see the lighting of the tree."

"Okay, I bet it's about time for Santa to come." Roland grabbed her hand and pulled her across the street after checking for cars. They landed breathless on the other side of the street. Puffs of cold air blew out around them. "It's quite a crowd this year. Let's go find the coffee and hot chocolate."

"Great idea." Keri was glad to be away from the beggars and get lost in the throng of people who took responsibility for their lives. After they got their hot drinks, they watched the children's excitement over Santa Claus's appearance. Then magically the lights of the tree appeared, showing off its grand beauty. Keri was always awed by the twinkling lights that shined so bright.

The sound of a guitar behind her interrupted her enjoyment of the tree lighting. And then, to add to her misery, the person started singing. Irritation rose within her. She was so sick of these street people begging for money. The voice floated through the air, surprisingly beautiful and familiar.

As the people around her—even Roland—started singing along with the person, Keri was embarrassed at her reaction. Obviously, this had been planned. But when she turned to see who the owner of this incredible voice was, she shook her head. She'd been correct. It was only a street person begging for money.

A very talented street person, though. Almost everyone around her sang along, and many people were dropping money into the case of the guitar. *It's too bad this talent isn't used for good, instead of paying for her drugs or alcohol.*

Keri wasn't surprised when Roland went and dropped money in the case. She was surprised to see him drop one of his VISA gift cards and a hundred-dollar bill. *Roland!* What on earth was she going to do with this man?

For once she kept her mouth shut and watched the lady as she performed one song after another. She hated to admit it, but it actually was fun to sing along with her. The voice, though, sounded so familiar it started to drive her crazy trying to place it. She tried to get a good look at the woman's face, but her head was lowered, and hair covered what Keri would've been able to see.

Keri closed her eyes, trying to remember where she'd heard the voice before. She finally determined she simply must have heard it on the streets. Suddenly, her eyes popped open wide as the name *Kathleen* went through her mind. The woman sounded just like her friend Kathleen. Well, they weren't friends anymore. It had been quite a few years since she'd seen her. Kathleen had gotten married, and after the second kid, they had grown apart. Keri was more into career than family at the time.

Wow! It sure was weird how much this lady sounded like her. Kathleen used to sing all the time. At church, in the car, at home—she just loved to sing, and people loved to hear her. Like this lady.

An odd feeling settled in her stomach. Keri remembered how Kathleen used to bring her guitar with them to the park on hot sunny days. She'd start singing contemporary songs, and not long after, they'd be surrounded by groups of people listening and singing. Many people would give her money. Kathleen and Keri would laugh afterward and go out to a nice dinner on the money.

Keri pushed her way closer to this mystery lady. She was so intent on seeing her face that she almost tripped over the guitar case. The mystery lady looked up and their eyes met.

"Kathleen?" Keri said in horror.

Kathleen stopped singing and put her guitar in the case and closed it.

The crowd groaned and booed. "Don't stop! Don't stop!" The crowd started cheering.

Kathleen stared at Keri again before vanishing into the crowd.

"Kathleen! Come back!" Keri ran in the same direction, but it seemed she had disappeared. Then she spotted her at the street corner. "Kathleen, wait!"

Kathleen turned in her direction, then ran across the street against the light. Keri followed her.

Finally, at the end of the block, Kathleen slowed and came to a stop. Her shoulders were heaving.

"Kathleen?" Keri stood next to her. "What on earth are you doing here?" She noticed the filth on her friend's jacket and her torn-up shoes. "Why are you dressed like this?"

"If you must know my business, I live in my car. I was hoping to make enough money tonight to get a motel since it's freezing out and I'm low on gas. But thanks to you. . ."

"Thanks to me? You didn't have to quit on my account."

"You stepped into the middle of my show. You could've waited to come up to me when I was done singing."

"I'm sorry. I didn't know it was you, for sure. I was just checking. What on earth are you doing—singing on the streets and dressed like this—anyway?"

"I told you. I live in my car, and I needed money."

"But. . .what about your husband and your kids?"

"He left soon after he lost his job. Moved to another state, filed for divorce, and now lives in a big fancy house with his new rich wife. My kids are staying with him until I get back on my feet. I lost our house about two years after he left. I couldn't get a job that paid enough to pay all my bills, but it paid more than the allowed amount for us to be eligible for food stamps or any assistance. I had trouble holding down a job because my youngest was sick a lot, and the doctor bills were incredible. My church helped me quite a bit, but they can only help so much. And now that I lost my home and my kids, I'm just trying to save some money so I can get a place. The shelters are usually full and have a waiting list and. . ." Kathleen's voice drifted into silence as she looked into the distance. "Well, now that you heard about your deadbeat friend. . ."

Keri didn't know what to say. All of the arguments she normally had for the homeless fell silent.

Roland came walking toward them. "There you are. I've been looking for you. Why are you chasing this poor girl?"

Keri frowned at him. "I know her."

"What?" Roland looked curiously at Kathleen. Then, in true Roland style, he held out his hand. Even though she wanted to give him some sanitizer, Keri found she wasn't repulsed by it. Instead, her heart swelled with love for him. "Hi, there. I'm Roland, Keri's fiancé."

"Fiancé? Wow, that's amazing. Miss Career Girl finally found a man to get domesticated with," Kathleen said sarcastically. Then she eyed Keri and her clothes. "It looks like you've been doing good."

Keri didn't know why, but she felt a bit self-conscious. "I started a business a few years ago. It was tough going at first, but this year, well. . .it really took off."

"I can see that. Good for you. Well, it was nice meeting you, Roland. My name's Kathleen, by the way. I need to see how much I got tonight, and hopefully I can get a motel."

"A motel?" Roland asked.

Kathleen nodded. "Yeah, it's a bit cold out tonight, and the car isn't going to work for me."

"Just for tonight?" Roland asked.

"Not sure; depends on how much money I earned."

"Well, would you mind if I paid for a motel for you? For a week or two?"

Kathleen stared at him. Then tears puddled in her eyes. "Why would you do that?"

"Hey, my grandfather was homeless once, and someone helped him get back on his feet, and then my grandfather passed it on and helped someone else get on their feet." Roland looked at Keri cautiously. "Me."

Keri stared wide-eyed at Roland. "What? You were. . ."

Roland nodded. "Yep, it's a long story."

"Which I hope to hear someday, Mr. Fiancé!"

"Wow, you've never told Keri! Whew hoo, dude. You're in trouble," Kathleen teased.

Keri glared at the two of them. "This isn't funny."

"No, you're right, dear, it isn't. Let's discuss it later. Meanwhile, Kathleen, let's get you to a motel and get you some food. Point us in the direction of your car."

Kathleen led the way, and soon Roland had her set up in a motel for two weeks. Then they all went over to the store and got her some groceries, shampoo, brushes—whatever she might need. Roland also let her know he'd placed a hundred-dollar VISA gift card in her case. He didn't mention the hundred-dollar bill, though.

"Listen, I know the clothes here aren't the best quality, but how about we get you some fresh things?" He let her pick out pajamas, undergarments, and some shirts and jeans. He didn't like the quality of the jackets, though, and promised he'd look into getting her something that would really keep her warm.

By the time they left her at the motel, Keri saw that the tired expression had disappeared from Kathleen's face. It actually made Keri feel good to be a part of this project, even though she didn't contribute anything to it and was just along for the ride.

On the cab ride back to their own car, Roland apologized for dumping that information about himself to her, in front of her friend.

Keri patted his arm. "I understand. If you hadn't said something like that, Kathleen may not have let you help her." Keri was glad he'd made something up like that.

Roland cleared his throat. "I didn't make it up."

He then went on to explain about some bad business decisions he'd made when he was in his early twenties. When he left for college, he'd informed his family he'd return a rich man. He had too much pride to let his family know he had failed and lost everything. He was living on the streets panhandling when his grandpa found him one day and did the same thing for him that Roland had done for Kathleen. And then he helped Roland get a place to live and get a job. Now I have more money than I know what to do with, thanks to my grandpa's inheritance. I've learned to invest wisely and to give wholeheartedly. It's his philosophy. He said a person can never out-give God."

"So that's why you give so much?" Keri asked.

"Yes, because I understand how it feels to be in their shoes. I also understand how it feels when someone puts that dollar or two in your hat. That's why I put a five or more." Roland's eyes were serious. Keri sat in a thoughtful silence, trying to digest everything she'd learned about the love of her life. It didn't make her love him any less. She just wished he'd been honest sooner.

"I have to admit, it actually felt good to help Kathleen tonight, but. . .Roland, I have to tell you, I still don't agree that merely dropping money in a person's hat is going to do anything."

Roland shrugged. "You've never been in that position to know how important that is to a person in need. Sure, there are other things to do. Like tonight, I think God opened the door wide for us to help Kathleen. But if I didn't have a heart to help homeless people, I wouldn't have even thought of doing what I did. I take advantage of the small moments and wait for the big moments like we experienced a few hours ago. But the little things count, too."

"Maybe it's not for me. I mean. . .all that filth grosses me out. But obviously, helping the poor is going to be a part of our life. Let me take time to pray and see what that's supposed to be for me."

"I'd like it if you did pray about it. I want us to be a team." Roland reached over and grabbed her hand. "I don't want to do this part of my life without you."

"Well. . .we'll see."

Over the course of the next few days, Keri was faithful to pray about it, as she'd promised. It wasn't until they were sitting in the Christmas Eve service, though, that she believed she heard God's voice. She could hardly wait to tell Roland when they got in the car after the service.

"Roland! I got it. Sure. . .you need to keep giving money and feeding the homeless and stuff, but. . .oh my word! When Mary and Joseph were looking for a place to stay, no one had a place for them, so they were given a place in a stable."

"Yeah. . ." Roland's brow creased.

"We need to *give* Kathleen a place to live. I wanted to pay my house off before we got married and keep it for an investment. Well, here is an investment. She can live there rent free, and we can help her find a job. After she gets a job, she can start taking on some responsibility for the place, but not so much that she can't afford it. If she's willing, we'll give her a little responsibility at a time. And if she gets a grant to go to school, we'll help her until she is out of school."

Roland's smile caused Keri's heart to swell with pride. She knew it was a great idea.

"Maybe she could get her kids back and start getting child support. Just think about this idea. I wonder if we started building houses to help the homeless. . .or, better yet, an apartment building where they learn to get back on their feet. Not a shelter, but a place they can live while they get reeducated or get a job and can. . ."

"I love it! And I love you!" Roland planted a long, drawn-out kiss on her lips.

Keri smiled as she pulled away. "Let's go bring Kathleen home tonight. She can live with me, until we're married. And maybe we should skip the big wedding and use the money. . ."

"To help build our first apartment building. I think that's a fabulous idea." Roland turned the key in the ignition.

They drove in silence to Kathleen's motel, both lost in their thoughts.

Jesus had no place to lay His head, and someone opened the door. Now the two of them *together* were going to open the door for someone to be able to have a place to lay their head, and a home.

Special Delivery for Christmas

Betty Ritchie

A kindly mailman is led to reach out to a lonely woman on his route, inviting her to a party where the guest of honor is a prince. This read-aloud story is a good reminder to children that God wants us to reach out with love to those around us.

Deliver de-letter, de-sooner de-better!" declared Mr. McMail to no one in particular as he rounded the corner onto Meadowbrook Lane. "How I love delivering the mail at Christmastime!"

Whistling his way from house to house, McMail delivered a wave and a nod to all the families on his route, even if there was nothing in the mail pouch for them that day. The cheerful greetings he brought with every card and package made Christmas a very joyful season indeed.

"Hello, Mrs. Cranberry!" said Mr. McMail as he handed her a stack of Christmas letters. "Are the little cranberries getting over that nasty flu they had last week? Wouldn't be right for them to miss all the Christmas festivities at church."

Mrs. Cranberry thanked him for his concern and for his prayers as McMail continued down the lane.

Pausing at the home of Mrs. Lola Lonely, the postman peered into his pouch, shook his head, and continued toward the next house. He walked briskly to keep warm in the crisp winter weather, so he was almost out of hearing range when Mrs. Lonely warbled, "Mr. McMail! Oh, Mr. McMail!"

Even before he turned, McMail recognized the voice. He knew she would be wearing her pearl necklace and a printed dress with a tired white sweater with lots and lots of buttons. Flashing a friendly smile, he greeted her warmly. "Merry Christmas to you, Mrs. Lonely."

"Aren't you forgetting something, Mr. McMail?" replied the silver-haired lady.

"Nothing for your house today, ma'am," he replied, patting his mailbag. "Perhaps tomorrow."

"But won't you check your bag one more time? Surely there's something with my name on it," pleaded Mrs. Lonely.

Glancing quickly at his bag, Mr. McMail had not even spoken when Mrs. Lonely continued. "Perhaps a little postcard from the library? Then again, there might be a Christmas card from my nephew in the big city. Such a good boy," she added.

"I'm afraid. . ." began the mailman.

"Not even a bill?" interrupted Mrs. Lonely. "Not even a super saver coupon book from the pharmacy?"

McMail was shaking his head, but she didn't give up. "You know, Mr. McMail, it can get very lonely for an old lady like me—especially at Christmastime when everyone is going to parties and having visitors. The mail you bring, even if it's junk mail, kind of keeps me company." She smiled, but her chin was quivering.

Mr. McMail hesitated. What could he do to cheer the heart of old Mrs. Lonely? What could he say to bring some real joy into her life?

In an instant, the idea came to him. *Thank You, Lord.* Clearing his throat to speak, he said to her, "I believe I do have something for you after all, ma'am."

Clutching her pearl necklace in surprise, she looked back. "Is it a package? I did order myself a new blouse from a catalog you brought. I thought I'd just pretend it was a Christmas present."

"Better than a package," he said. "Better than a letter or a Christmas card."

Mrs. Lonely looked stunned. How could anything be better than a Christmas card? "Wh–what is it, Mr. McMail?"

"An invitation. A special delivery invitation just for you."

"An invitation? Special delivery? That's wonderful!" She paused. "But who sent it?"

"A very special person, actually. He's a prince."

Mrs. Lonely stepped back in shock. "A prince! I've got an invitation from a prince?" She wrapped both arms around herself.

"Well, you see, Mrs. Lonely," began the mailman, "Christmas shouldn't be a time to feel lonely and left out. No, no, it should be a time for friends to be together. And this prince would like to be your friend."

"That would be wonderful—a prince for a friend. Amazing! What do you suppose he's inviting me to?"

"A caroling party this Saturday," he said. "Why don't you bundle up and come along? Mrs. McMail has baked lots of Christmas cookies to share at my house afterward."

"And the prince, will he be there?"

"He wouldn't miss it. When we have a get-together, he's always there. And he's very anxious to introduce himself to you."

Mrs. Lonely could hardly believe her ears. A day that had begun like any other lonely day had brought her a special delivery invitation from a prince who wanted to be her friend.

"Well, I need to go in and prepare for the party. My wool coat is in the cedar chest, and I'll have to find my gloves." She hesitated, then asked, "What does a person wear to meet a prince, Mr. McMail?"

"Just come as you are, ma'am. He doesn't really pay attention to your clothes; he cares more about your heart."

"My heart. . . ?" mumbled Mrs. Lonely, as she turned to go inside. "Why, I think my heart is fine. . .it's only a little lonely."

"See you Saturday, then!" exclaimed McMail brightly as he waved and headed down the lane.

When Mrs. Lonely awakened Saturday morning, there was a feeling in her heart that had not been there for a very long time. Instead of the hollow ache that usually plagued her, there was a sense of hope and something more. . .joy. Little shivers, like the ones that tickled her spine when she blew out her birthday candles, reminded her that something very special was going to happen this very day.

As she went about the daily chores, her mind replayed the conversation with Mr. McMail. An invitation from a prince. . .a prince who invited her to come just as she was. . .a prince who cared about her lonely heart.

Darkness fell early that December afternoon, but there was none of the usual darkness in Mrs. Lonely's heart as she prepared for the prince's party. Her excitement grew as she nibbled a sandwich for dinner and dressed in her nicest clothes. Clothes she hoped would be suitable for meeting a man of royalty.

She stood before the mirror, trying to smooth out the creases from her coat that had spent the last eight years in the cedar chest. Those were sad times back then. The coat had been a gift from her husband, who'd worked very hard to save for the surprise he'd planned that Christmas. But the illness had come suddenly, and he never did get to see her in his special surprise and never got to hear her say "thank you." The mere memory of that lonely Christmas brought tears to her eyes all over again.

But tonight would be different. She wouldn't be able to wear the coat for her beloved Mr. Lonely, but she would wear it to meet the prince.

Muffled voices from the porch interrupted her thoughts. The party! It was time to join the carolers. Reaching for her gloves, Mrs. Lonely opened the front door and stepped out into the crisp night air, her breath making little puffs as she breathed.

"Joy to the world, the Lord is come," sang the McMails and their friends.

Joy. Mrs. Lonely smiled as she picked up the tune. *I almost forgot that Christmas was supposed to be about joy,* she told herself.

As the rosy-cheeked carolers filed through the front door at the McMails, Mrs. Lonely looked around anxiously. Although she had not met all the people in the group, she was fairly certain the prince was not among them. How would she recognize him, anyway?

She watched as people hung up their coats and hats, but no one seemed to be dressed in clothing fit for a prince. She scanned the group again, but not one wore a crown.

Mrs. Lonely didn't want to bother Mr. McMail with foolish-sounding questions while he was taking care of his guests, so she said nothing. Probably the prince had last-minute business and had changed his plans. Pity. She really was looking forward to actually meeting this person of royalty.

On the other hand, the McMails and their friends were being very kind, and the evening was already the most pleasant time she'd enjoyed in years.

Shy as she was, Mrs. Lonely joined a group of women who were sipping hot cider and admiring the lovely Christmas decorations around the room. Gathering near a table with a carved wooden Nativity scene, they began to discuss ways to keep their holiday celebration centered on Jesus, the sweet little baby lying in the box of straw. They spoke as though they knew Him personally, as though He were real. Their faces glowed with warmth and joy. Mrs. Lonely felt very left out and alone.

Mr. McMail settled into a comfortable leather chair next to the table and invited his guests to listen to the Christmas story. Picking up a well-worn Bible, he began to read. It was apparent that the others in the room knew the story well, because their lips moved with the words he spoke. Often McMail lifted his eyes from the page and recited portions from memory.

As he closed the book, he finished the story saying, "...His name was called Jesus."

Heads nodded and listeners exchanged peaceful smiles.

Mrs. Lonely loved mysteries and puzzles of every kind. They were like friends that kept her company, day after day. But this puzzle was quite out of the ordinary. It seized her attention and demanded a solution. Why was this Jesus so important? Why did this baby in the straw seem so dear to everyone?

As questions ran through her mind, Mrs. Lonely heard Mr. McMail invite the group to pray. She bowed her head like the others and listened carefully for any clues that would help her solve the Jesus puzzle. Again and again she heard His name. Sometimes people said *Jesus*, sometimes *God*, and sometimes, *Lord*.

But the name that sent chills down her back was *Prince of Peace*. Were they talking about the prince she was supposed to meet tonight?

Gladly, Mrs. Lonely heard the group say, "Amen!" and normal conversation began again. Surely she would now have the opportunity to ask the questions that were on her mind. She turned timidly to the woman sitting next to her, the one who had kindly offered her arm when they were caroling from house to house.

"Ahem," began Mrs. Lonely, unsure how to ask her questions. "This Jesus. . .this Prince of Peace. . ."

A reassuring smile spread across the face of the kind woman. "Would you like to meet Him?" she offered.

"Mr. McMail said He would be here tonight, and I've gathered that you all know and respect Him. But tell me, why is He so important to you?"

"Jesus is the reason we celebrate Christmas, Mrs. Lonely. God loved the world so much that He sent His only Son, Jesus, to earth to pay for the sins of all people. When people invite Jesus into their lives and ask Him to forgive their sins, God welcomes them in His family."

A warmth filled Mrs. Lonely's heart. It had been eight years since she had thought about belonging to someone, about being part of a family. "Mr. McMail said that the prince wanted to meet me and be my friend," she said. "How is that even possible?"

"You can talk to Him anytime, just like we did a few minutes ago," encouraged the kind woman. "He always hears and understands. Tell Him that you'd like Him to forgive your sins. Tell Him you'd like to be in God's family. You will never be alone again."

The kind woman was right. When Mrs. Lonely returned to her home that night, she spent some time talking to Jesus. She asked Him to be her Friend, and He flooded her heart with joy and peace. She didn't feel empty and alone anymore. At last she belonged to someone.

Mr. McMail had been right. What a special delivery! Better than a package, better than a card or letter. Mrs. Lonely received the gift of peace and friendship from the Prince of Peace Himself!

A Note to the Reader

Betty Ritchie has worked with children her entire adult life. Her love of Jesus and enthusiastic service to her little flock at church are incredible gifts to the future leaders in the Body of Christ. She's creative, patient, and kind—just the example children need from a role model.

Conversation with the Moon: A Mother's Journal

Sharon Bernash Smith

Christmas Eve is full of holy reveries, and for one new mother, a prompting of thoughts filled with wonder and wondering. Alone with her son, she begins a very unusual conversation. . .one that might nudge your own heart and mind with holy imaginings.

My dearest son,

    On Christmas Eve, soon after your birth, with your daddy gone to war, I held you in my arms. Your skin next to mine was velvet, while tender moonlight rested on one of your perfect little cheeks. I'm not quite sure why, but in the wonder of the moment, I began a conversation with the moon.

Oh, dear Moon,

    I marvel at God's creation of you. What absolute splendor I see in your brilliance. How sweet the caress of your light, reaching like a lullaby. Though you've given no words, I hear your song just the same. So does my son. Tell me, are you shining on his daddy, too?

    Tonight, while the hour nears Christmas Day, I ask, oh, ancient Moon: "Do you remember the night Jesus was born?" I wonder if you were privileged to realize His entire destiny at the moment of His birth.

    I marvel at my child's perfect chin. . .his nose. . .and the dimple in his cheek. They are exactly like his father's. Amazing! Right here, do you see? Oh, I know every mother thinks their baby is perfect. Truly, I do, but he is wonderful. . .just like the man who serves so far away.

I can only imagine how Mary marveled at her baby boy. Did she count all His fingers, number all His toes, and joy in the sweetness of His newborn breath upon her cheek? Did she know that the tiny brow she kissed would one day hold a burden of cruel thorns?

Even as I hold my son, marveling in the perfection of his creation, my heart holds sorrow, for I know this boy will grow up. The day will come when he won't need me anymore. Perhaps he'll be a soldier, too, and go off to the ends of the earth. Which is why this moment of quiet reverie will be holy with remembrance.

Were you able to watch as Mary wondered about the God made Man who would someday save the world, yet came humbly to her tender care?

My child's father and I have promised to tell our son about that Man, the One who created the universe, and the One who made you, oh, dear Moon. Surely you know it's His power that keeps you shimmering and holds your resolute place in perfect order?

Talking and writing these words helps to pass the time while the two of us wait for our soldier's return home. Of course God knows I'm really talking with Him. Because, after all, who would have a conversation with the moon?

And she brought forth her firstborn Son,
and wrapped Him in swaddling cloths, and laid Him
in a manger, because there was no room for them in the inn.
LUKE 2:7 NKJV

Celebration on Gharbghar

LINDA J. REINHARDT
AS TOLD BY COLONEL DAN KERN OF THE US ARMY

Miles from home, in a war zone in Afghanistan, Colonel Dan Kern is given a surprising Christmas gift.

Colonel Dan Kern of the US Army was stationed in Afghanistan, responsible for educating the senior colonels and generals of one and two stars in the Afghan Army.

In Afghanistan they have what is called an Epidote, a command element of two to three hundred French soldiers, and the Epidote commander would lend him French soldiers. They were great teachers and soldiers. The colonel spent quite a bit of time with them and treated them as part of his own group, even eating with them every day. The French commander, appreciative of how Colonel Kern treated his soldiers, became good friends with him.

It was December 26th over in Afghanistan, but since they are twelve hours ahead, it was still Christmas in America. The Command General Staff College did patrols on this day. The French Epidote Commander, Colonel Pic, and Colonel Kern decided to take both of their soldiers for a Christmas hike on the treacherous, snow-packed Gharbghar, a mountain range in Kabul. All were dressed in their military gear since they were in a war zone and had to have their guns with them at all times.

Unbeknownst to Colonel Kern, though, Colonel Pic and his soldiers had brought along some items in their rucksacks.

It wasn't a secret that Colonel Kern was a man of faith. He covered his men by reading Psalm 91 with them whenever he could. Not only did he pray and attend church (both he and Colonel Pic are devout Catholics), but he treated others with kindness and spent time with them. Far from

419

home, in a war zone, he was responsible for the lives and education of their men.

After making their way up to the higher elevations of this rocky, snowy terrain, the men took a break and sent security out.

Then, suddenly, one man reached into his rucksack, pulled out a manger, and set it on one of the rocks.

What is going on? Colonel Kern wondered.

A baby Jesus followed out of another rucksack and was placed in the manger. Then a French flag was wrapped around the rock, along with an American flag.

A cupcake with a candle in it followed, along with champagne and plastic glasses. They even pulled out a Christmas tree and placed it all on this rock.

As they lit the candle, the French who were seasoned combat veterans and teachers along with the American soldiers, in their own languages, sang "Happy Birthday" to Jesus up on a treacherous, snow-covered mountainside in the middle of a war zone.

The words echoed off the mountains that day. . .what a beautiful sound.

As they finished their song, champagne was poured, and they gave a toast to their Lord Jesus. Colonel Kern tried to put into words to the French commander how much this meant, but words could never be enough. The commander knew, though, too, for he also had a strong faith in the Lord.

That Christmas Day, two men, wearing guns and bulletproof vests, responsible for the lives of many, took a moment to honor the One who gave His life for many.

It was the best gift Colonel Kern could've received that day.

Small Sacrifices

Sharon Bernash Smith

"...in our dark places we sacrifice and find faces
and light and happiness unexpected."
—Ann Voskamp

Every marriage begins with a wedding, and every wedding needs a bride and groom. Well, that's how it's supposed to happen, but one woman will find that every bride needs a plan B, with or without a groom.

Christmas Eve Day

What do you mean he's not answering?"

"Just what I said, Mother...he's not answering."

"What groom doesn't answer his bride's phone call on their wedding day?" Valerie Dutro paced the dressing room. "Beth, he should have been here an hour ago...all the groomsmen and the photographer are waiting on him for photos." One hand went to her throat. "Maybe he's gotten in a wreck or something."

"Or something," Beth said under her breath.

"Don't go all sarcastic on me now, please. I'd like you to remember how much money your father and I have spent on this wedding. Too much to have it ruined by a tardy groom. And"—big dramatic pause—"not to mention all the people who've taken time from their *own* Christmas celebrations just for the two of you." She stopped pacing, giving full attention to her daughter. "Really, Beth, you seem quite nonchalant and not very grateful."

Elizabeth Dawn Dutro counted to ten before speaking. "Mother, I could hardly forget about the money, because at least once a day since Donald and I got engaged you've reminded me of every last penny you spent, are spending, or will spend in the future." She checked herself in the full-length mirror so she wouldn't have to make eye contact.

"See, that's the attitude I'm talking about, Elizabeth. You're not only being ungrateful, but you're also very. . .very. . ."

"Rude? Is that the insult you were thinking of?" Beth sat down in exasperation.

The dressing room door opened wide enough for the wedding planner to stick her blond head inside. "Are we almost ready?"

Cheerfulness oozed—no, dripped—from every word, and for some reason, Beth found it annoying. Very. She said nothing.

"Uh, we may have a problem," Valerie said in her best I'm-going-to-remain-calm voice.

"Oh," the wedding planner responded in a not-so-cheery voice. "And that would be because. . . ?" Her face had drained of all color.

Valerie walked to the door and whispered, "The groom's gone missing."

"Oh my." The wedding planner stepped inside and closed the door. "Well, where do *we* think he's gone?" she said, her "cheerful" having now returned.

"*We* don't know." Beth shrugged.

"Let's go talk to the best man and see if he has any ideas."

Beth closed her eyes. *Lord, I so remember praying that I wanted Your perfect will to be done in my life because. . .because I'm not sure Donald is the ever-after man You want for me.*

There, she'd admitted it—even though, for some time now, she'd had serious doubts about Donald Mickelson being *the* man of her dreams. It wasn't because he wasn't charming; he was. It wasn't because he ever treated her with disrespect; that had never happened. *It's his relationship with You, Lord.*

They'd known each other since their sophomore year of college. Donald was a premed student, and Beth had been working on a nursing degree, when they'd discovered a myriad of mutual interests beyond the obvious ones of medicine. Time spent on hiking trails surrounding the university helped in getting to know one another. Often they'd stayed up too late on the weekends discussing books, movies, and current politics. . .she being more conservative than him.

Over time, the relationship grew deeper into a comfortable, reliable friendship. Beth couldn't remember when the conversation of marriage came up, or who had initiated it, but when both sets of parents had found out that the topic was on the table, elation and enthusiasm grew like wildfire. Before long, an engagement was announced and wedding plans blossomed. Now, thinking back, Beth could not recall Donald ever *really* proposing.

It was when they'd gone for premarital counseling at her church that niggling doubt set in. After filling out multiple questionnaires having to do with faith, future expectations, etc., Beth had been shocked to discover just how many differences existed between them. There were many, but one really big one for her.

When they'd left counseling session number three, she couldn't wait to get in the car. "Donald, how come you never told me you didn't want kids?" She struggled to hold back tears.

"I'm sure I told you. Come on, by the time I'm through medical school and my residency, I'll be too old anyway." He glanced sideways. "Won't I?" He patted her leg.

"Your dad was forty-five when you were born."

"My point exactly." He slapped the steering wheel for emphasis.

She tried to stay calm. "Donald, are you saying *never* to having children, or no to right now?" The big cry was about to spill over.

He'd pulled over to the side of the road and unbuckled, turning to look into her eyes. "What I'm saying is that I love you and want you to be happy. If you want kids when we're done with school, then I'll say 'maybe.'" He'd given her a big hug that relieved the anxiety. . .sort of. Though the "having children" issue went on hold, Beth never felt it had been settled.

As Donald's studies increased, he missed more and more of Sunday church services, while Beth grew in faith. Hungering after a deeper relationship with God, she became a true seeker, discovering that scripture was alive with meaning. What revelations!

She tried sharing her excitement with Donald, but his studies clearly took priority, and after a while, she didn't bother.

The doubts about marriage became stronger, but always the peacemaker, Beth didn't have the courage to stand up to her domineering mother. Expressing them to anyone but God was not an option.

Now two hundred people waited for her to walk into a future that at this point looked nonexistent. *Well, Donald, looks like you were the brave one*. Funny, with that thought came a wonderful peace. *This, Lord, could only be from You. Thanks.* She smiled. Peace is what she'd need, because her mother's frantic voice carried all the way down the hall.

"Elizabeth!"

The door flew open, and her mother landed inside. "My life is over! And I do mean over."

"Mom, it's *my* wedding, remember?"

"Okay, then, *our* lives are over." She flopped into a chair and mopped at the mascara trickling down both cheeks, resting somewhere close to her grimaced mouth. "What could you have possibly done to make Donald run out on you like this?" She blew her nose hard and continued the mopping.

"I prayed." Beth smiled, feeling genuinely sorry for her hysterical mother.

"What? Did you just say 'prayed'? Honestly, Beth, in times of crisis you never make sense." Her mother stood at the window, watching the last of the wedding guests filing in. It was raining.

"I did say I prayed, Mother. I asked God to show me if this wedding was in His plan."

"Well, of course it was. . .is. Are you crazy? Look around. There's probably 25,000 dollars' worth of *plan* all around you. See, you really are ungrateful. How can you be so obtuse?"

"Oh, Mom, you have no idea how very grateful I am, really." She walked over and turned her around until they faced one another. Beth felt nothing but unconditional compassion. *She's not going to understand this, Lord.*

Her pastor was a wonderful support when she'd asked him to come to the dressing room and pray. He offered no advice—only the prayer and any help she needed with plan B.

He'd been the one who walked out in front of the lovely crowd of guests still waiting. . .waiting and wondering what was happening. The maid of honor and best man had done their best to hold off all inquiries, but time had run out on the collective patience of everyone.

Immediately when the pastor picked up the mic, the crowd went silent. "Ladies and gentlemen, thank you for waiting. As I'm sure you've deduced, this day has not gone on as planned, at least by the bride." Her mother, sitting in the front row, hid her face behind both hands. "But," the pastor went on, "I believe you will want to stay and hear what Beth has to share."

A humming spread around the sanctuary when the bride stepped into view. She looked radiant.

Her father sat up straighter in the pew and tapped his wife on the shoulder. "Valerie, you won't want to miss this," he whispered.

Beth took the mic from the pastor. "Hello, everyone."

Silence.

"Like Pastor said, by now you've figured out that the wedding you came for has taken a wide detour." She laughed and then cleared her throat. "Please, I beg of you, don't feel sorry for me. Really, I mean it." She took two steps forward. "See, some time ago, I began to question. . . or at least think about what a forever marriage should look like. When I did, nagging thoughts dogged me. But instead of listening, I ignored the thoughts, pushing them away with all the plans there were for the wedding."

She put up one hand. "Let me make it clear. I am not blaming anyone for this but myself. At some point I began to pray that God would show me exactly what needed to be done. However, even after asking for His help, I ignored all the warning signs God gave me. I've only made these conclusions today, when Donald didn't show up. Obviously, he had the same doubts as me or he'd be here, right? I need to tell him thanks, because I admit it would have been all wrong for us to have gotten married today."

The audience remained completely silent, waiting for more.

"Hey, please don't look so shocked. . .it's going to be all right. I promise. I'm fine, and I know Donald will be as well."

A few people smiled, but when her father clapped, the entire sanctuary erupted in applause.

"I have a few more things to say, and then I'll be finished. Even though the wedding did not come off as planned, I want you to know there is still going to be a celebration. I chose this day for the wedding because it's my favorite holiday. . .and it will always be. Everyone loves Christmas, but there are those all around this city who have little or nothing. . .not at Christmas or ever." She choked back tears. "I've talked it over with Pastor, and with your help, we'd like to give all the food my lovely mother has had catered to the homeless shelter across town."

Her mother stifled a groan and hid her face again. "Even the five-thousand-dollar wedding cake?" she whispered.

"Even the wedding cake," Beth added with a giggle. "Now, that will have to be moved very carefully."

When the church exploded with cheers, she couldn't stop smiling.

Someone called a local news station, and by the time all the food started moving from the reception hall next door into waiting vehicles belonging to the wedding party and guests, cameras had arrived to record it all.

Amazingly, it was totally organized, thanks to the ever-cheerful wedding planner. Shocked at first, she came to realize Beth's vision and was able to handle everything but the bride's mother. That detail was left to the bride's father.

What the camera crew captured best was the shocked expressions on the shelter's residents' faces when all the beautifully dressed people walked through the worn doors of The Almighty Savior's Baptist Church. It was good they had a gym, because the former wedding party and guests needed the room for the several dozen tables that had been transported. Within an hour, each had been reset and decorated with shiny silver ribbon. Strands of white twinkling Christmas lights gave the entire space the holiday glow Beth had wanted all along.

She stood in the center, taking it all in. "Amazing, Lord," she whispered. "It's even more beautiful in this place than the other."

Her maid of honor and Donald's best man agreed to stand at the door in order to welcome the residents. . .a very different kind of reception line. Her mother refused the invitation to join them, as did the groom's parents, but her father eagerly accepted after taking her aside for a big embrace. "Beth, I've never been more proud of you in my life. Regardless of how this day has turned out, I want you to know you're an incredible woman."

The very last person in the door had been a little girl about six. She took Beth's hands and stared up into her face. "Are you an angel?"

Beth knelt to gaze into the child's eyes. "Why no, I'm not, honey, but what makes you think so?"

The child stepped close to whisper into Beth's ear. "Because you're all dressed in white." She smiled a toothless grin.

"I still don't understand," Beth whispered back.

"See, last night, before I went to bed, I asked God if He was real to please send a true, live, Christmas angel." She shrugged and pointed at Beth. "And today, here you are!" She threw both arms around Beth's neck, then pulled back to make eye contact.

Beth stood and picked up the child. "Well, I'm not an angel, but I can tell you for sure that God is real, because He sent us Jesus."

"On Christmas, right?" The little girl squirmed to get down but kept hold of Beth's hand.

"That's right."

"Well, even though you're *not* an angel, you still look like a nice one." She flashed another precious grin. "And that's good 'nough for me." She motioned for her new friend to bend down and stepped as close as she could get. "Thanks for coming, anyway," she said and then skipped away. Halfway to the other side, she turned and shouted with a wave, "Merry Christmas, Angel Lady."

For the first time that day, Beth finally cried. . .not because of sadness, but from the sweetest joy she'd ever known. She waved back, wiped the tears, and turned to see her mother serving wedding cake across the room.

Gifts That Hit the Mark

LINDA J. REINHARDT

Jan could hardly wait to get home from Christmas Eve service and open her present from her grandparents. Every year they gave the best gift ever. But she had no idea how this year's unexpected gift would transform her life.

I looked out the car door window at the brilliant display of Christmas decorations on the houses that we passed by. Ever since I was young, right after the Christmas Eve service, we had driven around town, admiring the Christmas decorations before going home and gathering with the family to open our gifts.

Even though the display fascinated me as a child, I would sit in the backseat of the car in apprehension, waiting to get home and open presents from my brothers, sisters, aunts, and uncles, and the one sent by my grandparents, which usually ended up being my favorite present (besides what I got from Santa on Christmas morning).

They lived thousands of miles away, yet every year their present ranked right up there with the one from Santa Claus. I didn't know how they were able to hit the mark, but they did, every Christmas.

This year, however, even more I couldn't wait to get home. Church was, well, church, and it was so boring driving around, looking at Christmas lights. I mean, how many different ways can you string brightly colored bulbs and position mangers and blown-up or plastic figures? The first house—okay, how pretty—but after the first block, all I could think was, *Let's go home already.*

And yes, I was excited to open presents—who wouldn't be?—but it was actually more fun to watch my nephews and nieces rip the paper off their packages. Then they wanted me to play with them for a while. I was at the age when people didn't really know what to buy me. I usually just got some money or gift cards, or sometimes someone would try to buy me an outfit I might like, which I usually returned during the day-after-Christmas sales with the excuse it didn't fit.

Still, Santa visited my house on Christmas morning, and I did look forward to the morning, but then we had to hurry and get ready. Now I had to help with the preparations for the holiday dinner. Ugh! It was a lot of work. And then the cleanup (yuck) seemed to take forever. It was hard being the only girl at home.

When we finally arrived at home, my older brothers and sisters had already arrived. "What took you so long?" they complained.

"You know Mom and Dad. They have to see every Christmas light display in the entire city," I muttered.

"Well, they're so beautiful," my mom exclaimed.

Soon my nieces and nephews gathered around me, fighting for my attention. "Jan, Auntie Jan," they cried out. (Okay, they were also vying for my two younger brothers' attention, too, but what does that matter?)

After we filled up our plates with munchies, we all squished together in the game room around the tree. There were so many packages it was hard to find a spot on the floor to sit down. My younger brothers, Jason and Jake (my mom had a thing for *J* names, as you can tell. My older brothers were Jeffrey and James, and my sisters were Jeannette and Josie), had the Santa Claus hats on, so they were responsible for passing out the presents. I sat with Brian, Tom, and Megan close to me, waiting in anticipation.

My older sister Jeannette didn't get herself a plate, so I tried to share mine, but she didn't want anything. I thought that was strange since she was super pregnant. My sisters and sisters-in-law usually pigged out on food when they were that far along. The due date was a week after New Year's, but we were all hoping the doctors were wrong and she would have the baby on New Year's Eve. You get lots of presents that way.

While my brothers were busy passing out the gifts, my sister stood and motioned to her husband, Daniel. "It's time?" he asked.

"Time?" My curiosity was aroused. Time for what? My sister was holding her back, and my dad made a beeline to open the door for her.

I soon realized it was time for the baby to be born. "Isn't it early?" I asked. No one answered me, since they were all too busy grabbing their coats, keys, and purses to head out the door to the hospital.

My sister stopped and turned just outside the door. "Why don't you all stay right here and finish opening presents instead of sitting in the boring waiting room? When the baby is born, we'll call and you can come see her."

That made sense. It was Christmas Eve, after all. Except for the little kids, the rest of us weren't really into the whole present-opening thing after that. Even so, when I was handed my present from my grandparents, I ripped it open with excitement and then opened the box. For the first time ever, I was a bit disappointed. Inside the box was a Bible. You know, the book that is in the book slot on the back of the pews at church. "Why would Grandma and Grandpa send me a Bible?" I asked. I looked up to discover my sisters and brothers pulling out the exact same thing from their presents that my grandparents gave them. All of us regarded each other with looks of dismay.

"Whatever." Josie put the cover back on the box her Bible had come in. "It will make a great coffee table book. People will think I'm really religious."

Barbara, Jeffrey's wife, snickered. "Everyone in town will wonder what happened to our family."

"Hey, we go to church," my mom declared. "We just went this evening. We even know all the words to the songs they sang tonight."

"Who doesn't? All you hear from Thanksgiving on is Christmas songs in the stores and offices around town. A person's bound to memorize them without even realizing it," Jeffrey piped in.

"Well, I think it's a thoughtful gift from your grandparents, and we should display it proudly." My mom held hers close to her chest.

"It wasn't on the top of my Christmas list, and they always send what is on the top of my list," I moaned. I opened the Bible, searching inside to see if she had put a check or some money inside it. "Bummer. I thought they'd at least put a check in the book."

"Jan, you should appreciate what they sent you," Mom admonished me. Although it was obvious she was less than thrilled about the gift too.

"'No matter how many gifts you receive, the greatest gift was given to the whole world many years ago. It's up to you to receive it. We hope you do, like we did this last year, Grandma and Grandpa,'" Jeffrey read and then gave a loud hoot. "Are you kidding me?"

I noticed I had the same note in my Bible, too, and a reference to read in some guy's book named Luke along with a list of some other weird names with numbers after them. I rolled my eyes and shut the book. My poor grandparents had struck out this year, not only with me, but with everybody.

Soon after that, the room was full of torn Christmas wrap and assorted gifts lying around. My job was to clean up the mess. Ugh! I hated it. But when I wadded some wrap up in a ball and, instead of throwing it in the garbage bag, threw it at my little brother, the cleanup became fun. Everyone joined in, trying to make it into the bag as I held it up in the air, or they'd try to hit me in the face or on top of the head. Finally, the room was picked up, the sleepy kids were put in their new Christmas jammies, and my older brothers and sisters decided to take their children home. Brian and Tom would stay with us, since Jeannette and Daniel were at the hospital.

After everyone left, my parents decided they would run over to the hospital to make sure everything was going okay. They said they wouldn't be able to sleep, anyway.

My nephews were crashed out on the floor, so I threw a blanket over them and decided to crash on the couch in case either woke up during the night and needed something.

I was awakened around 3:00 a.m. when my parents and Daniel returned. Daniel wore a bright smile. Obviously, the baby had been born. It was a boy, unlike what the doctor had predicted, and everything checked out fine with him despite the fact he was a couple of weeks early. My sister had sent Daniel home with my parents so the boys could have at least one parent with them on Christmas morning.

I thought of going and staying at the hospital with her, but only for a minute. I was too tired, and besides, I didn't have a ride at that hour of the night.

On Christmas morning I woke early, before everyone in the house, fortunately, because I noticed there were *no* presents under the tree, and my nephews would be devastated if Santa Claus forgot them. I felt a little sad that there wasn't a Santa present under the tree for me, even though

I don't believe in him anymore.

I got up to wake Daniel but couldn't find him anywhere. When I heard a light tapping coming from the front of the house, I went to find out what was causing it. I didn't want anything to wake up the boys until there were some presents under the tree.

After looking all around, I figured the tapping was coming from the front door. It wasn't an ordinary knock, so I guessed the screen door hadn't been shut tight. When I unlocked the big front door and reached for the screen, my eyes nearly popped out of my head. There was my brother-in-law, in his skivvies, standing on the porch with bags filled with presents.

"What on earth are you doing out there?" I whispered harshly. I moved aside to let him in the house. "Shhh...don't wake up the boys."

"I woke up earlier and realized the boys' Santa presents were at my house, so I ran over to our house to get their presents. When I returned, I realized I'd locked myself out. Here, take this. I'm freezing. I've been standing out there quite awhile. I was afraid if I knocked too loud or rang the bell the boys would wake up."

"Well...you could have made up a story, like Santa didn't know they were here and you had to go get the gifts or something like that. Man, I wonder if any of the neighbors saw you."

"Who knows? Can you slip these under the tree? I'm going to go crawl under a blanket and warm up."

"Yeah, sure." I grabbed the bags and tiptoed into the game room, careful not to wake the boys. After I put all of their gifts under the tree, I grabbed a blanket and curled up in the old recliner. The Bible my grandparents gave me was sitting on the table next to me. I started to wonder what they meant by the greatest gift was given to the world many years ago. I mean, last night had been pretty disappointing. I didn't get any gift that I jumped up and down about, and I didn't have a Santa present under the tree. What gift was so special in this Bible that my grandparents would give us all the same present?

Out of curiosity, I opened it, and after what seemed forever, I found the name Luke and the same number they had written on the front of the book.

I was kind of shocked to read a story about a baby who was born to a girl named Mary and a guy named Joseph. I remembered something about a baby—in fact, the people at churches I'd been to had sung about that and done skits about Mary and Joseph. But I didn't know the story was told in this book. My eyes started to get heavy as I read and I actually dozed off. . .

I was awakened a bit later by two very rambunctious little boys jumping all over me.

"Hey, you two, you're asking for it." I tickled their ribs and tried to blow raspberries on their cheeks. I loved hearing their squeals and giggles. I had them both wrapped in my arms when I opened my eyes big as I could. "Oh. . .oh. . .oh. . .I think Santa's been to our house. Look under the tree!" The two of them jumped out of my arms and ran for the tree. "Wait! Don't open them until you first go wake up your daddy!"

They groaned and whined, while they ran down the hall to the guest room. I took the time to brush my teeth real quick and pour myself a cup of coffee.

Then I sat back in my chair and watched with Daniel as the boys tore at their presents from Santa Claus. My mom and dad came in soon after they started. My mom gave me a sad smile before she gave me a hug and whispered, "Merry Christmas," in my ear. She then handed me a few small wrapped packages and sat on the floor next to me to watch me open my presents. The first was a watch. Then there were earrings with a matching necklace. I actually liked them. The last present I liked the most—a check for quite a bit of money!

"Mom! Really?"

She nodded.

"Wow! I'm going shopping tomorrow."

"I hoped you would. I knew you were so disappointed with your present from your grandparents and, well, you still live at home, so I thought I'd give you a little extra gift this year."

I looked over at my dad, who blew me a kiss. Catching it in the air, I planted it on my cheek. He smiled. "Thanks, you two," I said.

"Don't say anything to your little brothers when they wake up. Their gift is not quite as extravagant as yours. It's nice, but. . .well, we can only afford to make it up to one of you this year. Their time will come."

I knew my brothers had been hoping to get some money they could apply toward the new skateboards they were saving up for, so I hoped my parents would give them enough so they could go and buy them at the day-after-Christmas sales. But I promised I wouldn't tell and thanked my parents again with a beaming smile.

After my nephews had finished tearing open presents, I did my cleanup job and hurried to get ready for the day. I decided I wouldn't complain about having to help my mom after she had been so cool about the Christmas gifts.

Once we had everything pretty much set up for my aunts and uncles, my dad asked if I wanted to go visit my sister and my new nephew. Well, he didn't have to twist my arm to do that. And my sister—I don't know how she does it—looked like she was ready for a photo shoot, even after just having a baby. She's so naturally pretty and has such white teeth when she smiles. Her lips are a natural rose color so she only has to use some gloss when her lips feel chapped. Me, on the other hand? I need to put on the lip color and whiten my teeth. The beauty must have slipped out of the gene pool after she was born.

Her baby was, not surprisingly, beautiful. She named him Jim. He, too, has rose-colored lips. I hope he doesn't have a problem with that when he's older. . .being a boy and all.

Grandma called to congratulate my sister while I was holding Jim and cooing and gushing over him. "Hey, Jan. . ." My sister called to me and held out the phone. "It's Grandma. She wants to talk to you about the Christmas present she sent you."

I rolled my eyes before I exchanged the baby for the phone. "Hey, Grandma, thanks for the gift." My mom had taught me always to be grateful for a present even if I don't like it. "A gift is a gift," she would say, "and it means the person thought of you. If, for nothing else, be grateful for that."

"Oh. . .well. . .I know it's not the usual gift that I send you, but your grandpa and I recently had a life-changing experience. It blessed our lives so much that I had to let all of my sweeties know about it."

"Okay." I didn't know what else to say. I mean, what kind of life-changing experience could a book give you, especially one that's so big and hard to understand?

"I don't suppose you had a chance to read any parts of the Bible that I suggested you read?"

"Actually, I read some of it this morning." I was hoping this piece of information would appease her enough to change the subject.

"You did?" Grandma's voice had an excited lilt to it. This made me feel terrible because I still didn't get why she sent the Bible and I probably wouldn't read any more of it.

"Yes, but you know, Grandma, it really isn't my type of reading material. I like more romantic fiction, not history."

"Oh. . ." Grandma chuckled. "This is quite a different book. Will you do me a favor and please read the verses I asked you to and then call me back? You see, Christmas is so much more than getting Christmas presents and eating a very fattening dinner."

"Yeah, it's now also about celebrating little Jim's birthday."

Grandma chuckled. "Yes, yes, it is, and what a blessing for little Jim to be born on the day we celebrate our Lord's birthday."

"Our Lord's? Grandma, come on. . ." I didn't mean any disrespect, but really?

"Oh yes, honey, God loved the world so much, He sent Jesus to the world to save us from sin, and if you believe in Him, you will be saved forever. And when a person follows Him, oh, honey, their hearts and lives are changed. Believe me, your grandpa and I know."

"Okay, Grandma. . .I hope you have a great time celebrating His birthday, too." I rolled my eyes and twirled my finger like Grandma was loco to my sister. My sister giggled. "I'm going to go now so I can spend some time with Jim and Jeannette before I have to return home to be mom's slave for the day. I wish you were here with us. You really need to plan to come out for Christmas sometime. It's not that hard to fly."

"You know, I was thinking we should come out there for a visit, but not right now. Maybe for New Year's."

"New Year's?" I was only being polite. I wasn't really in the mood for my "changed life by God" Grandma and Grandpa to visit.

"You know, the more I think of it, the better it sounds. Oh, Jan, it will be wonderful to see all of you."

I groaned inwardly. *Me and my big mouth.* Jeannette was giving me a questioning look. I finally got off the phone and announced the news to Jeannette, who saw nothing wrong with the grandparents coming to visit. After all, there was a new grandson for them to meet. I left the hospital and went home with my dad. My mom was thrilled with the announcement of her parents coming and hummed through the rest of the afternoon.

As for me, I didn't hum. I looked at all the dishes on the table and dreaded having to do the cleanup when everyone was finished. I also dreaded my grandparents coming, knowing I would need to read that book before she came or I might hurt her feelings.

So after I spent over an hour scrubbing pots and pans and putting dishes in the dishwasher and emptying the dishwasher, I put on my nightie (which wasn't new, I might add. My mom forgot my annual pajama gift) and crawled into my bed to read. I figured I had better start now so I had plenty of time to get the chore done. Especially if it put me to sleep like it had that morning, I'd need the time.

I looked at the suggestions she wrote at the front of the Bible and then found a table of contents, which directed me to names she'd written, and then I figured out the code of the numbers. I started to read a few of them. They were short and actually kind of sweet words, but after a few of them, I put the book down on my lap and rubbed my eyes. I would really rather be reading another book or sleeping. What was the sense, anyway, of reading this book? Why did it make such a difference to them, and why didn't I get it?

I closed my eyes and gritted my teeth. I decided I would read one more on her list. I picked up the book, and before I turned the page, some words caught my eye.

> This is how we know what love is: Jesus Christ laid
> down his life for us. And we ought to lay down our lives
> for our brothers. If anyone has material possessions and
> sees his brother in need but has no pity on him, how can
> the love of God be in him? NIV

I thought of my brothers. Even though my parents did give them some money, it wasn't enough for them to purchase the new skateboards they wanted, unless they found an amazing sale. I really doubted they would find one so wonderful they'd get their skateboards.

I thought of the money my parents had given to me. Maybe I could take *pity* on my brothers tomorrow and help them out. I closed the book and giggled to myself. If this Bible wasn't good for anything else, it would be good for my brothers tomorrow. After a big yawn and a stretch, I decided I would do just that. Placing the book on my nightstand, I turned out the light.

The next day, I discovered it ended up making me feel really happy to help out my brothers. I even went out of my way and bought us all ice cream cones before I went shopping for my own things.

I was pretty tired by the end of the day and almost decided to skip reading the Bible, but I needed to get the list done before my grandparents arrived. So I opened it up and found the required reading. It was okay, but I didn't really understand it. Why would this guy named Jesus have to die for my sins? He didn't even know me. Wasn't this book written years ago? So I didn't see how it could be life-changing since it was obviously written for people who were already dead and gone.

I started to get bored, so I let my eyes skip over the pages and finally read, "Children, obey your parents. . .that it may go well with you and that you may enjoy long life on earth" NIV. *Wow! This is almost the secret to the fountain of youth!*

For the next couple of days I did whatever my parents asked. Not only did I do it, but I made sure they knew I was doing whatever they asked of me. I would say, "Yes, Mama," and "Yes, Dad," and then do it immediately with a big smile pasted on my face. Hey, I wanted long life—doesn't everybody?

The next couple of times I read the Bible I skipped over my grandma's list and merely browsed through the Bible, looking for more things I could do during the day. My family was beginning to wonder what was wrong with me. I'd spent the entire day giving my family glasses of water because the Bible said I was giving them to God.

One of the books caught my attention and I actually enjoyed reading it; it was like a bunch of poetry. While I was reading, a loud crashing sounded over my head and a flash of light followed. I was quick to hide under my covers. I'm so afraid of thunderstorms. Peeking out from under the covers, I noticed my lamp had gone out, so I reached into the drawer of my nightstand and got my nerdy head lamp out and put it on my head so I could see. I didn't want to be in the dark during the scary storm. I jumped when the next sound of thunder crashed overhead. I decided I'd try to read. Then maybe I wouldn't be so afraid.

I opened the book, shivering from fear, and read, "There is no fear in love. But perfect love drives out fear, because fear has to do with punishment. The one who fears is not made perfect in love" (NIV). *What is this? Perfect love puts fear out of our hearts?* I was so afraid as the thunder clapped again that I wanted to run down the hall and jump into my parents' lap. But I was too old for that. Was this perfect love from this Jesus I'd been reading about? And, even though it was written so long ago, could He take this fear out of my heart? I doubted it, but I did this silly thing and said in a whisper, "I know this is for other people, but I'm really scared, and I don't know if it's true anymore or not, but could You make Your perfect love take this fear out of my heart?"

The thunder clapped and I jumped. I sighed, disappointed. I closed the book and tore the head lamp off my head. I let it all drop to the floor beside my bed and put my head on my pillow. *Why am I disappointed? I know this book is for people who lived back then. Why is it so important to my grandparents to give each one of us one of these books?*

I rolled over on my back, contemplating their reasons for the present. Soon I noticed that I had completely stopped paying attention to the scary sound of the thunder. It was still making a loud crashing noise over my head, but yet. . .I sat up. Little goose bumps were all over my arm. *No way. Jesus didn't do that, did He?* Still I wondered, because I wasn't afraid. And I'm always terrified of storms.

I reached down and grabbed the dreaded book and my lamp. Opening the book, I started turning the pages looking for something to answer my question of why it was so important for me to have it as a Christmas present. And then I found something that began to answer my question: "My prayer is not for them alone. I pray also for those who will believe in me through their message" (NIV).

I wondered if that meant people reading the Bible hearing their message. *Could it mean people who are alive now?* I wanted to call up my grandparents and ask them, but it was too late. So I went back to the list she wrote and seriously paged to each thing she wanted me to read with the question: *Does this apply to me?*

*Did Jesus die on the cross thousands of years ago for my sins?

*Do I sin and fall short of the glory of God, but can receive salvation through Jesus?

*If I confess with my mouth and believe in my heart about Jesus, will I be saved?

*Can I be filled with this gift of the Holy Spirit?

*Did the whole world that Jesus died for mean me, too? And if I believed, would I be saved?

All of these questions ran like crazy through my head, and I needed to know the answer. I felt frustrated not knowing the answer. I read some more, believing it had to be in this book. Why else would they give it to us?

Once again I stopped and read:

> "For this reason I kneel before the Father, from
> whom his whole family in heaven and earth derives
> its name. . . . may have power, together with all the
> saints, to grasp how wide and long and high and
> deep is the love of Christ, and to know this love that
> surpasses knowledge. . . . Now to him who is able to
> do immeasurably more than all we ask or imagine,
> according to his power that is at work within us, to him
> be glory in the church and in Christ Jesus throughout all
> generations, for ever and ever! Amen." (NIV)

I had to work really hard to keep my eyes from bulging out of my head. All of this stuff I'd been reading all week was for me, too. It was for my whole family, for everyone. Now I knew why Grandma and Grandpa had given us the Bibles. They wanted us to know this Jesus *died* for our sins, even though we didn't know or care about Him.

"Oh, Jesus," I whispered, "I thank You for dying for me. I want to believe. I like all of this stuff I've read about love and forgiveness and how You would want us to treat others. Thank You for this gift I got for Christmas. Will You change my life, like You did my grandparents' lives?"

I could hardly sleep. I wondered if I would wake up completely different and not even know myself or if I would change gradually.

The next morning, I seemed to be the same person. I was a little disappointed, but then I remembered: I *had* changed. I had stopped being afraid of thunderstorms.

I suggested my brothers read the book my grandparents gave them. They surprised me by saying they'd been reading it all week long, ever since I helped them get the skateboards and they discovered I was reading it. They figured it must be a cool book to get me to do something as nice as that and to get them ice cream.

When I asked if they believed that Jesus had died for their sins, they showed me their Bibles. Theirs were a little different than mine and had this neat thing that walked them through a prayer if they chose to believe in Jesus and follow Him. I saw the prayer wasn't too far off from what I had prayed the night before, but I made sure to get it right and prayed the prayer in their Bible right then and there.

The three of us went and talked to my parents about it. They, too, had been reading their Bibles, ever since the day I did whatever they wanted, with a smile. Okay, it's not like I'm the worst kid in town, so I don't know why that impressed them so much, but it did. And guess what? They prayed the prayer, too.

My other brothers and sisters were reading but hadn't quite made it to the believing part yet. So we started praying for them.

I decided not to call my grandparents but instead decided to wait until I saw them face-to-face, when they stepped off the plane.

I couldn't wait to tell them that, yes, they did send me and my family the greatest gift of all.

Once again, they had hit the mark.

To the Least of These

LINDA J. REINHARDT

Bill thought he'd found an easy way to earn money for the extra expenses at Christmas. But he had no idea how much his new occupation would change him. . .or others.

T he wind blew like sharp, icy knives through my thin beat-up jacket. I forgot to wear my expensive thermal vest underneath the ragged one I had on. My face felt raw, and I couldn't stop shivering. I hadn't been prepared for the change in weather today. Still, I held up my sign and stood on the corner hoping someone would open their window to share some of their money with me.

Oh good! Here's someone now, flagging me over. As I approach their shiny red minivan, a hand sticks out the window holding a paper cup I can only assume is filled with coffee. I'm bummed it's not money but thankful for the warm drink. I take the cup and try my best to touch their fingers. It makes me chuckle. I rub my fingertips in some mud before I come out in the mornings and make sure it gets stuck in my fingernails. They are pretty disgusting looking. I like the looks I get. Behind their polite smiles and God bless you, I can see them mentally trying to remember where the hand sanitizer is.

I take the cup and give it a sip. I've had to learn to drink black coffee. Normally, I'm a three-shot espresso with heavy cream sort of guy from the local coffee shop.

I take a few sips and start feeling energized and a bit warmer. Why I didn't put warmer clothes on under these rags, I don't know.

Last month, a reporter did a story on me, where I foolishly admitted I had a pretty good day job but needed some extra money, so I decided to pretend to be a down-on-my-luck homeless person and stand on the corner to get some money.

When the reporter asked me what would make me do something like that, I'd answered that jobs were scarce, I can keep my own hours, and it was excellent money. There were days I made more money than I did working all week. So now I can buy my wife and kids some nice extras, and it makes my family happy.

She wanted to know why I picked begging for money, though. I explained that I normally give money to the guys and girls on the street corner because I want to help, but everyone knows they're going to go and spend it on a bottle of booze or some drugs. Besides, if they really needed help, well, they could go get some.

One time, I even hired one of the guys on the corner who said he'd work for money. And he did. He was a good worker. I gave him a clean outfit since he was my size and gave him some ideas of where he could find a job. He took the clothes and thanked me before he left. I saw him the following weekend on the same corner. When I asked him if he went to those places I suggested, he thanked me for the information but said he liked being self-employed like this because he made good money and kept his own hours. He admitted he lived in a pretty nice neighborhood just a few blocks from my own house.

So when I needed some extra money, I thought, *Well, why not? I'll put on a disguise and go to an area people most likely won't know me and be self-employed.*

I wouldn't let her take my picture, but since her article came out, the money has been a bit scarce. In the story, she had listed some ways to help those who find themselves on the streets. Now I get food, coffee, blankets, coats, and gift cards to restaurants. I usually take the coats and blankets downtown where the homeless people live. And I share the food with some of the others I see on the street corners.

I've been thinking of giving it a few more weeks. If the money doesn't pick up again, I'll quit for a while. Maybe people will forget about the reporter's suggestions and start passing out money again.

It really was a bummer, though, with Christmas in just a few days. I really wanted to spoil my family this year.

A guy tooted his car horn and waved me over. I gave him a big smile when I saw the bill in his hand that was hanging out the window. I barely made it in time before traffic started moving. People honked at me, I suppose in irritation.

"Hey buddy!" I turned in the direction of the voice. "You want this or not?" Another guy held out a bill for me.

I looked at the cars that were starting to move. He was in the far lane from me. It would be a risk getting to his car, but...I nodded and started walking toward him. The guy dropped the bill and took off. I rushed over to where he dropped it before it blew away. I heard laughter drift from his car as I got down on the ground and grabbed the bill before it got run over. Cars were honking as they slowly moved around me. And many were yelling things that would probably have hurt my feelings, if I really was down on my luck.

"Loser! Go get a job!"

"Hey, dirt bag, get out of the road."

I somehow made my way back without getting hurt. A few cars threw coins out at me and some of them hit me. But I retrieved them all. I unfolded the bill that had been dropped on the street and nodded. That had been worth it. It was a hundred-dollar bill. I hoped it wasn't counterfeit, but if it wasn't, good times were rolling again.

See, people can be really generous, especially around a holiday, and what better holiday than Christmas, where people are giving all the time? The church people are even more generous than normal. I've stood outside of many church parking lots after a service and earned some high wages.

After I collected all the coins off of the sidewalk, I picked my sign back up and wrapped myself up in a blanket someone had thrown out their window while I was desperately groping around for that bill. I decided it was time for a much-needed lunch break and to check in with the wife.

I followed a dirt path through the bushes that went down under the overpass. Lots of beggars went down there to eat, and some made drug deals. I learned early on to keep to myself or trouble could happen faster than a guy could blink. I usually tucked most of my money in my shoes and kept the change in my pockets in case I ever got mugged by any of them. There have been a few times when I've searched my pockets, in the pretense of buying drugs, just to keep the dealer from forcing me to give him money. I've only bought the smallest amount, so after a while he left me alone. I wasn't worth his time.

Today, I had quite a bit of food and gift cards. I thought I'd be generous and pass some out. Some of them took from me eagerly, and others just shook their heads as they dragged on a cigarette someone had given them. I reached into my pocket and passed out the cigarettes I'd been given, too.

When I finished eating, I went back up to my spot. Some lady had taken it. Once someone has a corner for the day, you respect that. That's a rule that is not broken.

I went over and sat down next to her. She was younger-looking up close. "How much you make so far?"

She scowled at me. "What's it to you, old man?"

"This is my corner."

"I don't see your name on it."

I didn't know what to say because I'm not really a tough street person, just pretending. I was actually afraid she'd hurt me or call someone over to hurt me.

"Well, I've been here all day."

"I know. I saw you. It looked good over here, so I moved."

"Where were you?" I asked.

"Over there." She pointed.

"Right on the other side of the street? How come I didn't see you?"

"Maybe you weren't paying attention."

"So why don't you go back over there? Why take my spot?"

The lady looked down at the street and bit at her lip. "That tough guy told me to leave or he'd make me leave. I was having a really good morning."

"You were? And what. . ." I looked over the cars and noticed a burly dude, dressed in leather with a shaved head. He made my skin crawl. "I'd have moved, too."

"Yeah, well, I've actually never done this before. And I don't want anything to happen to me."

"Why are you doing it now, then? Drugs? Alcohol? Lose your home because of it?" I rudely asked. I knew it was always the same old story.

The girl looked down again. This time I could see tears slipping down her cheeks and falling unchecked to the ground. I kind of felt bad but stayed guarded because I didn't know if this girl was a con artist or not. I mean, she could be in cohoots with the guy across the street.

"So what's your story?" I persisted.

She looked up at me with the saddest eyes. I felt my heart catch.

"My stepmom kicked me out of the house when my dad died. I have nothing. I need to find a way to get an attorney and fight her. I don't have a job, because I was going to college. My dad wanted me to have a good education. I do have my car and I had some money in my bank account, but it only went so far. Last night I needed money to pay the electric bill, so I sat at a corner and I was given enough money to pay it. So I thought I'd try again today so I can pay my rent and then maybe have money for an attorney. I also want to get a present for my grandma, who is in an adult care facility."

"Can't you talk to her or some other family member?"

"I only have my grandma and my dad. But now he's gone. We just moved here from back East last year, for my schooling. My grandma got too sick for us to be able to care for her, and my dad put her in an Alzheimer's unit. Then my dad got married again, and he died suddenly one night and, well. . .now it's just me."

I stood there for a moment wondering if I should believe this story or not when a car pulled up and parked.

A couple of people got out of the car and walked over to us. I rolled my eyes because I've been through this before. I was about to hear about Jesus again. It was worse over the Christmas holiday. Church people seemed destined to tell others why Christmas is celebrated. I mean, don't they know that people don't really care anymore? The church people say it's not really about the gifts that are bought at the store but rather the biggest gift ever given, and that is the birth of Jesus.

I usually tuned out about then, because for me, it *was* about the gifts I bought and also the meal. I loved a big holiday dinner. My wife is the best cook ever, and we have a pretty big family. Her sisters all have the same talent in the kitchen and we brothers-in-law, well, we are as, church people would say, blessed.

The two guys were joined by a woman, and they started talking to the young girl. I could hear the woman say they could help her if she really wanted to be helped. The girl was excited and agreed to follow them back to the church.

Meanwhile, one of the dudes was working hard to get my attention. I ignored him and held up my sign. It just happened to be a "blessed" time when one car after another held out a bill as they drove by.

The guy came up real close to me, making me feel a bit uncomfortable. Soon his face was next to mine. "Bill?"

My heart literally stopped beating for a moment. I didn't want to look at him. I knew that voice. It was my brother-in-law, Jim. My wife had told me a few weeks ago that her sister and Jim had started going to church. She just hoped they wouldn't start preaching at the family gatherings. I didn't respond, hoping he'd think I wasn't Bill.

"Come on, Bill, I know it's you. Does Bev know about this? Did you lose your job? And why are you dressed like that?"

I couldn't ignore him any longer. I lowered my sign. "Don't go blabbing to the family."

"But, Bill, what are you doing?"

"Making some extra money; I mean, why should all these drug addicts and alcoholics have it all? It's an easy job."

"Really? If it's such a great job, why do you hide it from your wife and the rest of the family?"

"Hey, don't start judging me. I heard you were starting to go to church and I know what comes with that—self-righteous, judgmental. . ."

Jim raised his hands up. "Sorry, was just asking. If this is something you want to continue to do, go ahead. But I'm going to leave you with this. No matter what you think of the homeless people, you are stealing from the poor and misleading all the people who take their hard-earned cash and give it to you."

I glared at him. What business was it of his?

"And I still love you, Bill, but please don't buy me a present with money you earned from this."

"Get out of here, would you?" I watched that self-righteous guy walk away and get in his van. The girl was picking up her stuff, getting ready to leave.

"Well, they think they may be able to help me. I'm so excited. I hope they can," she told me, like I cared what they were going to do for her. But I nodded politely. She waved at me. "Have a good day."

I started to watch the poor girl walk away, and then something stirred in my heart. I don't know what it was. And the stupid words my brother-in-law said, about ripping people off, rang in my head. "Hey!"

She turned around. "Yeah?"

I walked over to her and started pulling the money out of my boots.

"Here, take this money, and gift cards."

"What? I can't. . ."

"Yes, yes you can. I—I have a job. I do this. . .never mind. Just take it, and I hope things work out for you."

"Why thank you! You are the kindest man ever!" She surprised me by giving me a quick hug before she ran off. Well, now that I'd done my good deed, I was going home. I knew I had to tell my wife before my brother-in-law told his, because she'd be on that phone fast.

When I got home, my wife stood in the living room, furious. Obviously, her younger sister, Julie, had called her. After a few hours of arguing, I took off for a while. I don't know why, but I went over to Jim's. At first Julie wasn't going to get Jim. She'd heard about my fight with her sister. Finally, I convinced her.

Jim and I talked for a while, and I asked him why he was going to church. He told me about the trouble he was having at work. He'd gotten in trouble for mishandling money. After some deals made from his attorney, he wouldn't be doing any jail time, but he couldn't work in the same field and had to take a cut in pay.

When he went to church, he learned about sin. Sin is anything that doesn't please God. Obviously, what he'd done wouldn't please God. And then he learned that God loved the world so much, He sent His only Son to die for it. It was then that Bill realized how awesome it was that Jesus had died for his sin that had hurt so many people, including his family.

"So what I've been doing isn't too much different than what you did," I said.

"Nope. I have to still pay restitution to the company, but I don't have to pay anything to God. He wiped me clean for eternity."

I thought about it for a while. Jim told me some stories he'd heard from people as he talked to the homeless. Every day of their lives they fought to survive in one way or another, whether dealing with addictions or dealing with poor choices, or like the girl today, a victim of circumstance. "These people are so misunderstood. But when Jesus came, He came to help the poor, the sick, and the lost. He came for someone like me," Jim said calmly.

"I guess I've been a jerk. And I'm sorry for calling you all those names." Bill shrugged. "So, things are better now?"

"Things are hard, but I lean on Jesus every day to get me through. My wife knows I'm leaning on Him, and she trusts me again. We're going to get through this together."

I nodded. I finally admitted I'd like what he had, this Jesus. So Jim took my hand and led me in a prayer. I left their place knowing I'd done the right thing. It felt good that I knew Jesus forgave me and would help me with my life. I hoped with all my heart my wife would forgive me.

So I got in my car, and like all those other church-going people who get all generous around Christmastime, when I reached a corner where a person stood with a sign, I held out my hand with a bill in it. When the person came to my car, I gave them the bill and then reached out and touched them, like Jesus touched me.

Sometimes now I even stop my car and get out to talk to them. Just like those annoying church people who bugged me before, I let them know that Christmas is about the greatest gift of all. And He's there for them. His name is Jesus.

Wishing you a Merry Christmas,

LINDA, ROSANNE, AND SHARON

Other Treasured Books

By Sharon Bernash Smith, Linda J. Reinhardt, and Rosanne Croft

The Lost Loves of World War II
contains
"The Train Baby's Mother"
Sharon Bernash Smith

"The Short Life of Moths"
Sharon Bernash Smith

THE McLEOD FAMILY SAGA
Like a Bird Wanders
Sharon Bernash Smith, Rosanne Croft, Linda J. Reinhardt
Old Sins, Long Shadows
Sharon Bernash Smith

SISTER BLUE THREAD, by Linda J. Reinhardt
Hidden Song
Silenced Song
Lost Song

BELIEVE IN LOVE, by Rosanne Croft
A Gentile in Deseret
A Saint in the Eternal City

Acknowledgments

ONCE UPON A CHRISTMAS

I want to thank my granddaughters—Hayley, Noelle, and Zoey Smith. Because of them, I'm able to keep a childlike faith in the continued wonder of Christmas. Amazing! Merry Christmas, my little lovelies. I love you—Nana.

And always, I thank my Lord Jesus, who loves me and daily keeps my soul in His care. I am forever Your grateful daughter.

—Sharon Bernash Smith

Without my husband, Ray, and daughter, Caeli, life would be uninspiring. They help me grow closer to the Lord. Thank you, Ray, for the stories from your life and for allowing me to give them a different form. You are my greatest friend and encourager, along with Jesus.

For stirring my imagination through a flow of remembrances, I must recognize my siblings—Mary Cabelli, Christine Chenoweth, Kathleen Rechel, and Tom Black. Each of you means so much to me, more than I can say.

As always, thanks to the wonderful people at OakTara, especially Ramona Tucker and Jeff Nesbit.

—Rosanne Croft

Thank you, Sharon, for inviting me to participate in this fun project.

Thank you, Ramona and Jeff, for all you do to get these stories published. What a blessing.

And of course, thank you, my Ben, for how much you encourage me to follow my dreams no matter what.

Sarrah, you are the sweetest girl and encourager at such a young age.

Thank you to my sister, Wanda, for all the many, many extra things you do to help. You are an incredible blessing.

Brenda, you've read these stories a time or two. Thank you.

Thank you, Mom and Dad, for your encouragement and help. Merry Christmas!

—Linda J. Reinhardt

Thank you, Ramona, for asking us to write this second Christmas book; your confidence makes me a better writer.

I want to thank my Facebook "family" and others who surround me with encouragement on a daily basis. Your friendship and faithful prayers are never taken for granted.

Whenever I think about the privilege of being a writer, my heart fills with thanks to the Lord. Every day I walk the earth, I am surprised by the joy of His grace, mercy, and compassion. This makes me forever His grateful daughter.

—Sharon Bernash Smith

My heartfelt thanks to my steady and supportive husband, Ray, who has been by my side these 31 years and is the love of my life. I wouldn't be as inspired to write without him and our beautiful, almost grown-up daughter, Caeli. A special thanks to my mom, for her loving support. She loved Christmas so much that she left wrapped presents for me posthumously. What tender memories I will have of those last gifts now that she's with Jesus.

I must acknowledge my loyal friends and forever "sisters," Sharon Bernash Smith and Linda Reinhardt. What an exciting journey we've been on together. There's no way I could finish anything without your love and texts!

A sincere thanks to Jeanie Jenks, who helps me by reading my stories. I'm honored to have such a friend.

I am indebted to my sister, Liz Cabelli, for her help in completing a story. Thank you, Liz, for helping me write it so much better.

Thanks to the others who inspired me to keep writing: Stan Baldwin, Jeannie St. John Taylor, Helen Haidle, Julie Hymas in Utah, as well as everyone at Oregon Christian Writers.

Once again, thanks to the wonderful people at OakTara, especially the unstoppable Ramona Tucker, who first believed in us, and Jeff Nesbit, who does so much behind the scenes.

—Rosanne Croft

To my wonderful husband, Ben, my encourager, thanks for all the hours spent reading and editing my work. And for never complaining when I need space and time to put one of the stories dancing in my head into the computer.

To my little pumpkin, Sarrah, for working along with me while I'm writing a story. I can't wait to read some of your stories in print someday.

To my sister, Wanda, for cheering me on, doing all the side work, and being such a wonderful sister to me and auntie to Sarrah.

To my mom and dad, for always being my cheerleaders and for the listening ears.

To Ramona, for believing in this project and encouraging me as a writer.

To Sharon Bernash Smith and Rosanne Croft, it's wonderful to be a part of another project with you. I'm very grateful for that first day we met at Rosanne's house many years ago. What a path we have traveled together, huh?

To my friends, my Sister Blue Threads, who listen to my off-the-wall conversations whenever I get an idea about a story, or for encouraging me to keep on writing—Sylvia Stewart, Joan Alfsen, Bilinda Taylor, Brenda Conners, Nancy Garrett, Chris White, Deanne McOmie, Angie Taylor, Connie Jo Freeman, Darlene Holt, A. J. Lane, Anna Lund, and Sally Freese.

To my wonderful writers group: Carol, Marion, Patty, Carolyn, and Kathy.

And last, but definitely not least, to Jesus Christ, for my salvation and the desire and gift He has given me to write about it. To Him always be the glory.

—Linda J. Reinhardt

Starry, Starry, Christmas Night

I love the family of God! Thank you to my special circle of girlfriends for your faithfulness to the Lord and to me. Your constant willingness to lift me up, or rein me in, is never taken for granted, nor is the encouragement you pour out to me in generous abundance.

And *amazing* is the only word for my small group ladies at church. How I love you! Each of you is precious in your own miraculous way. To say you've made my life richer would be a complete understatement. You all are brave, funny, and faithful to our Lord. I cannot thank you enough for your willingness to pray, pray, pray. May God richly bless you, my beloved.

Once again, I so want to thank Ramona Tucker for her inspirational tenacity. You've had a year of incredible personal testing, friend, yet you've never given up on your dream and vision. I thank you and Jeff Nesbit for including me in the family that is OakTara.

Thank you, Linda Reinhardt and Rosanne Croft, for always being there to walk me through my writing challenges. . .maybe I should say crises. I love that we are still Sisters in Christ after all these years.

Thank you, Jesus, for calling me to write for Your kingdom and, most of all, for reminding me that I am Your daughter.

Gratefully,
—Sharon Bernash Smith

I'd like to thank Ramona of OakTara for having us put together another Christmas book project. What a fun blessing! Thank you for being an encouragement to me.

And, Sharon, here we go again. It's great to work on another project with you and the times we get to hang doing book signings!

And, Rosey, I do miss you on this project. Thanks for how you've encouraged my writing. I can't wait to read your book when you are finished.

Thank you, Ben; I wouldn't be able to do my dream without your support. You work hard so I can follow my dream and take care of our daughter. You constantly put us first and love us just like the Bible says to in Ephesians. I am forever grateful and love you.

Thank you also to my not-so-little pumpkin pie, Sarrah. You have the gift of encouragement and see things so clearly. God has given you wisdom beyond your age. Thanks for those times you are a team player so I can get some writing done. I hope and pray you will always be delighted when the rain drops on your face and want to dance through the puddles. You are a true PNW girl!

To my sister, Wanda, who encourages me through moments of texting, coffee drinking, movie nights, and. . .shopping. . .to keep the faith.

I want to thank my mom and dad for always being there with an encouraging word and hugs. I am really grateful to have a spectacular family, brothers, brothers-in-law, sisters-in-law, nieces, nephews.

And all of my Sister Blue Threads, you are fabulous, and may you be blessed right back with how you bless me.

Most of all, I humbly thank You, Jesus, for giving me a love to write and that I love to write about You!

—Linda J. Reinhardt

About the Authors

SHARON BERNASH SMITH wore many hats while raising two boys in rural Washington State—preschool owner/teacher, midwife's assistant in a home-birth practice, and a Pregnancy Resource Center volunteer for 25 years. Now as a writer and speaker, Sharon desires to touch lives for Christ through the written word and her own life experiences.

"Reality Fiction™ is my commitment to address the real-life struggles we all face," Sharon says. "There are no pat answers in life, and you won't find them in my books. However, God is just, and I will always portray Him as such."

Sharon is also the author of *Old Sins, Long Shadows,* Book Two in The McLeod Family Saga, and coauthor of the historical novel *Like a Bird Wanders,* Book One in The McLeod Family Saga, and the Christmas classics *Once Upon a Christmas, Always Home for Christmas,* and *Starry, Starry, Christmas Night* (all OakTara). *The Train Baby's Mother* (OakTara) was chosen as a top finalist in the Oregon Christian Writers' Cascade writing contest. She has also been published by Focus on the Family and AMG Publishers.

Sharon enjoys watercolor painting, land-sailing around the Pacific Northwest, and spending as much time as possible with friends and family, especially her four granddaughters. Sharon and her husband attend a large church in Washington State, where she serves as a Bible study leader in women's ministry.

See her on Facebook and at sharonbernashsmith.blogspot.com
www.oaktara.com

Raised in beautiful Washington State since age eight, LINDA J. REINHARDT has always enjoyed writing a poem, song, or story. She's contributed to church newsletters, a puppet ministry curriculum, and wrote/directed a Christmas play and women's Bible study play, and has written for *Girlfriend 2 Girlfriend* online magazine. Linda wrote a song performed at her wedding, which has now become a lullaby to her daughter before bed. She is now a speaker for StoneCroft Ministries and has also led writers' workshops.

On the top of the list of favorite pastimes is spending time with family, especially husband, Ben, and miracle daughter, Sarrah.

Besides the Sister Blue Thread series, Linda has coauthored the historical novel *Like a Bird Wanders*, Book One in The McLeod Family Saga, as well as the Christmas classics *Once Upon a Christmas, Always Home for Christmas,* and *Starry, Starry, Christmas Night* (all OakTara).

Linda is a stay-at-home mom. Her favorite activity is spending time with her best friend and husband and her miracle daughter. She also enjoys sitting over a cup of coffee with her sister or a friend, sharing the details of her heart. Passionate about ministering to post-abortive women, Linda is active in leading small group Bible studies: HEART (Healing and Encouragement for Abortion Related Trauma), Time to Heal, and Life Groups. As an avid believer in the power of prayer, she has met for the last ten years with a prayer group dedicated to supporting family and friends.

See her on Facebook and at www.lindajreinhardt.blogspot.com
www.sisterbluethread.blogspot.com
www.oaktara.com

ROSANNE CROFT, author of the Believe in Love series, is the coauthor of *Always Home for Christmas, Once Upon a Christmas,* and the historical novel *Like a Bird Wanders* (all OakTara). In addition, she contributed to *What Would Jesus Do Today? A One-Year Devotional* by Helen Haidle (Multnomah).

Residing near Bend, Oregon, Rosanne is a member of Central Oregon Writer's Guild and Oregon Christian Writers. She loves to quilt, hike, and have tea with friends.

www.rosannecroft.wordpress.com
www.oaktara.com